The Heritage of Literature Series
SUNSET SONG

The Heritage of Literature Series

Founder General Editor: E. W. Parker, M.C.

The titles in this series include modern classics, and a wide range of novels, short stories and drama

A selection from the series includes

ANIMAL FARM   *George Orwell*
THE WESKER TRILOGY   *Arnold Wesker*
GO TELL IT ON THE MOUNTAIN   *James Baldwin*
THE ROYAL HUNT OF THE SUN   *Peter Shaffer*
ROOTS   *Arnold Wesker*
SUNSET SONG   *Lewis Grassic Gibbon*
CRY THE BELOVED COUNTRY   *Alan Paton*
THE LONELINESS OF THE LONG-DISTANCE RUNNER   *Alan Sillitoe*
   BILLY LIAR   *Keith Waterhouse*   (in one volume)
THE WORLD OF THE SHORT STORY   An anthology chosen by
   A. H. M. Best and M. J. Cohen
FARMER'S BOY   *John R. Allan*
MISTER JOHNSON   *Joyce Cary*
BRAVE NEW WORLD   *Aldous Huxley*

A complete list of the series is available on request

Sunset Song

*Lewis Grassic
Gibbon*

with Commentary and Notes by
J. T. LOW

LONGMAN

LONGMAN GROUP LIMITED

London

*Associated companies, branches and representatives
throughout the world*

*This edition © Longman Group Ltd 1971
© This edition first published by Longman Group Ltd by arrangement
with Hutchinson Publishing Group Ltd 1971*

*First published 1971
Sixth impression 1979*

ISBN 0 582 34901 X

*Printed in Hong Kong by
Sheck Wah Tong Printing Press Ltd*

CONTENTS

ACKNOWLEDGEMENTS

I should like to thank Mrs Ray Mitchell, widow of the author, for the help she gave me so readily and for the interest she has shown in the work of preparing this edition. I should also like to say how grateful I am to Mr David Murison, editor of the Scottish National Dictionary, for discussing and helping me with problems of the glossary and the text. Of the books I have consulted I have found most valuable and useful Mr Ian S. Munro's biography *Leslie Mitchell: Lewis Grassic Gibbon* and his collection of Gibbon's essays and stories *A Scots Hairst*. For preparing the map of the Mearns and South Aberdeenshire I am greatly indebted to my colleague Mr Tom Masterton.

NOTE ON THE TEXT

The text used for this edition is substantially that of the first edition of 1932 which is free of the misprints that developed in later editions. I am glad, too, that we have been able to reprint the sketch map of Kinraddie that appeared at the beginning and end of the first edition. It is not to be expected that this 'map' should fit in exactly with the actual topography of the area; but it does give an interesting pictorial impression of the kind of setting the author had in mind. I have taken the liberty of rectifying, as far as I can, the compass indications.

J.T.L.

NOTE

If the great Dutch language disappeared from literary usage and a Dutchman wrote in German a story of the Lekside peasants, one may hazard he would ask and receive a certain latitude and forbearance in his usage of German. He might import into his pages some score or so untranslatable words and idioms—untranslatable except in their context and setting; he might mould in some fashion his German to the rhythms and cadence of the kindred speech that his peasants speak. Beyond that, in fairness to his hosts, he hardly could go—to seek effect by a spray of apostrophes would be both impertinence and mis-translation.

The courtesy that the hypothetical Dutchman might receive from German a Scot may invoke from the great English tongue.

L.G.G.

NOTE TO 1972 REPORT

I have taken the opportunity of correcting misprints that were discovered in the original 1971 edition.

John T. Low

Barmekin Hill

ECHT

Loch of Skene

ABERDEEN

River Dee

BANCHORY

North Sea

STONEHAVEN

DUNNOTTAR CASTLE

Bervie Water

DRUMLITHIE

MONDYNES

HAREDEN

BLOOMFIELD

ARBUTHNOTT School & Church

KINNEFF

INVERBERVIE

N
W — E
S

■ Standing Stone   ▲ Cairn
● Stone Circle   —·—· Slug Road
◆ Roman Camp   ---- Reisk Road

scale
0 1 2 3 4 5 miles
0 1 2 3 4 5 6 7 8 kilometres

*To
Jean Baxter*

THE PRELUDE

KINRADDIE

THE UNFURROWED FIELD

Kinraddie lands had been won by a Norman childe, Cospatric de Gondeshil, in the days of William the Lyon, when gryphons and such-like beasts still roamed the Scots countryside and folk would waken in their beds to hear the children screaming, with a great wolf-beast, come through the hide window, tearing at their throats. In the Den of Kinraddie one such beast had its lair and by day it lay about the woods and the stench of it was awful to smell all over the countryside, and at gloaming a shepherd would see it, with its great wings half-folded across the great belly of it and its head, like the head of a meikle cock, but with the ears of a lion, poked over a fir tree, watching. And it ate up sheep and men and women and was a fair terror, and the King had his heralds cry a reward to whatever knight would ride and end the mischieving of the beast. So the Norman childe, Cospatric, that was young and landless and fell brave and well-armoured, mounted his horse in Edinburgh Town and came North, out of the foreign south parts, up through the Forest of Fife and into the pastures of Forfar and past Aberlemno's Meikle Stane that was raised when the Picts beat the Danes; and by it he stopped and looked at the figures, bright then and hardly faded even now, of the horses and the charging and the rout of those coarse foreign folk. And maybe he said a bit prayer by that Stone and then he rode into the Mearns, and the story tells no more of his riding but that at last come he did to Kinraddie, a tormented place, and they told him where the gryphon slept, down there in the Den of Kinraddie.

But in the daytime it hid in the woods and only at night, by a path through the hornbeams, might he come at it, squatting in bones, in its lair. And Cospatric waited for the night to come and rode to the edge of Kinraddie Den and commended his soul to God and came off his horse and took his boar-spear in his hand, and went down into the

Den and killed the gryphon. And he sent the news to
William the Lyon, sitting drinking the wine and fondling
his bonny lemans in Edinburgh Town, and William made
him the Knight of Kinraddie, and gave to him all the wide
parish as his demesne and grant to build him a castle there,
and wear the sign of a gryphon's head for a crest and keep
down all beasts and coarse and wayward folk, him and the
issue of his body for ever after.

So Cospatric got him the Pict folk to build a strong castle
there in the lithe of the hills, with the Grampians bleak and
dark behind it, and he had the Den drained and he married
a Pict lady and got on her bairns and he lived there till he
died. And his son took the name Kinraddie, and looked out
one day from the castle wall and saw the Earl Marischal
come marching up from the south to join the Highlandmen
in the battle that was fought at Mondynes, where now
the meal-mill stands; and he took out his men and fought
there, but on which side they do not say, but maybe it was
the winning one, they were aye gey and canny folk, the
Kinraddies. And the great-grandson of Cospatric, he joined
the English against the cateran Wallace, and when Wallace
next came marching up from the southlands Kinraddie and
other noble folk of that time they got them into Dunnottar
Castle that stands out in the sea beyond Kinneff, well-
builded and strong, and the sea splashes about it in the high
tides and there the din of the gulls is a yammer night and
day. Much of meal and meat and gear they took with them,
and they laid themselves up there right strongly, they and
their carles, and wasted all the Mearns that the Cateran who
dared rebel against the fine English king might find no
provision for his army of coarse and landless men. But
Wallace came through the Howe right swiftly and he heard
of Dunnottar and laid siege to it and it was a right strong
place and he had but small patience with strong places. So,
in the dead of one night, when the thunder of the sea
drowned the noise of his feint, he climbed the Dunnottar
rocks and was over the wall, he and the vagabond Scots, and
they took Dunnottar and put to the slaughter the noble folk
gathered there, and all the English, and spoiled them of
their meat and gear, and marched away.

Kinraddie Castle that year, they tell, had but a young bride new home and she had no issue of her body, and the months went by and she rode to the Abbey of Aberbrothock where the good Abbot, John, was her cousin, and told him of her trouble and how the line of Kinraddie was like to die. So he lay with her, that was September, and next year a boy was born to the young bride, and after that the Kinraddies paid no heed to wars and bickerings but sat them fast in their Castle lithe in the hills, with their gear and bonny leman queans and villeins libbed for service.

And when the First Reformation came and others came after it and some folk cried *Whiggam!* and some cried *Rome!* and some cried *The King!* the Kinraddies sat them quiet and decent and peaceable in their castle, and heeded never a fig the arguings of folk, for wars were unchancy things. But then Dutch William came, fair plain a fixture that none would move, and the Kinraddies were all for the Covenant then, they had aye had God's Covenant at heart, they said. So they builded a new kirk down where the chapel had stood, and builded a manse by it, there in the middle of the yews where the cateran Wallace had hid when the English put him to rout at last. And one Kinraddie, John Kinraddie, went south and became a great man in the London court, and was crony of the creatures Johnson and James Boswell; and once the two of them, John Kinraddie and James Boswell, came up to the Mearns on an idle ploy and sat drinking wine and making coarse talk far into the small hours night after night till the old laird wearied of them and then they would steal away and as James Boswell set in his diary, *Did get to the loft where the maids were, and one Πεγγί Δννδας was φατ ιν τhε βυττοcκς ανδ I διδ λιε wιthhερ.*

But in the early days of the nineteenth century it was an ill time for the Scots gentry, for the poison of the French Revolution came over the seas and crofters and common folk like that stood up and cried *Away to hell!* when the Auld Kirk preached submission from its pulpits. Up as far as Kinraddie came the poison and the young laird of that time, and he was Kenneth, he called himself a Jacobin and joined the Jacobin Club of Aberdeen and there at Aberdeen was nearly killed in the rioting, for liberty and equality and fraternity, he called it. And they carried him back to Kinraddie a cripple, but he would still have it that all men were free and equal and he set to selling the estate and sending the money to France, for he had a real good heart. And the crofters marched on Kinraddie Castle in a body and bashed in the windows of it, they thought equality should begin at home.

More than half the estate had gone in this driblet and that while the cripple sat and read his coarse French books; but nobody guessed that till he died and then his widow, poor woman, found herself own no more than the land that lay between the coarse hills, the Grampians, and the farms that stood out by the Bridge End above the Denburn, straddling the outward road. Maybe there were some twenty to thirty holdings in all, the crofters dour folk of the old Pict stock, they had no history, common folk, and ill-reared their biggings clustered and chaved amid the long, sloping fields. The leases were one-year, two-year, you worked from the blink of the day you were breeked to the flicker of the night they shrouded you, and the dirt of gentry sat and ate up your rents but you were as good as they were. So that was Kenneth's leaving to his lady body, she wept right sore over the pass that things had come to, but they kittled up before her own jaw was tied in a clout and they put her down in Kinraddie vault to lie by the side of her man. Three of her bairns were drowned at sea, fishing off the Bervie braes they had been, but the fourth, the boy Cospatric, him that died the same day as the Old Queen, he was douce and saving and sensible, and set putting the estate to rights. He threw out half the little tenants, they flitted off to Canada and Dundee and parts like those, the others he couldn't move but slowly. But on the cleared land he had bigger steadings built and he let them at bigger rents and longer leases, he said the day of the fine big farm had come. And he had woods of fir and larch and pine planted to shield the long, bleak slopes, and might well have retrieved the Kinraddie fortunes but that he married a Morton quean with black blood in her, she smitted him and drove him to drink and death, that was the best way out. For his son was clean daft, they locked him up at last in an asylum, and that was the end of Kinraddie family, the Meikle House that stood where the Picts had builded Cospatric's castle crumbled to bits like a cheese, all but two-three rooms the trustees held as their offices, the estate was mortgaged to the hilt by then.

So by the winter of nineteen eleven there were no more than nine bit places left the Kinraddie estate, the Mains the biggest of them, it had been the Castle home farm in the long past times. An Irish creature, Erbert Ellison was the name, ran the place for the trustees, he said, but if you might believe all the stories you heard he ran a hantle more silver into his own pouch than he ran into theirs. Well might you expect it, for once he'd been no more than a Dublin waiter, they said. That had been in the time before Lord Kinraddie, the daft one, had gone clean skite. He had been in Dublin, Lord Kinraddie, on some drunken ploy, and Ellison had brought his whisky for him and some said he had halved his bed with him. But folk would say anything. So the daftie took Ellison back with him to Kinraddie and made him his servant, and sometimes, when he was real drunk and the fairlies came sniftering out of the whisky bottles at him, he would throw a bottle at Ellison and shout *Get out, you bloody dish-clout!* so loud it was heard across at the Manse and fair affronted the minister's wife. And old Greig, him that had been the last minister there, he would glower across at Kinraddie House like John Knox at Holyrood, and say that God's hour would come. And sure as death it did, off to the asylum they hurled the daftie, he went with a nurse's mutch on his head and he put his head out of the back of the waggon and said *Cockadoodledoo!* to some school bairns the waggon passed on the road and they all ran home and were fell frightened.

But Ellison had made himself well acquaint with farming and selling stock and most with buying horses, so the trustees they made him manager of the Mains, and he moved into the Mains farmhouse and looked him round for a wife. Some would have nothing to do with him, a poor creature of an Irishman who couldn't speak right and didn't belong to the Kirk, but Ella White she was not so particular and

was fell long in the tooth herself. So when Ellison came to
her at the harvest ball in Auchinblae and cried *Can I see
you home tonight, me dear?* she said *Och Ay*. And on the
road home they lay among the stooks and maybe Ellison
did this and that to make sure of getting her, he was fair
desperate for any woman by then. They were married next
New Year's Day, and Ellison had begun to think himself a
gey man in Kinraddie, and maybe one of the gentry. But the
bothy billies, the ploughmen and the orra men of the Mains,
they'd never a care for gentry except to mock at them and
on the eve of Ellison's wedding they took him as he was
going into his house and took off his breeks and tarred his
dowp and the soles of his feet and stuck feathers on them
and then they threw him into the water-trough, as was the
custom. And he called them *Bloody Scotch savages,* and was
in an awful rage and at the term-time he had them sacked,
the whole jing-bang of them, so sore affronted he had been.

But after that he got on well enough, him and his mistress,
Ella White, and they had a daughter, a scrawny bit quean
they thought over good to go to the Auchinblae School, so
off she went to Stonehaven Academy and was taught to be
right brave and swing about in the gymnasium there with
wee black breeks on under her skirt. Ellison himself began
to get well-stomached, and he had a red face, big and sappy,
and eyes like a cat, green eyes, and his mouser hung down
each side of a fair bit mouth that was chokeful up of false
teeth, awful expensive and bonny, lined with bits of gold.
And he aye wore leggings and riding breeks, for he was fair
gentry by then; and when he would meet a crony at a mart
he would cry *Sure, bot it's you, thin, ould chep!* and the
billy would redden up, real ashamed, but wouldn't dare say
anything, for he wasn't a man you'd offend. In politics he
said he was a Conservative but everybody in Kinraddie knew
that meant he was a Tory and the bairns of Strachan, him
that farmed the Peesie's Knapp, they would scraich out

> *Inkypoo, your nose is blue,*
> *You're awful like the Turra Coo!*

whenever they saw Ellison go by. For he'd sent a subscrip-
tion to the creature up Turriff way whose cow had been sold

to pay his Insurance, and folk said it was no more than a show off, the Cow creature and Ellison both; and they laughed at him behind his back.

So that was the Mains, below the Meikle House, and Ellison farmed it in his Irish way and right opposite, hidden away among their yews, were kirk and manse, the kirk an old, draughty place and in the winter-time, right in the middle of the Lord's Prayer, maybe, you'd hear an outbreak of hoasts fit to lift off the roof, and Miss Sarah Sinclair, her that came from Netherhill and played the organ, she'd sneeze into her hymn-book and miss her bit notes and the minister, him that was the old one, he'd glower down at her more like John Knox than ever. Next door the kirk was an olden tower, built in the time of the Roman Catholics, the coarse creatures, and it was fell old and wasn't used any more except by the cushat-doves and they flew in and out the narrow slits in the upper storey and nested there all the year round and the place was fair white with their dung. In the lower half of the tower was an effigy-thing of Cospatric de Gondeshil, him that killed the gryphon, lying on his back with his arms crossed and a daft-like simper on his face; and the spear he killed the gryphon with was locked in a kist there, or so some said, but others said it was no more than an old bit heuch from the times of Bonny Prince Charlie. So that was the tower, but it wasn't fairly a part of the kirk, the real kirk was split in two bits, the main hall and the wee hall, and some called them the byre and the turnip-shed, and the pulpit stood midway. Once the wee hall had been for the folk from the Meikle House and their guests and such-like gentry but nearly anybody that had the face went ben and sat there now, and the elders sat with the collection bags, and young Murray, him that blew the organ for Sarah Sinclair. It had fine glass windows, awful old, the wee hall, with three bit creatures of queans, not very decent-like in a kirk, as window-pictures. One of the queans was Faith, and faith she looked a daft-like keek for she was lifting up her hands and her eyes like a heifer choked on a turnip and the bit blanket round her shoulders was falling off her but she didn't seem to heed, and there was a swither of scrolls and fiddley-faddles all about her. And the second quean was Hope and she was near as unco as Faith, but had right bonny hair, red hair, though maybe you'd call it auburn, and in the winter-time the light in the morning service would come splashing through the yews in the kirkyard and into the wee hall through the red hair of Hope. And the third quean was Charity, with a lot of naked bairns at her feet and she looked a fine and decent-like woman, for all that she was tied about with such daft-like clouts.

But the windows of the main hall, though they were coloured, they had never a picture in them and there were no pictures in there at all, who wanted them? Only coarse creatures like Catholics wanted a kirk to look like a grocer's calendar. So it was decent and bare-like, with its carved old seats, some were cushioned and some were not, if you weren't padded by nature and had the silver to spend you might put in cushions to suit your fancy. Right up in the lithe of the pulpit, at angles-like to the rest of the kirk, were the three seats where the choir sat and led the hymn-singing; and some called it the calfies' stall.

The back door, that behind the pulpit, led out across the kirkyard to the Manse and its biggings, set up in the time of the Old Queen, and fair bonny to look at, but awful damp said all the ministers' wives. But ministers' wives were aye folk to complain and don't know when they're well off, them and the silver they get for their bit creatures of men preaching once or twice a Sunday and so proud they hardly know you when they meet you on the road. The minister's study was high up in the house, it looked out over all Kinraddie, at night he'd see from there the lights of the farmhouses like a sprinkling of bright sands below his window and the flagstaff light high among the stars on the roof of the Meikle House. But that nineteen eleven December the Manse was empty and had been empty for many a month, the old minister was dead and the new one not yet voted on; and the ministers from Drumlithie and Arbuthnott and Laurencekirk they came time about in the Sunday forenoons and took the service there at Kinraddie; and God knows for all they had to say they might well have bidden at home.

But if you went out of the kirk by the main door and took the road east a bit, and that was the road that served kirk and Manse and Mains, you were on to the turnpike then. It ran north and south but opposite to the road you'd just come down was another, that went through Kinraddie by the Bridge End farm. So there was a cross-roads there and if you held to the left along the turnpike you came to Peesie's Knapp, one of the olden places, no more than a croft of thirty-forty acres with some rough ground for pasture, but God knows there was little pasture on it, it was just a fair schlorich of whins and broom and dirt, full up of rabbits and hares it was, they came out at night and ate up your crops and sent a body fair mad. But it wasn't bad land the most of the Knapp, there was the sweat of two thousand years in it, and the meikle park behind the biggings was black loam, not the red clay that sub-soiled half Kinraddie.

Now Peesie's Knapp's biggings were not more than twenty years old, but gey ill-favoured for all that, for though the house faced on the road—and that was fair handy if it didn't scunner you that you couldn't so much as change your sark without some ill-fashioned brute gowking in at you—right between the byre and the stable and the barn on one side and the house on the other was the cattle-court and right in the middle of that the midden, high and yellow with dung and straw and sharn, and Mistress Strachan could never forgive Peesie's Knapp because of that awful smell it had. But Chae Strachan, him that farmed the place, he just said *Hoots, what's a bit guff?* and would start to tell of the terrible smells he'd smelt when he was abroad. For he'd been a fell wandering billy, Chae, in the days before he came back to Scotland and was fee'd his last fee at Netherhill. He'd been in Alaska, looking for gold there, but damn the bit of gold he'd seen, so he'd farmed in California till he was so scunnered of fruit he'd never look an orange or a pear in the face again, not even in a tin. And then he'd gone on to South Africa and had had great times there, growing real chief-like with the head one of a tribe of blacks, but an awful decent man for all that. Him and Chae had fought against Boers and British both, and beaten them, or so Chae said, but folk that didn't like Chae said all the fighting he'd

ever done had been with his mouth and that as for beaten,
he'd be sore made to beat the skin off a bowl of sour milk.

For he wasn't well liked by them that set themselves up for
gentry, Chae, being a socialist creature and believing we
should all have the same amount of silver and that there
shouldn't be rich and poor and that one man was as good
as another. And the silver bit of that was clean daft, of
course, for if you'd all the same money one day what would
it be the next?—Rich and Poor again! But Chae said the
four ministers of Kinraddie and Auchinblae and Laurencekirk and Drumlithie were all paid much the same money
last year and what had they this year?—Much the same
money still! *You'll have to get out of bed slippy in the
morning before you find a socialist tripping and if you give
me any of your lip I'll clout you in the lug, my mannie.* So
Chae was fell good in argy-bargying and he wasn't the
quarrelsome kind except when roused, so he was well-liked,
though folk laughed at him. But God knows, who is it they
don't laugh at? He was a pretty man, well upstanding, with
great shoulders on him and his hair was fair and fine and he
had a broad brow and a gey bit coulter of a nose and he
twisted his mouser ends up with wax like that creature the
German Kaiser, and he could stop a running stirk by the
horns, so strong he was in the wrist-bones. And he was one
of the handiest billies in Kinraddie, he would libb a calf or
break in a horse or kill a pig, all in a jiffy, or tile your dairy
or cut the bairns' hair or dig a well, and all the time he'd
be telling you that socialism was coming or if it wasn't then
an awful crash would come and we'd all go back to savagery,
Damn't ay, man!

But folk said he'd more need to start socialising Mistress
Strachan, her that had been Kirsty Sinclair of Netherhill,
before he began on anybody else. She had a fell tongue, they
said, that would clip clouts and yammer a tink from a door,
and if Chae wasn't fair sick now and then for his hut and a
fine black quean in South Africa damn the hut or the
quean had he ever had. He'd fee'd at Netherhill when he
came back from foreign parts, had Chae, and there had been
but two daughters there, Kirsty and Sarah, her that played
the kirk organ. Both were wearing on a bit, sore in the need

of a man, and Kistry with a fair let-down as it was, for it had seemed that a doctor billy from Aberdeen was out to take up with her. So he had done and left her in a gey way and her mother, old Mistress Sinclair, near went out of her mind with the shame of it when Kirsty began to cry and tell her the news. Now that was about the term-time and home to Netherhill from the feeing market who should old Sinclair of Netherhill bring but Chae Strachan, with his blood warmed up from living in those foreign parts and an eye for less than a wink of invitation? But even so he was gey slow to get on with the courting and just hung around Kirsty like a futret round a trap with a bit meat in it, not sure if the meat was worth the risk; and the time was getting on and faith! something drastic would have to be done. So one night after they had all had supper in the kitchen and old Sinclair had gone pleitering out to the byres, old Mistress Sinclair had up and nodded to Kirsty and said *Ah well, I'll away to my bed. You'll not be long in making for yours, Kirsty?* And Kirsty said *No*, and gave her mother a sly bit look, and off the old mistress went up to her room and then Kirsty began fleering and flirting with Chae and he was a man warm enough and they were alone together and maybe in a minute he'd have had her couched down right well there in the kitchen but she whispered it wasn't safe. So he off with his boots and she with hers and up the stairs they crept together into Kirsty's room and were having their bit pleasure together when *ouf!* went the door and in burst old Mistress Sinclair with the candle held up in one hand and the other held up in horror. *No, no,* she'd said, *this won't do at all, Chakie, my man, you'll have to marry her.* And there had been no escape for Chae, poor man, with Kirsty and her mother both glowering at him. So married they were and old Sinclair had saved up some silver and he rented Peesie's Knapp for Chae and Kirsty, and stocked the place for them, and down they sat there, and Kirsty's bairn, a bit quean, was born before seven months were past, well-grown and finished-like it seemed, the creature, in spite of its mother swearing it had come fair premature.

They'd had two more bairns since then, both laddies, and both the living spit of Chae, these were the bairns that

would sing about the Turra Coo whenever they met the
brave gig of Ellison bowling along the Kinraddie Road, and
faith, they made you laugh.

Right opposite Peesie's Knapp, across the turnpike, the
land climbed red and clay and a rough stone road went
wandering up to the biggings of Blawearie. *Out of the
World and into Blawearie* they said in Kinraddie, and faith!
it was coarse land and lonely up there on the brae, fifty-sixty
acres of it, forbye the moor that went on with the brae high
above Blawearie, up to a great flat hill-top where lay a bit
loch that nested snipe by the hundred; and some said there
was no bottom to it, the loch, and Long Rob of the Mill said
that made it like the depths of a parson's depravity. That
was an ill thing to say about any minister, though Rob said
it was an ill thing to say about any loch, but there the
spleiter of water was, a woesome dark stretch fringed rank
with rushes and knife-grass; and the screeching of the snipe
fair deafened you if you stood there of an evening. And
few enough did that for nearby the bit loch was a circle of
stones from olden times, some were upright and some were
flat and some leaned this way and that, and right in the
middle three big ones clambered up out of the earth and
stood askew with flat sonsy faces, they seemed to listen and
wait. They were Druid stones and folk told that the Druids
had been coarse devils of men in the times long syne, they'd
climb up there and sing their foul heathen songs around the
stones; and if they met a bit Christian missionary they'd gut
him as soon as look at him. And Long Rob of the Mill would
say what Scotland wanted was a return of the Druids, but
that was just a speak of his, for they must have been awful
ignorant folk, not canny.

Blawearie hadn't had a tenant for nearly a year, but now
there was one on the way, they said, a creature John Guthrie
from up in the North. The biggings of it stood fine and
compact one side of the close, the midden was back of them,
and across the close was the house, a fell brave house for a
little place, it had three storeys and a good kitchen and a
fair stretch of garden between it and Blawearie road. There
were beech trees there, three of them, one was close over

against the house, and the garden hedges grew as bonny with honeysuckle of a summer as ever you saw; and if you could have lived on the smell of honeysuckle you might have farmed the bit place with profit.

Well, Peesie's Knapp and Blawearie were the steadings that lay Stonehaven way. But if you turned east that winter along the Auchinblae road first on your right was Cuddiestoun, a small bit holding the size of Peesie's Knapp, and old as it, a croft from the far-off times. It lay a quarter-mile or so from the main road and its own road was fair clamjamfried with glaur from late in the harvest till the coming of Spring. Some said maybe that accounted for Munro's neck, he could never get the glaur washed out of it. But others said he never tried. He was on a thirteen years' lease there, Munro, a creature from down south, Dundee way, and he was a good six feet in height but awful coarse among the legs, like a lamb with water on the brain, and he had meikle feet that aye seemed in his way. He was maybe forty years or so in age, and bald already, and his skin was red and creased in cheeks and chin and God! you never saw an uglier brute, poor stock. For there were worse folk than Munro, though maybe they were all in the jail, and though he could blow and bombast till he fair scunnered you. He farmed his bit land in a then and now way, and it was land good enough, the most of it, with the same black streak of loam that went through the Peesie parks, but ill-drained, the old stone drains were still down and devil the move would the factor at Meikle House make to have them replaced, or mend the roof of the byre that leaked like a sieve on the head of Mistress Munro when she milked the kye on a stormy night.

But if anybody, chief-like, were to say, *God, that's an awful byre you have, mistress,* she would flare up in a minute *It's fine and good enough for the like of us.* And if that body, not knowing better, poor billy, were to agree that the place was well enough for poor folk, she'd up again *Who's poor? Let me tell you we've never needed anybody come to our help, though we don't boast and blow about it all over the countryside, like some I could mention.* So the

body would think there was no pleasing of the creature, and
she was right well laughed at in all Kinraddie, though not
to her face. And that was a thin one and she had black hair
and snapping black eyes like a futret, and a voice that fair
set your hackles on edge when she girned. But she was the
best midwife for miles around, right often in the middle of
the night some poor distracted billy would come chapping
at her window *Mistress Munro, Mistress Munro, will you get
up and come to the wife?* And out she'd get, and into her
clothes before you could whistle, and out into the cold of
Kinraddie night and go whipping through it like a futret,
and soon be snapping her orders round the kitchen of the
house she'd been summoned to, telling the woman in child-
bed she might easily be worse, and being right brisk and
sharp and clever. And the funny thing about the creature
was that she believed none spoke ill of her, for if she heard
a bit hint of such, dropped sly-like, she'd redden up like a
stalk of rhubarb in a dung patch and look as though she
might start to cry, and the body would feel real sorry for her
till next minute she'd be screeching at Andy or Tony, and
fleering them out of the little wits they had, poor devils.

Now, Andy and Tony were two dafties that Mistress
Munro had had boarded out on her from an Asylum in
Dundee, they weren't supposed to be dangerous. Andy was
a meikle slummock of a creature, and his mouth was aye
open, and he dribbled like a teething foal, and his nose
wabbled all over his face and when he tried to speak it was
just a fair jumble of foolishness. He was the daftest one,
but fell sly, he'd sometimes run away to the hills and stand
there with his finger at his nose, making faces at Mistress
Munro, and she'd scraich at him and he'd yammer back
at her and then over the moor he'd get to the bothy at
Upperhill where the ploughmen would give him cigarettes
and then torment him till he fair raged; and once tried to
kill one with an axe he caught up from a hackstock. And
at night he'd creep back to Cuddiestoun, outside he'd make
a noise like a dog that had been kicked, and he'd snuffle
round the door till the few remaining hairs on the bald
pow of Munro would fair rise on end. But Mistress Munro
would up and be at the door and in she'd yank Andy by

the lug, and some said she'd take down his breeks and skelp him, but maybe that was a lie. She wasn't feared at him and he wasn't feared at her, so they were a gey well-matched pair.

And that was the stir at Cuddiestoun, all except Tony, for the Munros had never a bairn of their own. And Tony, though he wasn't the daftest, he was the queer one, too, right enough. He was small-bulked and had a little red beard and sad eyes, and he walked with his head down and you would feel right sorry for him for sometimes some whimsy would come on the creature, right in the middle of the turnpike it might be or half-way down a rig of swedes, and there he would stand staring like a gowk for minutes on end till somebody would shake him back to his senses. He had fine soft hands, for he was no working body; folk said he had once been a scholar and written books and learned and learned till his brain fair softened and right off his head he'd gone and into the poorhouse asylum. Now Mistress Munro she'd send Tony errands to the wee shop out beyond the Bridge End, and tell him what she wanted, plain and simple-like, and maybe giving him a bit clout in the lug now and then, as you would a bairn or a daftie. And he'd listen to her and make out he minded the messages and off to the shop he'd go, and come back without a single mistake. But one day, after she'd told him the things she wanted, Mistress Munro saw the wee creature writing on a bit of paper with a pencil he'd picked up somewhere. And she took the paper from him and looked at it and turned it this way and that, but feint the thing could she make of it. So she gave him a bit clout in the lug and asked him what the writing was. But he just shook his head, read gowkéd-like, and reached out his hand for the bit of paper, but Mistress Munro would have none of that and when it was time for the Strachan bairns to pass the end of the Cuddiestoun road on their way to school down there she was waiting and gave the paper to the eldest, the quean Marget, and told her to show it to the Dominie and ask him what it might mean. And at night she was waiting for the Strachan bairns to come back and they had an envelope for her from the Dominie; and she opened it and found a note saying the writing was shorthand and that this was what it read when put in the ordinary way of writing: *Two pounds of sugar The People's Journal half an ounce of mustard a tin of rat poison a pound of candles and I don't suppose I can swindle her out of tuppence change for the sake of a smoke, she's certainly the meanest bitch unhung this side of Tweed.* So maybe Tony wasn't so daft, but he got no supper that night; and she never asked to see his notes again.

Now, following the Kinraddie road still east, you passed by Netherhill on your left, five places had held its parks in the crofter days before Lord Kenneth. But now it was a fair bit farm on its own, old Sinclair and his wife, a body that was wearing none so well—soured up the creature was that her eldest daughter Sarah still bided all unwed—lived in the farm-house, and in the bothy was foreman and second man and third man and orra lad. The Denburn lay back of the Netherhill, drifting low and slow and placid in its hollow, feint the fish had ever been seen in it and folk said that was just as well, things were fishy enough at Netherhill without the Denburn adding to them. Through the rank schlorich of moor that lay between the place and Peesie's Knapp were the tracks of an old-time road, some said it was old as Calgacus, him that chased the Romans all to hell at the battle of Mons Graupius, others said it was a Druid work, laid by them that set the stones above Blawearie loch. And God! there must have been an unco few idle masons among the creatures, they'd tried their hands at another stone circle in the Netherhill moor, right midway the old-time road. But there were no more than two-three stones above the ground in this later day, Netherhill's ploughmen swore the rest must have been torn up and broadcast over the arable land, the parks were as tough and stony as the heart of the old wife herself.

But it was no bad place for turnips and oats, the Nether-hill, sometimes the hay was fair to middling but the most of the ground was red clay and over coarse and wet for barley, if it hadn't been for the droves of pigs old Mistress Sinclair fed and sold in Laurencekirk maybe her man would never have sat where he did. She came of Gourdon stock, the old wife, and everybody knows what they are, the Gourdon fishers, they'd wring silver out of a corpse's wame and call stinking haddocks perfume fishes and sell them at a shilling a pair. She'd been a fishing quean before she took up with old Sinclair, and when they settled down in Netherhill on borrowed money it was she that would drive to Gourdon twice a week in the little pony lorry and come back with it stinking out the countryside for miles around with its load of rotten fish to manure the land. And right well it manured it and they'd fine crops the first six years or so and then the land was fair bled white and they'd to stop the fish-manure. But by then the pig-breeding was fine and paying, their debts were gone, they were coining silver of their own. He was a harmless stock, old Sinclair, and had begun to doiter and Mistress Sinclair would push him into his chair at night and take off his boots and put slippers on him there in front of the kitchen fire and say to him *You've tired yourself out again, my lad*. And he'd put his hand below her chin and say *Och, I'm fine, don't vex yourself. . . . Ay your lad still, am I, lass?* And they'd look at each other, daft-like, two wrinkled old fools, and their daughter Sarah that was so genteel would be real affronted if there were visitors about. But Sinclair and his old wife would just shake their heads at her and in their bed at night, hiddling their old bones close for warmth, give a bit sigh that no brave billy had ever shown inclination to take Sarah to *his* bed. She'd hoped and peeked and preened long years, and once there had seemed some hope with Long Rob of the Mill, but Rob wasn't the marrying sort. God! if Cuddiestoun's dafties were real dafties what would you say of a man with plenty of silver that bided all by his lone and made his own bed and did his own baking when he might have had a wife to make him douce and brave?

But Rob of the Mill had never a thought of what Kinraddie said of him. Further along the Kinraddie road it stood, the Mill, on the corner of the side-road that led to Upperhill, and for ten years now had Rob bided there alone, managing the Mill and reading the books of a coarse creature Ingersoll that made watches and didn't believe in

God. He'd aye two-three fine pigs about the Mill had Rob, and fine might well they be for what did he feed them on but bits of corn and barley he'd nicked out of the sacks folk brought him to the Mill to grind? Nor could a body deny but that Long Rob's boar was one of the best in the Mearns; and they'd bring their sows from as far afield as Laurencekirk to have them set by that boar of his, a meikle, pretty brute of a beast. Forbye the Mill and his swine and hens Rob had a Clydesdale and a sholtie beast he ploughed his twenty acres with, and a cow or so that never calved, for he'd never time to send them to the bull though well might he have taken the time instead of sweating and chaving like a daft one to tear up the coarse moorland behind the Mill and turn it into a park. He'd started that three years before and wasn't half through with it yet, it was filled with great holes and ponds and choked with meikle broom-roots thick as the arm of a man, you never saw a dafter ploy. They'd hear Rob out in that coarse ground hard at work when they went to bed, the rest of Kinraddie, whistling away to himself as though it were nine o'clock in the forenoon and the sun shining bravely. He'd whistle *Ladies of Spain* and *There was a young maiden* and *The lass that made the bed for me*, but devil the lass he'd ever taken to his bed, and maybe that was as well for the lass; she'd have seen feint the much of him in it beside her.

For after a night of it like that he'd be out again at the keek of day, and sometimes he'd have the Clydesdale or the sholtie out there with him and they'd be fine friends, the three of them, till the beasts would move off when he didn't want them or wouldn't move when he did; and then he'd fair go mad with them and call them all the coarsest names he could lay tongue to till you'd think he'd be heard over half the Mearns; and he'd leather the horses till folk spoke of sending for the Cruelty, though he'd a way with the beasts too, and would be friends with them again in a minute, and when he'd been away at the smithy in Drumlithie or the joiner's in Arbuthnott they'd come running from the other end of the parks at sight of him and he'd get off his bicycle and feed them with lumps of sugar he bought and carried about with him. He thought himself a

gey man with horses, did Rob, and God! he'd tell you stories
about horses till you'd fair be grey in the head, but he never
wearied of them himself, the long, rangy childe. Long he
was, with small bones maybe, but gey broad for all that,
with a small head on him and a thin nose and eyes smoky
blue as an iron coulter on a winter morning, aye glinting,
and a long mouser the colour of ripe corn it was, hanging
down the sides of his mouth so that the old minister had
told him he looked like a Viking and he'd said *Ah well,
minister, as long as I don't look like a parson I'll wrestle
through the world right content,* and the minister said he
was a fool and godless, and his laughter like the thorns
crackling under a pot. And Rob said he'd rather be a thorn
than a sucker any day, for he didn't believe in ministers or
kirks, he'd learned that from the books of Ingersoll though
God knows if the creature's logic was as poor as his watches
he was but a sorry prop to lean on. But Rob said he was
fine, and if Christ came down to Kinraddie he'd be welcome
enough to a bit meal or milk at the Mill, but damn the thing
he'd get at the Manse. So that was Long Rob and the stir at
the Mill, some said he wasn't all there but others said Ay,
that he was, and a bit over.

Now Upperhill rose above the Mill, with its larch woods
crowning it, and folk told that a hundred years before five
of the crofter places had crowded there till Lord Kenneth
threw their biggins down and drove them from the parish
and built the fine farm of Upperhill. And twenty years later
a son of one of the crofters had come back and rented the
place, Gordon was the name of him, they called him
Upprums for short and he didn't like that, being near to
gentry with his meikle farm and forgetting his father the
crofter that had cried like a bairn all the way from Kinraddie
that night the Lord Kenneth drove them out. He was a
small bit man with a white face on him, and he'd long,
thin hair and a nose that wasn't straight but peeked away
to one side of his face and no moustache and wee feet and
hands; and he liked to wear leggings and breeks and carry
a bit stick and look as proud as a cock on a midden. Mistress
Gordon was a Stonehaven woman, her father had been a bit

post-office creature there, but God! to hear her speak you'd think he'd invented the post office himself and taken out a patent for it. She was a meikle sow of a woman, but aye well-dressed, and with eyes like the eyes of a fish, fair cod-like they were, and she tried to speak English and to make her two bit daughters, Nellie and Maggie Jean, them that went to Stonehaven Academy, speak English as well. And God! they made a right muck of it, and if you met the bit things on the road and said *Well, Nellie, and how are your mother's hens laying?* the quean would more than likely answer you *Not very meikle the day* and look so proud it was all you could do to stop yourself catching the futret across your knee and giving her a bit skelp.

Though she'd only a dove's flitting of a family herself you'd think to hear Mistress Gordon speak that she'd been clecking bairns a litter a month since the day she married. It was *Now, how I brought up Nellie*—or *And the specialist in Aberdeen, said about Maggie Jean*—till folk were so scunnered they'd never mention a bairn within a mile of Upperhill. But Rob of the Mill, the coarse brute, he fair mocked her to her face and he'd tell a story *Now, when I took my boar to the specialist in Edinburgh, he up and said 'Mister Rob, this is a gey unusual boar, awful delicate, but SO intelligent, and you should send him to the Academy and some day he'll be a real credit to you.'* And Mistress Gordon when she heard the story she turned as red as a fire and forgot her English and said Rob was an orra tink brute.

Forbye the two queans there was the son, John Gordon, as coarse a devil as you'd meet, he'd already had two-three queans in trouble and him but barely eighteen years old. But with one of them he'd met a sore stammy-gaster, her brother was a gardener down Glenbervie way and when he heard of it he came over to Upperhill and caught young Gordon out by the cattle-court. *You'll be Jock?* he said, and young Gordon said *Keep your damned hands to yourself*, and the billy said *Ay, but first I'll wipe them on a dirty clout*, and with that he up with a handful of sharn and splattered it all over young Gordon and then rolled him in the greip till he was a sight to sicken a sow from its supper. The bothy men heard the ongoing and came tearing out but soon as they saw it was only young Gordon that was being mischieved they did no more than laugh and stand around and cry one to the other that here was a real fine barrow-load of dung lying loose in the greip. So the Drum-lithie billy, minding his sister and her shame, wasn't sharp to finish with his tormenting, young Gordon looked like a half-dead cat and smelt like a whole-dead one for a week after, a sore affront to Upperhill's mistress. She went tearing round to the bothy and made at the foreman, a dour young devil of a Highlandman, Ewan Tavendale, *Why didn't you help my Johnnie?* and Ewan said *I was fee'd as the foreman here, not as the nursemaid,* he was an impudent brute, calm as you please, but an awful good worker, folk said he could smell the weather and had fair the land in his bones.

Now the eighth of the Kinraddie places you could call hardly a place at all, for that was Pooty's, midway along the Kinraddie road between the Mill and Bridge End. It was no more than a butt and a ben, with a rickle of sheds behind it where old Pooty kept his cow and bit donkey that was nearly as old as himself and faith! twice as good-looking; and folk said the cuddy had bided so long with Pooty that whenever it opened its mouth to give a bit bray it started to stutter. For old Pooty was maybe the worst stutterer ever heard in the Mearns and the worst of that worst was that he didn't know it and he'd clean compel any minister creature organising a concert miles around to give him a platform part. Then up he'd get on the platform, the doitered old fool, and recite *Weeeee, ssss-leek-ed, cccccccowering TIMROUS BEASTIE* or such-like poem and it was fair agony to hear him. He'd lived at Pooty's a good fifty years they said, his father the crofter of the Knapp before that time, hardly a soul knew his name, maybe he'd forgotten it himself. He was the oldest inhabitant of Kinraddie and fell proud of it, though what there was to be proud of in biding all that while in a damp, sour house that a goat would hardly have stopped to ease itself in God knows. He was a shoe-maker, the creature, and called himself the Sutor, an old-fashioned name that folk laughed at. He'd grey hair aye falling about his lugs and maybe he washed on New Year's Days and birthdays, but not oftener, and if anybody had ever seen him in anything but the grey shirt with the red neckband he'd kept the fact a dead secret all to himself.

Alec Mutch was farmer of Bridge End that stood beyond the Denburn head, he'd come there up from Stonehaven way, folk said he was head over heels in debt, and damn it you couldn't wonder with a slummock of a wife like that to weigh him down. A grand worker was Alec and Bridge End not the worst of Kinraddie, though wet in the bottom up where its parks joined on to Upperhill. Two pairs of horses it was stabled for but Alec kept no more than three bit beasts, he'd say he was waiting for his family to grow up before he completed the second pair. And fast enough the family came, if she couldn't do much else, Mistress Mutch, fell seldom a year went by but she was brought to bed with a bairn, Mutch fair grew used to dragging himself out in the middle of the night and tearing off to Bervie for the doctor. And the doctor, old Meldrum he was, he'd wink at Alec and cry *Man, Man, have you been at it again?* and Alec would say *Damn it, you've hardly to look at a woman these days but she's in the family way.*

So some said that he must glower at his mistress a fell lot, and that was hard enough to believe, she was no great beauty, with a cock eye and a lazy look and nothing worried her, not a mortal thing, not though her five bairns were all yammering blue murder at the same minute and the smoke coming down the chimney and spoiling the dinner and the cattle broken into the yard and eating up her clean washing. She'd say *Ah well, it'll make no difference a hundred years after I'm dead,* and light up a bit cigarette, like a tink, for aye she carried a packet of the things about with her, she was the speak of half the Mearns, her and her smoking. Two of the five bairns were boys, the oldest eleven, and the whole five of them had the Mutch face, broad and boney and tapering to a chinney point, like the face of an owlet or a fox, and meikle lugs on them like the handles on a cream-jar. Alec himself had such lugs that they said he flapped them against the flies in the summer-time, and once he was coming home on his bicycle from Laurence-kirk, and he was real drunk and at the steep brae above the Denburn bridge he mistook the flow of the water for the broad road and in between coping and bank he went and head over heels into the clay bed twenty feet below; and often he'd tell that if he hadn't landed on a lug he might well have been brained, but Long Rob of the Mill would laugh and say *Brained? God Almighty, Mutch, you were never in danger of that!*

So that was Kinraddie that bleak winter of nineteen eleven and the new minister, him they chose early next year, he was to say it was the Scots countryside itself, fathered between a kailyard and a bonny brier bush in the lee of a house with green shutters. And what he meant by that you could guess at yourself if you'd a mind for puzzles and dirt, there wasn't a house with green shutters in the whole of Kinraddie.

THE SONG

I

PLOUGHING

Below and around where Chris Guthrie lay the June moors
whispered and rustled and shook their cloaks, yellow with
broom and powdered faintly with purple, that was the
heather but not the full passion of its colour yet. And in
the east against the cobalt blue of the sky lay the shimmer
of the North Sea, that was by Bervie, and maybe the wind
would veer there in an hour or so and you'd feel the change
in the life and strum of the thing, bringing a streaming
coolness out of the sea. But for days now the wind had been
in the south, it shook and played in the moors and went
dandering up the sleeping Grampians, the rushes pecked
and quivered about the loch when its hand was upon them,
but it brought more heat than cold, and all the parks were
fair parched, sucked dry, the red clay soil of Blawearie
gaping open for the rain that seemed never-coming. Up
here the hills were brave with the beauty and the heat of
it, but the hayfield was all a crackling dryness and in the
potato park beyond the biggings the shaws drooped red
and rusty already. Folk said there hadn't been such a drought
since eighty-three and Long Rob of the Mill said you
couldn't blame *this* one on Gladstone, anyway, and everybody laughed except father, God knows why.

Some said the North, up Aberdeen way, had had rain
enough, with Dee in spate and bairns hooking stranded
salmon down in the shallows, and that must be fine enough,
but not a flick of the greeve weather had come over the
hills, the roads you walked down to Kinraddie smithy or
up to the Denburn were fair blistering in the heat, thick
with dust so that the motor-cars went shooming through
them like kettles under steam. And serve them right, they'd
little care for anybody, the dirt that rode in motors, folk
said; and one of them had nearly run over wee Wat Strachan
a fortnight before and had skirled to a stop right bang in

front of Peesie's Knapp, Wat had yowled like a cat with a jobe under its tail and Chae had gone striding out and taken the motorist man by the shoulder. And *What the hell do you think you're up to?* Chae had asked. And the motorist, he was a fair toff with leggings and a hat cocked over his eyes, he'd said *Keep your damn children off the road in future.* And Chae had said *Keep a civil tongue in your head* and had clouted the motorist man one in the ear and down he had flumped in the stour and Mistress Strachan, her that was old Netherhill's daughter, she'd gone tearing out skirling *Mighty, you brute, you've killed the man!* and Chae had just laughed and said *Damn the fears!* and off he'd gone. But Mistress Strachan had helped the toff up to his feet and shook him and brushed him and apologised for Chae, real civil-like. And all the thanks she got was that Chae was summonsed for assault at Stonehaven and fined a pound, and came out of the courthouse saying there was no justice under capitalism, a revolution would soon sweep away its corrupted lackeys. And maybe it would, but faith! there was as little sign of a revolution, said Long Rob of the Mill, as there was of rain.

Maybe that was the reason for half the short tempers over the Howe. You could go never a road but farmer billies were leaning over the gates, glowering at the weather, and road-menders, poor stocks, chapping away at their hillocks with the sweat fair dripping off them, and the only folk that seemed to have a fine time were the shepherds up in the hills. But they swore themselves dry when folk cried that to them, the hill springs about a shepherd's herd would dry up or seep away all in an hour and the sheep go straying and baying and driving the man fair senseless till he'd led them weary miles to the nearest burn. So everybody was fair snappy, staring up at the sky, and the ministers all over the Howe were offering up prayers for rain in between the bit about the Army and the Prince of Wales' rheumatics. But feint the good it did for rain; and Long Rob of the Mill said he'd heard both Army and rheumatics were much the same as before.

Maybe father would have done better to keep a civil

tongue in his head and stayed on in Echt, there was plenty
of rain there, a fine land for rain, Aberdeen, you'd see it
by day and night come drenching and wheeling over the
Barmekin and the Hill of Fare in the fine northern land.
And mother would sigh, looking out from Blawearie's
windows, *There's no land like Aberdeen or folk so fine as
them that bide by Don.*

She'd bidden by Don all her life, mother, she'd been born
in Kildrummie, her father a ploughman there, he'd got
no more than thirteen shillings a week and he'd had thirteen
of a family, to work things out in due ratio, maybe. But
mother said they all got on fine, she was never happier
in her life than those days when she tramped bare-footed
the roads to the little school that nestled under the couthy
hills. And at nine she left the school and they packed a
basket for her and she bade her mother ta-ta and set out
to her first fee, no shoes on her feet even then, she hadn't
worn shoes till she was twelve years old. It hadn't been a
real fee that first one, she'd done little more than scare
the crows from the fields of an old bit farmer and sleep in
a garret, but fine she'd liked it, she'd never forget the singing of the winds in those fields when she was young or the
daft crying of the lambs she herded or the feel of the earth
below her toes, *Oh, Chris, my lass, there are better things
than your books or studies or loving or bedding, there's
the countryside your own, you its, in the days when you're
neither bairn nor woman.*

So mother had worked and ran the parks those days,
she was blithe and sweet, you knew, you saw her against
the sun as though you peered far down a tunnel of the
years. She stayed long on her second fee, seven or eight
years she was there till the day she met John Guthrie at
a ploughing-match at Pittodrie. And often once she'd tell of
that to Chris and Will, it was nothing grand of a match,
the horses were poor and the ploughing worse and a coarse,
cold wind was soughing across the rigs and half Jean
Murdoch made up her mind to go home. Then it was that it
came the turn of a brave young childe with a red head
and the swackest legs you ever saw, his horses were laced
in ribbons, bonny and trig, and as soon as he began the drill

you saw he'd carry off the prize. And carry it off he did, young John Guthrie, and not that alone. For as he rode from the park on one horse he patted the back of the other and cried to Jean Murdoch with a glint from his dour, sharp eye *Jump up if you like.* And she cried back *I like fine!* and caught the horse by its mane and swung herself there till Guthrie's hand caught her and set her steady on the back of the beast. So out from the ploughing match at Pittodrie the two of them rode together, Jean sitting upon the hair of her, gold it was and so long, and laughing up into the dour, keen face that was Guthrie's.

So that was beginning of their lives together, she was sweet and kind to him, but he mightn't touch her, his face would go black with rage at her because of that sweetness that tempted his soul to hell. Yet in two-three years they'd chaved and saved enough for gear and furnishings, and were married at last, and syne Will was born, and syne Chris herself was born, and the Guthries rented a farm in Echt, Cairndhu it was, and sat themselves down there for many a year.

Winters or springs, summers or harvests, bristling or sunning the sides of Barmekin, and life ploughed its rigs and drove its teams and the dourness hardened, hard and cold, in the heart of Jean Guthrie's man. But still the glint of her hair could rouse him, Chris would hear him cry in agony at night as he went with her, mother's face grew queer and questioning, her eyes far back on those Springs she might never see again, dear and blithe they had been, she could kiss and hold them still a moment alone with Chris or Will. Dod came, then Alec came, and mother's fine face grew harder then. One night they heard her cry to John Guthrie *Four of a family's fine; there'll be no more.* And father thundered at her, that way he had *Fine? We'll have what God in His mercy may send to us, woman. See you to that.*

He wouldn't do anything against God's will, would father, and sure as anything God followed up Alec with the twins, born seven years later. Mother went about with a queer look on her face before they came, she lost that sweet blitheness that was hers, and once, maybe she was ill-like, she said to father when he spoke of arranging a doctor and things, *Don't worry about that. No doubt your friend Jehovah will see to it all.* Father seemed to freeze up, then, his face grew black, he said never a word, and Chris had wondered at that, seeing how mad he'd been when Will used the word, thoughtless-like, only a week before.

For Will had heard the word in the kirk of Echt where the elders sit with shaven chins and the offering bags between their knees, waiting the sermon to end and to march with slow, sleeked steps up through the pews, hearing the penny of penury clink shy-like against the threepenny of affluence. And Will one Sunday, sitting close to sleep, heard fall from the minister's lips the word *Jehovah,* and treasured it for the bonniness and the beauty of it, waiting till he might find a thing or a man or beast that would fit this word, well-shaped and hantled and grand.

Now that was in summer, the time of fleas and glegs and golochs in the fields, when stirks would start up from a drowsy cud-chewing to a wild and feckless racing, the glegs biting through hair and hide to the skin below the tail-rump. Echt was alive that year with the thunder of herds, the crackle of breaking gates, the splash of stirks in tarns, and last with the groans of Nell, the old horse of Guthrie's, caught in a daft swither of the Highland steers and her belly ripped like a rotten swede with the stroke of a great, curved horn.

Father saw the happening from high in a park where the hay was cut and they set the swathes in coles, and he swore out *Damn't to hell!* and started to run, fleetly as was his way, down to the groaning shambles that was Nell. And as he ran he picked up a scythe-blade, and as he neared to Nell he unhooked the blade and cried *Poor quean!* and Nell groaned, groaning blood and sweating, and turned away her neck, and father thrust the scythe at her neck, sawing till she died.

So that was the end of Nell, father waited till the hay was coled and then tramped into Aberdeen and bought a new horse, Bess, riding her home at evening to the raptured starings of Will. And Will took the horse and watered her and led her into the stall where Nell had slept and gave to her hay and a handful of corn, and set to grooming her, shoulder to heel, and her fine plump belly and the tail of her, long and curled. And Bess stood eating her corn and Chris leant against the door-jamb, her Latin Grammar held in her hand. So, working with fine, strong strokes, and happy, Will groomed till he finished the tail, and then as he lifted the brush to hit Bess on the flank that she might move to the other side of the stall and he complete his grooming there flashed in his mind the fine word he had treasured. *Come over, Jehovah!* he cried, smiting her roundly, and John Guthrie heard the word out across the yard and came fleetly from the kitchen, wiping oatcake from his beard, and fleetly across the yard into the stable he came——

But he should not have stricken Will as he did, he fell below the feet of the horse and Bess turned her head, dripping corn, and looked down at Will, with his face bloody, and then swished her tail and stood still. And then John Guthrie dragged his son aside and paid no more heed to him, but picked up brush and curry-comb and cried *Whoa, lass!* and went on with the grooming. Chris had cried and hidden her face but now she looked again, Will was sitting up slowly, the blood on his face, and John Guthrie speaking to him, not looking at him, grooming Bess.

And mind, my mannie, if I ever hear you again take your Maker's name in vain, if I ever hear you use that word again, I'll libb you. Mind that. Libb you like a lamb.

So Will hated father, he was sixteen years of age and near a man, but father could still make him cry like a bairn. He would whisper his hate to Chris as they lay in their beds at night in the loft room high in the house and the harvest moon came sailing over the Barmekin and the peewits wheeped above the lands of Echt. And Chris would cover her ears and then listen, turning this cheek to the pillow and that, she hated also and she didn't hate, father, the land, the life of the land—oh, if only she knew!

For she'd met with books, she went into them to a magic land far from Echt, out and away and south. And at school they wrote she was the clever one and John Guthrie said she might have the education she needed if she stuck to her lessons. In time she might come out as a teacher then, and do him credit, that was fine of father the Guthrie whispered in her, but the Murdoch laughed with a blithe, sweet face. But more and more she turned from that laughter, resolute, loving to hear of the things in the histories and geographies, seldom thinking them funny, strange names and words like Too-long and Too-loose that convulsed the classes. And at arithmetic also she was more than good, doing great sums in her head so that always she was first in the class, they made her the dux and they gave her prizes, four prizes in four years she had.

And one book she'd thought fair daft, *Alice in Wonderland* it was, and there was no sense in it. And the second, it was *What Katy did at School*, and she loved Katy and envied her and wished like Katy she lived at a school, not tramping back in the spleiter of a winter night to help muck the byre, with the smell of the sharn rising feuch! in her face. And the third book was *Rienzi, the Last of the Roman Tribunes*, and some bits were good and some fair wearying. He had a right bonny wife. Rienzi had, and he was sleeping with her, her white arms round his neck, when the Romans came to kill him at last. And the fourth book, new given her before the twins came to Cairndhu, was *The Humours of Scottish Life* and God! if that stite was fun she must have been born dull.

And these had been all her books that weren't lesson-books, they were all the books in Cairndhu but for the Bibles grandmother had left to them, one to Chris and one to Will, and in Chris's one were set the words *To my dawtie Chris: Trust in God and do the right*. For grandmother, she'd been father's mother, not mother's mother, had been fell religious and every Sunday, rain or shine, had tramped to the kirk at Echt, sitting below some four-five ministers there in all. And one minister she'd never forgiven, for he'd said not GAWD, as a decent man would, but GOHD, and it had been a mercy when he caught a bit cold, laid up he was, and quickly passed away; and maybe it had been a judgment on him.

So that was Chris and her reading and schooling, two Chrisses there were that fought for her heart and tormented

her. You hated the land and the coarse speak of the folk
and learning was brave and fine one day; and the next you'd
waken with the peewits crying across the hills, deep and
deep, crying in the heart of you and the smell of the earth
in your face, almost you'd cry for that, the beauty of it and
the sweetness of the Scottish land and skies. You saw their
faces in firelight, father's and mother's and the neighbours',
before the lamps lit up, tired and kind, faces dear and close
to you, you wanted the words they'd known and used,
forgotten in the far-off youngness of their lives, Scots words
to tell to your heart how they wrung it and held it, the
toil of their days and unendingly their fight. And the next
minute that passed from you, you were English, back to the
English words so sharp and clean and true—for a while, for a
while, till they slid so smooth from your throat you knew they
could never say anything that was worth the saying at all.

But she sat for her bursary, won it, and began the conju-
gating Latin verbs, the easy ones only at first, *Amo, amas, I
love a lass* and then you laughed out loud when the Dominie
said that and he cried *Whist, whist* but was real pleased and
smiled at you and you felt fine and tingly and above all the
rest of the queans who weren't learning Latin or anything
else, they were kitchen-maids in the bone. And then there
was French, fair difficult, the u was the worst; and an
inspector creature came to Echt and Chris near dropped
through the schoolroom floor in shame when he made her
stand out in front of them all and say *o-oo, o-oo, o-oo-butin.*
And he said *Put your mouth as though you were going to
weesel, but don't do it, and say 'o-oo, o-oo, o-oo.'* And she
said it, she felt like a hen with a stone in its thrapple, after
the inspector creature, an Englishman he was with an awful
belly on him and he couldn't say whistle, only weesel. And
he went away, down to the gig that was waiting to drive
him to the station he went, and he left his brave leather
bag behind, and the Dominie saw it and cried *Whist,
Chrissie, run after the Inspector man with his bag.* So she
did and caught him up at the foot of the playground, he
gowked at her and said *Haw?* and then gave her a bit laugh
and saw *Haw?* again and then *Thenks.* And Chris went
back to the Dominie's room, the Dominie was waiting

for her and he asked if the Inspector had given her anything, and Chris said *No*, and the Dominie looked sore
disappointed.

But everybody knew that the English were awful mean
and couldn't speak right and were cowards who captured
Wallace and killed him by treachery. But they'd been beaten
right well at Bannockburn, then, Edward the Second hadn't
drawn rein till he was in Dunbar, and ever after that the
English were beaten in all the wars, except Flodden and
they won at Flodden by treachery again, just as it told in
The Flowers of the Forest. Always she wanted to cry when
she heard that played and a lot of folk singing it at a parish
concert in Echt, for the sadness of it and the lads that came
back never again to their lasses among the stooks, and the
lasses that never married but sat and stared down south to
the English border where their lads lay happed in blood and
earth, with their bloodied kilts and broken helmets. And
she wrote an essay on that, telling all ho wit happened, the
Dominie said it was fine and that sometime she should try
to write poetry; like Mrs Hemans.

But then, just after writing the essay, the twins were born
and mother had as awful a time as she'd always had. She
was sobbing and ill when she went to bed, Chris boiled
water in kettles for hours and hours and then towels came
down, towels clairted with stuff she didn't dare look at, she
washed them quick and hung them to dry. The doctor came
in with the evening, he stayed the whole night, and Dod and
Alec shivered and cried in their room till father went up
and skelped them right sore, they'd something to cry for
then but they didn't dare. And father came down the stairs
again, fleet as ever, though he hadn't been in bed for forty
hours, and he closed the kitchen door and sat with his head
between his hands and groaned and said he was a miserable
sinner, God forgive him the lusts of the flesh. Something
about the bonny hair of her also he said and then more
about lust, but he hadn't intended Chris to hear for he
looked up and saw her looking at him and he raged at her,
telling her to spread a table with breakfast for the doctor—
through in the parlour there, and boil him an egg.

And then mother began to scream, the doctor called down

the stairs *Man, it's a fair tough case, I doubt I'll need your help,* and at that father turned grey as a sheet and covered his face again and cried *I dare not, I dare not!* Then the doctor childe called him again *Guthrie man, do you hear me?* and father jumped up in a rage and cried *Damn't to hell, I'm not deaf!* and ran up the stairs, fleet as ever, and then the door in the room closed fast and Chris could hear no more.

Not that she wanted to hear, she felt real ill herself, cooking the egg and laying a meal in the parlour, with a white cloth spread above the green plush cloth and all the furniture dark and shadowed and listening. Then Will came down the stair, he couldn't sleep because of mother, they sat together and Will said the old man was a fair beast and mother shouldn't be having a baby, she was far too old for that. And Chris stared at him with horrified imaginings in her mind, she hadn't known better then, the English bit of her went sick, she whispered *What has father to do with it?* And Will stared back at her, shame-faced, *Don't you know? What's a bull to do with a calf, you fool?*

But then they heard an awful scream that made them leap to their feet, it was as though mother were being torn and torn in the teeth of beasts and couldn't thole it longer; and then a little screech like a young pig made followed that scream and they tried not to hear more of the sounds above them, Chris boiled the egg over and over till it was as hard as iron. And then mother screamed again, Oh God! your heart stopped to hear it, and that was when the second twin came.

Then quietness followed, they heard the doctor coming down the stairs, the morning was close, it hung scared beyond the stilled parks and listened and waited. But the doctor cried *Hot water, jugs of it, pour me a basin of water, Chris, and put plenty of soap near by it.* She cried *Ay, doctor,* to that but she cried in a whisper, he didn't hear and was fell angry. *D'you hear me?* And Will said to him, calling up the stair, *Ay, doctor, only she's feared,* and the doctor said *She'll have a damned sight more to fear when she's having a bairn of her own. Pour out the water, quick!* So they poured it and went through to the parlour while the doctor passed them with his hands held away from them, and the smell of his hands was a horror that haunted Chris for a day and a night.

That was the coming of the twins at Cairndhu, there'd been barely room for them all before that time, now they'd have to live like tinks. But it was a fell good farm, John Guthrie loath to part with it though his lease was near its end, and when mother came down from her bed in a fortnight's time with the shine of the gold still in the sweet hair of her and her eyes clear eyes again, he raged and swore when she spoke to him. *More rooms? What more room do we want than we have? Do you think we're gentry?* he cried, and went on again to tell that when he was a bairn in Pittodrie his mother had nine bairns all at home, nought but a butt and ben they had and their father nought but a plough-childe. But fine they'd managed, God-fearing and decent all he'd made them, and if one of Jean Murdoch's bairns were half as good the shame need never redden the face of her. And mother looked at him with the little smile on her lips. *Well, well, we're to bide on here, then?* and father shot out his beard at her and cried *Ay, that we are, content yourself.*

But the very next day he was driving back from the mart, old Bob in the cart, when round a corner below the Barmekin came a motor-car spitting and barking like a tink dog in distemper. Old Bob had made a jump and near landed the cart in the ditch and then stood like a rock, so feared he wouldn't move a step, the cart jammed fast across the road. And as father tried to haul the thrawn beast to the side a creature of a woman with her face all clamjamfried with paint and powder and dirt, she thrust her bit head out from the window of the car and cried *You're causing an obstruction, my man.* And John Guthrie roused like a lion: *I'm not your man, thank God, for if I was I'd have your face scraped with a clart and then a scavenger wash it well.* The woman nearly burst with rage at that, she fell back in the car and said *You've not heard the last of this. Take note of his name-plate, James, d'you hear?* And the shover looked out, fair shamed he looked, and keeked at the name-plate underneath Bob's shelvin, and quavered *Yes, madam,* and they turned about and drove off. That was the way to deal with dirt like the gentry, but when father applied for his lease again he was told he couldn't have it.

So he took a look at the *People's Journal* and got into his fine best suit, Chris shook the moth-balls from it and found him his collar and the broad white front to cover his working sark; and John Guthrie tramped into Aberdeen and took a train to Banchory to look at a small place there. But the rent was awful high and he saw that nearly all the district was land of the large-like farm, he'd be squeezed to death and he'd stand no chance. It was fine land though, that nearly shook him, fine it looked and your hands they itched to be at it; but the agent called him *Guthrie,* and he fired up at the agent: *Who the hell are you Guthrie-ing? Mister Guthrie to you.* And the agent looked at him and turned right white about the gills and then gave a bit laugh and said *Ah well, Mr Guthrie, I'm afraid you wouldn't suit us.* And John Guthrie said *It's your place that doesn't suit me, let me tell you, you wee, dowp-licking clerk.* Poor he might be but the creature wasn't yet clecked that might put on its airs with him, John Guthrie.

So back he came and began his searchings again. And the third day out he came back from far in the south. He'd taken a place, Blawearie, in Kinraddie of the Mearns.

Wild weather it was that January and the night on the Slug road smoring with sleet when John Guthrie crossed his family and gear from Aberdeen into the Mearns. Twice the great carts set with their shelvins that rustled still stray binder-twine from September's harvest-home laired in drifts before the ascent of the Slug faced the reluctant horses. Darkness came down like a wet, wet blanket, weariness below it and the crying of the twins to vex John Guthrie. Mother called him from her nook in the leading cart, there where she sat with now one twin at the breast and now another, and her skin bare and cold and white and a strand of her rust-gold hair draped down from the darkness about her face into the light of the swinging lantern: *We'd better loosen up at Portlethen and not try the Slug this night.*

But father swore at that *Damn't to hell, do you think I'm made of silver to put up the night at Portlethen?* and mother sighed and held off the wee twin, Robert, and the milk dripped creamily from the soft, sweet lips of him: *No, we're not made of silver, but maybe we'll lair again and all die of the night.*

Maybe he feared that himself, John Guthrie, his rage was his worriment with the night, but he'd no time to answer her for a great bellowing arose in the road by the winding scurry of peat-moss that lined the dying light of the moon. The cattle had bunched there, tails to the wind, refusing the Slug and the sting of the sleet, little Dod was wailing and crying at the beasts. Polled Angus and Shorthorns and half-bred Highland stirks who had fattened and feted and loved their life in the haughs of Echt, south there across the uncouthy hills was a world cold and unchancy. But John Guthrie dropped the tarpaulin edge that shielded his wife and the twins and the furnishings of the best room and gear good and plentiful enough; and swiftly he ran past the head of the horse till he came to where the cattle bunched. And he swung Dod into the ditch with one swipe of his hand and cried *Have you got no sense, you brat?* and uncoiled from his hand the length of hide that served him as a whip. Its crackle snarled down through the sting of the sleet, the hair rose in long serrations across the backs of the cattle, and one in a minute, a little Highland steer it was, mooed and ran forward and fell to a trot, and the rest followed after, slipping and sprawling with their cloven hooves, the reek of their dung sharp and bitter in the sleet smore of the night. Ahead Alec saw them coming and turned himself about again, and fell to a trot, leading up the Slug to Mearns and the south.

So, creaking and creaking, and the shelvins skirling under the weight of their loads, they passed that danger point, the carts plodded into motion again, the first with its hooded light and house gear and mother suckling the twins. In the next, Clyde's cart, the seed was loaded, potato and corn and barley, and bags of tools and implements, and graips and

forks fast tied with esparto twine and two fine ploughs and
a driller, and dairy things and a turnip machine with teeth
that cut as a guillotine cuts. Head down to the wind and her
reins loose and her bonny coat all mottled with sleet went
Clyde, the load a nothing to her, fine and clean and sonsy
she marched, following John Guthrie's cart with no other
thing or soul to guide but that ever and now, in this half-
mile and that she heard his voice cry cheerily *Fine, Clyde,
fine. Come on then, lass.*

Chris and Will with the last cart, sixteen Will and fifteen
Chris, the road wound up and up, straight and unwavering,
and sometimes they hiddled in the lithe and the sleet sang
past to left and right, white and glowing in the darkness.
And sometimes they clambered down from the shelvins
above the laboured drag of old Bob and ran beside him,
one either side, and stamped for warmth in their feet, and
saw the whin bushes climb black the white hills beside them
and far and away the blink of lights across the moors where
folk lay happed and warm. But then the upwards road
would swerve, right or left, into this steep ledge or that, and
the wind would be at them again and they'd gasp, climbing
back to the shelvins, Will with freezing feet and hands and
the batter of the sleet like needles in his face, Chris in worse
case, colder and colder at every turn, her body numb and
unhappy, knees and thighs and stomach and breast, her
breasts ached and ached so that nearly she wept. But of that
she told nothing, she fell to a drowse through the cold, and
a strange dream came to her as they plodded up through the
ancient hills.

For out of the night ahead of them came running a man,
father didn't see him or heed to him, though old Bob in the
dream that was Chris's snorted and shied. And as he came
he wrung his hands, he was mad and singing, a foreign
creature, black-bearded, half-naked he was; and he cried in
the Greek *The ships of Pytheas! The ships of Pytheas!* and
went by into the smore of the sleet-storm on the Grampian
hills, Chris never saw him again, queer dreaming that was.
For her eyes were wide open, she rubbed them with never a
need of that, if she hadn't been dreaming she must have
been daft. They'd cleared the Slug, below was Stonehaven

and the Mearns, and far beyond that, miles through the
Howe, the twinkling point of light that shone from the
flagstaff of Kinraddie.

So that was their coming to Blawearie, fell wearied all of
them were the little of the night that was left them, and slept
late into the next morning, coming cold and drizzly up from
the sea by Bervie. All the darkness they heard that sea, a
shoom-shoom that moaned by the cliffs of lone Kinneff. Not
that John Guthrie listened to such dirt of sounds, but Chris
and Will did, in the room where they'd made their shake-
down beds. In the strangeness and cold and the sighing of
that far-off water Chris could find no sleep till Will whispered *Let's sleep together*. So then they did, oxtering one
the other till they were real warm. But at the first keek
of day Will slipped back to the blankets of his own bed,
he was feared what father would say if he found them lying
like that. Chris thought of that angrily, puzzled and angry,
the English Chris as sleep came on her again. Was it likely
a brother and a sister would do anything if they slept
together? And besides, she didn't know how.

But Will back in his bed had hardly a minute to get
warm or a wink of sleep when John Guthrie was up and
about the place, rousing them all, and the twins were
wakened and crying for the breast, and Dod and Alec
trying to light the fire. Father swore up and down the
strange Blawearie stairs, chapping from door to door,
weren't they sick with shame lying stinking in bed and
half the day gone? Then out he went, the house quietened
down as he banged the door, and he cried back that
he was off up the brae to look at the loch in Blawearie
moor—*Get out and get on with the breakfast and get
your work done ere I come back else I'll warm your lugs
for you.*

And faith, it was queer that the notion took father to
climb the brae at that hour. For as he went up through
the broom he heard a shot, did John Guthrie, cracking the
morning so dark and iron-like, and he stood astounded,
was not Blawearie his and he the tenant of it? And rage
took him and he ceased to dander. Up through the hills

among the dead broom he sped like a hare and burst in sight
of the loch, grass-fringed and chill then under the winter
morning, with a sailing of wild geese above it, going out
east to the sea. All but one winged east in burnished strokes
under the steel-grey sky, but that one loped and swooped
and stroked the air with burnished pinions, and John
Guthrie saw the feathers drift down from it, it gave a wild
cry like a bairn smored at night below the blankets, and
down it plonked on the mere of the loch, not ten yards
from where the man with the gun was standing. So John
Guthrie he went cannily across the grass to this billy in
the brave leggings and with the red face on him, and who
was he standing so sure-like on Guthrie's land? He gave a
bit jump, hearing Guthrie come, and then he swithered
a laugh inside the foolish face of him, but John Guthrie
didn't laugh. Instead, he whispered, quiet-like, *Ay, man,
you're been shooting,* and the creature said *Ay, just that.*
And John Guthrie said *Ay, you'll be a bit poacher, then?*
and the billy said *No, I'll not be that, I'm Maitland, the
foreman at Mains,* and John Guthrie whispered *You may
be the archangel Gabriel, but you're not to shoot on MY
land, d'you hear?*

The Standing Stones reared up above the two, marled
and white-edged with snow they were, and a wind came
blowing fit to freeze the chilblains on a brass monkey as
they stood and glowered one at the other. Then Maitland
muttered *Ellison at Mains will see about this,* and made
off for all the world as if he feared the crack of a kick in
the dowp of him. And right fairly there, midmost his brave
breeks John Guthrie might well have kicked but that he
restrained himself, cannily, for the goose was still lying by
the side of the loch, jerking and slobbering blood through
its beak; and it looked at him with terror in its slate-grey
eyes and he waited, canny still, till Maitland was out of
sight, syne he wrung the neck of the bird and took it down
to Blawearie. And he told them all of the meeting with
Maitland, and if ever they heard a shot on the land they
were to run to him at once and tell him, he'd deal with any
damn poacher—Jew, Gentile, or the Prince of Wales himself.

So that was how father made first acquaintance with the Standing Stones, and he didn't like them, for one evening in Spring after a day's ploughing and tired a bit maybe, he went up on a dander through the brae to the loch and found Chris lying there, just as now she lay in the summer heat. Tired though he was he came to her side right fleet enough, his shoulders straight and his frightening eyes on her, she had no time to close the story-book she read and he snatched it up and looked at it and cried *Dirt! You've more need to be down in the house helping your mother wash out the hippens.* And he glanced with a louring eye at the Standing Stones and then Chris had thought a foolish thing, that he kind of shivered, as though he were feared, him that was feared at nothing dead or alive, gentry or common. But maybe the shiver came from his fleetness caught in the bite of the cold Spring air, he stood looking at the Stones a minute and said they were coarse, foul things, the folk that raised them were burning in hell, skin-clad savages with never a skin to guard them now. And Chris had better get down to her work, had she heard any shooting that evening?

But Chris said *No*, and neither she had, nor any other evening till John Guthrie himself got a gun, a second-hand thing he picked up in Stonehaven, a muzzle-loader it was, and as he went by the Mill on the way to Blawearie Long Rob came out and saw it and cried *Ay, man I didn't mind you were a veteran of the '45.* And father cried *Losh, Rob, were you cheating folk at your Mill even then?* for sometimes he could take a bit joke, except with his family. So home he brought the old gun and loaded it up with pellets and stuffed in wadding with a ram-rod; and by night he would go cannily out in the gloaming, and shoot here a rabbit and there a hare, no other soul must handle the gun but himself. Nor did any try till that day he went off to the mart at Laurencekirk and then Will took down the gun and laughed at the thing and loaded it and went out and shot at a mark, a herring box on the top of a post, till he was fell near perfect. But he wished he hadn't, for father came home and counted his pellets that evening and went fair mad with rage till mother grew sick of the subject and cried *Hold your whist, you and your gun, what harm was in Will that he used it?*

Father had been sitting at the neuk of the fire when he heard that, but he got to his feet like a cat then, looking at Will so that the blood flowed cold in Chris's veins. Then he said, in the quiet-like voice that was his when he was going to leather them, *Come out to the barn with me, Will.* Mother laughed that strange, blithe laugh that had come out of the Springs of Kildrummie with her, kind and queer in a breath it was, looking pityingly at Will. But Chris burned with shame because of him, he was over-old for that, she cried out, *Father, you can't!*

As well have cried to the tides at Kinneff to keep away from the land, father was fair roused by then, he whispered *Be quiet, quean, else I'll take you as well.* And up to the barn he went with Will and took down his breeks, nearly seventeen though he was, and leathered him till the weals stood blue across his haunches; and that night Will could hardly sleep for the pain of it, sobbing into his pillow, till Chris slipped into his bed and took him into her arms and held him and cuddled him and put out her hand below his shirt on to his body and made gentle her fingers to pass and repass across the torn flesh of his body, soothing him, and he stopped from crying after a while and fell asleep, holding to her, strange it seemed then for she knew him bigger and older than she was, and somehow skin and hair and body stranger than once they had been, as though they were no longer children. She minded then the stories of Marget Strachan, and felt herself in the darkness blush for shame and then think of them still more and lie awake, seeing out of the window as it wore on to midnight a lowe in mauve and gold that crept and slipt and wavered upon the sky, and that was the lowe of the night-time whin-burning up on the Grampians; and next morning she was almost too sleepy to stiter into her clothes and set out across the fields to the station and the College train for Duncairn.

For to the College she'd been sent and found it strange enough after the high classes in Echt, a little ugly place it was below Duncairn Station, ugly as sin and nearly as

proud, said the Chris that was Murdoch, Chris of the land.
Inside the main building of it was carved the head of a
beast like a calf with colic, but they swore the creature was
a wolf on a shield, whatever the brute might be doing
there.

Every week or so the drawing master, old Mr Kinloch,
marched out this class or that to the playground in front
of the wolf-beast; and down they'd all get on the chairs
they'd brought and try and draw the beast. Right fond
of the gentry was Kinloch, if you wore a fine frock and
your hair was well brushed and your father well to the fore
he'd sit beside you and stroke your arm and speak in a
slow sing-song that made everybody laugh behind his back.
Noooooooooooo, that's not quate raight, he would flute,
*More like the head of one of Chrissie's faaaaaaaather's pigs
than a heraaaaaaaaaaldic animal, I'm afraaaaaaaaaaaaaaaaaid.*
So he loved the gentry, did Mr Kinloch, and God knows
he was no exception among the masters there. For the
most of them were sons and daughters of poor bit crofters
and fishers themselves, up with the gentry they felt safe
and unfrightened, far from that woesome pit of brose and
bree and sheetless beds in which they had been reared.
So right condescending they were with Chris, daughter of
a farmer of no account, not that she cared, she was douce
and sensible she told herself. And hadn't father said that
in the sight of God an honest man was as good as any school-
teacher and generally a damned sight better?

But it vexed you a bit all the same that a creature like
the Fordyce girl should be cuddled by Mr Kinloch when
she'd a face like a broken brose-cap and a voice like a nail on
a slate. And but little cuddling her drawing warranted,
her father's silver had more to do with it, not that Chris
herself could draw like an artist, Latin and French and
Greek and history were the things in which she shone. And
the English master set their class an essay on *Deaths of the
Great* and her essay was so good that he was forced to read
it aloud to all the class, and the Fordyce quean had snickered
and sniffed, so mad she was with jealousy.

Mr Murgetson was the English master there, not that he
was English himself, he came from Argyll and spoke with

a funny whine, the Highland whine, and the boys swore he had hair growing up between his toes like a Highland cow, and when they'd see him coming down a corridor they'd push their heads round a corner and cry *Moo!* like a lot of cattle. He'd fly in an awful rage at that, and once when they'd done it he came into the class where Chris was waiting her lesson and he stood and swore, right out and horrible, and gripped a black ruler in his hands and glared round as if he meant to murder a body. And maybe he would if the French teacher, her that was bonny and brave, hadn't come simpering into the room, and then he lowered the ruler and grunted and curled his lip and said *Eh? Canaille?* and the French teacher she simpered some more and said *May swee*.

So that was the college place at Duncairn, two Chrisses went there each morning, and one was right douce and studious and the other sat back and laughed a canny laugh at the antics of the teachers and minded Blawearie brae and the champ of horses and the smell of dung and her father's brown, grained hands till she was sick to be home again. But she made friends with young Marget Strachan, Chae Strachan's daughter, she was slim and sweet and fair, fine to know, though she spoke about things that seemed awful at first and then weren't awful at all; and you wanted to hear more and Marget would laugh and say it was Chae that had told her. Always as Chae she spoke of him and that was an unco-like thing to do of your father, but maybe it was because he was socialist and thought that Rich and Poor should be Equal. And what was the sense of believing that and then sending his daughter to educate herself and herself become one of the Rich?

But Marget cried that wasn't what Chae intended, she was to learn and be ready for the Revolution that was some day coming. And if come it never did she wasn't to seek out riches anyway, she was off to be trained as a doctor, Chae said that life came out of women through tunnels of pain and if God had planned women for anything else but the bearing of children it was surely the saving of them. And Marget's eyes, that were blue and so deep they minded you of a well you peeped into, they'd grow deeper and darker and her sweet face grow so solemn Chris felt solemn herself. But that would be only a minute, the next and Marget was laughing and fleering, trying to shock her, telling of men and women, what fools they were below their clothes; and how children came and how you should have them; and the things that Chae had seen in the huts of the blacks in Africa. And she told of a place where the bodies of men lay salted and white in great stone vats till the doctors needed to cut them up, the bodies of paupers they were— *so take care you don't die as a pauper Chris, for I'd hate some day if I rang a bell and they brought me up out of the vat your naked body, old and shrivelled and frosted with salt, and I looked in your dead, queer face, standing there with the scalpel held in my hand, and cried 'But this is Chris Guthrie!'*

That was awful, Chris felt sick and sick and stopped midway the shining path that led through the fields to Peesie's Knapp that evening in March. Clean and keen and wild and clear, the evening ploughed land's smell up in your nose and your mouth when you opened it, for Netherhill's teams had been out in that park all day, queer and lovely and dear the smell Chris noted. And something else she saw, looking at Marget, sick at the thought of her dead body brought to Marget. And that thing was a vein that beat in Marget's throat, a little blue gathering where the blood beat past in slow, quiet strokes, it would never do that when one was dead and still under grass, down in the earth that smelt so fine and you'd never smell; or cased in the icy darkness of a vat, seeing never again the lowe of burning whins or hearing the North Sea thunder beyond the hills, the thunder of it breaking through a morning mist, the right things that might not last and so soon went by. And they only were real and true, beyond them was nought you might ever attain but a weary dream and that last dark silence—Oh, only a fool loved being alive!

But Marget threw her arms around her when she said that, and kissed her with red, kind lips, so red they were that they looked like haws, and said there were lovely things in the world, lovely that didn't endure, and the lovelier for that. *Wait till you find yourself in the arms of your lad,*

*in the harvest time it'll be with the stooks round about you,
and he'll stop from joking—they do, you know, and that's
just when their blood-pressure alters—and he'll take you
like this—wait, there's not a body to see us!—and hold you
like this, with his hands held so, and kiss you like this!*

It was over in a moment, quick and shameful, fine for
all that, tingling and strange and shameful by turns. Long
after she parted with Marget that evening she turned and
stared down at Peesie's Knapp and blushed again; and
suddenly she was seeing them all at Blawearie as though
they were strangers naked out of the sea, she felt ill every
time she looked at father and mother. But that passed in
a day or so, for nothing endures.

Not a thing, though you're over-young to go thinking
of that, you've your lessons and studies, the English Chris,
and living and eating and sleeping that other Chris that
stretches your toes for you in the dark of the night and
whispers a drowsy *I'm you*. But you might not stay from
the thinking when all in a day, Marget, grown part of
your life, came waving to you as you neared the Knapp with
the news she was off to Aberdeen to live with an auntie
there—*it's a better place for a scholar, Chae says, and I'll
be trained all the sooner.*

And three days later Chae Strachan and Chris drove
down to the station with her, and saw her off at the platform, and she waved at them, bonny and young, Chae
looked as numb as Chris felt. He gave her a lift from the
station, did Chae, and on the road he spoke but once, to
himself it seemed, not Chris: *Ay, Marget lass, you'll do fine, if
you keep the lads at bay from kissing the bonny breast of you.*

So that was your Marget gone, there seemed not a soul in
Kinraddie that could take her place, the servant queans
of an age with Chris were no more than gowks and gomerils
a-screech round the barn of the Mains at night with the
ploughmen snickering behind them. And John Guthrie
had as little use for them as Marget herself. *Friends? Stick
to your lessons and let's see you make a name for yourself,
you've no time for friends.*

Mother looked up at that, friendly-like, not feared of

him at all, she was never feared. *Take care her head doesn't soften with lessons and dirt, learning in books it was sent the wee red daftie at Cuddiestoun clean skite, they say.* And father poked out his beard at her. *Say? Would you rather see her skite with book-learning or skite with—* and then he stopped and began to rage at Dod and Alec that were making a noise in the kitchen corner. But Chris, a-pore above her books in the glow of the paraffin lamp, heeding to Cæsar's coming in Gaul and the stour the creature raised there, knew right well what father had thought to speak of—*lust* was the word he'd wanted, perhaps. And she turned a page with the weary Cæsar man and thought of the wild career the daftie Andy had led one day in the roads and woods of Kinraddie.

Marget had barely gone when the thing came off, it was fair the speak of the place that happening early in April. The sowing time was at hand, John Guthrie put down two parks with grass and corn, swinging hand from hand as he walked and sowed and Will carried the corn across to him from the sacks that lined the rigs. Chris herself would help of an early morning when the dew had lifted quick, it was blithe and lightsome in the caller air with the whistle of the blackbirds in Blawearie's trees and the glint of the sea across the Howe and the wind blowing up the braes with a fresh, wild smell that caught you and made you gasp. So silent the world with the sun just peeking above the horizon those hours that you'd hear, clear and bright as though he paced the next field, the ringing steps of Chae Strachan—far down, a shadow and a sunlit dot, sowing his parks behind the steadings of Peesie's Knapp. There were larks coming over that morning, Chris minded, whistling and trilling dark and unseen against the blaze of the sun, now one lark, now another, till the sweetness of the trilling dizzied you and you stumbled with heavy pails corn-laden, and father swore at you over the red beard of him *Damn't to hell, are you fair a fool, you quean?*

That morning it was that the daftie Andy stole out of Cuddiestoun and started his scandalous rampage through Kinraddie. Long Rob of the Mill was to say he'd once had a horse that would do that kind of thing in the early Spring, leap dykes and ditches and every mortal thing it would if it heard a douce little mare go by. Gelding though it was, the horse would do that, and what more was Andy, poor devil, than a gelding? Not that Mistress Ellison had thought him that—faith, no!

It was said she ran so fast after her meeting with the daftie she found herself down two stone in weight. The coarse creature chased her nearly in sight of the Mains and then scrabbled away into the rough ground, beyond the turnpike. She'd been out fell early for her, Mistress Ellison, and was just holding along the road a bit walk to Fordoun when out of some bushes Andy jumped, his ramshackle face all swithering and his eyes all hot and wet. She thought at first he was hurted and then she saw he was trying to laugh, he tore at her frock and cried *You come!* She nearly fainted, but didn't, her umbrella was in her hand, she broke it over the daftie's head and then turned and ran, he went louping after her along the road, like a great monkey he leapt, crying terrible things to her. When sight of the Mains put an end to that chase he must have hung back in the hills for an hour or so and seen Mistress Munro, the futret, go sleeking down the paths to the Mains and Peesie's Knapp and Blawearie, asking sharp as you like, as though she blamed every soul but herself, *Have you seen that creature Andy?*

While she was up Blawearie way he must have made his road back across the hills, high up above the Cuddiestoun, till Upperhill came in sight. For later one of the ploughmen thought he'd seen the creature, shambling up against the skyline, picking a great bunch of sourocks and eating them. Then he got into the Upperhill wood and waited there, and it was through that wood at nine o'clock that Maggie Jean Gordon would hold her way to the station—close and thick larch wood with a path through it, where the light fell hardly at all and the cones crunched and rotted underfoot and sometimes a green barrier of whin crept up a wood ditch and looked out at you, and in the winter days the deer came down from the Grampians and sheltered there. But in the April weather there were no deer to fright Maggie Jean, even the daftie didn't frighten her. He'd been

waiting high in the wood before he took her, but maybe
before that he ran alongside the path she was taking, keeping hidden from view of the lass, for she heard a little crackle
rise now and then, she was to remember, and wondered
that the squirrels were out so early. Gordon she was, none
the better for that it might be, but a blithe little thing,
thin body and bonny brown hair, straight to walk and
straight to look, and you liked the laugh of her.

So through the wood and right into the hands of the
daftie she went, and when he lifted her in his hands she
was frightened not even then, not even when he bore her
far back into the wood, the broom-branches whipped their
faces and the wet of the dew sprayed on them, coming into
a little space, broom-surrounded, where the sun reached
down a long finger into the dimness. She stood up and shook
herself when he set her down, and told him she couldn't
play any longer, she must really hurry else she'd miss her
train. But he paid no heed, crouching on one knee he
turned his head this way and that, jerking round and about,
listening and listening, so that Maggie Jean listened as well
and heard the ploughmen cry to their horses and her mother
at that moment calling the hens to feed—*Tickie-ae!*
Tickie-ae! —Well, I must go, she told him and caught her
bag in her hand and hadn't moved a step when he had
her in his hands again; and after a minute or so, though
she wasn't frightened even then, she didn't like him, telling
him mother only was allowed to touch her there, not anyone
else, and please she'd have to go. And she looked up at him,
pushing him away, his mad, awful head, he began to purr
like a great wild cat, awful it must have been to see him
and hear him. And God alone knows the next thing he'd
have done but that then, for it was never such a morning
before for that bright clearness, far away down and across
the fields a man began to sing, distant but very clear, with
a blithe lilt in the voice of him. And he broke off and
whistled the song and then he sang it again:

> *Bonny wee thing*
> *Canty wee thing,*
> *Lovely wee thing,*
> *Wert thou mine*

I would clasp thee
In my bosom
Lest my jewel
I should tyne

And at that, crouching and listening, the daftie took his
hands from Maggie Jean and began to sing the song himself;
and he took her in his arms again, but gently, fondling
her as though she were a cat, and he set her on her feet
and tugged straight the bit frock she wore; and stood up
beside her and took her hand and guided her back to the
path through the larch wood. And she went on and left
him and once she looked back and saw him glowering after
her; and because she saw he was weeping she ran back to
him, kind thing, and patted his hand and said *Don't cry!*
and she saw his face like that of a tormented beast and went
on again, down to the station. And only when she came
home that night did she tell the story of her meeting with
Cuddiestoun's Andy.

But as the day wore on and Long Rob, working in that
orra field above the Mill, still sang and sweated and swore
at his horses, the singing must have drawn the Andy creature
down from the larch wood, by hedges creeping and slipping
from the sight of the Upperhill men in the parks. And once
Rob raised his head and thought he saw a moving shadow
in a ditch that bounded the orra ground. But he thought
it a dog and just heaved a stone or so in case it was some
beast in heat or on chicken-killing. The shadow yelped and
snarled at that, but was gone from the ditch when Rob
picked up another stone; so he went on with his work;
and the daftie, tearing along the Kinraddie road out towards
the Bridge End, with the blood red trickling down his woesome face, was all unseen by him.

But right at the corner, close where the road jerked
round by Pooty's place, he near ran full tilt into Chris
herself, coming up from Auchinblae she was with the
messages her mother had sent her on, her basket over her
arm and her mind far off with the Latin verbs in -*are*.
He slavered at her, running towards her, and she screamed,
though she wasn't over-frightened; and then she threw the
basket clean at his head and made for Pooty's. Pooty him-

self was sitting just inside the door when she reached it, the louping beast was close behind, she heard the pant of his breath and was to wonder often enough in later times over that coolness that came on her then. For she ran fleet as a bird inside the door and banged it right in the daftie's face and dropped the bar and watched the planks bulge and crack as outside the body of the madman was flung against them again and again. Pooty mouthed and stuttered at her in the dimness, but he grew real brave when she made him understand, he sharpened two of his sutor's knives and prowled trembling from window to window—the daftie left them untouched. Then Chris took a keek from one window and saw him again: he was raking about in the basket she'd thrown at his head, he made the parcels dirl on the road till he found a great bar of soap, and then he began to eat that, feuch! laughing and yammering all to himself, and running back to throw himself against the door of Pooty's again, the foam burst yellow through the beard of him as he still ate and ate at the soap.

But he soon grew thirsty and went down to the burn, Pooty and Chris stood watching him, and then it was that Cuddiestoun himself came ben the road. He sighted Andy and cried out to him, and Andy leapt the burn and was off, and behind him went Munro clatter-clang, and out of sight they vanished down the road to Bridge End. Chris unbarred the door in spite of Pooty's stutterings and went and re-packed the bit basket, and everything was there except the soap: and that was down poor Andy's throat.

Feint the thing else he'd to eat that day, he was near the end of his tether; for though he ran like a hare and Cuddiestoun behind him was more than coarse in the legs, yet luck would have it that Mutch of Bridge End was just guiding his team across the road to start harrowing his yavil park when the two runners came in sight, real daft-like both of them, Andy running near double, soap and madness a-foam on his face, Cuddiestoun bellowing behind. So Mutch slowed down his team and called out to Andy, *Ay, man, you mustn't run near as fast as that*, and when Andy was opposite threw out a foot and tripped him up, and down in the stour went Andy, and Cuddiestoun was

c

on top of him in a minute, bashing in the face of him, but
Alec Mutch just stood and looked on, maybe working his
meikle ears a bit, it was no concern of his. The daftie's
hands went up to his face as the bashings came and then
Cuddiestoun gripped him right in the private parts, he
screamed and went slack, like a sack in Cuddiestoun's hands.
And that was the end of Andy's ploy, for back to the
Cuddiestoun he was driven and they said Mistress Munro
took down his breeks and leathered him sore; but you
never know the lies they tell, for others said it was Cuddiestoun himself she leathered, him having let the daftie out
of the house that morning to scandalize her name with his
coarse on-goings. But he'd no chance more of them, poor
stock, next day the asylum officials came out and took him
away in a gig, his hands fast tied behind his back; and that
was the last they ever saw of Andy in Kinraddie.

Father raged when he heard the story from Chris, queer
raging it was, he took her out to the barn and heard the
story and his eyes slipped up and down her dress as she
spoke, she felt sickened and queer. *He shamed you then?*
he whispered; and Chris shook her head and at that father
seemed to go limp and his eyes grew dull. *Ah well, it's the
kind of thing that would happen in a godless parish like
this. It can hardly happen again with the Reverend Gibbon
in charge.*

Three minister creatures came down to Kinraddie to try
for its empty pulpit. The first preached early in March,
a pernickety thing as ever you saw, not over five feet in
height, or he didn't look more. He wore a brave gown
with a purple hood on it, like a Catholic creature, and
jerked and pranced round the pulpit like a snipe with the
staggers, working himself up right sore about *Latter-Day
Doubt in the Kirk of Scotland*. But Kinraddie had never
a doubt of *him*, and Chris coming out of the kirk with Will
and father heard Chae Strachan say he'd rather sit under
a clucking hen than *that* for a minister. The second to try
was an old bit man from Banff, shaking and old, and some
said he'd be best, he'd have quietened down at his age,
not aye on the look for a bigger kirk and a bigger stipend.

For if there's a body on earth that would skin a tink for his sark and preach for a pension in purgatory it's an Auld Kirk minister.

But the poor old brute from Banff seemed fair sucked dry. He'd spent years in the writing of books and things, the spunk of him had trickled out into his pen, forbye that he read his sermon; and that fair settled his hash to begin with. So hardly a soul paid heed to his reading, except Chris and her father, she thought it fine; for he told of the long dead beasts of the Scottish land in the times when jungle flowered its forests across the Howe and a red sun rose on the steaming earth that the feet of man had still to tread; and he pictured the dark, slow tribes that came drifting across the low lands of the northern seas, the great bear watched them come, and they hunted and fished and loved and died, God's children in the morn of time; and he brought the first voyagers sailing the sounding coasts, they brought the heathen idols of the great Stone Rings, the Golden Age was over and past and lust and cruelty trod the world; and he told of the rising of Christ, a pin-point of the cosmic light far off in Palestine, the light that crept and wavered and did not die, the light that would yet shine as the sun on all the world, nor least the dark howes and hills of Scotland.

So what could you make of that, except that he thought Kinraddie a right coarse place since the jungles had all dried up? And his prayers were as short as you please, he'd hardly a thing to say of the King or the Royal Family at all, had the Reverend Colquohoun. So that fair put him out with Ellison and Mutch, they were awful King's men both of them, ready to die for the King any day of the week and twice on Sundays, said Long Rob of the Mill. And his preaching had no pleasure at all for Chae Strachan either, he wanted a preacher to praise up socialism and tell how Rich and Poor should be Equal. So the few that listened thought feint the much of the old book-writer from Banff, he stood never a chance, pleasing Chris and her father only, Chris didn't count, John Guthrie did, but his vote was only one and a hantle few votes the Banff man got when it came to the counting.

Stuart Gibbon was the third to make try for Kinraddie manse, and that Sunday when Chris sat down in the kirk and looked up at him in the pulpit she knew as well as she knew her own hand that he was to please all of them, though hardly more than a student he was, with black hair on him and a fine red face and shoulders strong and well-bulked, for he was a pretty man. And first his voice took them, it was brave and big like the voice of a bull, and fine and rounded, and he said the Lord's Prayer in a way that pleased gentry and simple. For though he begged to be forgiven his sins as he forgave those that sinned against him—instead, as was more genteel, crying to be forgiven his trespasses as he forgave those that trespassed against him —still he did it with a fine solemnity that made everybody that heard right douce and grave-like; and one or two joined in near the end of the prayer, and that's a thing gey seldom done in an Auld Kirk kirk. Next came his sermon, it was out of the *Song of Solomon* and well and rare he preached on it, showing that the Song had more meaning than one. It was Christ's description of the beauty and fine comeliness of the Auld Kirk of Scotland, and as such right reverently must it be read; and it was a picture of womanly beauty that moulded itself in the lithe and grace of the Kirk, and as such a perpetual manual for the women of Scotland that so they might attain to straight and fine lives in this world and salvation in the next. And in a minute or so all Kin-raddie kirk was listening to him as though he were promising to pay their taxes at the end of Martinmas.

For it was fair tickling to hear about things like that read out from a pulpit, a woman's breasts and thighs and all the rest of the things, in that voice like the mooing of a holy bull; and to know it was decent Scripture with a higher meaning as well. So everybody went home to his Sunday dinner well pleased with the new minister lad, no more than a student though he was; and on the Monday Long Rob of the Mill was fair deaved with tales of the sermon and put two and two together and said *Well, preaching like that's a fine way of having your bit pleasure by proxy, right in the stalls of a kirk, I prefer to take mine more private-like*. But that was Rob all over, folk said, a fair caution him and his Ingersoll that could neither make watches nor sense. And feint the voter it put off from tramping in to vote for Kinraddie's last candidate.

So in he went with a thumping majority, the Reverend Gibbon, by mid-May he was at the Manse, him and his wife, an English creature he'd married in Edinburgh. She was young as himself and bonny enough in a thin kind of way, with a voice as funny as Ellison's, near, but different, and big, dark eyes on her, and so sore in love were they that their servant quean said they kissed every time he went out a bit walk, the minister. And one time, coming back from a jaunt and finding her waiting him, the minister picked up his wife in his arms and ran up the stairs with her, both cuddling one the other and kissing, and laughing in each other's faces with shining eyes; and into their bedroom they went and closed the door and didn't come down for hours, though it was bare the middle of the afternoon. Maybe that was true and maybe it wasn't for the servant quean was one that old Mistress Sinclair had fee'd for the Manse in Gourdon, and before a Gourdon quean speaks the truth the Bervie burn will run backwards through the Howe.

Now every minister since Time was clecked in Kinraddie had made a round of the parish when he was inducted. Some did it quick, some did it slow, the Reverend Gibbon was among the quick. He came up to Blawearie just after the dinner hour on a Saturday and met in with John Guthrie sharpening a hoe in the close, weeds yammered out of Blawearie soil like bairns from a school at closing time, it was coarse, coarse land, wet, raw, and red clay, father's temper grew worse the more he saw of it. So when the minister came on him and cried out right heartily *Well, you'll be my neighbour Guthrie, man?* father cocked his red beard at the minister and glinted at him like an icicle and said *Ay, MISTER Gibbon, I'll be that*. So the minister held out his hand and changed his tune right quick and said quiet-like *You've a fine-kept farm here, Mr Guthrie, trig and trim, though I hear you've sat down a bare six months*. And he smiled, a big sappy smile.

So after that they were chief enough, sitting one the other on a handle on the sharn-barrow right in the middle of the close, the minister none feared for his brave, black clothes; and father told him the coarse land it was in Kinraddie, and the minister said he well believed him, it was only a man from the North could handle it so well. In a minute or so they were chief as brothers, father brought him over into the house, Chris stood in the kitchen and father said *And this quean's my daughter, Chris*. The minister smiled at her with his glinting black eyes and said *I hear you're right clever, Chrissie, and go up to the Duncairn College. How do you like it?* And Chris blushed and said *Fine, sir*, and he asked her what she was to be, and she told him a teacher, and he said there was no profession more honourable. Then mother came ben from putting the twins to sleep and was quiet and friendly, just as she always was with loon or laird, crowned with gold with her lovely hair. And she made the minister some tea and he praised it and said the best tea in his life he'd drunk in Kinraddie, it was the milk. And father asked whose milk they got at the Mains and the minister said *The Mains*, and father shot out his beard and said *Well may it be good, it's the best land in the parish they've a hold of, the dirt*, and the minister said *And now I'll have to be dandering down to the Manse. Come over and see us some evening, Chrissie, maybe the wife and I'll be able to lend you some books to help in your studies*. And off he went, swack enough, but no more fleet than father himself who swung alongside him down to where the turnip-park broke off from the road.

Chris made for the Manse next Monday night, she thought maybe that would be the best time, but she said nothing to father, only told mother and mother smiled and said *Surely*, far-off she seemed and dreaming to herself as so often in the last month or so. So Chris put on the best frock that she used for Sundays, and her tall lacing boots, and prigged out her hair in front of the glass in the parlour, and went up across the hill by Blawearie loch, with the night coming over the Grampians and the snipe crying in their hundreds beyond the loch's grey waters—still and grey, as though they couldn't forget last summer nor hope for another coming. The Standing Stones pointed long shadow-shapes into the east, maybe just as they'd done of an evening two thousand years before when the wild men climbed the brae and sang their songs in the lithe of those shadows while the gloaming waited there above the same quiet hills. And a queer uncanny feeling came on Chris then, she looked back half-feared at the Stones and the whiteness of the loch, and then went hurrying through the park paths till she came out above kirkyard and Manse. Beyond the road the Meikle House rose up in its smother of trees, you saw the broken walls of it, the flagstaff light was shining already, it would soon be dark.

She unsnecked the door of the kirkyard wall, passing through to the Manse, the old stones rose up around her silently, not old when you thought of the Standing Stones of Blawearie brae but old enough for all that. Some went back to the old, unkindly times of the Covenanters, one had a skull and crossed bones and an hour-glass on it and was mossed half over so that but hardly you could read the daft-like script with its esses like effs, and it made you shudder. The yews came all about that place of the oldest stone and Chris going past put out her hand against it and the low bough of a yew whispered and gave a low laugh behind her, and touched her hand with a cold, hairy touch so that a daft-like cry started up on her lips, she wished she'd gone round by the plain, straightforward road, instead of this near-cut she'd thought so handy.

So she whistled to herself, hurrying, and just outside the kirkyard stood the new minister himself, leaning over the gate looking in among the stones, he saw her before she saw him and his voice fair startled her. *Well, Chrissie, you're very gay*, he said, and she felt ashamed to have him know she whistled in a kirkyard; and he stared at her strange and queer and seemed to forget her a minute; and he gave an unco half-laugh and muttered to himself, but she heard him, *One's enough for one day*. Then he seemed to wake up, he mooed out at her *And now you'll be needing a book, no doubt. Well, the Manse is fair in a mess this evening, spring-cleaning or something like that, but if you just wait here a minute I'll run in and pick you something light and cheerful.*

Off he set, she was left alone among the black trees that bent over the greyness of the kirkyard. Unendingly the unseen grasses whispered and rustled above the stones' dim, recumbent shapes, and she thought of the dead below those stones, farmers and ploughmen and their wives, and little bairns and new-born babes, their bodies turned to skeletons now so that if you dug in the earth you'd find only their bones, except the new-buried, and maybe there in the darkness worms and awful things crawled and festered in flesh grown rotten and black, and it was a terrifying place. But at last came the minister, not hurrying at all but just drifting towards her, he held out a book and said *Well, here it is, and I hope you'll like it.* She took the book and looked at it in the dying light, its name was *Religio Medici,* and she mastered her shyness and asked *Did you sir?* and the minister stared at her and said, his voice just even as ever, *Oh, like hell!* and turned about and left her to go back through the terror of the yews. But they didn't terrify at all, climbing home and thinking of that word he used, swearing it had been and nothing else, should she tell of it to father?

No, that wouldn't do, a minister was only a man, and he'd loaned her a book, kind of him though he looked so queer. And besides, father didn't know of this errand of hers down to the Manse, maybe he'd think she was trying to hold in with gentry and would swear himself. Not that he swore often, father, she told herself as she hurried across the brae, and, hurrying, climbed out of the dimness into the last of the May daylight with the sunset a glow and a glimmer that danced about her feet, waiting for her; not often, except when things went clean over him, as that day in the sowing of the park below Blawearie when first the cart-shaft had broken and then the hammer had broken and then he'd watched the rain come on, and he'd gone nearly mad, raging at Will and Chris that he'd leather them till they hadn't enough skin to sit a threepenny bit on; and at last, fair skite, he'd shaken his fist at the sky and cried *Ay, laugh, you Mucker!*

Chris took a bit peep or so in *Religio Medici* and nearly yawned her head off with the reading of it, it was better fun on a spare, slow day to help mother wash the blankets. In the sun of the red, still weather Jean Guthrie had every bed in Blawearie cleared and the blankets piled in tubs half-filled with lukewarm water and soap, and Chris took off her boots and her stockings and rolled her knickers far up her white legs and stepped in the grey, lathered folds of blankets and tramped them up and down. It felt fine with the water gurgling blue and iridescent up through your toes and getting thicker and thicker; then into the next tub while mother emptied the first, lovely work, she felt she could trample blankets forever, only it grew hot and hot, a red forenoon while they did the washing. So next time mother was indoors she took off her skirt and then her petticoat and mother coming out with another blanket cried *God, you've stripped!* and gave Chris a slap in the knickers, friendly-like, and said *You'd make a fine lad, Chris quean,* and smiled the blithe way she had and went on with the washing.

But John Guthrie came home from the fields then, him and Will, and as soon as he saw her father's face went all shrivelled up and he cried *Get out of that at once, you shameful limmer, and get on your clothes!* And out she got, white and ashamed, shamed more for father than herself, and Will turned red and led off the horses, awkward-like but John Guthrie went striding across the close to the kitchen and mother and began to rage at her. *What would folk say of the quean if they saw her sit there, near naked? We'd be the speak and laughing-stock of the place.* And mother looked at him, sweet and cold, *Ah, well, it wouldn't be the first time you've seen a naked lass yourself; and if your neighbours haven't they must have fathered their own bairns with their breeks on.*

Father had been in a fair stamash at that, he left mother and went out with his face dead-white, not red, and he didn't say another word, he didn't speak to mother all that evening nor all the next day. Chris went to her bed that night and thought of the happening, lying close-up and alone, it had been as though she saw a caged beast peep from her father's eyes as he saw her stand in the tub. Like a fire that burned across the close, it went on and on as though she still stood there and he glowered at her. She hid her face below the blankets but she couldn't forget, next morning she was able to bear thinking of it no longer, the house had quietened with the folk gone out, she went to mother and asked her straight, she'd never asked anything of the kind before.

And then an awful thing happened, mother's face went grey and old as she stopped from her work at the kitchen table, she went whiter and whiter second on second. Chris near went out of her mind at the sight. *Oh, mother, I didn't mean to vex,* she cried and flung her arms round mother and held her tight, seeing her face then, so white and ill-looking it had grown in the last month. And mother smiled at her at last, putting her hands on her shoulders. *Not you, Chris quean, just life. I cannot tell you a thing or advise you a thing, my quean. You'll have to face men for yourself when the time comes, there's none can stand and help you.* And then she said something queerer, kissing Chris, *Mind that for me sometime if I cannot thole it longer*—and stopped and laughed and was blithe again. *We're daft, the two of us, run out and bring me a pail of water.* And Chris went out with the pail, out and up to the pump in the hot red weather, and then something came on her, she crept back soft-footed and there mother stood as she'd left her, white and lonely and sad, Chris didn't dare go into her, just stood and looked.

Something was happening to mother, things were happening to all of them, nothing ever stayed the same except maybe this weather and if it went on much longer the Reverend Colquohoun's bit jungles would soon be sprouting back across the parks of the Howe. The weary pleiter of the land and its life while you waited for rain or thaw! Glad she'd be when she'd finished her exams and was into Aberdeen University, getting her B.A. and then a school of her own, the English Chris, father and his glowering and girning forgotten, she'd have a brave house of her own and wear what she liked and have never a man vexed with sight of her, she'd take care of that.

Or maybe she wouldn't, queer that she never knew herself for long, grown up though she was, a woman now, near.

Father said that the salt of the earth were the folk that drove a straight drill and never looked back, but she was no more than ploughed land still, the furrows went criss and cross, you wanted this and you wanted that, books and the fineness of them no more than an empty gabble sometimes, and then the sharn and the snapping that sickened you and drove you back to books——

She turned over on the grass with a jerk when she came to that troubled thinking. The sunset was painting the loch, but hot as ever it was, breaking up for one of those nights when you couldn't bear a blanket above you and even the dark was a foul, black blanket. It had died off, the wind, while she lay and thought, feint the loss was that, but there was sign of nothing in the place of it, the broom stood up in the late afternoon, not moving, great faces massed and yellow like the faces of an army of yellow men, looking down across Kinraddie, watching for the rain. Mother below would be needing her help, Dod and Alec back from the school already, father and Will soon in from the fields.

There somebody was crying her already!

She stood up and shook out her frock and went through the grass to the tail of the brae, and looked down and saw Dod and Alec far below waving up at her. They were crying her name excitedly, it sounded like the lowing of calves that had lost their mother, she went slow to tease them till she saw their faces.

It was then, as she flew down the hill with her own face white, that the sky crackled behind her, a long flash zigzagged across the Grampian peaks, and far across the parks by the hills she heard the hiss of rain. The drought had broken at last.

II

DRILLING

Lying down when her climb up the cambered brae was done, panting deep from the rate she'd come at—skirt flying and iron-resolute she'd turn back for nothing that cried or called in all Blawearie—no, not even that whistle of father's!—Chris felt the coarse grass crackle up beneath her into a fine quiet couch. Neck and shoulders and hips and knees she relaxed, her long brown arms quivered by her side as the muscles slacked away, the day drowsed down an aureal light through the long brown lashes that drooped on her cheeks. As the gnomons of a giant dial the shadows of the Standing Stones crept into the east, snipe called and called——

Just as the last time she'd climbed to the loch: and when had that been? She opened her eyes and thought, and tired from that and closed down her eyes again and gave a queer laugh. The June of last year it had been, the day when mother had poisoned herself and the twins.

So long as that and so near as that, you'd thought of the hours and days as a dark, cold pit you'd never escape. But you'd escaped, the black damp went out of the sunshine and the world went on, the white faces and whispering ceased from the pit, you'd never be the same again, but the world went on and you went with it. It was not mother only that died with the twins, something died in your heart and went down with her to lie in Kinraddie kirkyard—the child in your heart died then, the bairn that believed the hills were made for its play, every road set fair with its warning posts, hands ready to snatch you back from the brink of danger when the play grew over-rough. That died, and the Chris of the books and the dreams died with it, or you folded them up in their paper of tissue and laid them away by the dark, quiet corpse that was your childhood.

66

So Mistress Munro of the Cuddiestoun told her that
awful night she came over the rain-soaked parks of
Blawearie and laid out the body of mother, the bodies
of the twins that had died so quiet in their crib. She nipped
round the rooms right quick and pert and uncaring, the
black-eyed futret, snapping this order and that, it was her
that terrified Dod and Alec from their crying, drove father
and Will out tending the beasts. And quick and cool and
cold-handed she worked, peeking over at Chris with her rat-
like face. *You'll be leaving the College now, I'll warrant,
education's dirt and you're better clear of it. You'll find
little time for dreaming and dirt when you're keeping the
house at Blawearie.*

And Chris in her pit, dazed and dull-eyed, said nothing,
she minded later; and some other than herself went searching and seeking out cloths and clothes. Then Mistress Munro
washed down the body that was mother's and put it in a
nightgown, her best, the one with blue ribbons on it that
she hadn't worn for many a year; and fair she made her
and sweet to look at, the tears came at last when you saw
her so, hot tears wrung from your eyes like drops of blood.
But they ended quick, you would die if you wept like that
for long, in place of tears a long wail clamoured endless,
unanswered inside your head *Oh, mother, mother, why did
you do it?*

And not until days later did Chris hear why, for they
tried to keep it from her and the boys, but it all came out
at the inquest, mother had poisoned herself, her and the
twins, because she was pregnant again and afraid with a
fear dreadful and calm and clear-eyed. So she had killed
herself while of unsound mind, had mother, kind-eyed and
sweet, remembering those Springs of Kildrummie last of
all things remembered, it may be, and the rooks that cried
across the upland parks of Don far down beyond the tunnels
of the years.

A month later Dod and Alec went back to school and as
they left to go home that night first one scholar cried after
them and others took it up *Daftie, daftie! Whose mother
was a daftie?* They ran for Blawearie and came stumbling

into the house weeping and weeping, father went fair mad at the sight of them and skelped them both, but skelping or not they wouldn't go back to the school next day.

And then Will spoke up, he cared not a fig for father now. All in a night it seemed the knowledge had come on him father wouldn't dare strike him again, he bought an old bicycle and would ride off in an evening as he pleased, his face cold and hard when he caught the glint of father's eye. Of a morning John Guthrie grumbled and girned at him, crying *Where do you wander each night like a tink?* But Will would say never a word, except once when John Guthrie made at him and then he swung round and whispered *Take care.* And at that father stopped and drew back, Chris watched them with angry eyes, angry and frightened in a breath as now when Will spoke up for his brothers.

Why should they go back? I wouldn't. Oh, and you needn't glower at me. You take damn good care you never go near a mart or a market yourself nowadays—I've to do all your dirty work for you!

Father louped to his feet at that, Will was on his as well, they stood with fists clenched in the kitchen and Dod and Alec stopped from their greeting and stared and stared. But Chris thrust the table in between the two, she made out she wanted it there for baking; and they dropped their fists and John Guthrie swore, but soft; and Will reddened up and looked foolish.

But father that night, he said never a word to the rest of them in Blawearie, he was over-proud for that, wrote off to his sister Janet in Auchterless and asked that she take Dod and Alec in her care and give them an Aberdeen schooling. In a week she was down from the North, Auntie Janet and her man. Uncle Tam he was, big and well-bulked and brave, and his watch-chain had rows and rows of wee medals on it he'd gotten for playing quoits. And they were fell kind, the two of them, Alec and Dod were daft with delight when they heard of the Auchterless plan. But Auntie and Uncle had never a bairn of their own and soon made plain if the boys went with them it would be for aye, they wanted to adopt the pair of them.

Father sneered and thrust out his beard at that *So you'd like to steal the flesh of my body from me!* and Auntie Janet nodded, right eye to eye, *Aye, John, just that, we've never a wean of our own, though God knows it's not for want of the trying*; and father said *Ill blood breeds ill*; and Auntie said *Ay, it'll be long ere I have to kill myself because my man beds me like a breeding sow*; and father said *You dirty bitch*.

Chris stuck the dirl of the row till her head near burst and then ran out of the kitchen, through the close into the cornyard, where Will was prowling about. He'd heard the noise and he laughed at them, but his eyes were angry as his arm went round her. *Never heed the dirty old devils, one's bad as the other, father, auntie, or that midden that's covered with its wee tin medals. Come off to the park with me and we'll bring home the kye.*

Deep in clover the cows as they came on them, Chris and Will; and they went in no hurry at all, unanxious to be back in Blawearie. And Will seemed angry and gentle and kind all at once. *Don't let them worry you, Chris, don't let father make a damned slave of you, as he'd like to do. We've our own lives to lead.* And she said *What else can I do but bide at home now?*

He said he didn't know, but he'd be libbed and pole-axed and gutted if *he* did for long, soon as he'd saved the silver he was off to Canada, a man was soon his own master there. Chris listened to that with eyes wide opened, she caught at the hope of it and forgot to smack at the kye that loitered and boxed and galumphed in their cloverful-foolishness up the brae. *Oh, Will, and you could send for me as your house-keeper!* He turned a dull red and smacked at the kye and Chris sighed and the hope went out, he'd no need to answer *Ay, maybe, but maybe it would hardly suit you.*

So then she knew for sure he'd a lass somewhere in Drumlithie, it was with her he planned to share a bed and a steading in the couthy lands of Canada.

And when they got back to Blawearie they found the row ended, father'd given in to his sister Janet, ill the grace though he did it with. In three days' time but three of them

were sitting to meat at the kitchen table, Chris listened for
days for voices of folk that were dead or gone, both far
enough from Blawearie. But even that lost strangeness in
time, the harvest drew on, she went out to the park to help
with it, lush and heavy enough it had sprung and yellowed
with the suns and rains of the last two months.

He'd no binder, father, wouldn't hear of the things, but
he'd brought an old reaper from Echt and with that they
cut the corn; though Will swore he'd be the fool of
Kinraddie seen driving a thing like that. Father laughed at
him over his beard, like a spitting cat, *If Kinraddie's laughing can make you a bigger fool than nature made you it'll
be a miracle; and don't fret the sark from your dowp, my
mannie, I'LL do the driving.* And though Will muttered at
that he gave in all the same, for every harvest there came
something queer and terrible on father, you couldn't handle
the thing with a name, it was as if he grew stronger and
crueller then, ripe and strong with the strength of the corn,
he'd be fleeter than ever and his face filled out, and they'd
hear him come up from the parks, astride the broad back of
Bess, singing hymns, these were the only things that he ever
sang, singing with a queer, keen shrillness that brought the
sweat in the palms of your hands.

Now in the park below Blawearie, steading and house, the
best crop, and that was the ley, was the first they cut, a great
swither of a crop with straw you could hardly break and
twist into bands for sheaves. Sore work Chris found it to
keep her stretch of each bout cleared for the reaper's coming,
the weather cool and grey though it was. But a sun was
behind the greyness and sometimes when you raised your
head from the sheaves you'd see a beam of light on the travel
far over the parks of Upperhill or lazing across the moor or
dancing a-top the Cuddiestoun stooks, a beam from the hot,
grey haze of that sky that watched and waited above the
sweat of the harvesting Howe.

First ere the cutting in the ley began there'd been roads
to clear all round the corn, wide bouts that father scythed
himself, he swore that the scythe would yet come back to
its own when the binders and reapers rotted in rust and folk
bred the old breed again. But its time was past or was yet

to come, the scythe's, out the reaper was driven and yoked, Chris followed down at the tail of it. The best of weather for harvest, folk said, it was ill to cut in a swither of heat; and so still was the air by morn and noon it reminded you of the days in Spring, you'd hear the skirl of the blades ring down the Howe for mile on mile, the singing of Long Rob of the Mill, the Cuddiestoun creatures swearing at Tony as he stood and gowked at the stooks. Then Blawearie's reaper clanged in through the gates with Bess and Clyde at the pole, and the blades flashed and brightened like the teeth of a beast and snarled in a famished freedom. And then John Guthrie cried *Get up!* and swung the horses down the bout, and the hungry snarl changed to a deep, clogged growling as the corn was driven on the teeth by the swinging reaper flails; and down the bout, steady and fine, sped the reaper, clean-cutting from top to bottom, with never a straggling straw as on other farms, John Guthrie saw to that.

But feint the time had you for glowering at rig or reaper, soon as the horses were off and the flail drove the first sheaf from the tail-board Chris had pounced on that sheaf and gathered and bound it and flung it aside before you could say *Glenbervie!* and had run to the next and twisted its band, and gathered and bound and bound and gathered with her hands like a mist below her eyes, so quick they were. Midway the bout Will met with her, working up from the foot, and flicking the sweat from his face. And just as they straightened and stretched and looked up to the head of the park the clong, clong of the empty reaper would change to the snarling engaging whirr as father guided the horses to the cutting again. Still the sun smouldered behind its mists and out by Kinneff the fog-horn moaned all hours, you felt like moaning like that yourself long ere the day was out and your back near cracked and broke with the strain of the bending.

But in three days' time the ley was cut, the yavil glowed yellow across the dykes and they moved to that without stop. And then suddenly the mists cleared up and the fog-horn stopped from its droning, it came on real blistering weather of heat, but hardly you'd bear to touch on the wood of the

reaper shaft when you loosed the horses, so hot it grew.
Kinraddie gasped and then bent to its chaving again, this
heat wouldn't last, the rain was due, God help the crops
that waited cutting then.

The second day of the yavil cutting a tink climbed up
the Blawearie road from the turnpike and cried to John
Guthrie for work, and father said *Maybe, maybe. Let's see
the work that you've in you first,* and the tink said *Ay, fine
that.* And he off with his coat and took the middle of the
bout, and was up it in a jiffy, gathering and binding to the
manner born, you might say, and giving Chris a bit smile
when he met with her. So, coming down the next bout father
cried to the tink that he'd take him on for a day or so, if the
weather held; and Chris could get up to the house and see
to the supper—*no idling, quean, mind that.* He was a black-
like, gipsy childe, the tink, father wouldn't have him into
the kitchen for meat, the creature might be all lice; and he
wouldn't have him sleep in the house.

So Chris made him a shake-down out in the barn, he said
he was real content with that. But when she carried him his
supper over to the barn the first night she felt shamed for
him suddenly, and told him she'd have had him eat in the
house if it hadn't been father. And he said *Don't let that
fash you, lass, I'm as little anxious for his company as he is
for mine. Forbye, he's only a Kinraddie clown!* Chris felt her
face flame at that, it just showed you there was no good
doing kindness to tinks, but she made out she hadn't heard
and turned back to go over the close. Then it was the tink
put out his arm, round her legs before she could move,
almost he pulled her down on the hay beside him. *You've
never lain with a man yet, lass, I can see, and that's a sore
waste of hot blood like yours. So mind I'm here if you want
me, I've deflowered more queans than I've years to my name
and sent none of them empty away.* He loosed her then,
laughing low, she couldn't do anything but stare and stare
at him, sick and not angry, something turned in her stomach
and her knees felt weak. The tink put out his hand and
patted her leg again. *Mind, if you want me I'll be here,* and
Chris shook her head, she felt too sick to speak, and slipped
out of the barn and crossed the close and washed and washed

at her hands and face with hot water till father lowered his
paper and asked *Have you gone clean daft?*

But up in her room that night, the room that was hers
and hers only now, Will slept where his brothers had slept,
she saw a great moon come over the Grampians as she
undressed for bed. She opened the window then, she liked
to sleep with it open, and it was as though the night had
been waiting for that, a waft of the autumn wind blew in,
it was warm and cool and it blew in her face with a smell
like the smell of late clover and the smell of dung and the
smell of the stubble fields all commingled. She leant there
breathing it, watching the moon with the hills below it but
higher than Blawearie, Kinraddie slept like a place in a
picture-book, drifting long shadows that danced a petronella across the night-stilled parks. And without beginning or
reason a strange ache came in her, in her breasts, so that
they tingled, and in her throat, and below her heart, and she
heard her heart beating, and for a minute the sound of the
blood beating through her own head. And she thought of
the tink lying there in the barn and how easy it would be to
steal down the stairs and across the close, dense black in its
shadows, to the barn.

But it was only for a second she thought of that, daftly,
then laughed at herself, cool and trim and trig, and closed
the window, shutting out the smells of the night, and slowly
took off her clothes, looking at herself in the long glass that
had once stood in mother's room. She was growing up
limber and sweet, not bonny, perhaps, her cheek-bones were
over high and her nose over short for that, but her eyes
clear and deep and brown, brown, deep and clear as the
Denburn flow and her hair was red and was brown by turns,
spun fine as a spider's web, wild, wonderful hair. So she saw
herself and her teeth clean-cut and even, a white gleam in
that grave brown stillness of face John Guthrie's blood had
bequeathed to her. And below face and neck now her clothes
were off was the glimmer of shoulders and breast and there
her skin was like satin, it tickled her touching herself. Below
the tilt of her left breast was a dimple, she saw it and bent
to look at it and the moonlight ran down her back, so queer
the moonlight she felt the running of that beam along her

back. And she straightened as the moonlight grew and looked at the rest of herself, and thought herself sweet and cool and fit for that lover who would some day come and kiss her and hold her, so.

And Chris saw the brown glimmer of her face grow sweet and scared as she thought of that—how they'd lie together, in a room with moonlight, and she'd be kind to him, kind and kind, giving him all and everything, and he'd sleep with his head here on her breast or they'd lie far into the mornings whispering one to the other, they'd have so much to tell! And maybe that third and last Chris would find voice at last for the whimsies that filled her eyes, and tell of rain on the roof at night, the terror and the splendour of it across the long slate roofs; and the years that faded and fell, dissolved as a breath, before those third clear eyes; and mother's face, lying dead; and the Standing Stones up there night after night and day after day by the loch of Blawearie, how around them there gathered things that wept and laughed and lived again in the hours before the dawn, till far below the cocks began to crow in Kinraddie and day had come again. And all that he'd believe, more than so often she believed herself, not laugh at, holding and kissing her, so. And faith! no more than a corpse he'd hold if she didn't get into her bed-gown and into her bed, you may dream of a lad till you're frozen as a stone, but he'll want you warmer than that.

So that was the harvest madness that came on Chris, mild enough it had been, she fell fast asleep in the middle of it. But it scored her mind as a long drill scores the crumbling sods of a brown, still May, it left neither pleasure nor pain, but she'd know that track all the days of her life, and its dark, long sweep across the long waiting field. Binder and reaper clattered and wheeped through the brittle weather that held the Howe, soon the weather might break and the stooking was far behind in Blawearie. But Will would have nothing to do with night-time work, he laughed in John Guthrie's face at the mention of it and jumped on his bicycle and rode for Drumlithie evening on evening. Father would wander out by the biggings and stare at the parks and then come glinting into the house and glower at Chris, *Get off to your bed when you've milked the kye;* and she made little protest at that, she was tired enough at the end of a day to nearly sleep in the straw of the byre.

But one night she didn't dare sleep, for up in the room he'd shared with mother she heard John Guthrie get out of bed and go slow padding about in his stocking soles, like a great cat padding there, a beast that sniffed and planned and smelled at the night. And once he came soft down the cowering creak of the stairs and stopped by her door, and she held her breath, near sick with fright, though what was there to be feared of? And she heard his breath come quick and gasping, and the scuffle of his hand on the sneck of the door; and then that stopped, he must have gone up or down, the house was quiet, but she didn't dare sleep again till Will came clattering home in the still, small hours.

For the harvest madness was out in Kinraddie if Chris had been quick to master hers. And though a lad and a quean might think their ongoings known to none but themselves, they'd soon be sore mistaken, you might hide with your lass on the top of Ben Nevis and have your bit pleasure there, but ten to one when you got up to go home there'd be Mistress Munro or some claik of her kidney, near sniggering herself daft with delight at your shame. First it was Sarah Sinclair and the foreman at Upperhill, Ewan Tavendale he was, that the speak rose round; they'd been seen coming out of the larch wood above the Upperhill, that wood where the daftie had trapped Maggie Jean, and what had they been doing there on their lone? It was Alec Mutch of Bridge End that met them, him taking a dander over the moor to the smithy with a broken binder-blade for mending. The two hardly saw him at first, Miss Sinclair's face was an unco sight, raddled with blushing it was like the leg of a tuberculous rabbit when you skinned the beast, Ewan slouched along at her side, hang-dog he looked as though it was his mother he'd bedded with, said Alec, and maybe that's how it had felt. Alec cried a *Good night!* to the pair, they near jumped out of their skins, and went on with the story to the smithy beyond the moor. And from there you may well be sure it went through Kinraddie fast enough, the smith could tell lies faster than he could shoe horses; and he was fell champion at that.

Truth or no, Chae Strachan got hold of the story and went over to Upperhill to see Ewan Tavendale and ask in a friendly way what he meant to do about Sarah, his sister-in-law, the daft old trollop. And maybe he'd have settled things canty and fine but that he came on Ewan at the wrong bit minute, he was sitting outside the bothy door with the rest of the bothy billies; and when Chae came up there rose a bit snigger, that fair roused Chae, he stopped bang in front of them and asked what the hell they were laughing at? And Sam Gourlay said *Little, damned little*, looking Chae from head to foot; and Ewan said he felt more in the way of weeping than laughing at such a sight, and he spoke in a slow, impudent way that fair roused Chae's dander to the boiling point. So, being a fell impatient man, and skilly with his hands, he took Sam Gourlay a clout in the lug that couped him down in the stour and then before you could wink he and Ewan were at it, ding-dong, like a pair of tinks, all round the Upperhill close; and Upprums came running in his leggings, the creature, fair scandalized, but he got a shove in the guts that couped him right down in the greip where once his son Jock had been so mischieved; and that was the end of *his* interfering. In a minute or so it was plain that Ewan, fight though he might, was like to have the worst of the sett, he was no match for that madman Chae. So the rest of the bothy lads up and went for Chae; and when he got back to Peesie's Knapp he'd hardly a stitch on his back. But Ewan, the coarse, dour brute, had a cut in the face that stopped *his* mouth for a while, and a black eye big enough to sole the boots on Cuddiestoun's meikle feet, folk said.

And faith! if it shouldn't be Cuddiestoun himself that began the next story, running into the middle of it himself, you might say, going up to the Manse to get a bit signature on some paper or other for his lawyer man. But Mr Gibbon they told him wasn't at home, Mistress Gibbon herself came out to tell him that, kind and fine as she was, but he didn't like her, the English dirt. So, fair disgruntled he turned from the door, maybe the poor brute's big sweating feet were fell sore already with a hot day's stooking. But just down at the end of the Manse's garden, where the yews bent thick above the lush grass their boughs that had sheltered the lost childe Wallace in the days before the coarse English ran him to earth and took him to London and there hanged and libbed him and hewed his body in four to hang on the gates of Scotland—there, in that grass in the half-dark was a rustling and squealing as though a drove of young pigs was rootling there. And Cuddiestoun stopped and picked up a handful of gravel from the minister's walk and flung it into the grass and cried *Away with you!* for maybe it was dogs in heat that were chaving there, big collies are none so chancy to meet when the creatures are set for mating. But instead of a collie up out of the grass rose the Gourdon quean, her that old Mistress Sinclair had fee'd for the Manse; and Munro saw her face then with a glazed look on it, like the face of a pig below the knife of its killer; and she brushed the hair from her face, daft-like, and went trailing past Munro, without a word from her, as though she walked half-asleep. But past him, going into the Manse, she began to whistle, and laughed a loud scraich of a laugh—as though she'd tried right desperately for something, and won, and beaten all the world in the winning of it. So it seemed to Cuddiestoun, and faith! you couldn't put that down to imagination, for he'd never had any, the ugly stock; so fair queer it must well have been, he stood and stared after her, dumbfoundered-like, and was just turning at last, to tramp down to the road, when he found Mr Gibbon himself at his elbow.

It had grown fell dark by then but not so dark that Cuddiestoun couldn't see the Minister was without a hat and was breathing in great deep paichs as though he'd come from the running of a race. And he barked out, *Well, speak up, man, what do you want?* Munro was sore took aback at hearing a fine childe like the minister snap at him that way. So he just said *Well, well, Mr Gibbon, you've surely been running a bit race?* and then wished he hadn't, for the minister went by him without another word, and then flung over his shoulder *If you want me, come tomorrow.*

And into the Manse he went and banged the door with a clash that fair made Cuddiestoun loup in his meikle boots. So there was nothing for him but to taik away home to

Mistress Munro, and faith! you might well believe the story lost nothing in the telling she gave it, and soon every soul in Kinraddie had a different version, Long Rob's was cried to John Guthrie as he went by the Mill. He never spread scandal about folk, Long Rob—only horses, was the joke they told of him—but maybe he classed ministers lower than them.

It seemed like enough to John Guthrie, the story, though he'd no coarse notions like Rob and his Ingersoll, the world was rolling fast to a hell of riches and the old slave days come back again, ministers went with it and whored with the rest. For the bitterness had grown and eaten away into the heart of him in his year at Blawearie. So coarse the land proved in the turn of the seasons he'd fair been staggered, the crops had fared none so bad this once, but he saw in a normal year the corn would come hardly at all on the long, stiff slopes of the dour red clay. Now also it grew plain to him here as never in Echt that the day of the crofter was fell near finished, put by, the day of folk like himself and Chae and Cuddiestoun, Pooty and Long Rob of the Mill, the last of the farming folk that wrung their living from the land with their own bare hands. Sign of the times he saw Jean Guthrie's killing of herself to shame him and make of his name a by-word in the mouths of his neighbours, sign of a time when women would take their own lives or flaunt their harlotries as they pleased, with the country-folk climbing on silver, the few, back in the pit, the many; and a darkness down on the land he loved better than his soul or God.

And next it was Will himself that started the claiks of Kinraddie, him and his doings in Drumlithie. But Chris met the story ere it reached Kinraddie, she met it in Drumlithie itself, in the yard of the gardener Galt. The tink had been gone from Blawearie that day she set out with her basket, no sign of the rain showed even then, the heat held still as the white, dull heat from a furnace door. Down in the turnpike the motor-cars went whipping by as she set her feet for Mondynes, there where the battle was fought in the days long syne. Below the bridge went the wash of the burn west to the Bervie Water, bairns cried and splashed in the bridge's lithe, they went naked there when they dared, she saw them glance white and startled in the shelter of the stones. Soon the heat grew such that she took off her hat and swung that in her hand and so climbed the road, and there to the left rose Drumlithie at last, some called it Skite to torment the folk and they'd get fell angry at that in Skite. No more than a rickle of houses it was, white with sunshine below its steeple that made of Skite the laugh of the Howe, for feint the kirk was near it. Folk said for a joke that every time it came on to rain the Drumlithie folk ran out and took in their steeple, so proud they were of the thing, it came from the weaver days of the village when damn the clock was there in the place and its tolling told the hour.

So that was Skite, it rose out of its dusts and its ancient smells, the berries hung ripe in the yard of the gardener Galt and he looked at Chris in a queer kind of way when he heard her name. Syne he began a sly hinting and joking as he weighed her berries, a great sumph of a man the creature was, fair running with creash in that hot weather, you near melted yourself as you looked at him. *And how's Will?* he asked. *We haven't seen much of him here of late—faith, the roses are fair fading from Mollie Douglas' cheeks.* And Chris said *Oh?* right stiff-like, and then *And I'll have two pounds of your blackberries too.* So he packed her that, hinting and gleying like a jokesome fat pig, she could have taken him a clout in the face, but didn't, it would only stir up more scandal, there seemed enough and to spare of that. Whatever could Will have been doing; and what had he done to his quean that he'd left her?

Right glad she was to be out from the stink of Skite with the road of Mondynes in front of her. Then she heard the bell of a bicycle far down the road behind and drew to one side, but the thing didn't pass, it slowed down and some-body called out, timid-like, *Are you Will Guthrie's sister?* Chris turned and saw her then, knew her at once Will's quean, young and white-faced and fair, and heard her own voice near troubled as the eyes that looked at her as she answered *Yes; and you'll be Mollie Douglas?*

The face of the girl blushed slow at that, slow and sweet, and she looked away back at the steeple of Skite as though she feared the thing spied on them; and then suddenly, near crying, she was asking Chris to tell Will he must ride over and see her again, come again that night, she couldn't bear it longer—she didn't care were she shameless or not, she couldn't! And then she seemed to read the question in Chris's eyes, the blood drained off from her face in a minute and then came back, it seemed to Chris she must be blushing all over under her clothes, right down to the soles of her feet as she herself sometimes blushed. But she cried *Oh, you think THAT, like all of them, but it isn't true!* Staring at her surprised and shamed Chris found she just couldn't speak up and deny that THAT was indeed what she'd thought, what else was a body to think? Then she found Mollie Douglas' face bent close to hers, sweet and troubled and shamed as her own. And Mollie tried to look at her and then looked away, blushing as though she'd sink into the ground, such a fool of herself she was making. *It's not that at all, only I love him so sore I can't live if I don't see Will!*

So there they were in the middle of the road, so shamed to look one at the other they'd nothing to say; and then a gig came spanking along from the station, at sight of it Mollie jumped on her bicycle again, and wheeled it about, and looked over her shoulder with a smile you couldn't forget, and stammered and cried *Ta-ta!*

But Chris couldn't forget that look in her eyes, she went home with that in her mind and at supper that night couldn't take her own eyes from Will. She saw him then for the first time in years, almost a man, with his fair hair waving across his head and spreading to his cheeks in a rust-red down, like the down on a new-hatched chick; and his eyes blue and dark as a quean's, and kind when they looked at her, sulky when they turned on father. Not that they turned there often, there was never a word between Will and father unless they were clean compelled to it; like dumb folk working and eating together that needed no speech for hate.

Father ate his supper and climbed down the hill with his gun, Will loitered from door to window, whistling and idle, till he saw right across the Howe, up on Drumtochty hills, something that rose and coiled ash-grey and then darker against the autumn sky, a great shape like a snake there in the quiet of the evening air, with its tail a glimmer that wasn't the sunset, burning up red in the lithe of the hills. *Whin-burning,* he called to Chris, *they're burning the whins up Drumtochty way, come on up the moor and have a try at ours. They're damned sore in the need of it.——But I've my jelly to make, you gowk!——Oh, to hell with your jelly, we'll soon be jelly and bones in a grave ourselves, come on!*

So she went, they gathered great piles of old papers for twisting in torches, and made up the brae to the moor. They sat down on the grass and breathed a while, Kinraddie below them all cut and close-stooked, waiting the coming of the night, the lowe of the Bervie lights as the glow of another whin-burning there by the sea. They spread out to left and right below the moor-gate, Chris held to the left and ran through the whins, stopping to kick holes down close to the ground wherever a meikle bush rose up. Then far round the knowe Will cried he was starting, she saw him a long way off with the sky behind him and called back *All right!* and knelt by the biggest bush she'd struck; and kindled her torch and set its light to the crackling dryness of the grass.

It whoomed in an instant, the whin, she set her torch into it and ran to the next and fired that; and so in and out, backwards and forwards worked round the brae, you'd to speed quick as your legs could carry you to fire the frontward bushes when those behind raged out with their flames and smoke at your hair. In the dry, quiet evening the fire crackled up and spread and roared through the bushes and caught on the grass and crept and smoked on quick, searching trains to bushes unlit, and fired them, half you thought those questing tongues alive and malignant as they lapped through the grass. By the time Chris met with Will at the moor-gate there spread before them a park like an upland sea on fire, sweeping the hill, now the sun had quite gone and the great red roaring beast of a thing hunted and postured unchallenged, all Kinraddie was lit with its glare.

Will was black as a nigger, his eyebrows scorched, he pulled Chris down to rest on the grass. *By God, I hope the fire doesn't catch on the fence up there, else old Guthrie will be casting me out of Blawearie for bringing his grey hairs in sorrow to the grave!*

He said that sneering-like, mocking at father's Aberdeen-shire voice, and Chris stirred half-angry, and sighed, and then asked *What would you do if he did put you out?* and Will said *Go.——Would you get a fee?——Damn the fears of that.*

But he didn't sound over-confident, Chris knew right well that he'd find it none so easy if it came to the push, with the harvest over now in the Howe. And then, for she'd clean forgot her in the excitement of the fires, she minded the quean Mollie Douglas—it was as though she saw her white face by Will's in the firelit dark. *I met Mollie Douglas in Drumlithie today, she asked me to ask you to go down and see her.*

He sat stock-still, he mightn't have heard, she pushed at his elbow *Will!* And at that he shook off her hand, *Oh, I hear. What's the good? I can't have a quean like other folk —I haven't even a fee.——Maybe she doesn't want your fee, just you. Will, they're saying things about her and you in Drumlithie—Galt and coarse tinks like that.——Saying things? What things?——What they aye say—that she's with a baby to you and you're biding away from her now.—— Galt said that?——Hinted at it, but he'll do more than hint when he's not speaking to a sister of yours.*

She'd never heard him swear as he did then, jumping to his feet with his fists tight-clenched. *That about Mollie— they said that, the orra swine! I'll mash that bloody Galt's head till his own mother won't know it!* But Chris told him that wouldn't help much, folk would just snigger and say there was something, sure, in the story of Mollie's condition. *Then what am I to do?* Will asked, raging still, and Chris blushed and said *Wait. Do you love her, Will?* But she might have known well enough how he'd take that question, maybe he blushed himself in the lithe of the dark, he threw down the paper torches he'd saved and muttered *I'm away to Drumlithie*, and was running down the hill before she could stop him.

Maybe, as he told Chris later, he went with no other inten-tion than seeing his Mollie herself. But as luck would have it, who should he near run down with his bicycle outside the Drumlithie Hotel but Galt himself, the great creash, gey drunk, and Alec Mutch in his company. And Alec cried, *Fine night, Will*, but Galt cried *Don't take her out tonight, Will lad, the grass is overwet for lying on*. Will stopped and jumped off and left his bicycle lying in the road and went up to Galt—*Speaking to me?* And the fat creash, panting like a sow in litter and sweating all down the great face of him, hiccoughed drunken-like *Who else?*——*Well take that then*, Will said and let drive at the great belly of Galt; but Mutch caught his arm and cried *Young Guthrie, you've fair gone daft, the man's old enough to be your father*. Will said if he'd a father like that he'd kill him and then go and drown himself; and tried to break away from Mutch and get at the Galt creash again. But Galt was right unkeen for that, in a minute he'd turned, for all his fat, and made off like a hare up the Drumlithie lanes, real swack with his girth and all, and was out of sight in a second.

Well, sure you may be there were claiks enough in Skite for Mutch to get all the story and drive home with it to the Bridge End. In a day or so it was all about the place, Will was the laughing-stock of Kinraddie. Father heard it first from the postman, who waved him down to the road to tell him, and soon's he heard it John Guthrie went back to Will stooking in the yavil field and said *What's this that I hear about you and some orra tink bitch in Drumlithie?*

Now Will had been in a fair fine temper all that day from seeing his Mollie again; and she'd made him swear he'd not fly in a rage or go making a fool of himself if he heard their coarse hinting at her. So he just went on with the stooking and said *What the devil are you blithering about?* Father shot out his beard and cried *Answer my question, Will!* and Will said *Put a question with sense in it, then. How am I to know what you've been hearing? I'm not a thought-reader*, and father said *Damn't to hell, you coarse brute, am I to stand your lip as well as your whoring every night? Is't true there's a tink called Mollie Douglas that's with a bairn by you?* and Will said *If you call Mollie Douglas a tink again, I'll knock the damned teeth down the throat of you, father though you be*.

And they stopped their stooking, glaring at each other,

and father made to strike at Will but Will caught his arm and cried *Mind!* So father lowered his arm, white as a ghost he'd turned, and went on with the stooking, Will stared at him, white himself, and then went on with the stooking as well. And that might well have been the end of it so far as Blawearie went; but that evening they heard a clatter outside in the close and there was the minister's bicycle and Mr Gibbon himself new off it; and into the kitchen he came and said *Good evening, Chris, good evening Mr Guthrie. Can I have a word with Will?*

So Chris was sent to bring Will from the byre where he bedded the kye, he came back with her grey in the gills, there sat the minister and father, solemn as two owls in the loft of a barn, it was plain they'd been taking the matter through hand together. Father said *Chris, go to your room,* and there was nothing else for her but go; and what happened after that she was never sure, for Will wouldn't tell her, but she heard the sound of the three of them, all speaking at once and Will getting in a rage; and then suddenly the kitchen-door banged and there was Will striding across the close to the· barn where he stored his bicycle. Mr Gibbon's voice cried after him, angry-like, with a boom, *Just a minute, Will, where are you going?* and Will looked back and said *You're so anxious I should lie with my lass and get her with a bairn that I'm off to try and oblige you.* And he wheeled his bicycle out by the honeysuckle hedge and pedalled away down the road and didn't come back to Blawearie till one o'clock in the morning.

Chris hadn't been able to sleep, she lay listening for him, and when she heard him come up the stairs she cried his name in a whisper *Will!* He stopped uncertain outside her door and then lifted the sneck and came in soft-footed and sat on the side of her bed. Chris raised herself on an elbow and peered at·him, there was little light in the room and no moon that night though the sky was white with stars, and Will no more than a shadow hunched on her bedside there, with a whitish blotch for a face. And Chris whispered *Will, I heard what you said when you went away. But you didn't do it?* and Will gave a low laugh, he wasn't in a rage, *It wouldn't be for want of prigging by half the*

*holy muckers in Kinraddie if I had. But you needn't be
feared for that, I'd as soon cut my own throat as do hurt
to—HER.*

So the minister's interfering brought no harm, faith! he'd
more need to roust round his own bit byre with a clart if
Cuddiestoun's story of the Gourdon quean were true. And
soon enough after that a worse scandal went on the rounds
about him, folk shook their heads and made out they were
fell affronted: all but Long Rob of the Mill, and he swore
B'God, it was the best he'd heard since Nebuchadnezzar
went out to grass!

And the way of it was that in early November a bit
daughter was born to the Manse, and the Reverend Gibbon
was proud as punch, he preached a grand sermon that
Sunday, *For unto us a child is born*; and it was so affecting
that old Mistress Sinclair of the Netherhill broke down and
cried in her hanky about it; but Long Rob of the Mill,
when he heard that, said: *She shouldn't take whisky sweeties
to the kirk with her.* Everybody else was fell impressed, folk
who'd been a bit off the Manse for months agreed he'd
maybe his faults, the Gibbon childe, but who hadn't these
days? and feint the many could wag a pow like that in a
Mearns pulpit. But damn't! if the next day he didn't go off
and spoil the whole thing, the Monday it was, he was just
setting out for the train to Aberdeen, Mr Gibbon, when the
nurse cried out to him he might bring a small chamber-pot
for the girlie, none in the Manse was suitable. He gave a bit
blush, the big, curly bull, and said *Very well, nurse,* in a bull-
like voice, and off to the station he went, it was Fordoun,
and left his bicycle there and caught his train.

About what happened after that some told one thing and
some another and some told both together. But it seems that
fair early in the day in Aberdeen the Reverend Gibbon fell
in with some friends of his; and they'd have it that a dram
there must be to celebrate the occasion. So off the whole lot
of them went to a public house and had their dram and syne
another on top of that to keep the first one down, syne two-
three more to keep the wind out, it was blowy weather on
the edge of winter. Some said that midway the carouse Mr

Gibbon had got up to make a bit prayer; and one of the barmaids had laughed at him and he chased her out of the bar up to her room and finished his prayer with her there. But you couldn't believe every lie you heard.

Sometime late in the afternoon he minded his train, the minister, and hired a cab and bought the bit chamber, and caught the train by the skin of the teeth. No sooner was he down in his carriage than, fell exhausted, he went fast asleep and blithely snored his way south through many a mile, right dead to the world he was.

Most of the story till then was maybe but guessing, ill-natured guessing at that, but the porter at the Bridge of Dunn, a good twenty miles south from Fordoun, swore to the rest. He was just banging the doors of the old 7.30 when out of a carriage window came a head, like a bull's head out of the straw, he'd fair a turn, had the porter, when he saw the flat hat that topped it. *Is this Fordoun?* the meikle head mooed, and the porter said *No, man, it's a damned long way from being that.*

So he opened the door for Kinraddie's minister, and Mr Gibbon came stumbling out and rubbed his eyes, and the porter pointed to a platform where he'd find a slow train back to Fordoun. This platform lay over a little bridge and the minister set out to cross; and the first few steps he managed fell well, but near the top he began to sway and missed his footing and flung out his hands. The next thing that the porter saw was the chamber-pot, burst from its paper, rolling down the steps of the bridge with the minister's hat in competition and the minister thundering behind.

And then, when the porter had picked him up and was dusting him the Reverend Gibbon broke down and sobbed on the porter's shoulder what a bloody place was Kinraddie! And how'd the porter like to live 'tween a brier bush and a rotten kailyard in the lee of a house with green shutters? And the minister sobbed some more about the shutters, and he said you couldn't lie down a minute with a quean in Kinraddie but that some half-witted clod-hopping crofter began to throw stones at you, they'd feint the respect for God or kirk or minister down in Kinraddie. And the porter said it was awful the way the world went, he'd thought of resigning from the railway himself and taking to preaching, but now he wouldn't.

Syne he helped the minister over to an up-going train and went home to his wife and told her the tale; and she told it to her sister from Auchinblae; and *she* told it to her man who told it to Mutch; and so the whole thing came out. And next time he rode down by the Peesie's Knapp, the minister, a head shot out of a hedge behind him, it was wee Wat Strachan, and cried loud as you like *Any chambers today?*

Not that they'd much to shout for that winter themselves, the Strachans; folk said it was easy to see why Chae was so strong on Rich and Poor being Equal: he was sore in need of the sharing out to start ere he went clean broke himself. Maybe old Sinclair or the wife were tight with the silver that year, but early as December Chae had to sell his corn, he brought the first threshing of the season down in Kinraddie. John Guthrie and Will were off at the keek of dawn when they saw the smoke rise from the engines, Chris followed an hour later to help Chae's wife with the dinner and things. And faith! broke he might be but he wasn't mean, Chae, when the folk came trampling in to eat there was broth and beef and chicken and oat-cakes, champion cakes they made at the Knapp; and loaf and jelly and dumpling with sugar and milk; and if any soul were that gutsy he wanted more he could hold to the turnip-field, said Chae.

The first three men to come in Chris hardly saw, so busied she was pouring their broth for them. Syne, setting the plates, she saw Alec Mutch, his great lugs like red clouts hung out to dry; and he cried *Ay, Chris!* and began to sup as though he hadn't seen food for a fortnight. Beside him was Munro of the Cuddiestoun, he was eating like a collie ta'en off its chain. Chae's thresh was a spree to the pair of them. Then more trampling and scraping came from the door, folk came drifting in two-three at a time, Chris over-busied to notice their faces, but some watched her and gave a bit smile and Cuddiestoun cried to father, *Losh, man,*

D

she's fair an expert getting, the daughter. The kitchen's more her style than the College.

Some folk at the tables laughed out at that, the ill-nature grinned from the faces of them, and suddenly Chris hated the lot, the English Chris came back in her skin a minute, she saw them the yokels and clowns everlasting, dull-brained and crude. Alec Mutch took up the card from Cuddiestoun then and began on education and the speak ran round the tables. Most said it was a coarse thing, learning, just teaching your children a lot of damned nonsense that put them above themselves, they'd turn round and give you their lip as soon as look at you. But Chae was sitting down himself by then and he wouldn't have that. *Damn't man, you're clean wrong to think that. Education's the thing the working man wants to put him up level with the Rich.* And Long Rob of the Mill said *I'd have thought a bit balance in the bank would do that.* But for once he seemed right in agreement with Chae—*the more education the more of sense and the less of kirks and ministers.* Cuddiestoun and Mutch were fair shocked at that, Cuddiestoun cried out *Well, well, we'll hear nothing coarse of religion,* as though he didn't want to hear anything more about it and was giving out orders. But Long Rob wasn't a bit took aback, the long rangy childe, he just cocked an eye at Cuddiestoun and cried *Well, well, Munro, we'll turn to the mentally afflicted in general, not just in particular. How's that foreman of yours getting on, Tony? Is he still keeping up with his shorthand?* There was a snicker at that, you may well be sure, and Cuddiestoun closed up quick enough, here and there folk had another bit laugh and said Long Rob was an ill hand to counter. And Chris thought of her clowns and yokels, and was shamed as she thought—Chae and Long Rob they were, the poorest folk in Kinraddie!

At a quarter past six the mill loosed off again from its bumble-bee hum, the threshers came trooping down to the tables again. More dumpling there was, cut up for tea, and bread and butter and scones and baps from the grocer, and rhubarb and blackberry jam, and syrup for them that preferred it, some folk liked to live on dirt out of tins. Most of the mill folk sat down in a right fine tune, well they might, and loosed out their waistcoats. Will was near last to come in from the close, a long, dark young childe came in at his heels, Chris hadn't set eyes on him before, nor he on her by the way he glowered. The two of them stood about, lost-like and gowked, looking for seats in the crowded kitchen till Mistress Strachan cried over to Chris *Will you lay them places ben in the room?*

So she did and took them their supper there, Will looked up and cried *Hello, Chris, how have you gotten on?* and Chris said *Fine, how've you?* Will laughed *Well, God, my back would feel a damned sight easier if I'd spent the day in my bed. Eh, Tavendale?* And then he minded his manners. *This is Ewan Tavendale from Upprums, Chris.*

So that was who; Chris felt queer as he raised his head and held out his hand, and she felt the blood come in her face and saw it come dark in his. He looked over young for the coarse, dour brute folk said he was, like a wild cat, strong and quick, she half-liked his face and half-hated it, it could surely never have been him that did THAT in the larch wood of Upperhill? But then if you could read every childe's nature in the way he wiped his nose, said Long Rob of the Mill, it would be a fine and easy world to go through.

So she paid him no more heed and was out of the Knapp a minute later and ran nearly all the way up to Blawearie to see to the milking there. The wind was still up but the frost was crackling below her feet as she ran, the brae rose cold and uncanny with Blawearie's biggings uncertain shadows high up in the cold mirk there. She felt tingling and blithe from her run, she said to herself if she'd only the time she'd go out every winter night and run up over hills with frost and the night star coming in the sky.

But that night as Blawearie went to its bed Will opened his bedroom door and cried *Father! Chris! See that light down there in the Knapp!*

Chris was over at her window then in a minute, bare-footed she ran and peered by the shadow of the great beech tree. And there was a light right plain enough, more than a light, a lowe that crackled to yellow and red and rose

in the wind that had come with the night. Peesie's Knapp
would be all in a blaze in a minute, Chris knew; and then
father came tearing down the stairs, crying to Will to get
on his clothes and follow him, Chris was to bide at home,
mind that. They heard him open the front door and go out
and go running right fleetly down the night of Blawearie
hill, Chris cried to Will *Wait for me, I'm coming as well,*
and he cried back *All right, but for Christ's sake hurry!*

She couldn't find her stockings then, she was trembling
and daft; and when found they were, her corsets were missing, slipped down the back of the kist they had, Will came
knocking at the door *Come on!*—*Light a match and come in,*
she called and in he came, knotting his muffler, and lighted a
match and looked at her in her knickers and vest, reaching
out for the new-seen corsets. *Leave the damn things where
they are, you're fine, you should never have been born a
quean.* She was into her skirt by then, and said *I wish I
hadn't,* and pulled on her boots and half-laced them, and
ran down the stairs after Will and put on her coat at the foot.
In a minute they were out in the dimness then, under the
starlight, it was rimed with frost, and running like mad
down to the lowe that now rose like a beacon against the
whole of Kinraddie. *God, I hope they've wakened!* Will
panted, for every soul knew the Strachans went straight to
bed at the chap of eight. Running, they could see by then
it was the barn itself that had taken alight, the straw sow
seemed burned to a cinder already, and the barn had caught
and maybe the house. And all over Kinraddie lights were
springing up, as they ran Chris lifted her eyes and saw
Cuddiestoun's blink and shine bright down through the
dark.

And faith, quick though they were, it was father that
saved Chae Strachan's folk. He was first down at the blazing
Knapp, John Guthrie; and he ran round the biggings and
saw the flames lapping and lowing at the kitchen end of
the house, not a soul about or trying to stop them though
the noise was fair awful, the crackling and burning, and
the winter air bright with flying sticks and straw. He banged
at the door and cried *Damn't to hell do you want to be
roasted?* and when he got no answer he smashed in the

window, they heard him then and the bairns scraiched,
there was never such a lot for sleep, folk said, Chae'd have
slept himself out of this world and into hell in his own
firewood if John Guthrie hadn't roused him then. But out he
came stumbling at last, he'd only his breeks on; and he
took a keek at John Guthrie and another at the fire and
cried out *Kirsty, we're all to hell!* and off he tore to the
byre.

But half-way across the close as he ran the barn swithered
and roared and fell, right in front of him, and he'd to run
back, there was no way then of getting at the byre. By then
Long Rob of the Mill came in about, he'd run over the
fields, louping dykes like a hare, and his lungs were panting
like bellows, he was clean winded. He it was that helped
Mrs Strachan with the bairns and such clothes as they could
drag out to the road while Chae and John Guthrie tried
to get at the byre from another angle; but that was no good,
the place was already roaring alight. For a while there was
only the snarling of the fire eating in to the wooden coup-
lings, the rattle of falling slates through the old charred
beams, and then, the first sound that Will and Chris heard
as they came panting down the road, a scream that was
awful, a scream that made them think one of the
Strachans was trapped down there. And at that sound Chae
covered his ears and cried *Oh God, that's old Clytie,* Clytie
was his little horse, his sholtie, and she screamed and
screamed, terrible and terrible, Chris ran back to the house
trying not to hear and to help poor Kirsty Strachan, snivelling and weeping, and the bairns laughing and dancing
about as though they were at a picnic, and Long Rob of
the Mill smoking his pipe as cool as you please, there was
surely enough smell and smoke without that? But pipe and
all he dived in and out of the house and saved chairs and
dishes and baskets of eggs; and Mistress Strachan cried *Oh,
my sampler!* and in Rob tore and rived that off a blazing
wall, a meikle worsted thing in a cracked glass case that
Mistress Strachan had made as a bairn at school.

And then came the clip-clop of a gig, it was Ellison down
from the Mains, him and two of his men, and God! he
might be little more than a windy Irish brute but he'd sense

for all that, the gig was crammed with ropes and pails,
Ellison strung out the folk and took charge, the pails went
swinging from hand to hand over the close from the well to
the childe that stood nearest the fire, and he pelted the fire
with water. But feint the much good that did for a while
and then there was an awful sound from the byre, the lowing
of the cattle with the flames among them, and Long Rob
of the Mill cried out *I can't stand it!* and took a pick-axe
and ran round the back of the close; and there he found
the sow was nothing but a black heap then, hardly burning
at all, and he cried back the news and himself louped
through the smoke and came at the back wall of the byre
and started to smash it in fast as he could. Chae followed
and John Guthrie, and the three men worked like madmen
there, Ellison's men splashed water down on the roof above
them till suddenly the wall gave way before them and
Chae's oldest cow stuck out its head and said *Moo!* right
in Chae's face. The three scrambled through into the byre
then, that was fell dangerous, the rafters were crumbling
and falling all about the stalls, and it was half-dark there
in spite of the flames. But they loosed another cow and two
stirks before the fire drove them out, the others they had to
leave, their lowing was fair demented and the smell of their
burning sickening in your throat, it was nearly a quarter
of an hour later before the roof fell in and killed the cattle.
Long Rob of the Mill sat down by the side of the road
and was suddenly as sick as could be, and he said *By God,
I never want to smell roasting beef again.*

So that was the burning of the Peesie's Knapp, there was
a great throng of folk in about by then, the Netherhill folk
and the Upperhill, the Cuddiestoun, and Alec Mutch with
his great lugs lit up by the fire, some had come on bicycles
and some had run across half Kinraddie and two had brought
their gigs. But there was little to do now but stand and
glower at the fire and its mischief. Ellison drove off to the
Mains with Mistress Strachan and the bairns, there for the
night they were bedded. The cattle he'd saved from the
byre, Chae drove to Netherhill, folk began to put on their
jackets again, it was little use waiting for anything else,
they'd away home to their beds.

Chris could see nothing of either father or Will, she turned to make for Blawearie then. Outside the radiance of the burning Knapp it was hard and cold, starless but clear, as though the steel of the ground glowed faintly of itself; beyond rose the darkness as a black wall, still and opaque. On the verge of its embrasure it was that she nearly ran into two men tramping back along the road, she hardly saw them till she was on them. She cried *Oh, I'm sorry,* and one of them laughed and said something to the other, next instant before she knew what was happening that other had her in his arms, rough and strong, and had kissed her, he had a face with a soft, grained skin, it was the first time a man had ever kissed her like that, dark and frightening and terrible in the winter road. The other stood by, Chris, paralysed, heard him breathing and knew he was laughing, and a far crackle rose from the last of the lowe in the burning biggings. Then she came to herself and kicked the man that held her, young he was with his soft, grained face, kicked him hard with her knee and then brought her nails down across his face. As he swore *You bitch!* and let go of her she kicked him again, with her foot this time, and he swore again, but the other said *Hist! Here's somebody coming,* and the two of them began to run, the cowardly tinks, it was father and Will on the road behind them.

And when Chris told Will of what happened, next morning it was that she told him when father wasn't by, he looked at her queerly, half-laughing, half-solemn, and made out he thought nothing of the happening, all ploughmen were like that, aye ready for fun. But it hadn't seemed fun to her, dead earnest rather; and lying that night in her bed between the cold sheets, curled up so that she might rub her white toes to some warmth and ease, it was in her memory like being chased and bitten by a beast, but worse and with something else in it, as though half she'd liked the beast and the biting and the smell of that sleeve around her neck and that soft, unshaven face against her own. Sweet breath he had had anyway, she thought, and laughed to herself, that was some consolation, the tink. And then she fell asleep and dreamed of him, an awful dream that made her blush even while she knew she was dreaming, she was

glad when morning came and was sane and cool and herself
again.

But that dream came to her often while the winter wore
on through Kinraddie, a winter that brought hardly any
snow till New Year's Eve and then brought plenty, darken
ing the sky with its white cascading. It was funny that
darkening the blind fall and wheep of the snow should
bring, like the loosening of a feather pillow above the hills,
night came as early as three in the afternoon. They redd
up the beasts early that evening, father and Will, feeding
them well with turnips and straw and hot treacle poured
on the straw; and then they came in to their supper and
had it and sat close round the fire while Chris made a fine
dumpling for New Year's Day. None of them spoke for long,
listening to that whoom and blatter on the window-panes,
and the clap-clap-clap of some loose slate far up on the roof,
till father whispered and looked at them, his whisper hurt
worse than a shout, *God, I wonder why Jean left us?*

Chris cried then, making no sound, she looked at Will
and saw him with his face red and shamed, all three of
them thinking of mother, her that was by them so kind
and friendly and quick that last New Year, so cold and
quiet and forgotten now with the little dead twins in the
kirkyard of Kinraddie, piling black with the driving of the
snow it would be under the rustle and swing and creak
of the yews. And Will stared at father, his face was blind
with pity, once he made to speak, but couldn't, always
they'd hated one the other so much and they'd feel shamed
if they spoke in friendship now.

So father took up his paper again and at ten o'clock Chris
went out to milk the kye and Will went with her over the
close, carrying the lantern, the flame of it leapt and starred
and quivered and hesitated in the drive of the snow. In the
light of it, like a rain of arrows they saw the coming of the
storm that night swept down from the Grampian heuchs,
thick and strong it was in Blawearie, but high in the real
hills a smoring, straight wall must be sweeping the dark,
blinding down against the lone huts of the shepherds and
the faces of lost tinks tramping through it looking for lights

the snow'd smothered long before. Chris was shaking, but not with cold, and inside the byre she leant on a stall and Will said *God, you look awful, what is't?* And she shook herself and said *Nothing. Why haven't you gone to see Mollie tonight?*

He said he was going next day, wasn't that enough, he'd be a corpse long ere he reached Drumlithie tonight—*listen to the wind, it'll blow the damn place down on our lugs in a minute!* And the byre shook between the lulls, it seemed to set its breath to rise and take from the hill-side into the air, there was such straining and creaking. Not that the calves or the stirks paid heed, they slept and snored in their stalls with never a care, there were worse things in the world than being a beast.

Back in the house it seemed to Chris she'd but hardly sieved the milk when the great clock ben in the parlour sent peal after peal out dirling through the place. Will looked at Chris and the two at father, and John Guthrie was just raising up his head from his paper, but if he'd been to wish them a happy New Year or not they were never to know, for right at that minute there came a brisk chap at the door and somebody lifted the sneck and stamped the snow from his feet and banged the door behind him.

And there he was, Long Rob of the Mill, muffled in a great grey cravat and with leggings up to his knees, covered and frosted from head to foot in the snow, he cried *Happy New Year to you all! Am I the first?* And John Guthrie was up on his feet, *Ay, man, you're fairly that, out of that coat of yours!* They stripped off the coat between them, faith! Rob's mouser was nearly frozen, but he said it was fine and laughed, and waited the glass of toddy father brought him and cried *Your Health!* And just as it went down his throat there came a new knock, damn't if it wasn't Chae Strachan, he'd had more than a drink already and he cried *Happy New Year, I'm the first foot in am I not?* And he made to kiss Chris, she wouldn't have minded, laughing, but he slithered and couped on the floor, Long Rob peered down at him and cried out, shocked-like, *God Almighty, Chae, you can't sleep there!*

So he was hoisted into a chair and was better in a minute

when he'd had another drink; and he began to tell what
a hell of a life it was he'd to live in Netherhill now, the
old mistress grew worse with the years, she'd near girn
the jaws from her face if the Strachan bairns so much as
gave a bit howl or had a bit fight—fell unreasoning that,
no bairns there were but fought like tinks. And Long Rob
said Aye, that was true, as it said in the hymn 'twas dog's
delight to bark and bite, and faith! the average human
could out-dog any cur that ever was pupped. Now, horses
were different, you'd hardly ever meet a horse that was
naturally a quarreller, a coarse horse was a beast they'd
broken in badly. He'd once had a horse—a three-four years
come Martinmas that would have been, or no! man, it was
only two—that he bought up in Auchinblae at the fall of
the year, a big roan, coarse as hell, they said, and he'd nearly
kicked the guts out of an old man there. Well, Rob had
borrowed a bridle and tried to ride home the beast to the
Mill, and twice in the first mile the horse threw him off
with a snort and stood still, just laughing, as Rob picked
himself up from the stour. But Rob just said to himself,
All right, my mannie, we'll see who'll laugh last; and when
he'd got that horse home he tied him up in his stall and
gave him such a hammering, by God he nearly kicked down
the stable. Every night for a week he was walloped like that,
and damn't man! in the shortest while he'd quietened down
and turned into a real good worker, near human he was,
that horse, he'd turn at the end of a rig as it drew to eleven
o'clock and begin to nicker and neigh, he knew the time
fine. Ay, canty beast that, he'd turned, and sold at a profit in
a year or so, it just showed you what a handless man did
with a horse, for Rob had heard that the beast's new owner
had let the horse clean go over him. A sound bit leathering
and a pinch of kindness was the only way to cure a coarse
horse.

Chae hiccupped and said *Damn't ay, man, maybe you're
right. It's a pity old Sinclair never thought of treating his
fish-wife like that, she'd deave a door-nail with her whines
and plaints, the thrawn old Tory bitch*. And Long Rob said
there were worse folk than Tories and Chae said if there
were they kept themselves damn close hidden, if he'd his

way he'd have all Tories nailed up in barrels full of spikes
and rolled down the side of the Grampians; and Long Rob
said there would be a gey boom in the barrel trade then,
the most of Kinraddie would be inside the barrels; and
Chae said *And a damned good riddance of rubbish, too.*

They were both heated up with the toddy then, and
raising their voices, but father just said, cool-like, that he
was a Liberal himself, and what did they think of this
bye-election coming off in the February? Chae said it would
make no difference who got in, one tink robber was bad
as another, Tory as Liberal; damn't if he understood why
Blawearie should be taken in by those Liberals. Long Rob
said *Why don't you stand as the Socialist man yourself,
Chae?* and winked at Chris, but Chae took it real serious
and said maybe he'd do that yet once Peesie's Knapp was
builded again. And Long Rob said *Why wait for that?
You're allowing your opinions to eat their heads off in
idleness, like a horse in a stall in winter. Losh, man, but
they're queer beasts, horses. There's my sholtie, Kate——*
But Chae said *Och, away to hell with your horses, Rob.
Damn't, if you want a canty kind of beast there's nothing
like a camel,* and maybe he'd have just begun to tell them
about the camel if he hadn't fallen off his chair then, nearly
into the fire he went, and John Guthrie smiled at him
over his beard, as though he'd really rather cut his throat
than smile. And then Will and Long Rob helped Chae to
his feet, Long Rob gave a laugh and said it was time they
went dandering back to their beds, he'd see Chae far
as the Netherhill. The storm had cleared a bit by then,
it was bright starlight Chris saw looking after the figures
of the two from her bedroom window—not very steady,
either of them, with shrouded Kinraddie lying below and
a smudge there, faint and dark, far down in the night, that
was the burned-out steading of Peesie's Knapp.

And there the smudge glimmered through many a week,
they didn't start on Peesie's new steading till well in the
February. But faith! there was clatter enough of tongues
round the place right from the night of the fire onwards.
All kinds of folk came down and poked in the ash with

their walking-sticks, the police and the Cruelty came from Stonehaven; and the factor came, he was seldom seen unless there was money in question; and insurance creatures buzzed down from Aberdeen like a swarm of fleas, their humming and hawing and gabbling were the speak of all Kinraddie. Soon all kinds of stories flew up and down the Howe, some said the fire had been lighted by Chae himself, a Drumlithie billy riding by the Knapp late that night of the fire had seen Chae with a box of spunks in his hand, coming from the lighting of the straw sow, sure; for soon as he saw the billy on the bicycle back Chae had jumped to the lithe again. Others said the fire had been set by the folk of Nether-hill, their only chance of recovering the silver they'd loaned to Chae. But that was just a plain lie, like the others, Chris thought, Chae'd have never cried for his burning sholtie like that if he'd meant it to burn for insurance.

But stories or no, they couldn't shake Chae, he was paid his claims up to the hilt, folk said he'd made two-three hundred pounds on the business, he'd be less keen now for Equality. But faith! if he'd won queer silver queerly, he'd lost feint the queer notion in the winning of it. Just as the building of the new bit Knapp began so did the bye-election, the old member had died in London of drink, poor brute, folk said when they cut his corpse open it fair gushed out with whisky. Ah well, he was dead then, him and his whisky, and though he'd maybe been a good enough childe to represent the shire, feint the thing had the shire ever seen of him except at election times. Now there came a young Tory gent in the field, called Rose he was, an Englishman with a funny bit squeak of a voice, like a bairn that's wet its breeks. But the Liberal was an oldish creature from Glasgow, fell rich he was, folk said, with as many ships to his name as others had fields. And real Radical he was, with everybody's money but his own, and he said he'd support the Insurance and to Hell with the House of Lords, *Vote for the Scottish Thistle and not for the English Rose*.

But the Tory said the House of Lords had aye been defenders of the Common People, only he didn't say aye, his English was a real drawback; and it was at the meeting where he said that, that Chae Strachan up and asked if it wasn't true that his own uncle was a lord? And the Tory said *Yes*, and Chae said that maybe *that* lord would be glad to see him in Parliament but there was a greater Lord who heard when the Tories took the name of poor folk in vain. The God of old Scotland there was, aye fighting on the side of the people since the days of old John Knox, and He would yet bring to an end the day of wealth and waster throughout the world, liberty and equality and fraternity were coming though all the damned lordies in the House of Lords should pawn their bit coronets and throw their whores back in the streets and raise private armies to fight the common folk with their savings.

But then the stewards made at Chae, he hadn't near finished, and an awful stamash broke out in the hall; for though most of the folk had been laughing at Chae they weren't to see him mishandled by an English tink and the coarse fisher brutes he'd hired from Gourdon; to keep folk from asking him questions. So when the first steward laid hands on Chae, John Guthrie, who was sitting near, cried *Ay, man, who'll you be?* And the fisher swore *You keep quiet as well*, and father rose and took him a belt in the face, and the fisher's nose bled like the Don in spate, and somebody put out a leg and tripped him up and that was the end of his stewarding. And when the other steward made to come to his help Long Rob of the Mill said *Away home to your stinking fish!* and took him by the lug and ran him out of the hall and kicked him into the grass outside.

Then everybody was speaking at once, Mr Gibbon was the Tory lad's chairman and he called out *Can't you give us fair play, Charles Strachan?* but Chae's blood was up, strong for the Kirk though he was in a way he clean forgot who he spoke to—*Come outside a minute, my mannie, and I'll fair-play you!* The minister wasn't such a fool as that, though, he said that the meeting was closed, fair useless it was to go on; and he said that Chae was a demagogue and Chae said that he was a liar, folk cried out *Wheest, wheest!* at that and began to go home. The Tory childe got hantle few votes in the end, Chae boasted it was his help put in the old Liberal stock; and God knows if he thought that fine he was easily pleased, they never saw the creature again in Kinraddie.

But that was the last time father struck a man, striking in cold anger and cold blood as was the way of him. Folk said he was an unchancy childe to set in a rage; but his next rage mischieved himself, not others. For a while up into the New Year, April and the turnip-time, things at Blawearie went fair and smooth, Will saying no more than his say at plate or park, never countering father, hardly he looked at him even; and father maybe thought to rule the roost as he'd done before when Will was no more than a boy that cowered when he heard that sharp voice raised, frightened and beaten and lying through nights with his sore wealed body in the arms of Chris. But Chris, knowing none of his plannings, guessed right well something new it was kept Will quiet, so quiet day on day, yet if you looked at him sudden you'd more likely than not see him smiling to himself, lovely the face that he smiled with, brown and clean, and his eyes were kind and clear and the hair grew down on his head in a bonny mop, Will took after mother with that flame of rusty gold that was hers.

Ah well, he kept to his whistling and his secret smiling, and every night after loosening and suppering was done, off down the road on his old bit bicycle he'd go, you'd hear through the evening stillness nothing but the sound of the old machine whirring down Blawearie road, and the weet-weet of the peewits flying twilit over Kinraddie, wheeling and circling there in the dark, daft creatures that made their nests in this rig and that and would come back next day and find them robbed or smothered away. So for hundreds of years they'd done, the peewits, said Long Rob of the Mill, and hadn't learned the sense of the thing even yet; and if you were to take that as a sample of the Divine Intelligence that had allotted a fitting amount of brain to each creature's needs then all you could suppose was that the Divine had more than a spite against the peesie.

Chris heard him say that one day she looked in at the Mill to ask when a sack of bruised corn, left there by Will, would be ready. But there on the bench outside the

Mill, in the shade from the hot Spring weather, sat Rob
and Chae and Mutch of Bridge End, all guzzling beer from
long bottles they were, Rob more bent on bruising their
arguments than on bruising Blawearie's corn. Peewits were
flying round the Mill fell thick, peewits and crows that
nested in the pines above the Mill, and the birds it was had
begun the argument. Chris waited for a while, pleased
enough with the shade and rest, hearkening to Long Rob
make a fool of God. But Alec Mutch wagged his meikle lugs,
*No, man, you're fair wrong there. And man, Rob, you'll
burn in hell for that, you know.* Chae was half on his side
and half wasn't, he said *Damn the fears, that's nothing but
an old wife's gabble for fearing the bairns. But Something
there IS up there; Rob man, there's no denying that. If I
thought there wasn't I'd out and cut my throat this minute.*
Then the three of them sighted Chris and Rob got up, the
long, rangy childe with the glinting eyes, and cried *Is't
about the bruised corn, Chris? Tell Will I'll do it tonight.*

But Will had unyoked and made off to Drumlithie, his
usual gait, when Chris got home, and father was up on the
moor with his gun, you heard the bang of the shots come
now and then. Chris had a great baking to do that night,
both father and Will would eat oatcakes and scones for a
wager, bought bread from the vans soon scunnered them
sore. Warm work it was when you'd heaped a great fire and
the girdle glowed below, you'd nearly to strip in fine weather
if you weren't to sweat yourself sick. Chris got out of most
things but a vest and a petticoat, she was all alone and could
do as she pleased, it was fine and free and she baked with a
will.

She was lifting the last cake, browned and good and
twice cross cut, when she knew that somebody watched her
from the door of the kitchen, and she looked, it was Ewan
Tavendale, him she hadn't seen since the day of the thresh
at Peesie's Knapp. He was standing against the jamb, long
and dark with his glowering eyes, but he reddened when
she looked, not half as much as she did herself, she could feel
the red warm blushing come through her skin from tip to
toe; *such a look he's taking,* she thought, *it's a pity I'm wearing a thing and he can't study the blush to its end.*

But he just said *Hello, is Will about?* and Chris said
No, in Drumlithie I think, and they stood and glowered
like a couple of gowks, Chris saw his eyes queer and soft
and shy, the neck of his shirt had fallen apart, below it
the skin was white as new milk, frothed white it looked,
and a drop of sweat stood there where the brown of his
tanning and the white of his real skin met. And then Chris
suddenly knew *something* and blushed again, sharp and
silly, she couldn't stop, she'd minded the night of the fire
at Peesie's Knapp and the man that had kissed her on the
homeward road, Ewan Tavendale it had been, no other,
shameless and coarse.

He was blushing himself again by then, they looked at
each other in a white, queer daze, Chris wondered in a kind
of a panic if he knew what she knew at last, half-praying
she was he wouldn't speak of it when he began to move
off from the door, still red, stepping softly, like father, like
a limber, soft-stepping cat. *Well, I was hoping I'd see him
in case he should leave us sudden-like.*

She stared at him all awake, that kissing on the winter
road forgotten. *Leave? Who said Will was leaving?—Oh,
I heard he was trying for a job in Aberdeen, maybe it's a
lie. Tell him I called in about. Ta-ta.*

She called *Ta-ta,Ewan,* after him as he crossed the close,he
half-turned round and smiled at her, quick and dark like
a cat again, *Ta-ta, Chris.* And she stood looking after him a
long while, not thinking, smiling, till the smell of a burning
cake roused her to run, just like the English creature Alfred.

And next morning she said to Will after breakfast, casual-
like, but her heart in her throat, *Ewan Tavendale was down
to see you last night, he thought you'd be leaving Blawearie
soon.* And Will took it cool and quiet, *Did he? God, they'd
haver the breeks from a Highlandman's haunches, the
gossipers of Kinraddie. Tavendale down to see me? More
likely he was down to take a bit keek at you, Chris lass. So
look after yourself, for he's Highland and coarse.*

In July it came to the hay-time, and John Guthrie looked
at Will and said he was going to have down the hay with a
scythe this year, not spoil the bit stuff with a mower. Fair
plain to Chris he expected Will to fly in a rage at that and

say he wasn't to chave and sweat in the forking of rig after
rig when a mower would clear Blawearie's park in a day
or two at the most. But Will just said *All right* and went on
with his porridge, and went out to the field in the tail of
father, a fork on his shoulder and whistling happy as a lark,
so that father turned round and snapped *Hold your damned
wheeber, you'll need your breath for the bout*. Even at that
Will laughed, as a man at a girning bairn, right off they were
worse friends than even the year before. But all that time,
Will was making his plans and on the morning of the
August's last Saturday, Chris aye remembered that morning
with its red sun and the singing of the North Sea over the
Howe, that morning he said to father *I'm off to Aberdeen
today.*

Father said never a word, he went on with his porridge
and finished it, he mightn't have heard Will speak, he
lighted his pipe and stepped out of the house, fleet as ever he
went, and began coling the hayfield in front of the house;
Will could see him then and be shamed of himself and
his idle jaunting. But Will wasn't ashamed, he looked after
father with a sneer, *The old fool thinks he can frighten me
still*, and said something else Chris didn't catch, syne looked
at her suddenly, his eyes bright and his lips moving, *Chris—
Lord, I wish you were coming as well!*

She stared at that amazed, pleased as well. *What, up to
Aberdeen? I'd like it fine but I can't. Hurry and dress, else
you'll miss your train.*

So he went and dressed, fell slow-like he seemed at the
business, she thought, the morning and a jaunt in front of
him. She went to the foot of the stairs and cried up to
ask if he were having a sleep before he set out? And instead
of answering her back with a jest and a fleer he laughed a
shaky laugh and called out All right, he'd soon be down.
And when he came she saw him in his Sunday suit, with his
new boots shining, he'd on a new hat that suited him fine.
Well, will I do? he asked and Chris said *You look fair brave,*
and he said *Havers!* and picked up his waterproof, *Well,
ta-ta, Chris*; and suddenly turned round to her and she
saw his face red and strange and he kissed her, they hadn't
kissed since they were children lying in a bed together on

a frosty night. She wiped her mouth, feeling shamed and pleased, and pushed him away, he tried to speak, and couldn't, and said *Oh, to hell!* and turned and ran out of the door, she saw him go down the Blawearie road fast as he could walk, looking up at the hills he was with the sun on them and the slow fog rising off the Howe, jerking his head this way and that, fast though he walked, but he didn't once look in father's direction nor father at him. Syne she heard him whistling bonny and clear, *Up in the Morning*, it was, they'd used that for a signal in the days when they went the school-road together, and down on the turnpike edge he looked round and stood still, and waved his hand, he knew she was watching. Then a queer kind of pain came into her throat, her eyes smarted and she told herself she was daft, Will was only off for the day, he'd be back at night.

But Will didn't come back that night, he didn't come back the next day, he came back never again to John Guthrie's Kinraddie. For up in Aberdeen he was wed to his Mollie Douglas, he'd altered his birth certificate for that; and the earth might have opened and swallowed them up after that, it seemed not a soul in Aberdeen had seen them go. So when father went into Aberdeen on the track of the two there wasn't a trace to be found, he went to the police and raged at them, but they only laughed—had he lain with the quean himself, maybe, that so mad he was with this son of his?

So father came home, fair bursting with rage, but that didn't help. And ten days went by before they heard of the couple again, it came in a letter Will sent to Chris at Blawearie; and it told that through Mollie's mother, old Mistress Douglas, Will had got him a job in the Argentine, cattleman there on a big Polled Angus ranch, and he and Mollie were sailing from Southampton the day he wrote; and oh! he wished Chris could have seen them married; and remember them kindly, they would write again, and Mrs Douglas at Drumlithie would aye be a friend to her.

So that was Will's going, it was fair the speak of the parish a while, folk laughed at father behind his back and said maybe that would bring down his pride a bit; and they asked Chae Strachan, that well-travelled childe, where was this Argentine, was it a fine place, would you say? And Chae said *Och*, fine, he'd never been actually there, you might say, but a gey fine place it was, no doubt, a lot of silver was there; and *Damn't, man, young Guthrie's no fool to spread his bit wings, I was just the same myself.* But most said it was fair shameful of Will to go off and leave his father like that, black burning shame he might think of himself; it just showed you what the world was coming to, you brought bairns into the world and reared them up and expected some comfort from them in your old age and what did you get? Nothing but a lot of damned impudence, it was all this education and dirt. You might well depend on it, that coarse young Guthrie brute would never thrive, there'd be a judgment on him, you'd see, him and his coarse tink quean.

Judgment or not on Will, it was hardly a week before his own rage struck down John Guthrie. He'd been setting up ricks in the cornyard when Chris heard a frightened squawk break out from the hens. She thought maybe some strange dog was among them and caught up a spurtle and ran out to the close and there saw father lying still in his blood, black blood it looked on his face where he'd fallen and mischieved himself against a stone. She cried out to him in fright and then cooled herself down, and ran for water from the spring and dipped her hanky in it and bathed his face. He opened his eyes then, dazed-like he seemed, and he said *All right, Jean lass*, and tried to rise, and couldn't. And rage came on him again, he put out his hand and gave Chris a push that near threw her down, he tried and tried to rise up, it was sickening to see. He chaved on the ground as though something tied him there, all one of his sides and legs, and the blood veins stood out blue on his face; and he cursed and said *Get into the house, you white-faced bitch!* he wouldn't have her looking at him. So she watched from behind the door, near sick she felt, it was as though a great frog were squattering there in the stour, and the hens gathered and squawked about him.

And at last he stood up and staggered to a stone, and Chris didn't look more, going on with her work as well as she could with hands that quivered and quivered. But when he came in for supper he looked much as ever, and grumbled at this and that, and ate his egg as though it would do him ill, syne got his gun and went off to the hill as fleet as ever. He was long up there, Chris went to the window and watched for him, seeing the August late night close in, Cuddiestoun's sheep were baaing high up in the Cuddiestoun moor and a sprig of the honeysuckle that made the Blawearie hedges so bonny through the summer tapped and touched against the window-pane, it was like a slow hand tapping there; and the evening was quiet in the blow of the night-wind, and no sign of father till Chris grew alarmed and nearly went out to look for him. But then she heard his step in the porch, in he came and put down his gun and saw her stand there and cried out *Damn't to hell, is that all you've to do, stand about like a lady?* So you could hardly believe there was much wrong with him then, except ill-nature, he'd plenty of that, you'd no foreseeing that next morning he'd try to get out of bed and lie paralysed.

She wouldn't in a hurry forget the sight of him then, nor the run she had down Blawearie brae till the new Knapp came in sight, brave with its biggings and house. But there at last was Chae Strachan, he was busied letting a strainer into the ground, smoking, the blue smoke of his pipe rose into the air, blue, like a pencil-stroke, a cock was crowing across the Denburn and he didn't hear her cry for a while. But then he did and was quick enough, he ran up to meet her, *What's wrong, Chris lass?* and she told him and he turned and ran down—*Go back to your father and I'll get to the doctor myself and send the wife up to Blawearie.*

And up she came, the fat, fusionless creature, all she could do was to stand and gowk at father, *Mighty me, Mr Guthrie, this is a sore, sore sight, whatever will you do now, eh?* And father mouthed and mowed at her from the bed as though the first thing he'd be keen on doing was braining her, paralysis or not he'd still plenty of rage. For when the doctor came up at last from Bervie and bustled into the room, peering and poking with the sharp, quick face of him, and his bald head shining, and snapped in his curt-like way, *What's this? what's wrong with you now, Blawearie?* father managed to speak out then right enough—*That's for you to find out, what the hell do you think you're paid for?*

So the doctor grinned behind his hand, *One of you women must help me strip him.* And he looked from Kirsty to Chris and said *You, Chris lass,* and that she did while Mrs Strachan went down to the kitchen to make him tea and trail around like a clucking hen, God! what mightn't be happening in Peesie's Knapp without her? Chris lost her temper at last, she lost it seldom enough, this time it went with a bang—*I don't know either what's happening in Peesie's Knapp but if you're in such tune about it you'd better go home and find out.* Mrs Strachan reddened up at that, bubbling like a bubbly-jock, that wasn't the way for a quean to speak to a woman that might well be her mother, she might think shame to curse and swear with her father lying at death's door there. And Chris said she hadn't sworn, but she was over-weary to argie about it, and knew right well that whatever she said now Mistress Strachan would spread a fine story about her.

And sure as death so she did, it was soon all over the Howe that that coarse quean at Blawearie had started to swear at Mistress Strachan while her father was lying near dead in the room above their heads. Only Chae himself didn't believe it, and when he came up to Blawearie next day he whispered to Chris, *Is't true you gave Kirsty a bit of a damning yesterday?* and when she said she hadn't he said it was a pity, it was time that somebody did.

So there father lay and had lain ever since, all those five weeks he'd lain there half-paralysed, with a whistle beside his bed when he wanted attention, and God! that was often enough. Creeping to her bed half-dead at night Chris would find herself thinking a thing that wouldn't bear a rethinking out here in the sun, with the hum of the heather-bees, heather-smell in her face, Lord! could she only lie here a day how she'd sleep and sleep! Fold over her soul and her heart and put them away with their hours of vexing and caring, the ploughing was done, she was set to her drilling, and faith! it was weary work!

She started and sighed and took her hands down from her face and listened again. Far down in Blawearie there rose the blast of an angry-blown whistle.

III

SEED-TIME

She'd thought, running, stumbling up through the moor, with that livid flush on her cheek, up through the green of the April day with the bushes misted with cobwebs, *I'll never go back, I'll never go back, I'll drown myself in the loch!* Then she stopped, her heart it seemed near to bursting and terribly below it moved something, heavy and slow it had been when she ran out from Blawearie but now it seemed to move and uncoil. Slow, dreadfully, it moved and changed, like a snake she had once seen up on this hill, and the sweat broke out on her forehead. Had anything happened with it? Oh God, there couldn't be anything! If only she hadn't run so, had kept herself quiet, not struck as she'd done, deaved and angry and mad she had been!

Sobbing, she fell to a slow walk then, her hand at her side, and through the gate into the moorland went with slow steps, the livid flush burning still on her cheek, she felt it was branded there. Tears had come in her eyes at last, but she wouldn't have them, shook them off, wouldn't think; and a pheasant flew up beneath her feet *whirroo!* as she came to the mere of the loch. She bent over there through the rushes, raising her hands to her hair that had come all undone, and parted it from her face and looked down at her face in the water. It rippled a moment, it was brown with detritus, at first she could see nothing of herself but a tremulous amorphousness in the shadow of the rushes; and then the water cleared, she saw the flush below her cheek-bone, her own face, strange to her this last month and stranger now. Below in Kinraddie the carts were rattling up every farm-road, driving out dung to the turnip-planting, somewhere there was a driller on the go, maybe it was Upperhill's, the chant was a deafening thing. Nine o'clock in the morning and here up on the hill she was, she didn't know where to go or where to turn.

There were the Standing Stones, so seldom she'd seen them this last nine months. Cobwebbed and waiting they stood, she went and leant her cheek against the meikle one, the monster that stood and seemed to peer over the water and blue distances that went up to the Grampians. She leant against it, the bruised cheek she leaned and it was strange and comforting—stranger still when you thought that this old stone circle, more and more as the years went on at Kinraddie, was the only place where ever she could come and stand back a little from the clamour of the days. It seemed to her now that she'd had feint the minute at all to stand and think since that last September day she'd spent up here, caught and clamped and turning she'd been in the wheel and grind of the days since father died.

But at the time a thing fine and shining it had been, she hadn't cared if folk deemed her heartless and godless—fine she thought it, a prayer prayed and answered, him dead at last with his glooming and glaring, his whistlings and whisperings. *Chris, do this,* and *Chris, do that* it went on from morn till night till but hardly she could drag herself to the foot of the stairs to heed him.

But a worse thing came as that slow September dragged to its end, a thing she would never tell to a soul, festering away in a closet of her mind the memory lay, it would die sometime, everything died, love and hate; fainter and fainter it had grown this year till but half she believed it a fancy, those evening fancies when father lay with the red in his face and his eye on her, whispering and whispering at her, the harvest in his blood, whispering her to come to him, they'd done it in Old Testament times, whispering *You're my flesh and blood, I can do with you what I will, come to me, Chris, do you hear?*

And she would hear him and stare at him, whispering also, *I won't,* they never spoke but in whispers those evenings. And then she'd slip down from his room, frightened and frightened, quivering below-stairs while her fancies raced, starting at every creak that went through the harvest stillness of Blawearie house, seeing father somehow struggling from his bed, like a great frog struggling, squattering across the floor, thump, thump on the stairs, coming down on her while she slept, that madness and tenderness there in his eyes.

She took to locking her door because of that wild fear. The morning of the day she woke to find him dead she leaned out from her bedroom window and heard Long Rob of the Mill, far ayont the parks of Peesie's Knapp, out even so early, hard at work with his chaving and singing, singing *Ladies of Spain* with a throat as young and clear as a boy's. She had slept but little that night, because of the fear upon her and the tiredness, but that singing was sweet to hear, sweet and heart-breaking, as though the world outside Blawearie were singing to her, telling her this thing in the dark, still house could never go on, no more than a chance and an accident it was in the wind-loved world of men.

She got into her clothes then, clearer-headed, and slipped down to the kitchen and put on the kettle and milked the kye and then made breakfast. Below the windows the parks stood cut and stooked and trim, Ellison and Chae and Long Rob had done that, good neighbours John Guthrie had, had he never aught else. There came no movement from father's room, he was sleeping long, and setting the tray with porridge and milk she hoped he'd have nothing to say, just glower and eat, she'd slip away then.

So she went up the stair and into his room without knocking, he hated knocking and all such gentry-like notions, she put down the tray and saw he was dead. For a moment she looked and then turned to the curtains and drew them, and took the tray in her hand again, no sense in leaving it there, and went down and ate a good breakfast, slowly and enjoyingly she ate and felt quiet and happy, even though she fell fast asleep in her chair and awoke to find it gone nine. She lay and looked at her outspread arms a while, dimpled and brown, soft-skinned with the play of muscles below them. Sleep? She could sleep as she chose now, often and long.

Then she tidied the kitchen and found a spare sheet and went out to the hedge above the road and spread the sheet there, the sign she'd arranged with Chae should she need him. In an hour or so, out in his parks he saw it and came hurrying up to Blawearie, crying to her half-way up *Chris, lass, what's wrong?* Then only she realized she hadn't yet spoken that day to a soul, wondered if her voice would shake and break, it didn't, was ringing and clear as a bell crying down to Chae, *My father's dead.*

It was fair a speak in Kinraddie, her coolness, she knew that well but she didn't care, she was free at last. And when Mistress Munro, her that came to wash down the corpse, poked out her futret face and said, *A body would hardly think to look at you that your father was new dead,* Chris looked at the dark, coarse creature and saw her so clearly as she'd never done before, she'd never had time to look at a soul through her own eyes before, Chris-come-here and Chris-go-there. Not a pringle of anger she felt, just smiled and said *Wouldn't you, now, Mistress Munro?* and watched her at work and watched her go, not caring a fig what she thought and did. Then she roused herself for a while, free yet she could hardly be for a day or so, and got ready the big room for Auntie Janet and her man to sleep in, medals and all, when they came down to the funeral.

Down the next day they came, the two of them, Auntie as cheery as ever, Uncle as fat, he'd another bit medal stuck on his chain; and when they saw she wasn't sniftering or weeping they put off the long decent faces they'd set for her sight, and told her the news, Dod and Alec did fine and had sent their love. And Auntie said they must sell up the things at Blawearie and Chris come and bide with them in the North, some brave bit farmer would soon marry her there.

And Chris said neither yea nor nay, but smiled at them, biding her time, waiting till she found if a will had been left by father. Chae Strachan and old Sinclair of Netherhill saw to the funeral, old Sinclair moving so slow up the road, you'd half think he'd stop and take root, clean agony it was to watch him, and his face so pitted and old, father had been young by the like of him. And Mr Gibbon came over to see her, he'd been drinking a fell lot of late, folk said, maybe that accounted for the fact that as he crossed the twilit brae he was singing out loud to himself, Auntie heard the singing and ran up and out and hid in the lithe of a stack to try and

make out what he sang. But he left off then and left her fair
vexed, she said later she could have sworn it was a song they
sang in the bothies about the bedding of a lad and a lass.

But Chris didn't care, keeping that secret resolve she'd
made warm and clean and unsoiled in her heart, taking it
out only alone to look at it, that old-time dream of hers.
She'd never looked at herself so often or so long as now she
did, the secret shining deep in her eyes, she saw her face
thinner and finer than of yore, no yokel face it seemed. So
she cared nothing for Mr Gibbon and his singing, the great
curly brute and his breath that smelt so bad, he went up
with her to father's room where father lay in his coffin, in a
fine white shirt and a tie, his beard combed out and decent
and jutting up, you'd say in a minute he'd raise those dead
eyelids and whisper at you. Down on his knees the minister
went, the great curly bull, and began to pray, Chris hesitated
a minute and looked at the floor, and then, canny-like, when
he wasn't seeing her, dusted a patch and herself knelt down.
But she didn't heed a word he was saying, honeysuckle smell
was drifting in on the air from the night, up on the hills the
dog of some ploughman out poaching was barking and barking itself to a fair hysteria following the white blink of some
rabbit's tail, in the closing dark she could see across the
brae's shoulder the red light of Kinraddie House shine like
a quiet star. So the curly bull prayed and boomed beside
her, it was what he was paid for, she neither listened nor
cared.

And that brought the funeral, it was raining early in the
dawn when they woke, a fine drizzle that seeped and seeped
from the sky, so soft and fine you'd think it snow without
whiteness; there was no sun at all at first but it came up at
last, a red ball, and hung there so till ten o'clock brought up
the first of the funeral folk, and that was Chae, and his
father-in-law, syne Ellison and Maitland in a gig they loosed
in the cornyard, setting the sholtie to graze. And Ellison
cried out, but low and decent, *I'll leave him here, me dear,
sure he'll be all right, won't he?* and Chris smiled and said
Fine, Mr Ellison, and he goggled his eyes, Irish as ever, you
could never change Erbert Ellison, not even for the worse,
folk said. Next there came a whole drove of folk, the factor,

the minister, Cuddiestoun with his ill-marled face like a
potato-park dug in coarse weather, but a fine white front,
new-starched, to cover his working sark, and cuffs that fair
chafed his meikle red hands, right decent, and he'd on fine
yellow boots on his meikle feet. Rob of the Mill and Alec
Mutch came next, you could hear their tongues from the
foot of Blawearie brae, folk were affronted and went out and
cried *Wheest-wheest!* down to them, and Rob called back
What is't? and faith! it would have been better if they'd been
left alone, what with the wheesting and whispering that
rose.

But they were real good, Rob bringing a bottle of whisky,
Glenlivet it was, and Alec a half-bottle, they whisked them
over to Uncle Tam when nobody looked; or anyway not a
body but looked the other way and spoke, canny-like, of the
weather. The kitchen was fair crowded, so was the room, like
a threshing-day, folk sat and each had a dram, Mr Gibbon
said *Spirits? Yes, thank you, I'll have a drop,* there'd have
been barely enough to go round but for Rob and Alec. Then
they heard another gig come up the hill, it was Gordon's
from Upperhill, him and his foreman. Uncle Tam winked
at the whisky, *You'll have a dram, Upperhill, you and your
man?* but Mr Gordon said, sniffy-like, *I hardly think it shows
respect and Ewan's tee-tee as well.*

Long Rob of the Mill sat next the door, he winked at
Chris and then at Ewan Tavendale, Ewan turned fair red
and said nothing. So he hadn't a dram, he'd have liked one
fine, Chris guessed, and felt mean and pleased and shy, and
then gave herself a shake inside, what did it matter to her?
Then the minister looked at his watch and the undertaker
came in about, and then last of all, they hadn't expected the
poor old stock, there was Pooty on the doorstep, he'd on a
clean collar and shirt and an old hat, green but well-
brushed; and when Uncle whispered if he'd have a dram he
said *Och, ay, it's the custom, isn't it?* and had two.

The undertaker had gone up by then, Uncle with him,
folk followed them one by one and came down, syne Auntie
beckoned Chris to the neuk of the stair and said *Would you
like to see him before he's screwed down?*

Uncle Tam and Long Rob of the Mill were there and

as Chris went in Long Rob said *Well, well, goodbye, Blawearie man,* and shook father's hand, his eyes looked queer when he turned away, he said *He was a fine neighbour* and went out and closed the door. Chris stood and looked at her father, seeing him so plain as never in life she'd seen him, he'd been over-restless for that and quick enough he'd have raged at you had you glowered at his face like this. Still enough now, never-moving there in the coffin, he seemed to have changed already since he died, the face sunk in, it wasn't John Guthrie and yet it was. Uncle whispered behind her, him and the undertaker, and then Auntie was beside her, *They're to screw it down now, kiss your father, Chris.* But she shook her head, she couldn't do that, the room was still as they looked at her, for a moment she felt almost sick again as in those evening hours when *that* in the coffin had lain and whispered that she should lie with it. Then she just said *Good-bye, father,* and turned from him and went down to her own room and put on her coat and hat, it wasn't decent for a quean to go to a funeral, folk said, but in Blawearie's case there was no son or brother to see him into the kirkyard.

Chae and Long Rob and Ellison and Gordon carried the coffin down to the stair-foot, and settled it on their shoulders there, and went slow with it out through the front door then; and the rain held off a little, wind blowing in their faces, though, as they held down the hill. Behind walked the Reverend Gibbon, bare-headed, all the folk were bare-headed but Chris, Long Rob and Chae stepping easily and cannily, Ellison as well, but Gordon quivering at his coffin corner, he'd have done better with a dram to steady him up. But Chris walked free and uncaring, soon as the burial was over she'd be free as never in her life she'd been, she lifted her face to the blow of the wet September wind and the world that was free to her. Then it was that she saw Ewan Tavendale walked beside her, he glanced down just then and straight and fair up into his eyes she looked, she nearly stumbled in the slow walk because of that looking. They came to the turnpike then, there Ewan took Gordon's corner and Alec Mutch Ellison's, and these two fell back beside the minister, but Chae and Long Rob shook their heads

when others offered to change with them, they'd manage
fine.

The rain still held off, presently the wind soughing down
the Howe died away and a little peek of sun came through,
not down the Denburn it came but high up in the hill peaks,
the lost, coarse ground where never a soul lived or passed
but some shepherd or gillie, you could see them far off, lone
and lonesome there on a still, clear day. Maybe so the dead
walked in a still clear, deserted land, the coarse lands of
death where only the chance wanderer showed his face,
Chris thought, and the dead lapwings wheeled and cried
against another sun. Then she ceased from that, startled out
a moment from the calm that had come to her with her
father's dying—daft to dream these things now when she
planned so much. Step, step, steadily and cannily went Long
Rob and Chae, Chae getting bald and sandy in the crown,
but Rob still with the corn hair clustered thick and the
great moustaches swinging from his cheeks as they turned
up the road that led to the kirkyard.

Then the sun went again, it was eleven o'clock perhaps,
and Chris raised her eyes and saw through the trees the
blinded windows of the Mains, the curtains were all drawn,
decent-like, in respect for the funeral; and she felt a queer,
sick thrill just below her left breast, not ill or sick, but just
like a starting of the blood there, as though she'd leant on
that place too long, and it had grown numb. It was dark
under the yews, they dripped on the coffin and Long Rob,
then there came a pattering as they passed by slow beneath,
and Chris saw the long, oval leaves suddenly begin to quiver,
it was as though a hand shook them, and through the leaves
was the sky, it had blackened over and the rain was coming
driving in a sheet down the brae from the Grampian haughs.
It came and whipped the wet skirts about her legs, she saw
Long Rob and Chae and Ewan stagger and then stand leaning against the drift, and then go on, not a soul put on his
hat, there'd be bad colds by night and ill-tunes over this
funeral yet.

That wasn't decent to think, but what did it matter to
her? She wished she were back in Blawearie, and hoped
the minister would not be over long-winded when he said

his say. There was the grave-digger, a man from the Mains, a big scrawny childe who lived ill with his wife, folk said, he had his coat collar up and came out below the eaves of the kirk and motioned them along a path. And ben it they went, then Chris saw the grave, red clay and bright it was, not as she'd expected his grave somehow to be, they weren't burying him in mother's grave. For that land was over-crowded, folk said that every time the grave-digger stuck his bit spade in the ground some bone or other from the dead of olden time would come spattering out, fair scunnering you. But this was an old enough bit as well, right opposite rose the stone with the cross-bones, maybe all the dead bodies had long mouldered away into red clay here, clay themselves, and folk were glad they left the earth free for new-comers.

Uncle had come to her elbow then and he stood with her, the others stood back, it was strange and silent but for the soft patter of the rain on the yews and the Reverend Gibbon shielding his Bible away from the wet drive of it, beginning to read. And Chris listened, her head bent against the rain's whisper, to the words that promised Resurrection and Life through Jesus Christ our Lord, who had died long syne in Palestine and had risen on the third day and would take from that thing that had been John Guthrie quick, and was now John Guthrie dead, the quickness and give it habitation again. And Chris thought of her dream looking up at the coarse lands of the hills and thinking of the lands of death, was that where Christ would meet with father? Unco and strange to think, standing here in the rain and listening to that voice, that father himself was there in that dark box heaped with the little flowers that folk had sent, father whom they were to leave here happed in red clay, alone in darkness and earth when the night came down. Surely he'd be back waiting her up in Blawearie, she'd hear his sharp, vexed voice and see him come fleetly out of the house, that red beard of his cocked as ever at the world he'd fought so dourly and well——

Somebody chaved at her hand then, it was the grave-digger, he was gentle and strangely kind, and she looked down and couldn't see, for now she was crying, she hadn't thought she would ever cry for father, but she hadn't known, she hadn't known this thing that was happening to him! She found herself praying then, blind with tears in the rain, lowering the cord with the hand of the grave-digger over hers, the coffin dirling below the spears of the rain. *Father, father, I didn't know! Oh father, I didn't KNOW!* She hadn't known, she'd been dazed and daft with her planning, her days could never be aught without father; and she minded then, wildly, in a long, broken flash of remembrance, all the fine things of him that the years had hidden from their sight, the fleetness of him and his justice, and the fight unwearying he'd fought with the land and its masters to have them all clad and fed and respectable, he'd never rested working and chaving for them, only God had beaten him in the end. And she minded the long roads he'd tramped to the kirk with her when she was young, how he'd smiled at her and called her his lass in days before the world's fight and the fight of his own flesh grew over-bitter, and poisoned his love to hate. *Oh father, I didn't know!* she prayed again, and then that was over, she was in the drive of the rain, hard and tearless, the grave-digger was pointing to the ground and she picked up a handful of soft, wet earth, and heard the Reverend Gibbon's voice drone out *Dust to dust, ashes to ashes,* and leant over the grave and dropped the wet earth; and then the grave-digger was throwing in the turf, the coffin rang as though it were hollow, she stared at it till Uncle had her by the elbow, speaking to her, and so was the Reverend Gibbon but she couldn't hear them at first; and folk were to say she must have been real fond of her father after all, the best of a coarse bit family in the end.

And then she was walking back through the kirkyard and the folk at the gate were stopping to shake her hand, Long Rob and Chae to say they'd aye help her, and Ellison, kind and solemn and Irish, and old Sinclair dripping in the rain, he should never have been out in a day like this. The last was Ewan Tavendale, he said *Ta-ta, Chris,* his hand was wet meeting hers as her own hand was, but he put up his left hand as well as his right and held both of hers a minute; and he didn't look ashamed and shy any more, but as though he was so sorry he'd help her in any way, not only the ways he could.

That was the last of them she saw and the end of father's funeral. Back in Blawearie Auntie Janet made her strip from her clothes and get into bed, *God be here, it's you that'll be next in your grave!* she cried. And Chris slept throughout the remainder of that day, undreaming, she didn't wake till late in the night, Blawearie listening and hearkening about her. And then she was afraid, awfully afraid, sitting up in bed and hearkening to that Something that walked the house with sharp, quick footsteps, running so fleetly up the stairs, impatient and unresting, a shadow with footfalls that were shadows; and into the night and far towards the dawn it roamed the house of Blawearie till the cocks were crowing and Uncle and Auntie moving, and Chris didn't feel afraid at all by then, only lay and wept softly for the father she'd never helped and forgot to love.

And the next forenoon the lawyer man came down from Stonehaven, it was Peter Semple, folk called him Simple Simon but swore that he was a swick. Father had trusted him, though, and faith! you'd be fell straight in your gait ere John Guthrie trusted you. Not that he'd listened to advice, father, he'd directed a will be made and the things to be set in that will; and when Mr Semple had said he was being fell sore on some of his family father had told him to mind his own business, and that was a clerk's. So Mr Semple drew up the will, it had been just after Will went off to the Argentine, and father had signed it; and now the Blawearie folk sat down in the parlour, with whisky and biscuits for Mr Semple, to hear it read. It was short and plain as you please, Chris watched the face of her uncle as the lawyer read and saw it go white in the gills, he'd expected something far different from that. And the will told that John Guthrie left all his possessions, in silver and belongings, to his daughter Christine, to be hers without let or condition, Mr Semple her guardian in such law matters as needed one, but Chris to control the goods and gear as she pleased. And folk were to say, soon as Kinraddie heard of the will, and faith! they seemed to have heard it all before it was well out of the envelope, that it was an unco will, old Guthrie had been fair spiteful to his sons, maybe Will would dispute his sister's tocher.

The money was over three hundred pounds in the bank, it was hard to believe that father could have saved all that. But he had; and Chris sat and stared at the lawyer, hearing him explain and explain this, that, and the next, in the way of lawyers: they presume you're a fool and double their fees. Three hundred pounds! And now she could do as she'd planned, she'd go up to the College again and pass her exams and go on to Aberdeen and get her degrees, come out as a teacher and finish with the filthy soss of a farm. She'd sell up the gear of Blawearie, the lease was dead, it had died with father, oh! she was free and free to do as she liked and dream as she liked at last!

And it was pity now that she'd all she wanted she felt no longer that fine thrill that had been with her while she made her secret plans. It was as though she'd lost it down in Kinraddie kirkyard; and she sat and stared so still and white at the lawyer man that he closed up his case with a snap. *So think it well over, Christine*, he said and she roused and said *Oh, I'll do that;* and off he went, Uncle Tam drew a long, deep breath, as though fair near choked he'd been *Not a word of his two poor, motherless boys!*

It seemed he'd expected Alec and Dod would be left their share, maybe that was why he'd been so eager to adopt them the year before. But Auntie cried *For shame, Tam, how are they motherless now that I've got them? And you'll come up and live with us when you've sold Blawearie's furnishings, Chris?* And her voice was kind but her eyes were keen, Chris looked at her with her own eyes hard, *Ay, maybe* and got up and slipped from the room, *I'll go down and bring home the kye.*

And out she went, though it wasn't near kye-time yet, and wandered away over the fields; it was a cold and louring day ,the sound of the sea came plain to her, as though heard in a shell, Kinraddie wilted under the greyness. In the ley field old Bob stood with his tail to the wind, his hair ruffled up by the wind, his head bent away from the smore of it. He heard her pass and gave a bit neigh, but he didn't try to follow her, poor brute, he'd soon be over old for work. The wet fields squelched below her feet, oozing up their smell of red clay from under the sodden grasses, and up in the hills she saw the trail of the mist, great sailing shapes of it, going south on the wind into Forfar, past Laurencekirk they would sail, down the wide Howe with its sheltered glens and its late, drenched harvests, past Brechin smoking against its hill, with its ancient tower that the Pictish folk had reared, out of the Mearns, sailing and passing, sailing and passing, she minded Greek words of forgotten lessons, Πάντα ῥεῖ, *Nothing endures*. And then a queer thought came to her there in the drooked fields, that nothing endured at all, nothing but the land she passed across, tossed and turned and perpetually changed below the hands of the crofter folk since the oldest of them had set the Standing Stones by the loch of Blawearie and climbed there on their holy days and saw their terraced crops ride brave in the wind and sun. Sea and sky and the folk who wrote and fought and were learnéd, teaching and saying and praying, they lasted but as a breath, a mist of fog in the hills, but the land was forever, it moved and changed below you, but was forever, you were close to it and it to you, not at a bleak remove it held you and hurted you. And she had thought to leave it all!

She walked weeping then, stricken and frightened because of that knowledge that had come on her, she could never leave it, this life of toiling days and the needs of beasts and the smoke of wood fires and the air that stung your throat so acrid, Autumn and Spring, she was bound and held as though they had prisoned her here. And her fine bit plannings!—they'd been just the dreamings of a child over toys it lacked, toys that would never content it when it heard the smore of a storm or the cry of sheep on the moors or smelt the pringling smell of a new-ploughed park under the drive of a coulter. She could no more teach a school than fly, night and day she'd want to be back, for all the fine clothes and gear she might get and hold, the books and the light and learning.

The kye were in sight then, they stood in the lithe of the freestone dyke that ebbed and flowed over the shoulder of the long ley field, and they hugged to it close from the drive of the wind, not heeding her as she came among them, the smell of their bodies foul in her face—foul and known and enduring as the land itself. Oh, she hated and loved in a breath! Even her love might hardly endure, but beside it the hate was no more than the whimpering and fear of a child that cowered from the wind in the lithe of its mother's skirts.

And again that night she hardly slept, thinking and thinking till her head ached, the house quiet enough now without fairlies treading the stairs, she felt cool and calm, if only she could sleep. But by morning she knew she couldn't go on with Uncle and Auntie beside her, they smothered her over with their years and their canny supposings. Quick after breakfast she dressed and came down and Auntie cried out, real sharp-like, *Mighty be here, Chris, where are you going?* as though she owned Blawearie stick and stone, hoof and hide. And Chris looked at her coolly, *I'm away to Stonehaven to see Mr Semple, can I bring you anything?* Uncle Tam rose up from the table then, goggling, with his medals clinking, *Away to Stonehive? What are you jaunting there for? I'll transact any business you have.* Their faces reddened up with rage, she saw plain as daylight how near it lay, dependence on them, she felt herself go white as she looked at them. *I'll transact my own business fine,* she said hardly, and called *Ta-ta* from the door and heard no answer and held down the Blawearie road and ran over the parks to the station, and caught the early scholars' train that went in to Stonehaven Academy.

It was crowded fell close, there were three-four scholars in the carriage she got in to, she didn't know any, they were learning French verbs. And she'd wanted to go back to things as silly!

They were past Drumlithie and the Carmont then, you could smell the woods of Dunnottar and look out at them from the window, girdling Stonehaven down to its bay, shining and white, the sun was out on the woods and the train like a weasel slipped through the wet smell of them. And there was Stonehaven itself, the home of the poverty toffs, folk said, where you might live in sin as much as you pleased but were damned to hell if you hadn't a white sark. She'd heard Chae Strachan say that, but it wasn't all true, there were fell poor folk in Stonehaven as well as the come-ups; and douce folk that were neither poor nor proud and had never a say when Stonehaven boomed of its braveness. And that it did fair often, the Mearns' capital, awful proud of its sarks but not of its slums; and it thought itself real genteel, and a fine seafront it had that the English came to in summer—daft, as usual, folk said, hadn't they a sea in England?

Because it was early in the day and the lawyer's office still shut Chris loitered on the road in the tail of the hasting scholars, the little things they were, all legs and long boots, funny how they tried to speak English one to the other, looking sideways as they cried the words to see if folk thought them gentry. Had Marget and she been daft as that?

But the sun was out now on the long Stonehaven streets and Chris went past the Academy down to the market, still at that hour with just a stray cat or so on the sniff around, genteel and toff-like, Stonehaven cats. Down through a lane she caught a glimmer of the North Sea then, or maybe it was the sunlight against the sky, but the smell of the sea came up. And she still had plenty of time.

So she went down to the shore, the tide was out, thundering among the rocks, not a soul on the beach but herself, gulls flying and crying, the sun strong and warm. She sat on a seat in the glow of it and shut her eyes and was happy. Below her feet the ground drummed and trembled with reverberations from that far-off siege of the rocks that the sea was making out there by the point of the bay, it was strange to feel it and be of it, maybe folk there were who felt for the sea as last night she had felt in the rain-drenched fields of Kinraddie. But to her it seemed restless, await-ing and abiding nowhither, not fine like the glens that nestled and listened high up the coarse country, or the parks sun-heavy with clover that waited your feet at evening.

She fell asleep then, she slept there two hours in the sun and woke feeling fresher than she'd done since father's funeral. So hungry also she felt she couldn't wait the ending

of the business she'd come on but went into a tea-house up
in the square, two women kept it, old bodies they were that
moved backward and forward the room, slow and rheu-
matic. One looked like the cats she'd seen in the square that
morning, sleeked and stroked, the other was thin as a lathe,
their tea-room looked scrubbed and clean and their tea had
a taste to match. They were sharp and stroked and genteel,
Chris thought for the first time then in her life how awful
it would be to grow old like them, old maids without men,
without ever having lain with a man, or had him kiss you
and hold you, and be with you, and have children of his, or
the arm of a man when you needed it, kind and steadfast
and strong. If she'd lived her plan to train as a teacher she'd
have grown like them.

She might grow so still! she thought, and daft-like suddenly felt quite feared, she paid for her tea in a hurry and
went out to the square again, thinking of herself as an old
maid, it wouldn't bear thinking about. So she hurried to
the office of Simple Simon and a little clerk asked her business, perky-like, and she looked at him coolly and said her
business was Mr Semple's. And then she minded the old
maids, was she herself one by nature? And in a cold fear she
smiled at the clerk, desperately, with her lips and eyes, it
was fine, the boy smiled also and blushed and thawed, and
said *Sit down, this is fine and comfortable*; and pulled out
a padded chair for her; and down she sat, light-hearted
again. Then the clerk came back and led her through a
passage to Semple's room, he looked busy enough, with a
telephone beside him and heaps of papers, and rows of
little black boxes round the shelves. Then he rose and shook
hands, *Well, well, it's Miss Guthrie come up; you've been
thinking of the will, no doubt?*

She told him, Yes, just that; and she was going to live on
at Blawearie a while, not roup the gear out at once, could
he see to that with the factor?

He stared at her with his mouth fallen open, *But you
can't live there alone!*

She told him she'd no such intention, couldn't he get her
some woman come live with her, some old bit body who'd be
glad of a home?

He said *Oh, God, there are plenty of them!* and began to chew at his mouser.

She told him it mightn't be for more than a month or so, till she'd made up her mind, just.

He said absent-like, *Just? Hell, a woman's mind just!* and then pulled himself up right sudden as she looked at him hardly and cool. Then he argued a bit, but Chris hardly listened, father's will had said she could do what she liked.

And presently, seeing she cared not a fig for him, Semple gave in and said he'd settle up with the factor, and he knew an old widow body, Melon, he'd send down to Blawearie the morn.

So Chris said *Thank you, good-bye*, and went out from the office, cool as she'd come, the sun was a fell blaze then and the streets chock-a-block with sheep, great droves of them, driven in to the weekly mart. Collies were running hither and yon, silent and cocked of ear, clean and quick as you'd wish, paying heed to none but shepherd and sheep. Drovers and beasts, they took a good look at Chris both, as she stood in her black clothes watching them; and just as she wondered what she'd do next, walk down to the sea and sit on a bench till it neared to dinner-time in the hotels, or go up to the station and take the 11.0, a gig going by slowed down of a sudden, a man jumped down and cried back to the driver.

The man that had jumped was the foreman at Upperhill, Ewan Tavendale, the driver old Gordon himself, he looked in a rage about something. And he cried *Mind the time then!* and gave Chris a sore glower and drove spanking away.

And then Ewan had crossed the pavement and was standing in front of her, he lifted his cap and said, shy-like, *Hello!* Chris said *Hello*, and they looked at each other, he was blushing, she minded the last time, she didn't like him half as she'd done at the funeral. He said *Are you in for the day?* and she mocked him, not knowing why she did that, it wasn't decent and father new dead, *Och ay, just that*. He blushed some more, she felt cool and queerly giddy in a breath, looking at the fool of a lad, folk were glowering at them both they were later to learn, not Gordon only but Ellison: and back the two of them went to Kinraddie and told every soul it was a sore shame there wasn't somebody about to heed to the Guthrie girl from the hands of that coarse tink brute, Ewan Tavendale.

But they hadn't known that and mightn't have cared, suddenly Chris felt herself hungry again, happy as well, not caring about Ewan himself but not wanting either he should leave her and go on to the mart. She said *I'm going up to the Inn for dinner,* and he looked at her, still shy, but with a kind of smoulder in the shyness, his eyes like the smoulder of a burning whin—*Maybe we can eat together?* And she said, as he turned by her side, *Oh, maybe. But what will Mr Gordon do?* And Ewan said he could dance a jig on the head of the mart with sheer rage, for all he cared.

So in they went to old Mother White's, not that they saw the old body herself; and there was a fine room to eat in, with white cloths set, and a canary that sang above them, the windows fast closed to the dust and dirt. And they'd broth, it was good, and the oat-cakes better; and then boiled beef and potatoes and turnip; and then rice pudding with prunes; and then some tea, Ewan found his tongue as they drank the tea and said today was his holiday, for he'd worked all the last Sunday on a job libbing lambs. And Chris said, it was out of her mouth before she thought, *So you're in no hurry to be back?* and Ewan leaned across the table, the smoulder near kindled to a fire, *Not unless you should be? What train are you taking up to Kinraddie?*

And then how it all came about, their planning to spend the day together and their walk to Dunnottar, Chris never knew, maybe neither did Ewan. But half an hour later, Stonehaven a blinding white glimmer behind, Dunnottar in front, they were climbing down the path that led to the island. The air was blind with the splash of the incoming tide, above you the rock rose sheer as the path wound downwards sheer; and high up, crowning the rock were the ruins of the castle walls, splashed with sunlight and the droppings of sea-birds. Gulls there were everywhere, Chris was deafened in the clamour of the brutes, but quiet enough in the castle it proved, not a soul seemed visiting there but themselves.

They paid their shillings and the old man came with them from room to room, a scunner to Ewan, Chris guessed, for his eyes kept wandering, wearied, to her from this ruin and that. In walls little slits rose up, through these it was that in olden times the garrisons had shot their arrows at besiegers; and down below, in the dungeons, were the mouldering clefts where a prisoner's hands were nailed while they put him to torment. There the Covenanting folk had screamed and died while the gentry dined and danced in their lithe, warm halls, Chris stared at the places, sick and angry and sad for those folk she could never help now, that hatred of rulers and gentry a flame in her heart, John Guthrie's hate. Her folk and his they had been, those whose names stand graved in tragedy:

HERE : LYES : IOHN : STOT : IAMES : ATCHISON : IAMES : RUSSELL : & WILLIAM : BROUN : AND ONE : WHOSE : NAME : WEE : HAVE : NOT : GOTTEN : AND : TWO : WOMEN : WHOSE : NAMES : ALSO : WEE : KNOW : NOT : AND : TWO : WHO : PERISHD : COMEING : DOUNE : THE : ROCK : ONE : WHOSE : NAME : WAS : IAMES : WATSON : THE : OTHER : NOT : KNOWN : WHO : ALL : DIED : PRISONERS : IN : DUNNOTTAR : CASTLE : ANNO : 1685 : FOR : THEIR : ADHERENCE : TO : THE : WORD : OF : GOD : AND : SCOTLANDS : COVENANTED : WORK : OF : REFORMA-TION :

                                    REV : II CH : 12 VERSE

But Ewan whispered, *Oh, let's get out of this,* though it was he himself that had planned they come to Dunnottar. So out in the sun, at the shelving entrance, they stood awhile in the cry of the gulls; and then Ewan said *Come down to the sea: I know a nook.*

And they climbed down and then up again, along the cliff-edge, it made you dizzy to look over and down at the incoming wash of froth, and sometimes, far under their feet, there rose a loud *boom!* like a gun going off. Ewan said that the rocks were sometimes hollow and the water ran far below the fields, so that ploughmen ploughed above the sea and in stormy weather they'd sometimes see their

furrows quiver from that storm that raged under their feet.
So they came to a crumbling path, it seemed to fall sheer
away, a seagull sailed up to meet them, and Ewan with his
feet already out of sight turned back and asked, *You'll not
be dizzy?* And Chris shook her head and followed him, it
seemed to her between sea and sky, down and down, and
then Ewan was gripping her ankle, she swung almost loose
for a moment, looking down in his face, it was white and
strained, then her foot and hand caught again, Ewan called
that it wasn't much further; and they got to the bottom
and sat and looked at each other on a ledge of sand.

The sun poured in there, the tide whispered and splashed
and threw out its hands at them on the sand, but it didn't
come further up. And Chris saw that the place was closed
in, you couldn't see a thing of the coast but the rocks over-
hanging, and only a segment of the sea itself, a mile or so
out a boat had tacked, it flashed its wings like a wheeling
gull; and Ewan was sitting beside her, peeling an orange.

They ate it together and Chris took off her hat, she felt
hot and uncouth in her sad black clothes. And suddenly,
for no reason, she thought of a time, years before, when
she'd been trampling blankets for mother a fine summer
day in May, and had taken off her skirts and her mother
had come out and laughed at her, *You'd make a fine lad!*
It was as though she heard mother speak, she looked up
and around, daftly, dazed-like a moment, but there was not
a soul near but Ewan Tavendale lying on an elbow, looking
at the sea, the sun in his face, young and smooth with its
smouldering eyes. And she found she didn't mislike him any
longer, she felt queer and strange to him, not feared, but
as though he was to say something in a moment that she
knew she couldn't answer. And then he said it, blushing,
but his smouldering eyes didn't waver, *Chris, do you like
me a bit?*

*Can't thole you at all, that's why we're out lazing in this
place together.*

But a nervousness came on her, not that she feared him,
she'd known all along she was safe with Ewan as Mollie
with Will in those long-gone days of the court at Drumlithie.
Only, it was as though her blood ran so clear and with such

a fine, sweet song in her veins she must hold her breath
and hark to it; and for the first time she knew the strange
thing her hand was, held there dripping sand, it seemed
as though all her body sat a little apart from herself, and
she looked at it, wondering. So it was that she knew she
liked him, loved him as they said in the soppy English books,
you were shamed and a fool to say that in Scotland. Ewan
Tavendale—that it should be him! And then she minded
something, it didn't matter at all, but she wanted to know
for all that. *Ewan, was it true that story they told about you
and old Sarah Sinclair?*

It was as though she had belted him in the face. He
went white then, funnily white leaving brown the red
tan in the little creases of his face that the coarse field
weather had made; and he sat up, angrily, and glowered
at her, the great black cat, so sleekéd and quick to anger.
And the feeling she'd had for him, that dizziness that
made earth and sea and her heart so light, quite went from
her. She said *Oh, I don't want to know,* and began to hum
to herself; and then Ewan reached out his hand and gripped
her arm, it hurt, he said *Damn well listen now that you've
asked me.* And it was awful, awful and terrible, she didn't
want to listen to him, covering her face with her hands,
he went on and on and then stopped at last—*Now you're
frightened, frightened that a woman should feel like that,
maybe some day you'll feel it yourself.*

She jumped to her feet then, angry as him, forgetting to
feel shamed. *Maybe I will, but when I do I'll get a better
man than you to serve me!* And before he could answer
that she had caught up her hat and was up the cliff path
so quick she didn't know how she did it, her fingers and
feet were nimble and sure, she heard Ewan cry below her
and paid no heed. He was barely half-way up when she
reached the top and looked down, and then the rage quite
went from her, she leaned over the edge instead, holding
down her hand, and he caught it and smiled, and they stood
and panted and smiled one at the other, fools again as they'd
been in the market-square of Stonehaven.

But suddenly Ewan whipped out his watch, *God it must
be getting fell late,* and as he said it the sunshine went.

Chris raised her head and saw why, they'd been sitting down there in the last of it, the gloaming was down on the country-side and the noise of the gulls rising up through the mirk. Ewan caught her hand and they ran by the cliff-edge of the gloaming-stilled parks, there were great dappled kye that stopped their grazing to look; and up in front, dark and uncanny, they saw Dunnottar rise on its rock. And then they reached the main road and slowed down, but she still left her hand in Ewan's.

And in Stonehaven they caught by the skin of the teeth the six o'clock train, the mart was long over and folk gone home. In the carriage were only themselves all the way to Kinraddie, Ewan sat on the opposite seat, she liked him sit there, liked him not wanting to hold her hand, she'd have hated him touch her now. And they didn't say a word till they neared Kinraddie, and then he said *Chrissie! Tired?* and she said *Losh, no, and my name's Chris, Ewan.* Then she saw him blush again in the flicker of the gaslight; and a strange, sweet surge of pity came on her, she leant over and patted his knee, he was only a boy in spite of his Sarah Sinclair.

But she thought of Sarah all the same that night, lying listening in bed to the coming of the rain again, a wet winter it promised the Howe. So women were like that when they didn't have the men they wanted?—many of them maybe like that, hiding it away even from themselves till a summer of heat drove on here and there to such acts as affronted Kinraddie. But she didn't feel affronted, it was maybe because she was over young, had read over many of the books, had been the English Chris as well as this one that lay thinking of Ewan; and the old ways of sinning and winning, having your own pleasure and standing affronted at other folk having theirs, seemed often daft to her. Sarah Sinclair might well have obliged her and met with some other lad than Ewan that August night; but then she wasn't to know Chris Guthrie would ever lie and think of him in her bed, hearing the batter of the rain against her window and the swish of the great Blawearie trees.

It was then, in a lull of the swishing, she heard the great crack of thunder that opened the worst storm that had struck the Howe in years. It was far up, she thought, and yet so close Blawearie's stones seemed falling about her ears, she half-scrambled erect. Outside the night flashed, flashed and flashed, she saw Kinraddie lighted up and fearful, then it was dark again, but not quiet. In the sky outside a great beast moved and purred and scrabbled, and then suddenly it opened its mouth again and again there was the roar and the flash of its claws, tearing at the earth, it seemed neither house nor hall could escape. The rain had died away, it was listening—quiet in the next lull, and then Chris heard her Auntie crying to her. *Are you all right, Chrissie?* and cried back she was fine. Funny Uncle Tam had cried never a word, maybe he was still in the sulks, he'd plumped head-first in when he'd heard of the old woman that Semple was sending to help keep house in Blawearie. They were off to Auchterless the morn, and oh! she'd be glad to see them go, she'd enough to do and to think without fighting relations.

The thunder clamoured again, and then she suddenly sat shivering, remembering something—Clyde and old Bob and Bess, all three of them were out in the ley field there, they weren't taken in till late in the year. Round the ley field was barbed wire, almost new, that father had put up in the Spring, folk said it was awful for drawing the lightning, maybe it had drawn it already.

She was out of bed in the next flash, it was a ground flash, it hung and it seemed to wait, sizzling, outside the window as she pulled on stockings and vest and knickers and ran to the door and cried up *Uncle Tam, Uncle Tam, we must take in the horses!* He didn't hear, she waited, the house shook and dirled in another great flash, then Auntie was crying something, Chris stood as if she couldn't believe her own ears. Uncle Tam was feared at the lightning, he wouldn't go out, she herself had best go back to her bed and wait for the morning.

She didn't wait to hear more than that, but ran to the kitchen and groped about for the box of matches and lighted the little lamp, it with the glass bowl, and then found the littlest lantern and lighted that, though her fingers shook and she almost dropped the funnel. Then she found old

shoes and a raincoat, it had been father's and came near
to her ankles, and she caught up the lamp and opened the
kitchen door and closed it quick behind her just as the
sky banged again and a flare of sheet lightning came flowing
down the hill-side, frothing like the incoming tide at Dunnottar. It dried up, leaving her blinded, her eyes ached and
she almost dropped the lantern again.

In the byre the kye were lowing fit to raise the roof, even
the stirks were up and stamping about in their stalls. But
they were safe enough unless the biggings were struck, it was
the horses she'd to think of.

Right athwart her vision the haystacks shone up like great
pointed pyramids a blinding moment, vanished, darkness
complete and heavy flowed back on her again, the lantern-
light seeking to pierce it like the bore of a drill. Still the
rain held off as she stumbled and cried down the sodden
fields. Then she saw that the barbed wire was alive, the
lightning ran and glowed along it, a living thing, a tremulous, vibrant serpent that spat and glowed and hid its head
and quivered again to sight. If the horses stood anywhere
near to that they were finished, she cried to them again
and stopped and listened, it was deathly still in the night
between the bursts of the thunder, so still that she heard
the grass she had pressed underfoot crawl and quiver erect
again a step behind her. Then, as the thunder moved away
—it seemed to break and roar down the rightward hill,
above the Manse and Kinraddie Mains,—something tripped
her, she fell and the lantern-flame flared up and seemed
almost to vanish; but she righted it, almost sick though she
was because of the wet, warm thing that her body and face
lay upon.

It was old Bob, he lay dead, his tongue hanging out, his
legs doubled under him queerly, poor brute, and she shook
at his halter a minute before she realized it was useless
and there were still Bess and Clyde to see to. And then
she heard the thunder and clop of their hooves coming across
the grass to her, they loomed suddenly into the light of the
lamp, nearly running her down, they stood beside her and
whinnied, frightened and quivering so that her hand on
Bess's neck dirled as on the floor of a threshing-machine.

Then the lightning smote down again, quite near, though the thunder had seemed to move off, it played a great zig-zag over the field where she stood with the horses, and they pressed so near her she was almost crushed between them; and the lantern was pressed from her hand at last, it fell and went out with a crash and a crinkle of breaking glass. She caught Bess's bridle with one hand, Clyde's with another, and the lightning went and they began to move forward in the darkness, she thought she was in the right direction but she couldn't be sure. The next flash showed a field she didn't know, close at hand, with a high, staked dyke, and then she knew she had gone utterly wrong, it was the dyke on the turnpike.

The thunder growled satisfiedly and Clyde whinnied and whinnied, she saw then the reason for that, right ahead was the waving of a lantern, it must be Uncle come out to look for her at last, she cried *I'm here!* and a voice cried *Where?* She cried again and the lantern came in her direction, it was two men climbing the dyke. The horses started and whinnied and dragged her forward and then she found herself with Chae Strachan and Ewan, they had seen to their own horses on Upperhill and the Knapp, and had met and had minded hers on Blawearie; and up they had come to look for them. In the moment as they recognised one the other the lightning flared, a last sizzling glow, and then the rain came again, they heard it coming far up in the moors, it whistled and moaned and then was a great driving swish. Chae thrust his lantern upon Ewan, *Damn't man, take that and the lass and run for the house! I'll see to the horse!*

Ewan caught Chris under the arm, he swung the lantern in his other hand, they ran for a gate that led to the turnpike, the horses galloped behind them, Chae dragging at their halters and cursing them; and the rain overtook them as they gained the road, it was a battering wet hand that beat at them, Chris was soaked to the skin in a moment.

But in another they'd gained the new biggings of Peesie's Knapp, there shone a light in the kitchen, Ewan opened the door and pushed Chris in, *Bide here and I'll off and help Chae!* He disappeared into the blackness, the door closed behind him, Chris went forward into the kitchen and the glow of the fire. She felt daft and deaf in the sudden silence and out of the rain, in the stillness of the new kitchen with its meikle clock wagging against the wall, and its calendars and pictures all spaced about, it looked calm and fine. Then she realised how wetted she was and took off the raincoat, it rained a puddle on the kitchen floor, she was dressed below only in knickers and vest, she'd not remembered that!

There came a rattle and clatter outside in the close as the men ran to the house, Chris slipped on the coat again and was tugging at the buttons as the two came stamping in. Chae cried, *Damn't, Chris, get out of that coat, you must fair be soaked. Here, I'll stir up the fire, the old wife's in bed, she'd sleep through a hundred storms.*

He bent over the fire then, poking it up, Chris found Ewan beside her, his hair black with the rain, the great cat, to help her off with her coat. She whispered, *I can't Ewan, I've nothing on below!* and he blushed as red as a girl himself, and dropped his hands, and looked like a foolish boy so that she lost her own shyness at once, and told the same thing to Chae when he turned him round. He laughed at her with his twinkling eyes, *What, nothing at all?—Well, not very much, Chae——Then come ben and I'll get you a coat of the wife's, you can slip into that.*

The rain was pelting on the roof as she followed him through to Mistress Strachan's new parlour, it sounded loud enough to wake the dead let alone her that had been Kirsty Sinclair. Chae opened the wardrobe and brought out a fine coat, Mistress Strachan's best for the Sunday, lined and fine and smelling of moth-balls; and then a pair of her slippers. *Get out of your things, Chris lass, and bring them to dry. I'll have something warm for you and Ewan to drink.*

Left alone with the candle she wished she'd asked for a towel; Chae was kind but a man had no sense. But she managed without, though stripping from vest and knickers and stockings felt like parting wetly from her own skin, almost, so soaked she had been. Then she put on the coat and slippers and gathered up the wet underthings and went through with them to the kitchen; and there was Chae one side of the fire with a bottle of whisky at his elbow, making toddy, and Ewan at the other, with his coat off, warming his hands and looking at the door for her to come ben. They didn't look at her over-close, either of them, Chae pulled in one chair for her to sit on and another for her things to dry on, and when she'd spread them out he stopped in his toddy-making and said *Damn't, Chris, was that ALL you'd on?* And she nodded and he said *You'll have your death of cold, sit closer.*

And that was fine, sitting next to Ewan, close to the blaze of the meikle larch logs that Chae had put on, they were swack with resin. Syne Chae had the toddy made and he handed a glass to Ewan first, as was right with a man, and another to Chris, with three spoonfuls of sugar in it, Mistress Strachan might have had something to say about that if she'd seen such wastry. But she was fast asleep up in Chae's bed and knew nothing of it all till the morning, she made up for it then, folk said she accused both Chae and Ewan of cuddling and sossing with the Guthrie quean all the hours of the night.

So that was the ongoing there was that night of lightning, nor was it the only one in Kinraddie, for the lightning, and maybe it was the big flash Chris had seen as she gained the brae leading down to the horses, drove a great hole through the Manse spare bedroom, and let in the rain and fair ruined the place. Folk said that when the Reverend Gibbon heard the bolt strike the house, he'd been awake and listening, he dived like a rabbit below the blankets and cried *Oh, Christ, keep it away from me!* Which wasn't the kind of conduct you'd have expected from a minister, but there was a fair flock of folk the lightning scared that night in one place or another, Jock Gordon at Upperhill ran to his mother's bedroom and wept all over the counterpane there like a bairn. And Alec Mutch of Bridge End went out about midnight to look for his sheep, but he was half-drunk when he went and got drunker every minute as he chaved about, not seeing a thing. And at last he came to a big stook out in the corn-parks and crawled into that, it was a stook that stood near the turnpike, and feint the thing else was seen of him till late the next morning when the postman was going by and the sun was shining fine, and out Alec's face and meikle lugs were stuck from the stook and gave the postman such a turn in the wame he was nearly sick on the spot.

But of all that Chris knew nothing, she'd plenty to think of with her own bit ploys. For after the rain cleared and her under-things dried she went through to the parlour and got in them again, and into the raincoat of father's, and Chae lighted a lantern, fair yawning with sleep was Chae, and Ewan was to guide home to Blawearie both Chris and the horses. So out to the night again, the rain had cleared and freshened it, there was a wind from off the sea blowing in the stars, and clouds like the drifting of great women's veils, fisher-wives' veils, across the sad faces of the coarse high hills. Then the horses champed in the courtyard, Ewan had their halter-ropes in his hand, Chris was beside him swinging the lantern, they cried *Ta-ta!* to Chae and Chae nearly uncovered the back of his gums, so sleepy he was, poor stock; and he started to cry something to Chris about coming up the morn and seeing to old Bob whom the lightning had killed, they'd be able to sell him to the knacker in Brechin. But a yawh put an end to whatever he'd to say, it hardly mattered, it was morn already, you could see far down by Bervie a band of greyness stroke the horizon, as though an idle finger stroked it there on a window-pane.

Tramp, tramp, with a nicker now and then and long snortings through their nostrils, the horses, glad to be roaded up to Blawearie, Ewan big by the side of Chris, she hadn't realised before how big he was. He said nothing at all, except shy-like, once *Are you warm enough?* and she laughed and said *Fine,* she'd never again be shy with Ewan Tavendale. And it seemed to her even then it would be long before she forgot this walk through the night that was hardly night at all, an hour poised on the edge of the morning, like a penny on its rim, the flutter of the wind in their faces and the wet country sleeping about them, it smelt like Spring, not a morning in fore-winter. Then she was yawning, stopping from that, it was still a bit way to the house, she wondered if Uncle or Auntie had known she went out to the horses in the lightning. But she needn't have worried, not a thing they'd guessed and didn't till the morning came,

Blawearie was black as the inside of a lum-hat when they climbed to it, the kye quietened down, it hardly seemed home at all she had come to, a strange place this, with Ewan beside her. She opened the stable door for him, he led in the horses and made a shake-down, and came out and closed and barred up the door, she held him the lantern to see to that. And then he turned round, they were standing there in the close, his arms went round her, below her arms, and she said *Oh, don't!* and turned away her face; and he did nothing and she turned up her face to him again, peeping to see what he did.

Dark still it was but she saw his teeth, laughing at her, and then she put down the lantern and somehow resistance went from her, she hadn't wanted to resist, he was holding her close to him, kissing her, her cheeks and the tip of her nose because he couldn't see well in the darkness. And then he waited a moment and his lips came to hers and they were trembling as her own were, she wanted to cry and she wanted to laugh in a breath, and have him hold her for ever, so, in the close, and his trembling lips that came into hers, sweet and terrible those lips in hers. There was a great power of honeysuckle that year, the smell of it drenched all the close in wet, still weather, it perfumed the night and that kiss, she wouldn't ever forget them both though she lived unkissed again till she died. And then she knew they were near to other things, both of them, Ewan's breath was quicker than it should, he'd stopped from kissing her that kiss in the lips, his lips were urgent on her neck and breast; and she let him, she pulled aside the coat for him, standing so still, it was warm and sweet, she was his, he hers, for all things and everything, she never wanted better than that.

And then, in that ultimate moment, close at hand Chris heard the Blue Wyandotte, already so cocky that he was, stir on his ree, he gave a bit squawk before he stirred and peeked for the day he would crow so lustily. Somehow that stirring brought Chris to her senses, she wasn't afraid, only this could wait for another night's coming, it was sweet and she wanted it to live and last, not snatch it and fumble it blindly and stupidly. And she caught Ewan's hand and kissed him, he stopped with that kiss of hers on his cheek, his cheek with the soft brown skin; and she whispered *Wait, Ewan!*

He let her go at once, shamed of himself, he had little need to be that, she saw him troubled and uncertain in the dim light and put her arms about him and kissed him again and whispered *Come down and see me tomorrow evening*, and he said *Chris, when'll you marry me?* and she quivered strangely and sweetly as he said that, his hands holding her again, but gently. And then something happened, and the happening was a yawn, she yawned as though her head would fall off, she couldn't stop yawning; and a laugh came in the middle of it and that only made it worse. And Ewan let go of her again, maybe he was nearly in a rage at first, and then he yawned himself, they stood like two daft geese, yawning, and then they were laughing together, holding hands, not laughing too loud in case they'd be heard. And five minutes after that Ewan was far on his way to the steading of Upperhill and Chris lying in her bed, she'd hardly touched it when she thought of Ewan, she wanted to think of him long and long, only next minute she was fast asleep.

It didn't seem that minute had passed when she heard Uncle Tam come chapping at her door, fair testy, *Come away, come away, now; there's a fire to light and your Auntie wants her tea.* She sat up in bed, still sleepy and dazed, *All right, Uncle Tam,* and yawned and didn't move for a minute, remembering the things of the night and day she'd forgotten in sleep. And then she threw off the blankets and got out from the bed, and stretched till each muscle was taut and quivering, she felt light and free and fine, not at all Chris Guthrie with the grave brown face and heavy hair, light and free as a feather; and without a stitch on she did a little dance at her window in the splash of early sun that came there—what a speak for Kinraddie were she seen! And she was singing to herself as she dressed and went slipping downstairs, Uncle was kneeling at the kitchen fire, like a cow with colic, and fair sour in the face. *You're in fine tune this morning,* he glowered, and she said *Ay, Uncle, I'm that, give the sticks to me,* and had them out of his hand and the fire snapping into them all in a minute.

Uncle went out to the close then, to look over the fields for the horses, and came back at a run, his little quoit medals swinging and clashing from his meikle belly, *Mighty, Chris, there's no sign of a horse!* She didn't turn round, just said *You could hardly have looked in the stable,* and heard him stop and breathe a great breath, and then go out again. And not a word more he said at the breakfast, he went up to their room to pack; but Auntie asked how the horses came to be in and was told Chris had done it herself, with Chae Strachan and Ewan to help. She seemed fair shamed to hear that, Auntie Janet, but angry as well, she whisked round the house like a wasp, *Ah well, it's plain you've no use for your relatives here, I only pray you don't come to disaster.* And Chris said *That's awfully fine of you, Auntie,* and that made her madder than ever, but Chris didn't care, she didn't care though all the world, all Kinraddie and the Howe, went mad and choked itself with its bootlaces over the things that had been between her and Ewan.

If it wasn't in a rage it was fair in a stir of scandal by postman time, Kinraddie. Not a thing but it knew of her day in Stonehaven with that coarse tink brute, Ewan Tavendale, they'd been seen to go wandering out to Dunnottar together, they'd hidden away down in a hole by the sea—what did they that for if they'd nothing to hide? The postie told this to Auntie while Chris meated the chickens, Auntie fair grew worked up and forgot to rage, near crying she was as she told the story to Chris. How funny were folk! Chris thought, standing and fronting that trembling face. You knew them, saw through them, tied them up in little packets stowed away in your mind, labelled COARSE or TINKS or FINE; and they came tumbling from the packets at the very first shake, mixed and up-jumbled, she'd never known a soul bide neat and sure in his packet yet. For here was Auntie near crying because she thought her niece had been raped by Ewan Tavendale overnight, ashamed for her, sorry for her, fair set to carry her off to Aberdeen and cover her shame. But Chris said *There's nothing to cry about yet, Auntie Janet, Ewan and I haven't lain together. We'll wait till we're married,* and laughed at her Auntie's face, it was funny and pitiful both at once. And Auntie said *He's to*

marry you then? and Chris said she hoped so, but you never
knew, and Auntie fell in a fearsome stew again, it wasn't fair
to torment her like that, but that was the mood of Chris that
morning.

Then Chae Strachan came up from the Knapp and
looked at old Bob lying dead in his park. He shook his
head over him, he doubted if the knacker would pay more
than a pound—the closest muckers in Scotland, knackers,
and *that* was fair saying a lot. Syne he promised to drive
Auntie and her man to the station, and went back to the
Knapp for his gig and was up and waiting before you could
blink. And Chris helped her relatives up in the gig, and sent
them her love to her brothers, and off the gig spanked, they
looked over their shoulders and saw her stand laughing, she
didn't care a button, coarse quean that she was.

And fair a relief was the riddance, the place to herself
again; and then as she watched the gig whip round the
corner into the turnpike it came on her that it wasn't *again*,
it was just the first time! Blawearie was hers, there wasn't
a soul in the place but herself, nobody had a right to come
near it but if she allowed. The honeysuckle was blinding
sweet in the sun, wet still, and she stood beside it and
buried her face in it, laughed into it, blushed in it, remembering herself of the night before. And Ewan would be up
to see her soon, to see her . . . and she wouldn't think of
more! she had hundreds of things to do.

By noon she had dinner set for the old wife sent from
Stonehaven. And then she heard Chae's gig come driving
up to Blawearie and there was Chae and an old bit body,
fair tottery she seemed as she got from the gig, with a black
mutch on and a string bag gripped in her hand But when
she reached the ground she was none so tottery, she said
that the heights aye feared her legs; and she looked Chris all
over as though to make sure of her, living or dead, and asked
Where'll I put my box, Mem? And Chris blushed for shame
that any old soul should *Mem* at her, *Maybe Chae will carry
it up for us?* And Chae said *Och, fine that,* and hoisted the
old tin thing on his shoulder, and went swaggering into the
house, and Mrs Melon followed after and Chris turned to
Chae's gig.

By the time Chae came down she had nearly unyoked it, Chae cried *Damn't, Chris, what's on?* and she told him *Dinner, you're to stay for that.* So he was fell pleased, though he hummed and hawed a minute about rousting back to the Knapp. But she smiled at him, that way she had done to the boy in Semple's office, and Chae stared at her and wound up his waxed mouser and twinkled his eyes and gave her shoulder a slap, *Lord, Chris, they'll right soon be after you, the lads, with your eyes like that!* And he gave a bit sigh as though, other times, other ways, he'd have headed the band himself.

So into the kitchen he came and sat himself down with old Mistress Melon, and Chris dished up the rabbit stew and they had a great dinner, Mistress Melon was a funny old wife as soon as she saw you put on no airs. She'd a great red face as though she'd just unbended from a day's hard baking, and pale blue eyes like a summer sky, and faded hair that had once been brown, and Chris soon saw she was maybe the biggest gossip that had ever come into Kinraddie, and faith! that meant the challenging of many a champion. But her stories of Stonehaven had a lilt and a laugh, and the best was the one of the Provost that had lost his stud in his tumbler when speaking to a teetotal gathering. And Chae said that was a fine one, *Damn't, mistress, when I was in Africa . . .* and he told them a story of a man he knew, a black he'd been, real brave, and he found a diamond, on his own ground too, but as soon as the British heard of it they sent to arrest him for't. And what had that black childe done? Swallowed the damned thing and nothing of him could the British make, and they couldn't arrest him, and the black got his diamond back in a day or so in the course of nature, they were awful constipated folk, the blacks.

All the time he was telling the story Chae had been tearing into his rabbit and oat-cake; and soon's he'd finished one plate he took a look over the pot and cried *God, that was right fine, Chris quean. Is there more on the go?* Chris liked that, it was fine to have somebody that was hungry and liked his meat and didn't make out he was gentry or polite, there was less politeness about Chae than about a potato fork. Mistress Melon was eating right heartily too, and syne Chae told them another story, about a lion that he and the black head childe had hunted, they'd been awful chief together . . . And Mistress Melon asked *What, you and the lions?* and winked at Chris, but Chae wasn't a bit put out, he just said *Damn't no, mistress, me and the head man,* and went on with the story again, it was plain Mistress Melon thought he was a bit of a liar till suddenly, casual-like, Chae opened the front of his sark and finished up. *And that was the bit memento the damned beast left on me.* Syne they saw the marks on his chest, the marks of great raking claws they were they had torn fair deep and sure, and Chae's dark body-hair didn't grow in them. So Mistress Melon was fair stammy-gastered at that; and said so to Chris when Chae was gone.

Soon as that was Chris set to arranging with the Melon wife how the two of them would partition the work, Mistress Melon could do the cooking and cleaning, Chris preferred the outside, she'd milk and see to the kine; and they'd get on bravely, no doubt. Mistress Melon was a fell good worker in spite of her awful tongue, she'd cleared up the dinner things and washed them and put them away ere Chris was well out of the house. Then down on her knees she went and was scrubbing the kitchen floor, Chris was glad enough to see her at that, she hated scrubbing herself. If only she'd been born a boy she'd never had such hatings vexing her, she'd have ploughed up parks and seen to their draining, lived and lived, gone up to the hills a shepherd and never had to scunner herself with the making of beds or the scouring of pots. But neither would she ever have had Ewan hold her as last night he had.

And then she blushed and went on in silence with the cleaning of the byre, thinking of his coming and what she would say to him and the thing it was they'd arrange. Before she knew it the new plan came shaping up bravely in her mind, neat and trim and trig, and when she looked out and saw the gloaming near and went over the close and down through the parks for the kye, she had everything fixed, it didn't matter a fig what folk might say.

So when Ewan came in by at last she waited him ben in the parlour, with a great fire kindled there and the two big leather chairs drawn close. It was Mistress Melon that

brought him through, her meikle red face fair shaking
with ill-fashionce, agog to know what was toward. But Chris
just said *Thank you, Mistress Melon*, and ticed Ewan over
to his chair, and took his cap from him and made him sit
down and fair closed the door in the old wife's face. It was
bright and warm in the room, she turned round and saw her
lad sit so; and then she raised her head and saw herself in
the long, old mirror of the parlour wall, and thought how
she'd changed, it crept on you and you hardly noticed, in
ways you were still as young as the quean with the plaits that
had run by Marget to catch the scholars' train. But she saw
herself then in her long green skirt, long under the knee,
and her hair wound in its great fair plaits about her head,
and her high cheekbones that caught the light and her
mouth that was well enough, her figure was better still; and
she knew for one wild passing moment herself both frightened and sorry she should be a woman, she'd never dream
things again, she'd live them, the days of dreaming were by;
and maybe they had been the best; and there was Ewan waiting for her, the great quiet cat, reddening and turning his
head up with its smouldering eyes.

She went to him then and put her hand on his shoulder
and before she knew it they were close together and so stayed
long after they had finished with kissing, just quiet, in the
firelight, his arms about her, her head on his shoulder,
watching the fire. And when at last they began to speak she
put her hands over his lips, whispering to him to whisper
in case Mistress Melon should be listening out by. Maybe
she wasn't but in the shortest while they heard her go
stamping about in the kitchen, singing a hymn fell loud,
and that was a bit suspicious.

But they ceased from heeding her soon enough, they'd a
hundred things to plan and discuss, there in the fire-glow,
they lit no lamp, Chris listened with her head down-bent
as he told her he couldn't marry, he'd no more than a
hundred pounds saved up, they'd have to wait. And she told
him *she* had three hundred pounds, no credit to her, it was
her father's saving, but if she and Ewan married fair soon
he could take over Blawearie's lease, they could stay where
they were, *and that would be fine, no need for you any day*

then to go back through the parks to Upperhill. He kissed
her again at that, hurting her lips, but she didn't heed, it
was fine to be hurt like that; but she wouldn't kiss back till
he'd put him his Highland pride in his pouch and muttered
All right.

They'd planned to be married in December and as they'd
planned so the thing worked out without any hitch at all.
In November Ewan found and fee'd a substitute foreman
for Upperhill, a quiet-like childe James Leslie; and though
old Gordon was none so pleased he couldn't well afford to
fall out with so near a neighbour as the new Blawearie.
Chris went into Stonehaven again with Ewan and saw the
man Semple, he was fair suspicious, at first, but she argued
him soon from that, and he got the lease changed to Ewan's
name, and well-feathered his own nest in the changing, no
doubt.

By then the news was no news, Kinraddie knew all, and
when they came from the station that night they met in with
Ellison down from the Mains, he'd been waiting them there
to go by and he wouldn't have it but that they go up to the
house and drink their own healths in a dram. Mistress Ellison
was gentry and nice, more gentry than nice, poor thing, she
was still no more than a servant quean and fleered and arched
to make Chris and Ewan blush, she managed with Ewan.
But Chris kept cool as ice, and nearly as friendly, she didn't
see that a joke was less dirty if a neighbour spoke it. She
and Ewan fair quarrelled over that when they left the
Mains, it was their first quarrel and she wouldn't let him
touch her, she said *If you like foul stories, I don't,* and he
said, prigging at her, *Oh don't be a fool, Chris quean,* and
she said *There's no need for you marry a fool, then,* and the
Highland temper quite went with him then, he flared up
like a whin with a match at it, *Don't be feared, I've no such
intention!* and off he went, up over the hill through the
evening parks. Chris walked on prim and cold and quick,
it was near to sunset, she turned her head, she couldn't but
help it, to see if he wasn't looking back, he wasn't; and that
was too much, she stopped and cried *Ewan!* and he wheeled
like a shot and came running to her, she was crying in

earnest by then, she cried up against his coat while he held her and panted and swore at himself, *Oh, Chris, I didn't mean to hurt you!* And she sniffed *You didn't, it was myself*; and they made it all up again. She walked home subdued-like that night, it wouldn't be always plain sailing, they'd awful tempers, both of them. Then she saw the light of Blawearie shine steadfast across the parks and her heart kindled to a queer, quiet warmth at that.

They'd arranged to be married on New Year's Eve, most folk would be free to come that day. For three evenings they sat in Blawearie parlour and wrote their invitations to folk they knew and some they didn't, nearly every soul in Kinraddie was asked, they couldn't well miss out one of them. And to Auntie and Uncle and Dod and Alec they wrote, and to Ewan's friend, McIvor, a Highlandman out of Ross. He hadn't any near relatives, Ewan, and faith! they were feint the loss.

Chris knew that some would be sore affronted she should marry so close to her father's death, and with all the stir they intended, too. But Ewan said *Damn it, you're only married once as a general rule, and it won't hurt the old man in Kinraddie kirkyard.* So when Uncle wrote down from Auchterless that he'd think black, burning shame to attend such a marriage, Ewan said he could blacken and burn till he was more like a cinder heap than a man, for all they need care.

Chris was sorry they wouldn't let her brothers come, but it couldn't be helped, she wasn't to weep for that. So they planned out a wedding they'd mind on when they grew old, ordering food enough to feed the French, as the saying went, Mistress Melon near burst her meikle face with amaze as the packages came pouring in; and she spread the story of Chris's extravagance out through the Howe, she'd soon see the end of old Guthrie's silver. Folk shook their heads when they heard of that, it was plain that the quean wouldn't store the kiln long.

When Ewan went over to see to the banns the Reverend Gibbon tried to read him a lecture about such a display so close to John Guthrie's death. But he gave it up quick enough when Ewan began to spit like a cat and say the service he wanted was a wedding, not a sermon. Syne it grew plain they couldn't meet so often, Ewan would have to bide at the Upperhill all the day before the marriage. Chris kissed him good-bye that evening and told him to look after himself, and herself looked after him, troubled, knowing the kind of coarse things they might try him with in the bothy. And try they did, but Ewan couped one of them in to the midden and threw young Gordon into the horse-trough when that brute was trying the same on Ewan himself; so they let him be, dour devils to handle, those Highlandmen.

And down in Blawearie next day, what with cooking and chaving and tending to beasts, and wrestling with the worry of the barn, it wasn't half spruced for the dance, Chris might well have gone off her head if Chae and Long Rob of the Mill hadn't come dandering up the road in the afternoon, shy-like, bringing their presents. And Rob's was fine, two great biscuit barrels in oak and silver; and Chae's was from him and Kirsty, sheets and pillows, kind of Mistress Strachan, that, when you minded how the two of you'd fallen out over father ill. And when they heard of the barn they cast off their coats, *Leave it to us, Chris lass, just tell's what you want;* and they set to with ladders and tow and fancy frills and worked till near it was dark, redding up the place, it looked fine as a fairy-palace in a picture-book when they finished. Chae said *And who's your musician?* Chris nearly dropped through the floor with shock, she and Ewan had fair forgot about music. But Chae said it didn't matter, he'd bring his melodeon and Long Rob his fiddle; and faith! if that didn't content the folk they were looking for a church parade of the Gordons, not a wedding.

Syne they bade good night to Chris, and they laughed at her, kind-like, and said *This time the morn you'll be a married woman, Chris, not a quean. Sleep sound tonight!* And she laughed back and said *Oh, fine that;* but she blushed when Long Rob began to glint his grey eyes at her, he'd have to think of getting married himself, he said, fine it must be to sleep with a slim bit the like of herself those coldrife winter nights. And Chae said *Away, Rob, feint the much sleep you'd give her!*

And then they cried their good nights again and went off,

leaving Chris with such lonesome feeling as she'd seldom
had, all had been done that could be done, she wanted sleep
but couldn't sleep; and she wandered from room to room
till Mistress Melon was fair upset and cried *For God's sake
gang to your bed, lass, I'll tend to the rest; if you don't lie
down you'll look more like a bull for the butcher's than a
bride the morn.* And Chris laughed, she heard her laugh
funny and faint-like, and said she supposed so, and went off
to her room, but not to bed. She sat by the window, it was
a night that was rimed with a frost of stars, rime in the sky
and rime on the earth, the Milky Way shone clear and hard
and the black trees of Blawearie waved their leafless boughs
up against the window, sparkling white with the hoar; and
far across the countryside for hours she watched the winking
of the paraffin-lights in the farmhouses, till they sank and
went out, and she was left in a world that might well have
been dead but that she lived. Strange and eerie it was,
sitting there, she couldn't move from the frozen flow of
thoughts that came to her then, daft things she'd no need to
think on her marriage eve ... that this marriage of hers was
nothing, that it would pass on and forward into days that
had long forgotten it, her life and Ewan's, and they pass also,
and the face of the land change and change again in the
coming of the seasons and centuries till the last lights sank
away from it and the sea came flooding up the Howe, all her
love and tears for Ewan not even a ripple on that flood of
water far in the times to be. And then she found herself cold
as an icicle and got to her feet and at last began to get from
her clothes—strange to think that tomorrow and all the
tomorrows Ewan would share her room and her bed with
her.

She thought that cool and unwarmed, still in the grip of
the strange white dreaming that had been hers, looking
down at herself naked as though she looked at some other
than herself, a statue like that of the folk of olden time that
they set in the picture galleries. And she saw the light white
on the satin of her smooth skin then, and the long, smooth
lines that lay from waist to thigh, thigh to knee, and was
glad her legs were long from the knee to the ankle, that
made legs seem stumbling and stumpy, shortness there. And

still impersonally she bent to see if that dimple still hid there under her left breast, it did, it was deep as ever. Then she straightened and took down her hair and brushed it, standing so, silly to stand without her night-gown, but that was the mood she was in, somehow it seemed that never again would she be herself, have this body that was hers and her own, those fine lines that curved from thigh to knee hers, that dimple she'd loved when a child—oh, years before!

And then a clock began to strike, it struck two, and suddenly she was in a panic to be bedded and snug and herself again; and was in between the sheets in an instant, cuddling herself to some warmth and counting how many hours it would be till morning. And oh! it was still so long!

It came in snow that morning; she looked out from her window and saw it sheeting across the countryside, all silent; but still the daft peewits wheeped and wheeled against the hills, looking for the nests they'd lost in the harvest and couldn't forget. In the race and whip of the great broad flakes the leafless trees stood shivering; but down below Mistress Melon was already at work, Chris heard the clatter of the breakfast things, it was time she herself was into her clothes, there were hundreds of things to do.

Then she took out of the chest of drawers her under-things, there was no need to wait to change them, and looked at them, the silken vest, awful price it had been, and knickers and petticoat, vest, knickers and petticoat all of a shade, blue, with white ribbon; and they looked lovely and they smelt fine, she buried her face in them, so lovely they were and the queer feeling they brought her. And she changed her mind, she couldn't wear anything now she'd be wearing when she was married, she put on her old things and her old skirt and went down the stairs; and there was Mistress Melon smiling at her, *How do you feel on your marriage-morn, Chris?*

And Chris said *Fine*, and Mistress Melon said that was a good job, too, she'd known creatures of queans come down fair hysterical, others that just shook with fright, still others that spoke so undecent you knew fine a man's bed was no unco place for *them*. She hoped Chris would be awful happy, no fear of that, and soon have a two-three bairns keep her out of longer. And Chris said *You never know*, and she ate her porridge and Mistress Melon hers, and they cleared the table and scrubbed the kitchen and then Chris went out and tended the beasts, the very horses seemed to guess there was an unco thing on the go, Bess nozzled up against her shoulder; and there in the barn when she peeked in it, right in the middle of the floor were two great rats, sitting up on their tails, sniffing at each other's mouths, maybe kissing, and that was so funny, she tried not to laugh, but gave a choked gurgle and flirt! the rats were out of sight and into their holes.

In the cornyard the hens came tearing about her, mad with hunger, she gave them meat hot from the pot and then a bushel of corn, they liked that fine. But first the little bit Wyandotte got up on the cartshaft and gave a great crow that might have been heard in the Upperhill; and he cocked a bright eye on her, first one eye and then the other, and Chris laughed again.

She didn't feel hurried after that, then the postman came, fell dry, they gave him a dram and he licked his lips and said *Here's to you, Chris!* as blithe to drink to her health as to blacken her character. He'd brought him two parcels, one was a lovely bedspread from Mistress Gibbon of the Manse, nice of the quiet-voiced English thing, and the other from the Gordons of Upperhill, a canteen of cutlery, full enough of knives and forks and things to keep you cleaning them a week on end and not be finished, said Mistress Melon.

Then up the road came the wife of the grave-digger, Garthmore, him that had buried father. Sore made as always she was, poor thing, they'd asked her to come and lend them a hand more out of pity than anything else; and when the three sat down to dinner she said *Eh, me! it's fine to be young and be married, and maybe he'll treat you all right, but mine, my first man, him that's now dead, God! he was a fair bull of a man and not only the first night, either. He was aye at it, near deaved me to death he would if he hadn't fallen over the edge of a quarry on the road from the feeing-market some nine-ten years come Martinmas. But*

Mistress Melon said, *Havers, are you trying to frighten the lass? She'll be fine, her lad's both blithe and kind;* and Chris loved her for that, she'd never seemed to see and know Mistress Melon before, thinking her just a hard-working, hard-gossiping old body, now she saw the kindliness of her shine out, her gossiping no more than the dreams she aye dreamt and must tell to others. And then Mistress Melon cried *Away and get into your dress now, Chris, before the folk come up.*

It had left off snowing, Chris, dressing, saw from her window, a sunless day; and a great patching of clouds was upon the sky, the light below bright and sharp, flung by the snow itself; and the smoke rose straight in the air. Far over the braes by Upperhill where Ewan would be getting set in his clothes—unless he'd done that long before in the morning—the sheep were baaing in their winter buchts. Then Chris took off her clothes, and stood white again, and put on the wedding things, mother'd have liked to see them, mother lying dead and forgotten in Kinraddie kirkyard with the twins beside her. She found herself weep then, slowly, hardly, lost and desolate a moment without mother on her marriage-day. And then she shook her head, *Oh, don't be a fool, do you want to look a fright before Ewan and the folk?*

She peered at her face in the glass, then, fine! her eyes were bright, the crying had helped them. Pretty in a way, not only good-looking, she saw herself, dour cheek-bones softened for the hour in their chilled bronze setting. And she combed out her hair, it came far past her middle, thick and soft and sweet-smelling and rusty and tarnished gold. Then last was her dress, blue also, but darker than her under-clothes because so short was the time since father had died, she threaded the neck with a narrow black ribbon but round her own neck put nothing, her skin was the guerdon there.

So, ready, she turned herself round a minute, and held back the skirt from her ankles and liked them, they were neat and round, she had comely bones, her feet looked long and lithe in the black silk stockings and shoes. She found herself a hanky, last, and sprinkled some scent in that, only a little; and hid it away in her breast and went down the stairs just as she heard the first gig drive up.

That was the Strachans from Peesie's Knapp, Mistress Strachan fell long in the face at first. But Chae soon kindled her up with a dram, he whispered to Chris that he'd look after the drink; and Mistress Melon said it was aye best to have a man body at that end of the stir. And before they could say much more there came a fair stream of traffic up from the turnpike, all Kinraddie seemed on the move to Blawearie: except the old folk from Netherhill, and they sent their kind wishes and two clucking hens for Chris's nests. The hens broke the ice, you might say, for they got themselves loose from the gig of the Netherhill folk and started a wild flutter and chirawk everywhere, anywhere out of Blawearie. Long Rob of the Mill was coming up the road at that minute, in his Sunday best, and he met the first hen and heard the cry-out that followed her, and he cried himself, *Shoo, you bitch!* The hen dodged into the ditch, but Rob was after her, grabbing her, she squawked fair piercing as he carried her up to the house, his fine Sunday coat was lathered with snow; and he said that such-like work would have been nothing to Chae, who had chased the bit ostriches out in the Transvaal, but he'd had no training himself. Syne he took up the dram that Chae had poured him and cried *Here's to the bonniest maid Kinraddie will mind for many a year!*

That was kind of him, Chris had been cool and quiet enough until then, but she blushed at that, seeing Rob stand like a Viking out of the picture books with the iron-grey glint in his eyes. Mistress Munro, though, was right sore jealous as usual, she poked her nose in the air and said, and not over-low, *The great fool might wait for the tea before he starts his speechifying;* she was maybe mad that nobody had ever said *she* was bonny; or if anybody ever had, he was an uncommon liar.

Then the Bridge End folk came up, then Ellison and his wife and their daughter, and then the Gordons, and then the minister, riding on his bicycle, it looked as though he'd had a fall or two and he wasn't in the best of temper, he wouldn't have a dram, *No, thank you, Chae,* he said, real stiff-like. And when Rob gave him a sly bit look, *You've been communing with Mother Earth, I see, Mr Gibbon,* he just turned his back and made out he didn't hear, and folk looked fair uncomfortable, all except Long Rob himself and Chae, they winked one at the other and then at Chris.

She thought the minister a fusionless fool, and went to the door to see who else was coming; and there, would you believe it, was poor old Pooty toiling up through the drifts with a great parcel under his oxter, his old face was white with snow and he shivered and hoasted as he came in, peeking out below his old, worn brows for Chris. *Where's the bit llllass!* he cried, and then saw her and put the parcel in her hands, and she opened it then, as the custom was, and in it lay a fine pair of shoes he had made for her, shoes of glistening leather with gay green soles, and a pair of slippers, soft-lined with wool, there wouldn't be a grander pair in Kinraddie. And she said *Oh, thank you,* and she knew that wasn't enough, he stood peering up at her like an old hen peers, she didn't know why she did it but she put her arms round him and kissed him, folk laughed at that, all but the two of them, Pooty blinked and stuttered till Long Rob reached out a hand and pulled him into a chair and cried *Wet your whistle with this, Pooty man, you've hardly a minute ere the wedding begins.*

And he was right, for up the road came walking the last two, Ewan and his best man, the Highlander McIvor, near six feet six, red-headed, red-faced, a red Highlandman that bowed so low to Chris that she felt a fool; and presented his present, and it was a ram's horn shod with silver, real bonny and unco, like all Highland things. But Ewan took never a look at Chris, they made out they didn't see one the other, and Mistress Melon whispered to her to go tidy her hair, and when she came down again all the place was quiet, there was hardly a murmur. She stopped at the foot of the stairs with the heart beating so against her skin it was like to burst from her breast; and there was Chae Strachan waiting her, he held out his arm and patted her hand, when she laid it on his arm, and he whispered *Ready then, Chris?*

Then he opened the parlour door, the place was crowded,

F

there were all the folk sitting in chairs, solemn as a kirk congregation, and over by the window stood the Reverend Gibbon, very stern and more like a curly bull than ever; and in front of him waited Ewan and his best man, MacIvor. Chris had for bridesmaids the little Ellison girl and Maggie Jean Gordon, they joined with her, she couldn't see clear for a minute then, or maybe too clear, she didn't seem to be seeing with her own eyes at all. And then Chae had loosed her hand from his arm and she and Ewan stood side by side, he was wearing a new suit, tweed it was, and smelt lovely, his dark face was solemn and frightened and white, he stood close to her, she knew him more frightened than she was herself. Something of her own fear went from her then, she stood listening to the Reverend Gibbon and the words he was reading, words that she'd never heard before, this was the first marriage she'd ever been at.

And then she heard Chae whisper behind her and listened more carefully still, and heard Ewan say *I will*, in a desperate kind of voice, and then said it herself, her voice was as happy and clear as well you'd have wished, she smiled up at Ewan, the white went from his face and the red came in spate. The Red Highlander behind slipped something forward, she saw it was the ring, and then Ewan fitted it over her finger, his fingers were hot and unsteady, and Mr Gibbon closed his eyes and said, *Let us pray*.

And Chris held on to Ewan's hand and bent her head and listened to him, the minister; and he asked God to bless their union, to give them courage and strength for the difficulties that the years might bring to them, to make fruitful their marriage and their love as pure and enduring in its fulfilment as in its conception. They were lovely words, words like the marching of a bronze-leafed beech on the lips of a summer sky. So Chris thought, her head down-bent and her hand in Ewan's, then she lost the thread that the words were strung on, because of that hand of Ewan's that still held hers; and she curved her little finger into his palm, it was hard and rough there and she tickled the skin secretly, and his hand quivered and she took the littlest keek at his face. There was that smile of his, flitting like a startled cat; and then his hand closed firm and warm and sure on hers, and hers lay quiet in his, and the minister had finished and was shaking their hands.

He hesitated a minute and then bent to kiss Chris; close to hers she saw his face older far than when he came to Kinraddie, there were pouches under his eyes, and a weary look in his eyes, and his kiss she didn't like. Ewan's was a peck, but Chae's was fine, it was hearty and kind though he reeked of the awful tobacco he smoked, and then Long Rob's, it was clean and sweet and dry, like a whiff from the Mill itself; and then it seemed every soul in Kinraddie was kissing her, except only Tony, the daftie, he'd been left at home. Everybody was speaking and laughing and slapping Ewan on the back and coming to kiss her, those that knew her well and some that didn't. And last it was Mistress Melon, her eyes were over bright but careful still, she nearly smothered Chris and then whispered *Up to your room and tidy yourself, they've messed your hair.*

She escaped them then, the folk trooped out to the kitchen where the fire was roaring, Chae passed round the drams again, there was port for the women if they wanted it and raspberry drinks for the children. Soon's the parlour was clear Mistress Melon and Mistress Garthmore had the chairs whisked aside, the tables put forward and the cloths spread; and there came a loud tinkling as they spread the supper, barely past three though it was. But Chris knew it fell likely that few had eaten much at their dinners in Kinraddie that day, there wouldn't have been much sense with a marriage in prospect; and as soon as they'd something solid in their bellies to foundation the drink, as a man might say, the better it would be. In her room that wouldn't be her room for long Chris brushed her hair and settled her dress and looked at her flushed, fair face, it was nearly the same, hard to believe though you thought it. And then something felt queer about her, the ring on her hand it was, she stood and stared at the thing till a soft whispering drew her eyes to the window, the snow had come on again, a scurry and a blinding drive from down the hills; and below in the house they were crying *The bride, where is she?*

So down she went, folk had trooped back in the parlour by then and were sitting them round the tables, the minister at the head of one, Long Rob at the head of another, in the centre one the wedding cake stood tall on its stand with the Highland dirk beside it that Ewan had gotten from McIvor to do the cutting. The wind had risen storming without as Chris stood to cut, there in her blue frock with the long, loose sleeves, there came a great whoom in the chimney and some looked out at the window and said that the drifts would be a fell feet deep by the morn. And then the cake was cut and Chris sat down, Ewan beside her, and found she wasn't hungry at all, about the only soul in the place that wasn't, everybody else was taking a fair hearty meal.

The minister had thawed away by then, he was laughing real friendly-like in his bull-like boom of a voice, telling of other weddings he'd made in his time, they'd all been gey funny and queer-like weddings, things that you laughed at, not fine like this. And Chris listened and glowed with pride that everything at hers was just and right; and then again as so often that qualm of doubt came down on her, separating her away from these kindly folk of the farms—kind, and aye ready to believe the worst of others they heard, unbelieving that others could think the same of themselves. So maybe the minister no more than buttered her, she looked at him with the dark, cool doubt in her face, next instant forgot him in a glow of remembrance that blinded all else: she was married to Ewan.

Beside her: He whispered *Oh, eat something, Chris, you'll fair go famished,* and she tried some ham and a bit of the dumpling, sugared and fine, that Mistress Melon had made. And everybody praised it, as well they might, and cried for more helpings, and more cups of tea, and there were scones and pancakes and soda-cakes and cakes made with honey that everybody ate; and little Wat Strachan stopped eating of a sudden and cried *Mother, I'm not right in the belly!* everybody laughed at that but Kirsty, she jumped to her feet and hurried him out, and came back with him with his face real frightened. But faith! It didn't put a stop to the bairn, he started in again as hungry as ever, and Chae cried out *Well, well, let him be, maybe it tasted as fine coming up as it did going down!*

Some laughed at that, others reddened and looked real

affronted, Chris herself didn't care. Cuddiestoun and his wife sat opposite her, it was like watching a meikle collie and a futret at meat, him gulping down everything that came his way and a lot that didn't, he would rax for that; and his ugly face, poor stock, fair shone and glimmered with the exercise. But Mistress Munro snapped down at her plate with sharp, quick teeth, her head never still a minute, just like a futret with a dog nearby. They were saying hardly anything, so busied they were, but Ellison next to them had plenty to say, he'd taken a dram over much already and was crying things across the table to Chris, Mistress Tavendale he called her at every turn; and he said that she and Mistress Ellison must get better acquaint. Maybe he'd regret that the morn, if he minded his promise: and that wasn't likely. Next to him was Kirsty and the boys and next to that the minister's table with Alec Mutch and his folk and young Gordon; a real minister's man was Alec, awful chief-like the two of them were, but Mistress Mutch sat lazy as ever, now and then she cast a bit look at Chris out of the lazy, gley eyes of her, maybe there was a funniness in the look that hadn't to do with the squint.

Up at Rob's table an argument rose, Chris hoped that it wasn't religion, she saw Mr Gordon's wee face pecked up to counter Rob. But Rob was just saying what a shame it was that folk should be shamed nowadays to speak Scotch —or they called it Scots if they did, the split-tongued sourocks! Every damned little narrow dowped rat that you met put on the English if he thought he'd impress you— as though Scotch wasn't good enough now, it had words in it that the thin bit scraichs of the English could never come at. And Rob said *You can tell me, man, what's the English for sotter, or greip, or smore, or pleiter, gloaming or glunch-ing or well-kenspeckled? And if you said gloaming was sunset you'd fair be a liar; and you're hardly that, Mr Gordon.*

But Gordon was real decent and reasonable, *You can't help it, Rob. If folk are to get on in the world nowa-days, away from the ploughshafts and out of the pleiter, they must use the English, orra though it be.* And Chae cried out that was right enough, and God! who could you blame? And a fair bit breeze got up about it all, every soul in the parlour seemed speaking at once; and as aye when they spoke of the thing they agreed that the land was a coarse, coarse life, you'd do better at almost anything else, folks that could send their lads to learn a trade were right wise, no doubt of that, there was nothing on the land but work, work, work, and chave, chave, chave, from the blink of day till the fall of night, no thanks from the soss and sotter, and hardly a living to be made.

Syne Cuddiestoun said that he'd heard of a childe up Laurencekirk way, a banker's son from the town he was, and he'd come to do farming in a scientific way. So he'd said at first, had the childe, but God! by now you could hardly get into the place for the clutter of machines that lay in the yard; and *he* wouldn't store the kiln long. But Chae wouldn't have that, he swore *Damn't, no, the machine's the best friend of man, or it would be so in a socialist state. It's coming and the chaving'll end, you'll see, the machine'll do all the dirty work.* And Long Rob called out that he'd like right well to see the damned machine that would muck you a pigsty even though they all turned socialist tomorrow. And they all took a bit laugh at that, Chris and Ewan were fair forgotten for a while, they looked at each other and smiled. Ewan reached down and squeezed her hand and Chris wished every soul but themselves a hundred miles from Blawearie.

But then Chae cried *Fill up your glasses, folk, the best man has a toast.* And the red Highlander, McIvor, got up to his feet and bowed his red head to Chris, and began to speak; he spoke fine, though funny with that Highland twist, he said he'd never seen a sweeter quean than the bride or known a better friend than the groom; and he wished them long and lovely days, a marriage in the winter had the best of it. For was not the Spring to come and the seed-time springing of their love, and the bonny days of the summer, flowering it, and autumn with the harvest of their days? And when they passed to that other winter together they would know that was not the end of it, it was but a sleep that in another life would burgeon fresh from another earth. He could never believe but that two so young and fair as his friend and his friend's wife, once made one flesh

would be one in the spirit as well; and have their days built
of happiness and their nights of the music of the stars. And
he lifted his glass and cried *The bride!* looking at Chris
with his queer bright eyes, the daft Highland poet, they
were all like that, the red Highlanders. And everybody
cried *Good luck to her!* and they all drank up and Chris
felt herself blush from head to foot under all the blue things
she wore.

And then Long Rob of the Mill was making a speech,
different from McIvor's as well it might be. He said he'd
never married himself because he'd over-much respect for
those kittle folk, women; but if he'd been ten years younger
he was damned if his respect would have kept him from
having a try for Chris Guthrie, and beating that Highland
childe, Ewan, at his own fell game. That was just Ewan's
luck, he thought, not his judgment, and Chris was clean
thrown away on her husband, as she'd have been on any
husband at all: but himself. Ah well, no doubt she'd train
him up well, and he advised Ewan now, from the little that
he knew of marriage, never to counter his wife; not that he
thought that she wasn't well able to look after herself, but
just that Ewan mightn't find himself worsted though he
thought himself winner. Marriage, he took it, was like
yoking together two two-year-olds, they were kittle and brisk
on the first bit rig—unless they'd fallen out as soon as they
were yoked and near kicked themselves and their harness to
bits—but the second rig was the testing time, it was then
you knew when one was pulling and one held back, the one
that had sheer sweirty—and, that was a word for Mr Gordon
to put into English—in its bones, and the one with a stout
bit heart and a good guts. Well, he wouldn't say more
about horses, though faith! it was a fascinating topic, he'd
just come back to marriage and say they all wished the best
to Chris, so sweet and trig, and to Ewan, the Highland
cateran, and long might they live and grow healthy, wealthy,
and well content.

Then they all drank up again, and God knows who
mightn't have made the next speech if Chae then hadn't
stood up and cried *The night's near on us. Who's game for
a daylight dance at Chris's wedding?*

So out they all went to the kitchen, it was cold enough there from the heat of the room, but nothing to the cold-rife air of the barn when the first of them had crossed the close and stood in the door. But Mistress Melon had kindled a brazier with coal, it crackled fine, well away from the straw, Rob tuned up his fiddle, Chae squeaked on his melodeon, it began to feel brisk and warm even while you stood and near shivered your sark off. Chris was there with the men, of course, and the children and Mistress Gordon and Mistress Mutch and Mistress Strachan were there, Mistress Munro had stayed behind to help clear the tables, she said, and some whispered it was more than likely she'd clear most of the clearings down her own throat, by God she couldn't have eaten a mouthful since Candlemas.

But then Chae cried *Strip the Willow*, and they all lined up, and the melodeon played bonnily in Chae's hands, and Long Rob's fiddle-bow was darting and glimmering, and in two minutes in the whirl and go of *Strip the Willow*, there wasn't a cold soul in Blawearie barn, or a cold sole either. Then here, soon's they'd finished, was Mistress Melon with a great jar of hot toddy to drink, she set it on a bench between Chae and Long Rob. And whoever wanted to drink had just to go there, few were bashful in the going, too; and another dance started, it was a schottische, and Chris found herself in the arms of the minister, he could dance like a daft young lad. And as he swung her round and around he opened his mouth and cried *Hooch!* and so did the red Highlander, McIvor, *Hooch!* careering by with fat Kirsty Strachan, real scared-like she looked, clipped round the waist.

Then Chae and Long Rob hardly gave them a breather, they were at it dance on dance; and every time they stopped for a panting second Chae would dip in the jar and give Rob a wink and cry *Here's to you, man!* and Rob would dip, solemn-like as well, and say *Same to you!* and off the fiddle and melodeon would go again, faster than ever. Ewan danced the schottische with prim Mistress Gordon, but for waltzing he found a quean from the Mains, a red-faced daft-like limmer, she screamed with excitement and every-body laughed, Chris laughed as well. Some were watching to see if she did, she knew, and she heard a whisper she'd have all her work cut out looking after him, coarse among the queans he was, Ewan Tavendale. But she didn't care, she knew it a lie, Ewan was hers and hers only; but she wished he would dance with her for a change. And here at the *Petronella* he was, he anyway hadn't been drinking, in the noise of the dance as they swayed up and down the barn he whispered *Well, Chris?* and she whispered back *Fine,* and he said *You're the bonniest thing ever seen in Kinraddie, Long Rob was right.* And she said she liked him to think so, and he called her back in the darkness away from the dancers, and kissed her quickly and slowly, she didn't hurry either, it was blithe and glad to stand there kissing, each strained to hear when they'd be discovered.

And then they were, Chae crying *Where's the bride and the groom? Damn't, they're lost!* and out they'd to come. Chae cried was there anyone else could play the melodeon? and young Jock Gordon cried back to him *Ay, fine that,* and came stitering across the floor and sat himself down by the toddy jar, and played loud and clear and fine. Then Chae caught Chris, he said to Ewan *Away, you greedy brute, wait a while till she's yours forever and aye,* and he danced right neatly, you didn't expect it from Chae, with his grey eyes laughing down at you. And as he danced he said suddenly, grave-like, *Never doubt your Ewan, Chris, or never let him know that you do. That's the hell of a married life. Praise him up and tell him he's fine, that there's not a soul in the Howe can stand beside him, and he'll want to cuddle you till the day he dies; and he'll blush at the sight of you fifty years on as much as he does the day.* She said *I'll try,* and *Thank you, Chae,* and he said *Och, it must be the whisky speaking,* and surrendered her up to Ellison, and took the melodeon from Gordon again, but staggered and leant back against the sack that hung as a draught-shield behind the musician's place. Down came the sack and there among the hay was the minister and the maid from the Mains that had scraiched so loud, she'd her arms round him and the big curly bull was kissing the quean like a dog lapping up its porridge.

Chris's heart near stopped, but Chae snatched up the

sack, hooked it back on its hook again, nobody saw the sight except himself and Chris and maybe Long Rob. But you couldn't be sure about Rob, he looked as solemn as five owls all in one, and was playing as though, said Chae, he was paid by piece-work and not by time.

Between eight and nine Mistress Melon came out to the barn and cried them to supper, the storm had left off, all but a flake that sailed down now and then like a sailing gull in the beam from the barn door. On the ground the snow crinkled under their feet, frost had set in, the folk stood and breathed in the open air, and laughed, and cried one to the other, *Man, I'll have aching joints the morn!* The women ran first to the house, to tidy their hair, Ewan saw everybody in, except Munro of the Cuddiestoun, he was nowhere to be seen.

And then Ewan heard a funny bit breathing as he passed by the stable; and he stopped and opened the door and struck a match, and there was Munro, all in his Sunday-best, lying in the stall beside Clyde the horse, and his arms were round the beast's neck, and faith! the beast looked real disgusted. Ewan shook him and cried *Munro, you can't sleep here,* but Munro just blinked the eyes in his face, daft-like, and grumbled *Why not?* Syne Alec Mutch turned back from the house to see what all the stir was about, and both he and Ewan had another go at the prostrate Munro, but damn the move would he make, Alec cried *To hell with him, leave him there with the mare, she's maybe a damned sight kinder a bed-mate then ever was that futret of a wife of his.*

So they closed the door of the stable and went in to their supper, everybody ate near as well as at tea-time, fair starved they were with the dancing and drink. Chris had thought she herself was tired till she ate some supper, and then she felt as fresh as ever, and backed up Long Rob, who looked twice as sober as any of the men and had drunk about twice as much as any three of them, when he cried *Who's for a dance again?* Mistress Melon had the toddy jar filled fresh full and they carried that out, everybody came to the barn this time except Mistress Munro, *No, no, I'll clear the table.*

And young Elsie Ellison, wondering for why the creature should stay behind, stayed herself and took a bit keek round the corner of the door; and there was Mistress Munro, with a paper bag in her hand, stuffing it with scones and biscuits and cake, and twisting her head this side and that, like the head of a futret. So Elsie, fair scared, ran off to the barn and caught at her father's tails and cried *The Cuddiestoun wife's away home with the pieces,* and Ellison, he was whiskied up to high tune by then, cried *Let her run to hell and be damned to her.*

Syne he started a tale about how once she insulted him, the dirty Scotch bitch. But Long Rob and Chae were striking up a dance again and Chris heard no more of the Ellison story, dancing a waltz with young Jock Gordon, it was like flying, Jock's face was white with excitement. The fourth dance, Alec Mutch, the fool, began to stiter the floor, backwards and forwards, he was a real nuisance till he passed Long Rob and then Rob cried *Hoots, Alec, man, your feet are all wrong!* and thrust out a foot among Alec's and couped him down and Chae shoved him aside to the straw with a foot and a hand, and played on with the other foot and hand, or maybe with a foot and his teeth, a skilly man, Chae.

Mistress Mutch said nothing, just standing and laughing and smoking at her cigarette. There were more men than women in the barn, though, even when the men made do with a little quean, and soon Chris found herself dancing with Mistress Mutch, the great, easy-going slummock, she spoke slow and easy as though she'd just wakened up from her sleep. Chris couldn't tell what way she looked with that gleying eye, but what she spoke was *Take things easy in married life, Chris, but not over-easy, that's been MY ruin. Though God knows it'll make not a difference in a hundred years time and we're dead. Don't let Ewan saddle you with a birn full of bairns, Chris, it kills you and eats your heart away, forbye the unease and the dirt of it. Don't let him Chris, they're all the same, men; and you won't well steer clear of the first or the second. But you belong to yourself, mind that.*

Chris went hot and cold and then wanted to ask something of Mistress Mutch and looked at her and found she couldn't, she'd just have to find the thing out for herself. Long Rob came down to dance with her next, he'd left the fiddle to old Gordon, and he asked what that meikle slummock had been saying to her? And Chris said *Oh, just stite,* and Rob said *Mind, don't let any of those damned women fear you, Chris; it's been the curse of the human race, listening to advice.* And Chris said *But I'm listening to yours, Rob, now, amn't I?* He nodded to her, solemn, and said, *Oh, you've your head screwed on and you'll manage fine. But mind, if there's ever a thing you want with a friend, not to speak it abroad all over Kinraddie, I'll aye be there at the Mill to help you.* Chris thought that a daft-like speak for Rob, kind maybe he meant it, but she'd have Ewan, who else could she want?

And then the fun slackened off, the barn was warm, folk sat or lay on the benches or straw, Chris looked round and saw nothing of the minister then, maybe he'd gone. She whispered to Chae about that, but he said *Damn the fears, he's out to be sick, can't you hear him like a cat with a fishbone in its throat?* And hear him they could, but Chris had been right after all, he didn't come back. Maybe he was shamed and maybe he just lost his way, for next noon there were folk who swore they'd seen the marks of great feet that walked round and round in a circle, circle after circle, all across the parks from Blawearie to the Manse; and if these weren't the minister's feet they must have been the devil's, you could choose whichever you liked.

No sooner was the dancing done than there were cries *Rob, what about a song now, man?* And Rob said *Och, ay, I'll manage that fine,* and he off with his coat and loosened his collar and sang them *Ladies of Spain;* and then he turned round to where Chris stood beside her Ewan and sang *The Lass that Made the Bed to Me:*

> Her hair was like the link o' gowd,
>   Her teeth were like the ivorie,
> Her cheeks like lilies dipt in wine,
>   The lass that made the bed to me.

> Her bosom was the driven snaw,
>   Two drifted heaps sae fair to see,
> Her limbs, the polished marble stane,
>   The lass that made the bed to me.

> I kissed her owre and owre again,
>> And aye she wist na what to say.
> I laid her between me and the wa',
>> The lassie thought na long till day.

Folk stared and nodded at Chris while Rob was singing, and Ewan looked at first as though he'd like to brain him; and then he blushed; but Chris just listened and didn't care, she thought the song fine and the lass lovely, she hoped she herself would seem as lovely this night—or as much of it as their dancing would leave. So she clapped Rob and syne it was Ellison's turn, he stood up with his meikle belly a-wag and sang them a song they didn't know:

> Roses and lilies her cheeks disclose,
>> But her red lips are sweeter than those,
> Kiss her, caress her,
>> With blisses her kisses,
> Dissolve us in pleasure and soft repose.

and then another, an English one and awful sad, about a young childe called Villikins and a quean called Dinah, and it finished:

> For a cup of cold pizen lay there on the ground
>
> With a tooril-i-ooril-i-oorily-i-ay.

Chae cried that was hardly the kind of thing that they wanted, woeful as that; and they'd better give Chris a rest about her roses and lips and limbs, she had them all in safe-keeping and would know how to use them; and what about a seasonable song? And he sang so that all joined in seasonable enough, for the snow had come on again in spite of the frost:

> Up in the morning's no for me,
>> Up in the morning early,
> When a' the hills are covered wi' snaw
> I'm sure it's winter fairly!

Then Mistress Mutch sang, that was hardly expected, and folk tittered a bit; but she had as good a voice as most and better than some, she sang *The Bonnie House o' Airlie,* and then *Auld Robin Gray* that aye brought Chris near to weeping, and did now, and not her alone, with Rob's fiddle whispering it out, the sadness and the soreness of it, though it was long, long syne:

> When the sheep are in the fauld, and the kye are a' at hame
> And a' the weary world to its rest has gane,
> The tears o' my sorrow fa' in shooers frae my e'e
> And Auld Robin Gray he lies sound by me.

and all the tale of young Jamie who went to sea and was thought to be drownded in an awful storm; and his lass married Auld Robin Gray; and syne Jamie came back but couldn't win his lass away from the auld man, though near broken-hearted she was:

> I gang like a ghaist, and I carena' to spin,
> I daurna' think o' Jamie, for that wad be a sin,
> But I'll try aye my best a guid wife to be,
> For Auld Robin Gray he is kind to me.

Old Pooty was sleeping in a corner; he woke up then, fell keen to recite his TIMROUS BEASTIE; but they pulled him down and cried on the bride herself for a song. And all she could think of was that south country woman crying in the night by the side of her good man, the world asleep and grey without; and she whispered the song to Rob and he tuned his fiddle and she sang, facing them, young and earnest, and she saw Ewan looking at her solemn and proud, *The Flowers of the Forest:*

> I've heard them lilting at our ewe-milking,
>   Lasses a' lilting before dawn o' day;
> But now they are moaning on ilka green loaning,
>   The Flooers o' the Forest are a' wede away

> Dool and wae for the order sent oor lads tae the Border!
>   The English for ance, by guile wan the day,
> The Flooers o' the Forest, that fought aye the foremost,
>   The pride o' oor land lie cauld in the clay.

Chae jumped up when she finished, he said *Damn't, folk, we'll all have the whimsies if we listen to any more woesome songs! Have none of you a cheerful one?* And the folk in the barn laughed at him and shook their heads, it came on Chris how strange was the sadness of Scotland's singing, made for the sadness of the land and sky in dark autumn evenings, the crying of men and women of the land who had seen their lives and loves sink away in the years, things wept for beside the sheep-buchts, remembered at night and in twilight. The gladness and kindness had passed, lived and forgotten, it was Scotland of the mist and rain and the crying sea that made the songs—And Chae cried *Let's have another dance, then, it's nearly a quarter to twelve, we must all be off soon as midnight chaps.*

And they all minded what midnight would bring, and Chae and Rob had the melodeon and fiddle in hand again, and struck up an eightsome, and everybody grabbed him a partner, it didn't matter who was who, McIvor had Chris and danced with her as though he would like to squeeze her to death, he danced light as thistle-down, the great red Highlander; and no sooner was one dance finished than Rob and Chae swept forward into another, they played like mad and the lights whipped and jumped as the couples spun round and round; and the music went out across the snowing night; and then Chae pulled out his great silver watch, and laid it beside him, playing on.

And suddenly it was the New Year, the dancing stopped and folk all shook hands, coming to shake Chris's and Ewan's; and Long Rob struck up the sugary surge of *Auld Lang Syne* and they all joined hands and stood in a circle to sing it, and Chris thought of Will far over the seas in Argentine, under the hot night there. Then the singing finished, they all found themselves tired, somebody began to take down the barn lights, there was half an hour's scramble of folk getting themselves into coats and getting their shivering sholts from out the empty stalls in the byre. Then Chris and Ewan were handshook again, Chris's arm began to ache, and then the last woof-woof of wheels on snow thick-carpeted came up the Blawearie road to them, it was fell uncanny that silence in the place after all the noise and fun of the long, lit hours. And there was Mistress Melon in the kitchen-door, yawning fit to swallow a horse, she whispered to Chris *I'm taking your room now, don't forget,* and cried them *Good night, and a sound sleep, both!* and was up the stairs and left them alone.

He hardly seemed tired even then, though, Ewan, prowling locking the doors like a great quiet cat till Chris called to him softly *Oh, sit by me!* So he came to the chair she sat in and picked her out of it, so strong he was, and himself sat down, still holding her. They watched the fire a long time and then Chris's head drooped down, she didn't know she had been asleep till she woke to find Ewan shaking her, *Chris, Chris, you're fair done, come on to bed.* The fire was dying then and the paraffin had run low in the lamp, the flame swithered and went out with a plop! as Ewan blew on it; and then they were in the dark, going up the stairs together, past the room that had been Chris's and where Mistress Melon slept for a night ere she went back to Stonehaven.

And to Chris going up that stair holding the hand of her man there came a memory of one with awful eyes and jutting beard, lying in that room they came to, lying there and whispering and cursing her. But she put the memory away, it had never happened, sad and daft to remember that, she was tired. Then, with her hand on the door, Ewan kissed her there in the dark, sweet and wild his kiss, she had not thought he could kiss her like that, not as though he wanted her as a man might do in that hour and place, but as though he minded the song he had heard her sing. She put up her face to the kiss, forgetting tiredness, suddenly she was wakeful as never she had been, the sleep went out of her head and body and the chill with it, Ewan's hand came over hers and opened the door.

A fire burned bright in the fireplace, they had thought the place would be black and cold, but Mistress Melon had seen to that. And there was the bridal bed, pulled out from the wall, all in white it was, with sheet and blanket turned back, the window curtains were drawn, and in the moment they stood breathing from their climb of the stairs, Chris heard the sound of the snow that stroked the window, with quiet, soft fingers, as though writing there.

Then she forgot it, standing by the fire getting out of her blue things, one by one. She found it sweet to do that, so slowly, and to have Ewan kiss her at last when there was no bar to his kisses, lying with him then, with the light put out and the radiance of the fire on the walls and ceiling. And she turned towards him at last, whispering and tender for him, *We're daft, we'll catch cold without anything on!* and then she saw his face beside her, solemn and strange, yet not strange at all. And he put his left hand below her neck, and he took her close to him, and they were one flesh, one and together; and far into the morning she woke, and was not cold at all, him holding her so, and then she heard again the hand of winter write on the window, and listened a moment, happy, happy, and fell fast asleep till morning brought Mistress Melon and two great cups of tea to waken Ewan and herself.

So that was her marriage, not like wakening from a dream was marrying, but like going into one, rather, she wasn't sure, not for days, what things they had dreamt and what actually done—she and this farmer of Blawearie who would stir of a morning at the jangle of the clock and creep from bed, the great cat, and be down the stairs to light the fire and put on the kettle. She'd never be far behind him, though, she loved even the bitterness of those frozen mornings, and a bitter winter it was, every crack and joist of the old house played a spray of cold wind across the rooms. He'd be gone to the byre and stable as she came down and sought out the porridge meal and put it to boil, Blawearie's own meal, fine rounded stuff that Ewan so liked. She'd leave it to hotter there on the fire and then bring the pails from the dairy and open the kitchen door on the close and gasp in the bite of the wind, seeing a grey world on the edge of morning, the bare stubble of the ley riding quick on the close, peering between the shapes of the stacks, the lights of the lanterns shining in byre and stable and barn as Ewan feeded and mucked and tended horses and kye.

And the byre would hang heavy with the breaths of the kye, they'd have finished their turnips as she came in, and Ewan would come swinging after her with a great armful of straw to spread them in front, he'd tickle her neck as she sat to milk and she'd cry *Your hand's freezing!* and he'd say *Away, woman, you're still asleep. Up in the morning's the thing!* and go whistling out to the stable, Clyde

and Bess stamping there, getting fell cornfilled and frolic-
some, they more than wanted exercise. She would carry the
milk back herself most mornings and make the breakfast,
but sometimes Ewan would come with her, so young and
daft they were, folk would have laughed to see them at that,
both making breakfast and sitting them close to eat it.
Then Ewan would light his pipe when he'd done and sit
and smoke while she finished more slowly; and then he'd
say that he'd meat the hens, and she'd tell him not to haver,
she'd do that herself, and he'd argue, maybe sulk, till she
kissed him back to his senses again. Then he'd laugh and
get up and get down John Guthrie's gun, and be out and up
in the moors till eleven, sometimes he'd bring a great bag
and Chris would sell the spare rabbits to the grocer that
came on Tuesdays.

There was little to be done, such weather on Blawearie.
Ewan tidied the barn they'd danced in, it seemed years
ago since that night, and got ready plough and sock and
coulter for the time when the weather would break. And
then he found the bruised corn running low in the great
kist there, that was his first out-going from the place
since his marriage, Chris watched him go, sitting in the
front of the box-cart, Clyde in the shafts, the cart loaded
down with corn for the Mill, and Ewan turning to wave
to her from the foot of Blawearie brae. And all that afternoon he was away she fretted from room to room, oh! she
was a fool, there was nothing could happen to him! And
when at last he came back she ran out to him, fair scared
he was at the way she looked, and thought her ill, and when
she cried she had missed him so he went white and then
blushed, just a boy still, and forgot to unyoke Clyde left
in the cold, he was kissing Chris instead. And faith! for the
bairns of farmers both they might well have had more
sense.

But, and it crept into her mind that night and came
often in the morning and days that followed, somehow that
going of Ewan's to the Mill had ended the foolishness that
shut them in fast from Kinraddie and all the world, they
two alone, with all the gladness that was theirs alone and
her kisses the most that Ewan'd ever seek and his kisses

ending days and nights, and almost life itself for her. Kinraddie came in again, something of her own cool reliance came back, the winter wore on to its close, and mid-February brought the sun, weather that might well have come out of a May. Looking out from her window as every morning still she did, Chris saw the steam of the lands below the house, it was as though the earth had swung round the fields of Kinraddie into the maw of the sun, a great furnace, and left them there to dry. The hills marched their great banners of steam into the face of each sunrise and through the whisper and wakening and shrouding of the morning came presently the moan of the foghorn at Todhead, a dreadful bellow, like a sore-sick calf, it went on and on, long after the mist had cleared, it rose and faded into the sun-dazzle overhead as great clouds of gulls came wheeling in from the sea. They knew what was toward on Kinraddie's land, Chris heard the call of them as she went about the day's work, and looked out on the ley field then, there was Ewan with the horses, ploughing his first rig, bent over the shafts, one foot in the drill, one the rig side, the ploughshare, sharp and crude and new, cleaving the red-black clay. The earth wound back like a ribbon and curved and lay; and the cloud of gulls cawed and screamed and pecked on the rig and followed Ewan's heels again.

All over Kinraddie there were horse-pairs out, though none so early as Ewan's, it seemed, folk had stayed undecided about the weather, they'd other things to do, they'd say, than just wait about to show off like that young Blawearie. But, when the day rose and at nine Chris set her a jug of tea in a basket, and set by it scones well buttered and jammed, and carried out the basket to Ewan *wishing* up the face of the rig, Chae Strachan, far away and below, was a-bend above his plough-shafts at the tail of his team, Upperhill had two pairs in the great park that loitered up to the larchwood, and there was Cuddiestoun's pair, you guessed it him and his horses, though they never came full in sight, their heads and backs just skimmed the verge of the wood and hill.

Spring had come and was singing and rilling all over the fields, you listened and heard, it was like listening to

the land new wake, to the burst and flow of a dozen burns
in this ditch and that; and when you turned out the cattle
for their first spring dander, in case they went off the legs,
they near went off the face of the earth instead, daft and
delighted, they ran and scampered and slid, Chris was feared
that the kye would break their legs. She tried driving them
down to the old hayfield, but the steers broke loose and held
down the road, and Ewan saw them and left his plough
and chased them across the parks, swearing blue murder at
them as he ran; and faith! if it hadn't been for the postman
meeting them and turning them at the end of the road they
might well have been running still.

Chris had known then mazes of things to do in that bright
coming of the weather, the house was all wrong, it was foul
and feckless, Ewan unyoking at midday would come in and
make hardly his way through the kitchen, heaped high
with the gear of some room, Chris saw her long hands grow
sore and red with the scrubbing she did on the sour old
walls. Ewan said she was daft, the place was fine, what more
did she want? And she said *Less dirt;* and that maybe he
liked dirt, she didn't; and he laughed *Well, maybe I do,
I like you right well!* and put his arm round her shoulders
and they stood and kissed in the mid of the heaped and
littered kitchen—awful to be like that, said Chris, they
could hardly be sane.

In March the weather broke, the rain came down in
plashing pelts, you could hardly see a hand's-length in front
of your face if you ran through the close. Ewan sat in the
barn, winnowing corn or tying ropes, or just smoking and
swearing out at the rain. Chae Strachan came up for a talk
on the second day, all in oilskins he came; and he sat in the
barn with Ewan and said he'd seen it rain like this in Alaska,
and the mountains move when the snows were melting. And
Ewan said he didn't care a damn though Alaska moved
under the sea the morn, when would it clear on Blawearie?
Munro came next, then Mutch of Bridge End, they'd
nothing on their hands but watch the rain and shake their
heads and swear they were all fair ruined.

But at last it went, the unending rain of a fortnight went,

and that morning they woke and found it fine, Ewan took him a look at the land from the bedroom window and prompt lay back in the bed again. *Damn Blawearie and all that's on't, let's have a holiday the day, Chris quean.* She said *I can't, I'm cleaning the garret,* and Ewan got angered, she'd never seen him angry like that before, Highland and foreign then, spitting like a cat. *Are you to spend all your days cleaning damned rooms? You'll be old and wizened and a second Mistress Munro before you're well twenty. Off on a holiday we're going today.*

And, secretly glad, she lay back, lying with her hands under her head, lazy, and looking at him, thinking how different he was from that lad she'd tramped to Dunnottar with, so close she knew him now, the way he thought and the things he liked and his kindness and slowness to take offence, and the bitter offence, how it rankled in him, once it was there! Like and not like what she'd thought and wanted in those days before they had married. Spite of their closest moments together, Ewan could still blush at a look or a touch of hers; she touched him then to make sure, and he did! He said *Hold off! you're a shameless limmer, for sure, and not nineteen yet. Come on, let's get out and get off.*

So they raced through the morning's work and by nine were down at the Peesie's Knapp, and borrowed Chae's gig and heard Chae promise to milk and take in Blawearie's kye. Then out they drove and swung left through Kinraddie, into the Laurencekirk road, the sun shining and the peewits calling, there were snipe in a loch they passed, the North Sea was gloom-away by Bervie as the sholtie trotted south. You could see then as the land rose higher the low parks that sloped to the woods and steeple of Drumlithie, beyond that the hills of Barras, the Reisk in its hollow among its larch-woods. West of that rose Arbuthnott, a fair jumble of bent and brae, Fordoun came marching up the horizon in front of them then, and they were soon going through it. Ewan said if he bided in Fordoun he'd lay his neck on the railway line and invite the Flying Scotsman to run over it, so tired he'd be of biding in a place that looked like a barn painted by a man with nothing but thumbs and a squint in both eyes.

But Chris liked the little place, she'd never seen it before
and the farms that lay about it, big and rich, with fine black
loam for soil, different from the clay of bleak Blawearie.
Ewan said *To hell with them and their fine land too, they're
not farmers, them, only lazy muckers that sit and make
silver out of their cotters*; and he said he'd rather bide in
a town and wear a damned apron than work in this countryside. And then they were near Laurencekirk, the best of
weather the day held still, Laurencekirk looked brave in the
forenoon stir, with its cattle mart and its printing office
where they printed weekly the *Kincardineshire Observer*,
folk called it *The Squeaker* for short. It had aye had a hate
for Stonehaven, Laurencekirk, and some said that it should
be the county capital, but others said God help the capital
that was entrusted to it; and would speak a bit verse that
Thomas the Rhymour had made, how ere Rome——

> became a great imperial city
> 'Twas peopled first, as we are told,
> By pirates, robbers, thieves, banditti:
> Quoth Tammas: 'Then the day may come
> When Laurencekirk shall equal Rome.'

And when Laurencekirk folk heard that they would
laugh, not nearly cry as they did in Drumlithie when you
mocked at their steeple, or smile sick and genteel as they did
in Stonehaven when you spoke of the poverty toffs. Ewan
said it was a fine town, he liked Laurencekirk, and they'd
stop and have dinner there.

So they did, it was fine to eat food that another had
cooked. Then they looked at the day and saw how it wore
and planned to drive over to Edzell Castle—*There's nothing
to see there but a rickle of stones*, said Ewan, *but you'll like
them fine, no doubt*.

So they did as they'd planned, the afternoon flew, it was
golden and green. Under Drumtochty Hill they passed,
Ewan told that in summer it came deeper with the purple
of heather than any other hill in Scotland; but it hung dark
and asleep like a great cloud scraping the earth as they
trotted past. There was never a soul at the castle but themselves, they climbed and clambered about in the ruins, stone

on stone they were crumbling away, there were little dark chambers in the angle walls that had sheltered the bowmen long syne. Ewan said they must fair have been fusionless folk, the bowmen, to live in places like that; and Chris laughed and looked at him, queer and sorry, and glimpsed the remoteness that her books had made.

She was glad to be out in the sun again, though, clouds were racing it up from the North and Ewan said they'd not need to loiter long. In the garden of the castle they wandered from wall to wall, looking at the pictures crumbling there, balls and roses and rings and callipers, and wild heraldic beasts without number, Ewan said he was glad that they'd all been killed. But Chris didn't laugh at him, she knew right well that such beasts had never been, but she felt fey that day, even out here she grew chill where the long grasses stood in the sun, the dead garden about them with its dead stone beasts of an ill-stomached fancy. Folk rich and brave, and blithe and young as themselves, had once walked and talked and taken their pleasure here, and their play was done and they were gone, they had no name or remembered place, even in the lands of death they were maybe forgotten, for maybe the dead died once again, and again went on. And, daft-like, she tried to tell Ewan that whimsy, and he stared at her, pushing his cap from his brow, and looked puzzled and said *Ay*, half-heartedly; he didn't know what she blithered about. She laughed then and turned away from him, angry at herself and her daftness; but once she'd thought there wouldn't be a thing they wouldn't understand together. . . .

And the rain that had held away all the day came down at last and caught them on their way back home, overtaking them near to Laurencekirk, in a blinding surge that they watched come hissing across the fields, the sholtie bent its head to the storm and trotted on cannily, it grew dark all of a moment and Ewan found there was never a lamp on Chae's bit gig. He swore at Chae and then drove in silence, and the wind began to rise as they came on the long, bare road past Fordoun, near lifting the sholt from its feet; and out in the darkness they heard the foghorn moaning by Todhead lighthouse. They were a pair of drookéd rats when

they turned the gig into the close at Peesie's Knapp, and
Chae cried to them to come in and dry, but they wouldn't,
they ran all the way to Blawearie and the wet trees were
creaking in the wind as they reached to their door.

Now that was the last wet day of the Spring and to Chris
the weeks began to slip by like posts you glimpse from the
fleeing window of a railway train in a day of summer—light
and shade and marled wood, light and shade and the whoom
of the train, life itself seemed to fly like that up through
the Spring, Ewan had the corn land all ploughed and sown
himself almost early as was the Mains; only in the yavil did
Chris go out and carry the corn for him.

And that she liked fine, not a chave and a weariness
as it was with father, Ewan brisk and cheerful with the
smoulder gone from his eyes, they had settled to a clear, slow
shining, it seemed to Chris, now he had his own home and
wife. Then in the days of the harrowing Chris drove the
harrows while he carted manure to the turnip-land, she was
glad that she hadn't that work, glad to tramp behind the
horses instead, with kilted skirts, a switch in her hand and
the reins there and the horses plod-plodding steadily, they
knew her fine, and she spoiled them with bits of loaf and
jam so that Ewan, coming to drive them himself, cried
vexedly, *Hold up your head from my pockets, Clyde! What
the hell are you sniff-sniff-sniffing for?*

Then he went down to Stonehaven and bought a new
sower and sowed the turnips; and the night he finished and
unloosed and came back to the biggings for his supper, he
couldn't find Chris though he called and called. She heard
him calling and didn't answer, herself lying out in the
garden under the beeches, brave and green and rustling
their new Spring leaves, whispering without cease over her
head that was buried in the grass while she lay and thought.
A little insect ran over her hand and she hated it, but it
mightn't disturb her for this time at the least, nothing might
do that, she lay so certain and still because of this thing that
had come to her. She felt neither gladness nor pain, only
dazed, as though running in the fields with Ewan she had
struck against a great stone, body and legs and arms, and lay

stunned and bruised, the running and the fine crying in the
sweet air still on about her, Ewan running free and careless
still, not knowing or heeding the thing she had met. The
days of love and holidaying and the foolishness of kisses—
they might be for him yet but never the same for her, dreams
were fulfilled and their days put by, the hills climbed still
to sunset but her heart might climb with them never again
and long for tomorrow, the night still her own. No night
would she ever be her own again, in her body the seed of
that pleasure she had sown with Ewan burgeoning and
growing, dark, in the warmth below her heart. And Chris
Guthrie crept out from the place below the beech trees
where Chris Tavendale lay and went wandering off into the
waiting quiet of the afternoon, Chris Tavendale heard her
go, and she came back to Blawearie never again.

But she did not tell Ewan, not that night nor the week
that followed, nor the weeks after that, watching her own
body with a secret care and fluttering eyes for the marks
and stigmata of this thing that had come to her. And she
saw her breast nipples change and harden and grow' soft
again, the breasts that Ewan had kissed and thought the
wonder of God, a maid's breasts a maid's no longer,
changing in slow rhythm of purpose with the sway and
measure of each note in the rhythm, her belly rounding to
plumpness below the navel, she looked in the glass and saw
also her eyes changed, deeper and most strange, with red
lights and veinings set in them. And in the silences of the
night, when the whit-owl had quieted out by the barn, once
something moved there under her heart, moved and stirred
drowsily, a sleeper from dreams; and she gasped and cried
and then lay still, not wakening Ewan, for this was her rig
and furrow, she had brought him the unsown field and the
tending and reaping was hers, even as with herself when
she lay in her own mother's body. And she thought of that,
queer it seemed then how unclearly she had thought of that
aforetime, shamed, indecent and coarse for a quean to think
of such things—that her mother had once carried her as seed
and fruit and dark movingness of flesh hid away within her.

And she wakened more fully at that, lying thinking while
Ewan slept at her side, turned away from him, thinking of

mother, not as her mother at all, just as Jean Murdoch, another woman who had faced this terror-daze in the night. They went sleepless in the long, dark hours for the fruitage of love that the sower slept all unaware, they were the plants that stood dark and quiet in the night, unmoving, immobile, the bee hummed home and away, drowsy with treasure, and another tomorrow for the hunting his. So was the way of things, there was the wall and the prison that you couldn't break down, there was nothing to be done— nothing, though your heart stirred from its daze and suddenly the frozenness melted from you and still you might not sleep. . . . But now it was because of that babble of words that went round and around in your mind, soundless and scared of your lips, a babble of hours in the hills and loitering by lochs and the splendour of books and sleeping secure—babble of a world that still marched and cried beyond the prison walls, fair and unutterable its loveliness still outside the doors of Blawearie house, mocked by its ghost, a crying in the night for things that were lost and foregone and ended.

It quietened away then, morning came tapping at the window, she turned and slept, sleeping exhausted, rising with white face and slow steps so that she was long in the kitchen. And Ewan came hasting in, hurried that morning, the first of the turnips were pushing their thin, sweet blades of grass above the drills, he wanted to be out to them. *Damn't, Chris, are you still asleep?* he cried, half-laughing, half-angry, and Chris said nothing, going back to the dairy, Ewan stared and then moved uneasily and followed her with hesitant feet, *What's wrong? What's up?*

Turning to look at him, suddenly Chris knew that she hated him, standing there with the health in his face, clear of eyes—every day they grew clearer here in the parks he loved and thought of noon, morning and night; that, and the tending to beasts and grooming of horses, herself to warm him at night and set him his meat by day. *What are you glowering for?* he asked, and she spoke then at last, calmly and thinly, *For God's sake don't deave me. Must you aye be an old wife and come trailing after me wherever I go?*

He flinched like a horse with the lash on its back, his eyes kindled their smoky glow, but he swung round and away from her. *You're out of bed the wrong side this morning,* and out he went. She was sorry then, wanted to cry to him, dropped the pails to run after him, when he spoilt it all, crying from the middle of the close: *And I'd like my breakfast before the night comes down.*

It was as though she were dry whin and his speech a fire set to it, she ran out and overtook him there in the close, catching his shoulder and whirling him round, so surprised he was that he almost fell. *Speak to me like that?* she cried, *Do you think I'm your servant? You're mine, mind that, living off my meal and my milk, you Highland pauper!* . . . More than that she said, so she knew, no memory of the words abided with her, it was a blur of rage out of which she came with Ewan holding her shoulders and shaking her! *You damned bitch, you'd say that to me? To me?* . . . he was glaring like a beast, then he seemed to crumple, his hands fell from her. *Och, you're ill, you should be in your bed!*

He left her in the close then, striding to the barn, she stood like a fool with the tears of rage and remorse blinding her eyes. And as she went back to the kitchen and came out with the pails Ewan went striding away over the fields, his hoe on his shoulder, it was barely yet light, he was going to the parks without his breakfast. Milking the kye she hurried, her anger dying away, hurrying to be finished and have the breakfast ready, for he'd sure to be back again soon.

So she planned; but Ewan didn't come back. The porridge hottered to a thick, tough mess, beyond the raised blind the day broke thick and evilly red, hot like a pouring of steam across the hills; the tea grew cold. Herself half-desperate with hunger she waited, couldn't sit, wandering from fire to door and door to table; and then she caught sight on the dresser of the whistle that had lain by father while he lay in paralysis in bed, and snatched it down, and all in a moment had run over the close to the lithe of the corn ricks.

Shading her eyes she saw Ewan then, down in the turnip-park, swinging steady and quick in lunge and recovery, Kinraddie's best hoer. Then she whistled to him loud and clear down through the morning, half Kinraddie must have heard the blast, but he took no notice. Then she went desperate in a way, she stopped from whistling and screamed to him, *Ewan, Ewan!* and at her first scream he looked up and dropped his hoe—he'd heard her whistling all right, the thrawn swine! She screamed again, he was running by then over the parks to the close; him not ten yards away she screamed a third time, hurting her throat, but she did it calmly, anger boiled in her, yet in a way she was cool enough.

And Ewan cried *God, Chris, have you gone clean daft? What are you screaming for, what do you want?* He towered up above her, angry, amazed, it was then that she knew for sure, she gathered up all the force in her voice and body for the reply that sprang to her lips and the thing that followed it. *That!* she said, and struck him across the face with her arm's full force, her fingers cried agony and then went numb, on Ewan's face a great red mark sprang up, the clap of the blow went echoing around the Blawearie biggings.

So she saw and heard, only a moment, next minute he was at her himself like a cat, her head rang and dirled as he struck her twice, she tried to keep her footing and failed and fell back, against the rick-side, clutching at the thing, staring feared at Ewan, the madness on his face, his fists coming again. *Get up, get up!* he cried, *Damn you, get up!* and she knew he would strike her again, and rising shielded her face with her arm, trying to cram back the sobs in her throat, too late for that. Dizzy, she saw him in front of her swaying and moving, she couldn't see him but she cried *No, no!* and turned then and ran stumbling up through the close, up the hill to the moor. Twice he called as she ran, the second time so that nearly she stopped, *Chris, Chris, come back!* in a voice that was breaking as her own had been. But she couldn't stop running, a hare that the snare had whipped, *Never again, never again, the loch, the loch!* she sobbed as she ran and panted, the Standing Stones wheeling up from the whins to peer with quiet faces then in her face.

A quarter of an hour, half an hour, how long had she lain and dozed? Still morning in the air, she was soaked with

dew. She turned and half-rose, heard the whistling of the
broom and sank down again.

It was Ewan by the moor-gate, searching, he'd stopped to
stare at the loch, thinking the thing she had thought, not
seeing her yet. She sighed. She felt tired as though she had
worked a great day in the sweat of the land, but Ewan would
see to her, Ewan would take heed.

So she raised her voice and called to him and he came.

IV

HARVEST

It seemed to her that but hardly could she have left the place since that May-day more than six years ago when Ewan had come seeking her through the red, evil weather. She closed her eyes and put out a hand against the greatest of the Standing Stones, the coarse texture of the stone leapt cold to her hand, for a shivering wind blew down the hills. She started at thought of another thing then, opening her eyes to look round; but there he was, still and safe as he stood and looked at her. She cried *Stay by me, Ewan!* and he came running to her side; and she caught his hand and closed her eyes again, praying in a wild compassion of pity for that Ewan whose hand lay far from hers.

Six years: Spring rains and seeding, harvests and winters and springs again since that day that Ewan had come seeking her here with his white, chill face that kindled to warmth and well-being when she called him at last. She'd cried in his arms then, tired and tired, as he carried her down the hill; and the rage was quite gone from him, he bore her into the house and up to their bed, and patted her hand, and said *Bide you quiet!* and went off down the hill at a run.

So she learned he had run, and to Peesie's Knapp, but she didn't know then, she sank and sank away into sleep, and awakened long after with Ewan and still another man come in the room, it was Meldrum from Bervie, the doctor. He peeled off his gloves from his long white hands, and peered at her like a hen with his gley, sharp eye. *What's this you've been doing, Chris Guthrie?*

He didn't wait a reply but caught up her hand and wrist and listened, still like a hen, head on one side while Ewan stared at him greyly. Then he said *Well, well, that's fine, let's see a bit more of you, young Mistress Tavendale.*

While he listened with the funny things at his ears and the end of it on her chest, she closed her eyes, ill no longer though drowsy still, and peeked sideways at Ewan, smiling at him. And then the doctor moved his stethoscope further down, it tickled her bared skin there and she knew he knew, and he straightened up *And you tell me you didn't know what the thing was, Chris Tavendale?*

She said *Oh, yes,* and he said *But not Ewan?* and she shook her head and they both laughed at Ewan standing there staring from one to the other, black hair unbrushed, she had gone near to killing him that morning. And then Dr Meldrum shook him by the arm, *You're going to be a father, Blawearie man, what think you of that? Away and make me a cup of tea while Chris and I go into more intimate details—you needn't bide, she's safe enough with an old man, bonny though she be.*

All that he said as canny as ordering a jug of milk, Ewan gasped, and made to speak, and couldn't, but his face was blithe as he turned and ran down the stairs. They heard him singing below and old Meldrum cocked his head to the side and listened, *Damned easy for him to sing, eh, Chris? But you'll sing yourself when this bairn of yours comes into the world. Let's see if everything's right.*

It was. He put his hand on her shoulder when he finished and gave her a shake. *A body as fine and natural and comely as a cow or a rose, Chris Guthrie. You'll have no trouble and you needn't fret. But look after yourself, eat vegetables, and be still as kind to Ewan as the wear of the months will let you be. Good for him and good for you.* She nodded to that, understanding, and he gave her another shake and went down to Ewan, and drank the tea that Ewan had made, if tea it was, which you doubted later when you smelt the cups.

Ewan knowing, Meldrum knowing, it was as though a bank had gone down behind which she had dreamt a torrent and a storm would burst and blind and whelm her. But there was nothing there but the corn growing and the peewits calling, summer coming, marching up each morning with unbraided hair, the dew rising in whorling mists from the urgent corn that carpeted Ewan's tri:. fields. Nothing to fear and much to do, most of all to tell Ewan not to fret, she wasn't a doll, she'd be safe as a cow though she hoped to God she didn't quite look like one. And Ewan said *You look fine, bonnier than ever,* saying it solemnly, meaning it, and she was glad, peeking at herself in the long mirror when she was alone, seeing gradually that smooth rounding of belly and hips below her frock—lucky, she had never that ugliness that some poor folk have to bear, awful for them. She took pleasure in being herself, in being as before, not making a difference, cooking and baking and running to the parks with the early morning piece for Ewan, he'd cry *Don't run!* and she'd cry *Don't blether!* and reach beside him, and sink down beside him midway the long potato rows he was hoeing, growing low and broad and well-branched, the shaws, it was set a fine year for potatoes. And as he sat and ate she'd gather his coat below her head for a pillow, and lean back with her arms outspread in the sun and make of that few minutes her resting-time, listening to Ewan on the crops and the weather that was so good folk didn't believe it could last, there must soon be a break of the fine interplay of the last two months.

That was late in June he said that, and all the dour Howe watched the sky darkly, certain some trick was on *up there.* For the rain that was needed came in the night, just enough, not more, as though cannily sprinkled, and the day would be fine with sun, you couldn't want better; but it wasn't in the nature of things it would last. And Chris said, dreamily, *Maybe things are changing for the better all round,* and Ewan said *Damn the fears!* his gaze far off and dark and intent, the crops and the earth in his bones and blood, and she'd look in his face and find content, not jealous or curious or caring though she herself found in his eyes a place with the crops and land. And she'd close her eyes in the sun-dazzle then, in the smell, green, pungent, strong and fine, of the coming potato shaws, and sometimes she'd doze and waken sun-weary, Ewan working a little bit off, not clattering his hoe lest she wake.

She made up her mind she'd have the baby born in the

room that had once been her own. So she rubbed it and
scrubbed it till it shone again and brought out the bed
mattress and hung it to air, in the garden, between the
beeches, all in leaf they were, so thick. You could hardly see
the sky looking up in that malachite, whispering dome; and
by as she looked came Long Rob of the Mill to settle his bills
with Ewan, he saw Chris then and came to lean on the
hedge, hatless, and long as ever, with the great moustaches
and the iron blue eyes.

And he picked a sprig of the honeysuckle and bit it
between his teeth. *This'll be for the son, eh, Chris? And
when are you having him born?* She said *Late September
or early October, I think,* and Rob shook his head, it wasn't
the best time for bairns, though feint the fear for hers. And
he laughed as he leaned there, minding something and he
told Chris of the thing, his own mother it was, the wife of a
crofter down in the Reisk. She'd had her twelve children
in sixteen years, nine of them died, Rob was the oldest and
only a lad and he'd seen the youngest of his brothers born.
Seen? I helped, think of that, Chris quean! And think she
did and she shivered, and Rob said *That was daft, the
telling of that. But things are fair right with you, then,
Chris?*

So maybe, going home, he told of Blawearie's news; soon
Kinraddie knew more than did Chris herself. Folk began to
trail in about in the quiet of an evening, out of ill-fashionce,
and nothing much more, they'd gley sidewise at Chris as
they'd argue with Ewan, syne home they would go and tell
it was true, *Ay, there'll soon be a family Blawearie way,
Chris must fair have taken at the first bit sett.* But others
knew better, Mutch and Munro, and the speak went round
that the taking was well ere the marriage, Ewan had married
the quean when she threatened him with law. Kinraddie
mouthed that over, it was toothsome and tasty, and the
speak came creeping up to Blawearie, Chris never knew how
she heard it. But she did, Ewan did, and he swore to go out
and kick the backsides of Mutch and Munro till they'd
dream of sitting as a pleasure and a passion. And off he'd
have set in the rage of the moment but Chris caught him
and held him, that would only be daft, folk would think it

the truer, the scandal; and if it made them the happier to think as they did, let them think!

And then it seemed to Chris that her world up Blawearie brae began to draw in, in and about her and the life she carried, that moved now often and often, turning slow under her heart in the early days, but jerking with suddenness, a moment at a stretch now, sometimes, so that she would sit and gasp with closed eyes. In, nearer and nearer round herself and the house the days seemed to creep, Will in Argentine was somebody she'd met in a dream of the night, Aberdeenshire far away, nothing living or moving but shadows in sunlight or night outside the circle of the hills and woods she saw from Blawearie's biggings. Then fancies came on her and passed, but were daft and straining and strange while they lasted, she couldn't break herself of the things, they'd to wear and fade at their own bit gait.

One night it was that she couldn't touch kye, Ewan had to do the milking himself, sore puzzled and handless he was but she couldn't help that, though next morning she laughed at herself, what was there to fear in the milking of kye? Then came the day when they drove Chae Strachan's sheep to the buchts and the libbing of the lambs went on till it nearly drove her mad, the thin young baaing that rose an unending plaint, the folk with their pipes and knives and the blood that ran in the sunlight. All in a picture it rose to her on the sound of that baaing, and she hid in the dairy at last, the only place that shut out the sound.

But another fad, and the one that lasted the longest, was fear that all sounds would go, fear of the night when it might be so nearly still, Ewan sleeping with his head in his arm as he sometimes did, soundless, till she'd think him dead and shake him to a sleepy wakefulness; and he'd ask *What's wrong? Have I been stealing the blankets from you?* and she'd say *Yes*, ashamed to let him know of that fear of hers.

So she found the days blithe enough then, the scraich and scratch of hens in the close, the sound of the mower that Ewan drove up and down the rigs of the hay, the mooing of the calves wild-plagued with flies, Clyde's neighing to a passing stallion. Only night was the time to be feared, if she woke and there was that stillness; but even the quietest night if she listened hard she'd hear the wisp-wisp of the beech leaves near to the window, quietening her, comforting her, she never knew why, as though the sap that swelled in branch and twig were one with the blood that swelled the new life below her navel, that coming day in the months to be a thing she'd share with that whisperer out in the darkness.

And oh! but the time was long! She could almost have wished that she and Ewan had bedded unblessed as Mutch said they had, the baby would have been here by now and not still to come, still waiting harvest and stooking and the gathering of stooks. But it lay with her, warm and shielded, and saw with her the growth and ripening of that autumn's corn, yellow and great, and the harvest moons that came so soon in that year, red moons a-slant and a-tilt on the rim of the earth they saw as they went to bed, you felt it another land and another world that hung there in the quietness of the sky.

One night, the mid-days of August as they sat at meat, the door burst open and in strode Chae Strachan, a paper in his hand, and was fell excited, Chris listened and didn't, a war was on, Britain was to war with Germany. But Chris didn't care and Ewan didn't either, he was thinking of his coles that the weather might ruin; so Chae took himself off with his paper again, and after that, though she minded it sometimes, Chris paid no heed to the war, there were aye daft devils fighting about something or other, as Ewan had said; and God! they could fight till they were black and blue for all that he cared if only the ley field would come on a bit faster, it was near fit for cutting but the straw so short it fair broke your heart. And out he'd go in the evening light, down to the ley park and poke about there, rig to rig, as though coaxing the straw to grow and grow in the night for his delight in the morning. A bairn with a toy, Chris thought, laughing as she watched him then; and then came that movement in her body as she watched Ewan still—a mother with his child he was, the corn his as this seed of his hers, burgeoning and ripening, growing to harvest.

The corn was first. Up and down the rigs on his brave new
binder, Clyde and Bess each aside the pole, rode Ewan; and
the corn bent and was smitten on the fly-board, and gathered
up on the forking teeth and wound and bound and ejected.
Up and down went the whirling arms, and fine harvest
weather came then in Kinraddie, though it rained in Dee,
folk said, and down in Forfar the year was wet. Park by park
Ewan rode it down, Chris still could carry him a piece as he
worked, but she walked slow now, careful and slow, and
he'd jump from the binder and come running and meet her,
and down he would sit her in the lithe of a stook while he
stood and ate, his gaze as ever on the fields and sky, there was
still the harvest to finish.

But finished it was, September's end, and there came a
blatter of rain next day, Chris saw the coming of the rain
and the bright summer went as the stooks stood laden and
tall in the fields. And Chris found herself sick, a great pain
came and gripped at her breast, at her thighs, she cried
Ewan! and nearly fell and he ran to her. They stared in
each other's faces, hearing the rain, and then again the
pain drove through and through Chris like a heated sword,
and she set her teeth and shook Ewan free, she knew the
things she'd to do. *It'll maybe be a long time yet, but get
Chae to drive for the doctor and nurse. He'll bring the
nurse back from Bervie, Chae.*

Ewan stood and stared and his face was working, she
smiled at him then though the pain of the sword was as
nothing now, iron hooks were tearing in her body instead,
rusty and dragging and blunt. She held up her face to be
kissed and kept her teeth fast and said *Hurry, though I'm
fine!* and syne watched him run down the road to the Knapp.
Then, white, in a daze of pain, she began to walk backwards
and forwards on the kitchen floor, as she knew she must do
to bring on the birth quick, everything else was ready and
waiting in the room upstairs. And after a while the pain
waned and went, but she knew it would soon be back. So
she filled her a hot-water bottle and almost ran up the stairs
to put it in the bed, almost running lest the pain come
midway and catch her unaware. But it held off still, she
smoothed out the sheets, brought out the rubber one she'd

had bought, and tied that down, firm and strong, and set the great basin on the rug by the window and wondered what else there might be. Then she saw her face in the glass, it was flushed and bright and her eyes all hot; and suddenly she thought how strange it would be if she died, like the many women who died in chidlbed, she felt well and strong, they had felt the same, strange to think that her face might be dead and still in another day, that face that she looked at now, it couldn't be hers, it was still the face of a quean.

From the window she saw Ewan running back and as she reached to the foot of the stairs to meet him the pain came on her again, she had to sit down. But that was daft, it would make it last longer, she struggled to her feet and walked in the kitchen again, Ewan was in the doorway, a white blur of a face and nothing else unless she looked at him hard and hard. He kept saying *Chris, go and lie down!* and she opened her mouth and gasped and meant to tell him she was fine; and instead found herself swearing and swearing, terrible words she hadn't known she knew, they were wrung from her lips as she went stumbling to and fro, better than screaming, women screamed, but she wouldn't.

And then came relief again, the kitchen straightened and she sat down, Ewan emerged from his blur and made her tea. Something kept worrying her—what was he to have for his dinner? She couldn't remember the thing she'd intended, and gave it up, her tormentors were near-by again. *Boil yourself an egg, Ewan!* she gasped, and he didn't understand, he thought it something she wanted—*Boil what?* And at that a frenzy of irritation came on her, *Oh, boil your head if you like!* and she dragged herself to her feet, the clock on the mantelshelf was expanding and contracting, its dial blurred and brightened as she stood. And then she was sure, she cried *Ewan, help me up to the room,* for she knew that her time had come.

What happened then she didn't know, there came a clear patch and she found herself nude, all but a stocking, it wouldn't come off, she sat on the bedside and tried, Ewan tried, it was so funny she giggled in spite of the pain. And then she saw Ewan's face, it had grown to the face of an old man, now, she must lie and get him out of the room. She cried *Mind the fire, Ewan, there's no wood there, run and hack some*, and when he was out of the room she could heed to herself and her agony at last; and she bit the sheets, she rolled herself tight in a ball, the pain seemed to go for a moment, maybe she had smothered the baby, she didn't care, she couldn't abide it, not through hours and hours and days and days, for weeks it had gone on now, she had seen the room darken and lighten and night come, tormented by Ewan and father her body, and Will was dead, they had tortured him first.

She cried *Will!* then and opened her eyes from an hour-long sleep. In the room was the doctor and the nurse from Bervie, he came over to her side, old Meldrum, *Well, Chris lass, how do you feel? Fine to send for us in such a stour, and here we coming tearing up to find you sleeping like a lamb! This is Mrs Ogilvie, you've heard of her.*

Chris tried to speak, and managed, her body was a furnace, but she managed to speak, she didn't get it clear and she tried again. And Mrs Ogilvie patted her and said *Don't bother with that. Do you feel you're getting on fine?* Dr Meldrum came back then, *Well, let's see*; and Chris poised herself on the rim of a glistening cup of pain while they looked at and felt at and straightened something alien and white, it was her own body she remembered. Meldrum said *Fine, fine, it shouldn't be long, I'll wait below*, and went out and closed the door, he hated confinements. Mrs Ogilvie sat down and next minute jumped to her feet again, *Don't do that, Mrs Tavendale, don't grip yourself up! Slacken and it's easy, wish it to come, there's a brave girl!*

Chris tried: it was torment: the beast moved away from her breasts, scrabbled and tore and returned again, it wasn't a beast, red-hot pincers were riving her apart. Riven and riven she bit at her lips, the blood on her tongue, she couldn't bite more, she heard herself scream then, twice. And then there were feet on the stairs, the room rose and fell, hands on her everywhere, holding her, torment-ing her, she cried out again, ringingly, deep, a cry that ebbed to a sigh, the cry and the sigh with which young

Ewan Tavendale came into the world in the farm-house of
Blawearie.

So quick as all that, she was lucky, folk said, bringing
a birth in a forenoon, just; it was twelve when Ewan was
born. Some folk, Mrs Ogilvie told, had to thresh from dawn
to dusk and through another night to another day, and
Chris lay and nodded and said *Yes, I know*, and fell fast
asleep, she didn't dream at all. And, waking, she found
herself washed and dried, a new nightgown put on her and
Mrs Ogilvie knitting by the side of the bed, nothing else,
oh! she couldn't have dreamt and not known it. She whispered, scared, *My baby?* and Mrs Ogilvie whispered *Beside
you, don't crush him*, and Chris turned round her head
and saw then beside her a face as small as though carved
from an apple, near, perfect and small, with a fluff of black
hair and a blue tinge on long eyelids, and a mouth that was
Ewan's and a nose her own, and she nearly cried out *Oh,
my baby!*

So she lay and wondered, near cried again, and put out
her hand, it felt strong and quick, only heavy, and her
fingers passed up and along, under its swathings, a body as
small and warm as a cat's, with a heart that beat steady and
assured. And the baby opened his eyes and fluttered them
at her and yawned and she saw a tongue like a little red
fish in the little red mouth; and the blue-shaded eyelids went
down again and young Ewan Tavendale slept.

Sweet to lie beside him in the hours that went by, sleeping
herself now and then and wakening to watch him, not ugly
as she'd thought he'd be, lovely and perfect. And then he
moved and whimpered, unrestful, and was picked from the
bed in Mrs Ogilvie's hands, and fluttered his eyelids at her,
Chris saw, and opened his mouth and weeked like a kitten.
And Mrs Ogilvie said *He's hungry now*, Chris found him in
her arms at last, and hugged him, just once, and held him to
her breast. The blind little mouth came kissing and lapping,
he wailed his disappointment, his little hands clawing at
her. Then his lips found her nipple, it hurt and it didn't, it
was as though he were draining the life from her body, there
was nothing better than to die that way, he was hers close

and closer than his father had been, closer than again could any child be. And she wondered above him and kissed his black hair, damp still from the travail of birth; and looked at the eyes that stared so unwinkingly as the hungry lips clung to her breast. So at last he was finished, then Ewan came up, he'd come while she slept before and he bent and kissed her and she cried *Mind the baby!* and he said *By God, am I like to forget?* And he wiped his forehead, poor Ewan!

In a week Mrs Ogilvie was gone and Chris felt so well she was up and about, it was daft to lie wearied and feckless when she felt so fine. So down to the kitchen and the shining of the October sun she came, she and her baby, into the whisper and murmur of that war that had so excited Chae Strachan.

For it was on, not a haver only, every soul that came up to look at young Ewan began to speak of it sooner or later. Chae came and looked at young Ewan and tickled his toes and said *Ay, man!* And he told them they'd brought out a fine bit bairn between them, every man might yet have to fight for bairn and wife ere this war was over; and he said that the Germans had broken loose, fair devils, and were raping women and braining bairns all over Belgium, it was hell let loose. And Ewan said *Who'll win, then?* and Chae said if the Germans did there'd be an end of both peace and progress forever, there wouldn't be safety in the world again till the Prussians—and they were a kind of German, with meikle spiked helmets, awful brutes, and the very worst— were beaten back to the hell they came from. But Ewan just yawned and said *Oh, to hell with them and their hell both, Chae! Are you going to the mart the morn?*

For he didn't care, Ewan; but the mart was as bad, nobody spoke of anything but war, Munro of the Cuddiestoun was there, and Mutch, they'd a fair drink in their bellies, both, and swore they'd 'list the morn were they younger, by God. That was just the drink speaking, no doubt, but the very next day the Upperhill foreman, James Leslie he was that had taken Ewan's place, went into Aberdeen and joined in the Gordons, he was the first man to go from Kinraddie and was killed fell early. But folk thought him fair daft, showing off and looking for a holiday, just, there was no use coming to such stir as that when the war would so soon be over. For the papers all said that it would, right fierce they were, *Man, some of those editors are right rough creatures, God pity the Germans if they'd their hands on them!* And folk shook their heads, and agreed that the newspaper billies were ill to run counter.

But the Germans didn't care—maybe they didn't read the papers, said Long Rob of the Mill; they just went on with their raping of women and their gutting of bairns, till Chae Strachan came up to Blawearie one night with a paper in his hand and a blaze on his face, and he cried that he for one was off to enlist, old Sinclair could heed to the Knapp and to Kirsty. And Ewan cried after him, *You're havering, man, you don't mean it!* but Chae cried back *Damn't ay, that I do!* And sure as death he did and went off, by Saturday a letter came to Peesie's Knapp that told he had joined the North Highlanders and been sent to Perth.

So there was such speak and stir as Kinraddie hadn't known for long, sugar was awful up in price and Chris got as much as she could from the grocer and stored it away in the barn. Then Ewan heard funny things about the sermon that the Reverend Gibbon had preached the Sunday before, and though he couldn't bear with a kirk he broke his habit and put on his best suit and went down to the service next Sabbath. There was a fell crowd there, more than Ewan had heard of the last week's sermon, and the place was all on edge to hear what the Reverend Gibbon would say. He looked bigger and more like a bull than ever, Ewan thought, as he mounted the pulpit, there was nothing unusual as the gave out the hymn and the prayer. But then he took a text, Ewan couldn't mind which, about Babylon's corruptions, they'd been right coarse there. And he said that God was sending the Germans for a curse and a plague on the world because of its sins, it had grown wicked and lustful, God's anger was loosed as in the days of Attila. How long it would rage, to what deeps of pain their punishments would go, only God and His Anger might know. But from the chastisement by blood and fire the nations might rise anew, Scotland

not the least in its ancient health and humility, to tread
again the path to grace.

And just as he got there, up rose old Sinclair of the
Netherhill, all the kirk watched him, and he put on his hat
and he turned his back and went step-stepping slow down
the aisle, he ·wouldn't listen to this brute defending the
German tinks and some friend that he called Attila. Hardly
had he risen when Mutch rose too, syne Cuddiestoun, and
they too clapped on their hats; and Ellison half made to rise
but his wife pulled him down, he looked daft as a half-
throttled turkey then, Ella White wasn't to have him make
himself a fool for any damned war they waged. But the
minister turned red and then white and he stuttered when
he saw folk leaving; and his sermon quietened down, he
finished off early and rattled off the blessing as though it was
a cursing. Outside in the kirkyard some young folk gathered
to clout him in the lug as he came from the kirk, but the
elders were there and they edged them away, and Mr
Gibbon threaded the throngs like a futret with kittle, and
made for the Manse, and padlocked the gate.

But Ewan didn't care one way or the other, as he told to
Chris. The minister might be right or be wrong with his
Babylons and whores and might slobber Attila every night
of the week, Blawearie had its crop all in and that was what
mattered. And Chris said *Yes, what a blither about a war,
isn't it, Ewan?* and tickled young Ewan as he lay on her lap.
And he laughed and kicked and his father sat down and
looked at him, solemn, and said it was fair wonderful, *Did
you see him look up at me then, Chris quean?*

So they were douce and safe and blithe in Blawearie
though Kinraddie was unco with Chae Strachan gone.
Kirsty came up on a visit and cried when she sat in the
kitchen beside the crib, Chris made her tea but she wouldn't
take comfort. She said she knew well enough Chae'd never
come back, he was in such a rage with the Germans he'd
just run forward in his bit of the front and kill and kill till
he'd fair lost himself. Chris said *And they're maybe not such
bad folk as the papers make out*, and at that Kirsty Strachan
jumped up *So, you're another damned pro-German as well,
are you? There's over-many of your kind in Kinraddie*. Chris

stared clean amazed, but out Kirsty Strachan went running, still crying, and that was the last they saw of her in many a week, maybe she was ashamed of her outburst.

Whether or not *she* was, there could be never a doubt about the Reverend Gibbon. For the next Sabbath day, when another great crowd came down to the kirk to hear him preach, they got all the patriotism they could wish, the minister said that the Kaiser was the Antichrist, and that until this foul evil had been swept from the earth there could be neither peace nor progress again. And he gave out a hymn then, *Onward, Christian Soldiers* it was, and his own great bull's voice led the singing, he had fair become a patriot and it seemed likely he thought the Germans real bad But Long Rob of the Mill, when he heard the story, said it was a sight more likely that he thought the chance of losing his kirk and collections a damned sight worse than any German that was ever yet clecked.

For, and it grew a fair scandal all through the Howe, you could hardly believe it, it was funny enough, Long Rob of the Mill didn't hold with the war. He said it was a lot of damned nonsense, those that wanted to fight, the M.P.s and bankers and editors and muckers, should all be locked up in a pleiter of a park and made to gut each other with graips: there'd be no great loss to the world and a fine bit sight it would make for decent folk to look on at. But for folk with sense to take part in the soss and yammer about King and country was just plain hysteria; and as for Belgium invaded, it got what it needed, what about the Congo and your Belgians there? Not that the Germans weren't as bad, they were all tarred with the same black brush.

But, though folk weren't patriots as daft as Chae Strachan, that didn't look when he was being laughed at, they knew right well that Long Rob couldn't lie like that, the long, rangy childe, without being pro-German, as the papers called it. For all the papers were full of pro-Germans then, British folk that thought that the German rascals were right; and in England folk went and smashed in their windows, such a rage they were in with the pro-Germans for being so coarse. There was little danger that they'd smash

Rob's windows, there were few that cared to tackle the
childe except Chae Strachan that was training in Perth. So
the whole stour might well have blown over, Rob was a well-
liked billy and you needn't heed his blithers, if the Reverend
Gibbon hadn't taken to the business and preached a
sermon about tinks and traitors, and a lot he preached
about a jade called Jael, fell unchancy she'd been, right
holy, though, and she'd killed a childe Sisera that she
couldn't thole, because he was coarse to the Jews. And the
Reverend Gibbon boomed out she was fine, a patriot and
a light unto Israel she'd been, and we in like manner must
act the same, right here in our midst were traitors that sided
with the Anti-Christ, shame on Kinraddie that it should be
so!

Folk listened to the sermon and fair got excited, and after
dinner that Sabbath a horde of billies, some came from
Kinraddie though most did not, but Upperhill's new foreman was there, and an awful patriot childe just like Gordon
himself, they went down to the Mill, and there was Long
Rob sitting out by his door, smoking at his pipe and reading
in a book, coarse stite about God and God knows what. And
the Upperhill foreman cried out *Here's the Kaiser's crony,
let's duck the mucker!* and the lot made a run at Rob and
got him gripped in their hands, Rob thought it some joke
and he laughed at them, setting by his bit book. But they
soon let him know they were serious enough, they were
clean worked up about the sermon and Long Rob the Anti-
christ's friend, and they started to haul Rob over to the mill-
course then, where the water was sparkling and raging from
a good bit spate in the hills.

Syne at last Rob knew they meant what they said, folk
told that he gave a great cry that wasn't a curse and wasn't
a shout, it was both together; and as they dragged him he
lifted his foot, real coarse-like, and he kicked the foreman
at the Upperhill right in the private parts then, and the
foreman at the Upperhill he screamed like a fell stuck pig;
and God! folk laughed right well when they heard about
that. Well, the next thing that happened was that Rob got
a hand free then, and he took a childe near him, a meikle
man from the Mains, a clout in the ear that stretched him

flat; and then Rob was free and he ran, all the rest at his heels, for the house. But he could run right well, could Rob, and fair outdistanced the pack, and he leapt inside and he barred the door.

So they threw some stones and rammed at the door with their shoulders, half-shamed by then at the stour they were raising, and maybe they knew they'd feel fools by Monday; and they might have gone home in another minute if it hadn't been that the meikle Mains man, him that Rob had couped on the ground with a clout in the ear, crawled up to his feet and picked up a great stone; and crack! through the kitchen window it went with a bang and a splinter inside!

Next minute the door flung open, they turned and looked and there was Long Rob, a gun in his hand and his face grey with rage. Some cried *Take care, man, now, put down that gun!* but they edged away back for all that. And Rob cried out *Smash in my window you would, then, would you, you scum?* and he swung the gun at the nearest billy and let drive at him. The pellets sang past the billy's head and he'd had enough of the war, he turned and ran like a rabbit; and the others scattered and ran as well, and Long Rob ran after them, and his gun went bang! again and again, you could hear it all over Kinraddie. Folk ran to their doors, they thought the Germans had landed and were looting the Mearns; Chris, who had run across the Blawearie cornyard, shaded her eyes and looked over the country and at last she saw them, the running figures, like beetles in the distance, they fanned out and ran from the Mill as focus. And behind ran another that stopped now and then, and a puff of smoke went up at each stopping, and there came the bang of the gun. Mist was coming down and it blinded the battlefield, and through it the attacking army ran in an awful rout, Chris saw them vanish into its coming and Long Rob, still shooting, go scudding in chase.

So that was the result of the Reverend Gibbon's sermon, Kinraddie fair seethed with the news next day, all about the attack on the Mill and how Rob had chased the childes that came up against him, some could hardly sit down for a week after that, so full were their backsides with pellets.

And some said that Long Rob was a coarse tink brute, if he was willing to fight like that at the Mill it was him that should go out to France and fight; but others, though they weren't so many, Chris and Ewan were among them, liked Long Rob and sided with him, and said it was a damn poor show for Scotland if her patriots aye ran as they had at the Mill. That had been the Sunday, but on Wednesday was another happening, and God knows what mightn't have come of *it* but for the interfering of the daftie Tony, him that bided at Cuddiestoun.

He'd been stitering along the Denburn road, had Tony, when he rounded a bend and there, on the road outside the Mill, was the Reverend Gibbon, his bicycle was lying in the stour and Long Rob had him gripped by the collar, and if he wasn't in danger of a bash in the face appearances were sore deceptive. For Long Rob had seen the minister come riding in the distance and knew his black coat and stopped the Mill and ran down to the road to ask what the hell the Reverend had meant by saying he was friends with the Antichrist. And the Reverend Gibbon turned red with rage and cried *Stand out of my way there, Rob*, and Rob cried, *Stand still you first, my man, for we've a bit bone to pick!* and as the minister tried to ride him down Rob caught the handles and twisted them sore, and off the minister came, like a sack of corn, right flump in Rob's hands.

And Rob gave him a bit shake and asked *Who's pro-German?* and the minister swore himself blue and made at Rob, and Rob shook him like a futret a rabbit, and syne stood back and looked close at his face, and made up his mind that he'd smash in the minister's bit nose right then, he'd seen that kind of thing done before and it fair sossed up a pretty man, you just struck and struck till the bone gave way. So Rob was just starting to mash up the minister childe when round the bend with a funny bit screech came the daftie Tony, he scraiched like a hen with a seed in its throat and ran and caught at Rob's arm. *He's only a half-witted cieric, Rob, you'll dirty your hands on him*, he cried, and both Rob and minister, sore astounded, stopped from their fighting and stared at the creature, the impudence of him with his wee red beard, and him only a daftie, like. But he nodded to the minister *Get while the going's good and your hide's still intact*, he said; and if you'd believe it the minister louped on his bicycle without a word, and off he rode; and Long Rob turned and asked the daftie where he'd hidden his sense all the time they'd known him, but Tony stood still like a stock of rags, a daft-like look on his face. And when Rob spoke to him again he just smiled like a gowk, and went shuffling away through the stour.

Some said that if all things were true that wouldn't be a lie, but Rob swore to it, he wasn't boasting what he'd done to the minister, he said, he was just so astonished at Tony he'd to tell them the story to make Tony's part plain. Cuddiestoun swore 'twas a lie from beginning to end, the thing you'd expect from a damned pro-German, like; but he didn't say that to Long Rob, he was over coarse in the feet, Munro, to run as fleet as the other billies had when Rob got in action. But he stopped his trade with Long Rob and he carted his corn for crushing and bruising over to the mill at Mondynes, syne Mutch of Bridge End did the same. Ah well, they might do that if they liked, folk as a rule were hardly so daft as leave the best miller for miles around just because of his saying that all the Germans could hardly be tinks. Maybe, you know, there was something in what the man said, coarse devils though most of the Germans were.

But Chris didn't care, sitting there at Blawearie with young Ewan at her breast, her man beside her, Blawearie theirs and the grain a fine price, forbye that the stirks sold well in the marts. Maybe there was war and bloodshed and that was awful, but far off also, you'd hear it like the North Sea cry in a morning, a crying and a thunder that became unending as the weeks went by, part of life's plan, fringing the horizon of your days with its pelt and uproar. So the new year came in and Chris watched young Ewan change and grow there at her breast, he was quick of temper like his father, good like his mother, she told Ewan; and Ewan laughed *God, maybe you're right! You could hardly be wrong in a thing after bringing a bairn like that in the world.* And she laughed at him *But you helped a little!* and he blushed as red as he always did, they seemed daft as ever in their love as the days wore on. It was still as strange and as kind to lie with him, live with him, watch the sweat on his forehead when he came from tramping a day in the parks at the heels of his horses; still miracle to hear beside her his soundless breathing in the dark of the night when their pleasure was past and he slept so soon. But she didn't herself, those nights as the Winter wore to March, into Spring: she'd lie and listen to that hushed breathing of his one side of her, the boy's quicker breath in his cradle out by—content, content, what more could she have or want than the two of them, body and blood and breath? And morning would bring her out of her bed to tend young Ewan and make the breakfast and clean out the byre and the stable, singing; she worked never knowing she tired and Long Rob of the Mill came on her one morning as she cleaned the manure from the stable and he cried *The Spring of life, eh, Chris quean? Sing it and cherish it, 'twill never come again!*

Different from the old Rob he looked, she thought, but thought that carelessly, hurried to be in to young Ewan. But she stopped and watched him swing down the rigs to Ewan by the side of his horses, Ewan with his horses halted on the side of the brae and the breath of them rising up like a steam. And she heard Ewan call *Ay, man, Rob*, and Rob call *Aye, man, Ewan*, and they called the truth, they seemed fine men both against the horizon of Spring, their feet deep laired in the wet clay ground, brown and great, with their feet on the earth and the sky that waited behind. And Chris looked at them over-long, they glimmered to her eyes as though they had ceased to be there, mirages of men dreamt by a land grown desolate against its changing sky. And the Chris that had ruled those other two selves of herself, content, unquestioning these many months now, shook her head and called herself daft.

That year's harvest fell sharp away, but the price of corn made up for it, other prices might rise but farming folk did well. So it went in the winter and into the next year too, Ewan took in a drove of Irish steers to eat up the lush green grass of nineteen-sixteen. They grew fat and round in the shortest while, Chris proud to see them, so many beasts had Blawearie. You'd hardly believe 'twas here father had

chaved and fought for a living the way he did; but that was
before the War.

For it still went on, rumbling its rumours like the thunder
of summer beyond the hills. But nobody knew now when
it would finish, not even Clae Stratchen come home, a
soldier all the way from the front, as they called it; in the
orra-looking khaki he came, with two stripes sewn on his
arm, he said they had made him a corporal. He came up to
Blawearie the night he got home and scraped his feet on
the scraper outside and came dandering into the kitchen as
aye he had done, not knocking but crying through the door,
Ay, folk, are you in?

So there was Chae, Chris gave a loud gasp to see him,
Chae himself, so altered you'd hardly believe it, Chae himself, thin, his fine eyes queered and strained somehow. Even
his laugh seemed different, hearty as it was, and he cried
God, Chris, I'm not a ghost yet! and syne Chris and Ewan
were shaking his hands and sitting him down and pouring
him a dram and another after that. And young Ewan came
running to see and cried *soldier!* and Chae caught him and
swung him up from the floor and cried *Chris's bairn—God,
it can't be, I mind the day he was born, just yesterday it was!*

Young Ewan took little to strangers, most, not frightened
but keep-your-distance he was, but he made no try to keep
distant from Chae, he sat on his knee as Chris spread them
supper and Chae spoke up about things in the War, it wasn't
so bad if it wasn't the lice. He said they were awful, but
Chris needn't be feared, he'd been made to stand out in the
close by Kirsty and strip off everything he had on, and
fling the clothes in a tub and syne get into another himself.
So he was fell clean, and God! he found it a change not trying to reach up his shoulders to get at some devil fair sucking and sucking the life from his skin.

And he gave a great laugh when he told them that, his
old laugh queerly crippled it was. And Ewan asked what he
thought of the Germans, were they truly coarse? And Chae
said he was damned if he knew, he'd hardly seen one alive,
though a body or so you saw now and then, gey green and
feuch! there's a supper on the table! Well, out there you
hardly did fighting at all, you just lay about in those damned

bit trenches and had a keek at the soil they were made of. And man, it was funny land, clay and a kind of black marl, but the French were no good as farmers at all, they just pleitered and pottered in little bit parks that you'd hardly use as a hanky to wipe your neb. Chae didn't like the French at all, he said they were damned poor folk you'd to fight for, them, meaner than dirt and not half so sweet. And Ewan listened and said *So you don't think that I should join up, Chae?* and Chris stared at him, Chae stared at him, young Ewan stared, and they all three stared till Chae snorted *There are fools enough in the fighting as it is.* Chris felt something holding her throat, she'd to cough and cough, trying to speak, and couldn't, and Ewan looked at her shamed-like and blushed and said *Och, I was asking, only.*

Chae went round all Kinraddie on his leave that time and found changes enough to open his eyes, maybe he was fell wearied with the front, folk thought, there was nothing on there but their pleitering and fighting. And the first change he saw the first morning, did Chae, lying down on his bed for the pleasure of it and Kirsty at the making of his breakfast. And Chae sat up in his bed to reach for his pipe when he looked from the window and he gave a great roar; and he louped from his bed in his sark so that Kirsty came running and crying *What is't? Is't a wound?* But she found Chae standing by the window then, cursing himself black in the face he was, and he asked how long had *this* been going? So Mistress Strachan looked out the way he looked and she saw it was only the long bit wood that ran by the Peesie's Knapp that vexed him, it was nearly down the whole stretch of it, now. It made a gey difference to the look-out faith! but fine for Kinraddie the woodmen had been, they'd lodged at the Knapp and paid high for their board. But Chae cried out *To hell with their board, the bastards, they're ruining my land, do you hear!* And he pulled on his trousers and boots and would fair have run over the park and been at them; but Kirsty caught at his sark and held him back and cried *Have you fair gone mad with the killing of Germans?*

And he asked her hadn't she got eyes in her head, the fool, not telling him before that the wood was cut? It would lay

the whole Knapp open to the north-east now, and was fair
the end of a living here. And Mistress Strachan answered
up that she wasn't a fool, and they'd be no worse than the
other folk, would they? all the woods in Kinraddie were due
to come down. Chae shouted *What, others?* and went out to
look; and when he came back he didn't shout at all, he said
he'd often minded of them out there in France, the woods,
so bonny they were, and thick and brave, fine shelter and
lithe for the cattle. Nor more than that would he say, it
seemed then to Kirsty that he quietened down, and was
quiet and queer all his leave, it was daft to let a bit wood
go vex him like that.

But the last night of his leave he climbed to Blawearie
and he said there was nothing but the woods and their fate
that could draw his eyes. For over by the Mains he'd come
on the woodmen, teams and teams of them hard at work on
the long bit forest that ran up the high brae, sparing nothing
they were but the yews of the Manse. And up above Upperhill they had cut down the larch, and the wood was down
that lay back of old Pooty's. Folk had told him the trustees
had sold it well, they got awful high prices, the trustees did,
it was wanted for aeroplanes and such-like things. And over
at the office he had found the factor and the creature had
peeked at Chae through his horn-rimmed glasses and said
that the Government would replant all the trees when the
War was won. And Chae had said that would console him
a bloody lot, sure, if he'd the chance of living two hundred
years and seeing the woods grow up as some shelter for beast
and man; but he doubted he'd not last so long. Then the
factor said they must all do their bit at a sacrifice, and Chae
asked *And what sacrifices have you made, tell me, you
scrawny wee mucker?*

That wasn't fair to the factor, maybe, who was a decent
childe and not fit to fight, but Chae was so mad he hardly
knew what he said, and didn't much care. So when he fell
in with old Ellison things were no better. For Ellison'd
grown fair big in the mind and the pouch, folk said he was
making silver like a dung-heap sourocks; and he'd bought
him a car and another piano; and he said *Ow, it's you,
Charles lad! Are you home for long?* and he said *And I'll bet*

you want back to the front line, eh? And Chae said that he'd
be wrong in the betting, faith ay! *Did you ever hear tell of a
body of a woman that wanted a new bairn put back in her
womb?* And Ellison gowked and said *No.* And Chae said
And neither have I, you gowk-eyed gomeril, and left him at
that; and it was hardly a kindly remark, you would say.

But it seemed the same wherever he went in Kinraddie,
except at the Mill and his father-in-law's; every soul made
money and didn't care a damn though the War outlasted
their lives; they didn't care though the land was shaved of
its timber till the whole bit place would soon be a waste
with the wind a-blow over heath and heather where once
the corn came green. At Cuddiestoun he came on the Munro
pair, they were rearing up hundreds of chickens that year
and they sold them at great bit prices to the Aberdeen
hospitals. So busy they were with their incubators they'd
but hardly time to take notice of him, Mistress Munro
snapped and tweeted at him, still like a futret, and the
creature wrinkled its long thin neb: *Ah well, we'll have to
get on with our work. Fine being you and a soldier, Chae,
with your holidays and all. But poor folk aye have to work.*
Munro himself looked shamed at that and coloured all over
his ugly face, poor stock, but he'd hardly time to give Chae
a dram, so anxious he was with a new brood of hens. So
Chae left him fell quick, the place got on his stomach and
syne as he held through the parks he came bang on Tony,
standing right mid-way the turnip-field. And his eyes were
fixed on the ground and God! he might well have stood there
for days by the look of him. Chae cried out to him *Ay, then,
Tony man* not expecting any reply, but Tony looked up and
aside, *Ay, Chae, so the mills of God still grind?*

And Chae went on, and he thought of that, a real daft-like
speak he thought it at first, but further up the brae as he
held by Upprums, he scratched his head, was the thing so
daft? He stopped and looked back, and there, far below,
was the Tony childe, standing, glued to the ground. And
Chae shivered in a way, and went on.

So Chae wandered his round of Kinraddie, a strange place
and desolate with its crash of trees and its missing faces.
And not that alone. for the folk seemed different, into their

bones the War had eaten, they were money-mad or mad
with grief for somebody killed or somebody wounded—like
Mistress Gordon of the Upperhill, all her pride gone now
because of the Jock she had loved and aye called John. But
it was Jock she called him when Chae sat with her in the
parlour then, and she told him the news of her blinded son
in the hospital in England. He wouldn't ever see again, it
wasn't just a nervous trouble or anything like that, he'd
drawn back the bandages when she went to see him and
shown her the great red holes in his head; and syne he'd
laughed at her, demented like, and cried: *What think you
of your son now, old wife?—the son you wanted to make a
name for you with his bravery in Kinraddie? Be proud, be
proud, I'll be home right soon to crawl round the park and
I'll show these holes to every bitch in the Mearns that's looking for a hero.* He'd fair screamed the words at his mother
and a nurse had come running and soothed him down, she
said he didn't know what he said, but Mistress Gordon had
never a doubt about that. And she told Chae about it
and wept uncovered, her braveness and her Englishness all
fair gone; and when Gordon came into the room he looked
different too, shrivelled up he was, he'd taken to drink,
folk said.

So Chae went out across the parks to the Bridge End then
and half-wished that he'd missed the Upperhill. But across
the nethermost park below the larch wood he ran into young
Maggie Jean, her that Andy the daftie had near mischieved,
grown a gey lass, and he hardly knew her. But she knew him
fine and smiled at him, blithe and open. *It's Chae Strachan!
You look fine as a soldier, Chae! And please can I have a
button?* So he cut off a button from his tunic for her and
they smiled at each other, and he went out across the fields
with a lighter heart then, she was sweet as a sprig of
Blawearie 'suckle.

Bridge End he found with Alec away, he'd gone selling
sheep in Stonehaven. But Mistress Mutch was there and she
sat and smoked at a cigarette and told him that Alec was
still a fell patriot, he'd enrolled in the volunteers of Glenbervie and every other night went down to Drumlithie for
drill, a sight for sore eyes, the gowks, prancing about like

dogs with diarrhœa, that's what they minded her of. And
she asked Chae when the War was to end, and Chae said
God only knows and she asked *And you still believe in Him?*
And Chae was real shocked, a man might have doubts and
his disbelief, you expected a woman to be different, they
needed more support in the world. But now that he thought
of God for himself he just couldn't say, there was more of
his Enemy over in France, that minded him now he must
give the Reverend Gibbon a look up at the Manse. But
Mistress Mutch said *Haven't you heard, then? Mr Gibbon's
gone, he's a Colonel-chaplain in Edinburgh now, or something like that; and he wears a right brave uniform with a
black hanky across the neck of it. His father's come down to
take his place, an old bit stock that drinks German blood
by the gill with his porridge, by the way he preaches.*

At Pooty's Chae knocked and knocked and got feint the
answer. And folk were to tell him that wasn't surprising,
old Pooty had taken to locking himself in nowadays, he got
queerer and queerer, he said every night he heard men
tramping the roads in the dark, chill hours, and they crept
off the roads and slithered and slipped by the hedges and
fields, and he knew who they were, they were Germans, the
German dead from out of the earth that had come to work
ill on Scotland. And even in the daytime if you but looked
quick, right sharp and sudden between the bending of a
bough or the bar of a gate, you'd see a white German
face, distorted still in the last red pain, haunting the
Scottish fields. And that was queer fancying well you might
say.

But Chae knew nothing of the business, he near knocked
in the door of the little house ere he gave it up and went ben
the road to Long Rob's. And Rob saw him coming and
turned off the Mill and ran to meet him, and they sat and
argued the rest of the day, Rob brought out his bottle and
they had a bit dram; and then Rob made them their supper
and they'd another long dram, and they argued far to the
wee, small hours. And Chae swore that he still believed the
War would bring a good thing to the world, it would end
the armies and fighting forever, the days of socialism at last
would dawn, the common folk had seen what their guns

could do and right soon they'd use them when once they came back.

And Rob said *Havers, havers. The common folk when they aren't sheep are swine, Chae man; you're an exception, being a goat.*

Well, it was fine enough that long arguing with Rob, but out in the dark by the side of Chae as they walked along the road together Rob cried *Oh man, I'd go back with you the morn if only*—and the words fair seemed to stick in his throat. And Chae asked *If only, what, man?* and Rob said *If only I wanted to be easy—easy and a liar. But I've never gone that gait yet and I'm damned if I'll begin for any bit war!*

And what he meant by that Chae didn't know, he left him then and held over the moor land towards the Knapp under the rising moon. And it was there that a strange thing happened to him, maybe he'd drunk over much of Long Rob's whisky, though his head was steady enough as a rule for thrice the amount he'd drunk. Ah well, the thing was this, that as he went over an open space of the vanished Standing Stones he saw right in front of him a halted cart; and a man had got out of the cart and knelt by the axle and looked at it. And Chae thought it some carter billy from the Netherhill taking the near cut through the moor, and steered out to go by and cried *Good night, then.* But there wasn't an answer, so he looked again, and no cart was there, the shingly stones shone white and deserted under the light of the moon, the peewits were crying away in the distance. And Chae's hackles fair stood up on end, for it came on him that it was no cart of the countryside he had seen, it was a thing of light wood or basketwork, battered and bent, low behind, with a pole and two ponies yoked to it; and the childe that knelt by the axle had been in strange gear, hardly clad at all, and something had flashed on his head, like a helmet maybe. And Chae stood and swore, his blood running cold, and near jumping from his skin when a pheasant started under his feet with a screech and a whirr and shot away into the dimness. And maybe it was one of the men of old time that he saw there, a Calgacus' man from the Graupius battle when they fought the Romans up from the south; or maybe it had only been the power of Long Rob's Glenlivet.

So that was Chae's round of the countryside, in a blink his leave was gone and Chae had gone with it, folk said he was still the same old Chae, he blithered still about Rich and Poor, you'd have thought the Army would have taught him better. But Chris stuck up for him, Chae was fine, not that she herself cared for the Rich and Poor, she was neither one nor the other herself. That year the crops came so thick Ewan said they must hire some help, and that they did, an oldish stock from Bervie he was, gey handless at first, John Brigson his name. But he soon got into the set of Blawearie, sleeping in the room that had once been Chris's, and making rare friends with young Ewan, it was lucky they had him. And the harvest came fine and Chris thought it near time that another baby should come to Blawearie. They'd been careful as blithe in the thing so far, but now it was different, Ewan'd love to have another.

And one night went on and then another, and she whispered to herself *In the Spring I'll tell him*; and the New Year went by; and then news came up to Blawearie in a wave of gossip from all over the Howe. For the Parliament had passed the Conscription Act, that meant you'd to go out and fight whatever you said, they'd shoot you down if you didn't. And sure as death Ewan soon had his papers sent to him, he'd to go up to Aberdeen and be there examined, he'd been excused before as a farmer childe. Long Rob got his papers on the very same day and he laughed and said *Fine, I'll like a bit jaunt*.

And into Aberdeen they all went, a fair crowd of them then, all in one carriage; and the ploughmen all swore that they didn't care a button were they taken or not; and Ewan knew right well that they wouldn't take him, they didn't take folk that farmed their own land; and Long Rob said nothing, just sat and smoked. So they came to Aberdeen and went to the place and sat in a long bare room. And a soldier stood near the door of the room and cried out their names one after the other; and Long Rob sat still and smoked his pipe. So they finished at last with the ploughmen childes, the whole jing-bang were passed as soldiers. And they called Long Rob, but he just sat still and smoked his pipe, he wouldn't stir out of his jacket, even. So there was a great bit stir at that, they danced around him and swore at him, but he blew his smoke up in their faces, calm, like a man unvexed by midges met on a summer day.

They gave up the try, they did nothing to him then, he came back to the Howe and sat down at the Mill. But next he was called to appear at Stonehaven, the Exemption Board sat there for the cases; and Rob rode down on his bicycle, smoking his pipe. So they called out his name and in he went and the chairman, a wee grocer man that worked night and day to send other folk out to fight the Germans, he asked Long Rob how he liked the idea that folk called him a coward? And Long Rob said *Fine, man, fine. I'd rather any day be a coward than a corpse.* And they told him he couldn't have exemption and Long Rob lit up his pipe and said that was sad.

Home to the Mill he came again, and that night folk saw him on the round of his parks, standing and smoking and looking at his land and sky, the long rangy childe. Ewan went by fell late that evening and saw him and cried *Ay, Rob!* but the miller said never a word, Ewan went home to Blawearie vexed about that. But Chris said it was just that Long Rob was thinking of the morn, he'd been ordered to report to the Aberdeen barracks.

And the next day passed and all Kinraddie watched from its steadings the ingoings and outgoings of Rob at the Mill; and damn the move all the day long did he make to set out as they'd ordered him. The next day came, the policeman came with it, he rode up to the Mill on his bicycle and bided at the Mill a good two hours and syne rode out again. And folk told later that he'd spent all that time arguing and prigging at Rob to set out. But Rob said *If you want me, carry me!* and faith! the policeman couldn't very well do that, angered though he was, it would look fair daft wheeling Rob along the roads on his bicycle tail. So the policeman went off to Stonehaven and out from it late in the evening there drove a gig, the policeman again, and two home-time soldiers, it needed all three to take Rob of the Mill away

to the war. He wouldn't move even then, though he made
no struggle, he just sat still and smoked at his pipe, and
they'd to carry him out and put him in the gig. And off they
drove, that was how Long Rob went off to the War, and
what happened to him next there rose this rumour and
that, some said he was in jail, some said he'd given in, some
said he'd escaped and was hiding in the hills; but nobody
knew for sure.

And to Chris it seemed then, Chae gone, Rob gone, that
their best friends were out of Kinraddie now, friends close
and fine, but they had themselves, Ewan and her and young
Ewan. And she held close to them both, working for them,
tending them, seeing young Ewan grow straight and strong,
with that slim white body of his, like his father's, just; and
it made a strange, sweet dizziness go singing in her heart as
she bathed him, he stood so strong and white, she would
mind that agony that had been hers at the birth of this body,
it had been worth it and more. And now she wanted another
bairn, Spring was coming, fast and fast, the land smelt of it,
the caller sea winds came fresh with the tang that only in
Spring they brought, it was nineteen-seventeen. And Chris
said in her heart that in April their baby would be
conceived.

So she planned and went singing those days about the
kitchen of Blawearie toun, busy with this plot, she planned
fresh linen and fresh clothes for herself, she grew young and
wayward as before she married, and she looked at Ewan
with secret eyes. And old John Brigson would cry *Faith,
mistress, you're light of heart!*

But Ewan said nothing, strange enough that. She knew
then that something troubled him, maybe he was ill and
would say nothing about it, sitting so silent at meat and
after, it grew worse as the days went on. And when he looked
at her no longer was the old look there, but a blank, dark
one, and he'd turn his face from her slowly. She was vexed
and then frightened and out in the close one morning, over
the stillness of the hen's chirawk, she heard his voice raised
in cursing at Brigson, it was shameful for him to do that
and not like Ewan at all to do it. Then he came back from

the steading with quick stepping feet, as he passed through the kitchen Chris cried *What's wrong?* He muttered back *Nothing*, and went up the stairs, and he took no notice of young Ewan that ran after him, bairn-like, to show him some picture in a book he had.

Chris heard him rummage in their room, and then he came down, he was fully dressed, his dark face heavy and stranger than ever, Chris stared at him *Where are you going?* and he snapped *To Aberdeen, if you'd like to know*, and off he went. He had never spoken to her like that—he was EWAN, hers! . . . She stood at the window, dazed, looking after him, so strange she must then have looked that little Ewan ran to her, *Mother, mother!* and she picked him up and soothed him and the two of them stood and watched Ewan Tavendale out of sight on the bright spring road.

It seemed to Chris he had hated her that minute when he looked at her in the kitchen, she went through the day with a twist of sickness about her heart. To old Brigson, shamed for her man, she said that Ewan had been worried with this business and that, he'd been out of his temper that morning and had gone to Aberdeen for the day. And John Brigson said cheerily *Never heed, mistress. He'll be right as rain when he's back the night*, and he helped her wash up the supper things, and they had a fine long talk. Syne off he went to tend to the beasts, and Chris grew anxious, looking at the clock, till she minded that there was a later train still, the ten o'clock train. So she bedded young Ewan and milked the kye, and came back to the kitchen, and waited. John Brigson had gone to his bed, Blawearie was quiet, she went out and walked down to the road to meet Ewan in the fresh-fallen dew of the night—so young the year and so sweet, she'd make it this night, the night with Ewan that she'd planned!

By Peesie's Knapp a snipe was sounding, she stood and listened to the bird, and saw in the starlight the skeleton timbers of the great wood that once fronted the north wind there. A hare scuttled over the road, the ditches were running and trilling, hidden, filled with the waters of Spring, she smelt the turned grass of the ploughlands and shivered in the blow of the wind, Ewan was long on the road. At the turnpike bend she stopped and listened for the sound of his feet, and minded a thing out of childhood then, if you put your ear to the ground you'd hear far off steps long ere you'd hear them when standing and upright. And she laughed to herself, remembering that, and knelt on the ground, agile and fleet, as the Guthries were, and put close her ear to the road, it was cold and crumbly with little stones. She heard a flock of little sounds going home to their buchts, far and near, each sound went home, but never the sound of a footstep.

And then, Stonehaven way, a great car came flashing down through the night, its headlights leaping from brae to brae, Chris stood back and aside and she saw it go by, there were soldiers in it, one bent on the wheel, she saw the floating ends of his Glengarry bonnet, the car whirled past and was gone in the night. She stared after it, dazed and dreaming, and shivered again. Ewan must have held over the hills and was already at Blawearie, it was daft to be here, he'd be anxious about her and go out seeking *her*!

So she ran back to Blawearie and she got there panting. But her heart was light, she'd play a trick on Ewan, creep in on him quiet as quiet, come up behind him sudden in the kitchen and make him jump. And she padded softly across the close to the kitchen door and looked in, and the lamp stood lit on the table, and the place was quiet in its glow. She went up the stairs to their room, there was no sign of Ewan, young Ewan lay sleeping with his face in the pillow, she righted him away from that and went down to the kitchen again. She sat in a chair there, waiting, and her heart froze and froze with the fears that came up in it, she saw Ewan run over by a car in the streets, and why hadn't they sent her a telegram? But maybe she was wrong, maybe he'd missed the last train and taken one out to Stonehaven instead and was tramping from there in the darkness now. She piled new logs on the fire and sat and waited, and the night went on, she fell fast asleep and waking found the lamp gone out, in the sky between bar and blind was a sharp, dead whiteness like the hand of a corpse. And as she stretched herself, chilled and queer, up in John Brigson's room the alarum clock went. It was half-past five, the night had gone, and still Ewan had not come back.

Nor came he back that day, nor many a day beyond that. For the postman at noon brought Chris a letter, it was from Ewan and she sat in the kitchen and read it, and didn't understand, and her lip hurt, and she put up the back of her hand to wipe it and looked at the hand and saw blood on it. Young Ewan came playing about her, he took the letter out of her hand and ran off with it, screaming with laughter in his young, shrill voice, she sat and did not look after him and he came back and laughed in her face, surprised that she did not play. And she took him in her arms and asked for the letter again, and again she tried to read it. And what Ewan wrote was he'd grown sick of it all, folk laughing and sneering at him for a coward, Mutch and Munro aye girding at him. He was off to the War, he had joined the North Highlanders that day, he would let her know where they sent him, she wasn't to worry; and *I am yours truly Ewan.*

When John Brigson came in at dinner-time he found Chris looking white as a ghost, but she wasn't dazed any longer, it just couldn't be helped, Ewan was gone but maybe the war would be over before he had finished with his training. And John Brigson said *Of course it will, I see the Germans are retreating on all the fronts, they're fair scared white, they say, when our men take to the bayonet.* Little Ewan wanted to know what a bayonet was and why the Germans were scared of them, and John Brigson told him and Chris was sick, she'd to run out to be sick, for if you've ever gutted a rabbit or a hen you can guess what is inside a man, and she'd seen a bayonet going into Ewan there. And John Brigson was awful sorry, he said he hadn't thought, and she wasn't to worry, Ewan would be fine.

Oh, but that Spring was long! Out in the parks in the day-time she'd go to help John Brigson and ease her weariness, she took little Ewan with her then and a plaid to wrap him in for sleep, under the lithe of a hedge or a whin, when he grew over-tired. And the fields were a comfort, the crumble of the fine earth under your feet, swinging a graip as you walked, breaking dung, the larks above, the horses plodding by with snorting breath, old Brigson a-bend above the shafts. He made fair poor drills, they were better than none, and he aye was pleasant and canty, a fine old stock, he did lots of the things that Ewan had done and asked no more pay for the doing of them. That was as well, he wouldn't have got it, the weather was bitter, corn spoiled in the planting.

Early in the year, about May that was, the rain came down and it seemed it never would end, there was nothing to be done out of doors, the rain came down from the north-east across Kinraddie and Chris wasn't the only one that noted its difference from other years. In Pessie's Knapp there was Mistress Strachan vexing herself in trying to make out the change; and then she minded what Chae had said would happen when the woods came down; once the place had been sheltered and lithe, it poised now up on the brae in whatever storm might come. The woodmen had all finished by then, they'd left a country that looked as though it had been shelled by a German army. Looking out on those storms that May, Chris could hardly believe that this was the place she and Will had watched from the window that first morning they came to Blawearie.

And then the very next day as she made the butter, young Ewan was up the stairs with his blocks and books, John Brigson had gone to Mondynes with a load of corn, Chris heard a step in the close, somebody running in a hurry from the rain. Then the door burst open and a soldier came in, panting, in the queerest uniform, a hat with gold lacing and red breeches and leggings, Chris stared at the hat and then at the face. And the soldier cried *Oh, Chris, I believe you don't know me!* and she cried then, *Will!* and her arms went round him, they cuddled one the other like children, Chris crying, Will near to crying himself, patting her shoulder and saying *Oh, Chris!*

Then she pushed him away and looked at him and they cuddled each other again and Will danced her all round the kitchen, and little Ewan up the stairs heard the stir and came tearing down and when he saw a strange man holding his mother in his arms he made at Will and whacked his legs and cried, *Away, man!* Will cried *God almighty, what's this you've got, Chris?* and swung Ewan high and stared in his face and shook his head *You're a fine lad, ay, but you've over much of your father in you ever to be as bonny as your mother!*

That wasn't true but fine to hear, Chris could hardly get any work done or a meal made ready, so many the things they'd to take through hand. Will sat and smoked and every now and then they'd look one at the other and Will would give a great laugh *Oh Chris, mind this . . . mind that . . . !* And his laughter had tears in it, they were daft, the pair of them. And when old John Brigson came home, they heard the noise of the wheels in the close and Will went out to lend him a hand, the old stock jumped off the cart and made for a fork that was lying to hand, he thought Will a German in that strange bit uniform. But he laughed right heartily when Will said who he was, and the two of them came in for dinner and Will sat at the table's head, in Ewan's place. And as he ate he told them how he came in the uniform, and all the chances and wanderings that were his and Mollie's when they went from Scotland.

And faith! he'd had more than enough of both, for in Argentine, as he'd told Chris already by letter, he'd left his first work after a while, he and Mollie had both learned up the Spanish, and he took a job with a Frenchman there, an awful fine stock. He liked Will well and Will liked him, and he gave Will half of his house to bide in, it was a great ranch out in the parks of that meikle country. So there they had lived and were happy and blithe till the Frenchman had to go to the War. Will had thought of going himself more than once but the Frenchman had told him he'd be a fair fool, he might well be glad there wasn't British conscription; besides, some body or other had to look to the ranch. But in less than two years the Frenchman came back, sore wounded he'd been, and soon as he came Will told him it was *his* turn now, he'd see some of this War for himself. And the Frenchman told him he was fair a fool, but he'd get him a job with the French. So he did after cables and cables to Paris, and Will said goodbye to Mollie and the Frenchman and the Frenchman's wife, and sailed from

Buenos Ayres to Cherbourg; and in Paris they knew all about him, he found himself listed as a sergeant-major in the French Foreign Legion, an interpreter he was, for he knew three languages fine. Then they'd given him a fortnight's leave and here he was.

And when he was alone with Chris that evening and she told him about Ewan down training in Lanark, he said Ewan was either soft or daft or both. *Why did you marry the dour devil, Chris? Did he make you or were you going to have a bairn?* And Chris didn't feel affronted, it was Will that asked, he'd treat her just the same if she owned up to a fatherless bairn once a year, or twice, if it came to that. So she shook her head, *It was just because he was to me as Mollie to you,* and Will nodded to that, *Ah, well, we can't help when it gets that way. Mind when you wanted to know . . . ?* And they stood and laughed in the evening, remembering that, and they walked arm in arm up and down the road and Chris forgot all her worries remembering the days when she and Will were bairns together, and the dourness and the loveliness then, and Will asked *Did you mind when we slept together—that last time we did it when the old man had near killed me up in the barn?* And his face grew dark, he still couldn't forgive, he said that folk who ill-treated their children deserved to be shot, father had tormented and spoiled him out of sheer cruelty when he was young. But Chris said nothing to that, remembering the day of father's funeral and how she had wept by his grave in Kinraddie kirkyard.

But she knew she could never tell Will of that, he'd never understand, and they spoke of other things, Will of the Argentine and the life out there, and the smell of the sun and the warm weather and the fruit and flowers and flame of life below the Southern Cross. Chris said *But you'll come back, you and Mollie, to bide in Scotland again?* and Will laughed, he seemed still a mere lad in spite of his foreign French uniform, *Havers, who'd want to come back to this country? It's dead or it's dying—and a damned good job!*

And, daftly, Chris felt a sudden thrust of anger through her heart at that; and then she looked round Kinraddie in the evening light, seeing it so quiet and secure and still,

thinking of the seeds that pushed up their shoots from a
thousand earthy mouths. Daft of Will to say that: Scotland
lived, she could never die, the land would outlast them all,
their wars and their Argentines, and the winds come sailing
over the Grampians still with their storms and rain and the
dew that ripened the crops—long and long after all their
little vexings in the evening light were dead and done. And
her thoughts went back to the kirkyard, she asked Will
would he like to come to the kirk next day, she hadn't been
there herself for a year.

He looked surprised and then laughed *You're not getting
religious, are you?* as though she had taken to drink. And
Chris said *No*, and then thought about that, time to think
for once in the pother of the days with Blawearie so quiet
above them, young Ewan and old Brigson asleep. And she
said *I don't believe they were ever religious, the Scots folk,
Will—not really religious like Irish or French or all the rest
in the history books. They've never BELIEVED. It's just
been a place to collect and argue, the kirk, and criticise God.*
And Will yawned, he said maybe, he didn't care one way or
the other himself, Mollie in the Argentine had taken up with
the Catholics, and faith! she was welcome if she got any fun.

So next day they set out for the kirk, the weather had
cleared, blowing wet and sunny in a blink, there were teeth
of rainbows out over Kinraddie, Chris said it was Will's
uniform that messed up the sky. But she was proud of him
for all that, how folk stared as the two of them went down
the aisle! Chris was in her blue, with her new short skirt
and long boots, and Will in *his* blue and red trousers and
leggings, and his jacket with the gold lace on it and the high
collar and the soft fine hat with the shiny peak. Old Gibbon,
him that preached for his son, near fell down the stairs of the
pulpit at sight of Will. But he recovered fell soon and
preached them one of the sermons that had made such stir
throughout the Howe a year or so back, he told how the
German beasts now boiled the corpses of their own dead
men and fed the leavings to pigs. And he ground his teeth
at the Germans, they were so coarse; and he said that GUD
would assuredly smite them.

But folk had grown sick of him and his ragings, there was

H

only a small attendance to hear him and when they came out in the end Will said *It's good to be out of that creature's stink!* Syne Ellison recognised Will and came swaggering over, redder than ever and fatter than ever, and he cried *If it ain't Will Guthrie! How are you?* and Will said *Fine.* Most of the folk seemed pleased to see him, even Mutch and Munro, excepting the Munro wife herself, she snapped, *And what would you be, then, Will? They've a man at the picture palace in Stonehaven that wears breeks just like that.* And Will said *Faith, Mistress Munro, you're an authority on breeks. I hear you still wear them at the Cuddiestoun.* Folk standing round gave a snicker at that, real fine for the futret, she'd met her match.

And Will's leave went by like a shot, he was all over the Howe in the first few days, up in Fordoun and down in Drumlithie, and everywhere folk made much of him. But after that he bided nearly all the time by Chris, he helped her or Brigson in old clothes of Ewan's she'd raked out for him. He went shooting with father's gun fell often, up in the moor it was blithe to hear him and his singing, young Ewan would go wandering up to meet him. And when it came to the end and the last day, young Ewan in bed and they sat by the fire and the June night came softly down without, Chris didn't fear at all for Will, he was clean and happy and quick, things went well with him. And next morning only young Ewan cried at the parting, and off he went, it seemed then at Blawearie that more than Will had gone out of their lives, it was a happy voice that had sung for itself a chamber in their hearts those weeks he had been with them.

But the hills flowed up and down, day after day, in their dark and sunshine, and even those weeks were covered and laid past, and Chris saw the harvest near, so near, a good harvest again in spite of the weather; and still the War went on. Sometimes she'd a note or postcard from Ewan in Lanark, sometimes she wouldn't hear for week on week till she grew fair alarmed. But he just said it was that he never could write, he didn't know how, they were awfully busy and she wasn't to worry.

And then through Kinraddie a motor came driving one day, it turned at the cross-roads and drove down by the Denburn. It stopped at the Mill and folk ran to their doors and wondered who it could be, the place was locked up and deserted-like. And when the motor stopped a man got out, and another came after, slow, and he took the arm of the first one, and they went step-stepping at snail's pace up to the Mill-house and folk could see no more. But soon the story of it was known all over the place, it was Long Rob himself come back, he had never given in, they had put him in prison and ill-used him awful; but he wouldn't give in whatever they did, he laughed in their faces, *Fine, man, fine.* Last he went on the hunger-strike, that was when you just starved to death to spite them, and grew weaker and weaker. So they took him from prison to a doctor childe and the doctor said it was useless to keep him, he'd never be of use to his King and country.

So home at last he had come, folk told he was fairly a wreck, he could hardly stand up and walk or make his own meat, God knows how he ever got into his clothes. And Mutch and Munro wouldn't go near him, neither would Gordon, they said that it served him right, the coarse pro-German. And when Chris heard that there came a stinging pain in her eyes and she called old John Brigson to yoke a cart and put corn in it, as though taking it to Rob for bruising; and Chris got into the cart as well and took young Ewan on her knee, and off they set from Blawearie. Outside the Mill-house Chris cried on Brigson to stop, and found the basket she'd laid on the bottom of the cart and ran through the close to the kitchen door. It stood half-open, the place was dark with hardly a glimmer from the fire, but she saw someone sitting, she stopped and stared, an old man it seemed with a white, drawn face, his hands fumbling at the lighting of a pipe.

She called *Rob!* and he looked up and she saw his eyes, they were filled with awful things, he cried *Chris! God is't Chris Guthrie?* She was shaking his hand and his shoulder then, minding things about him, not looking at him, minding the fine neighbour he'd been to her and Ewan in the days they married. And she asked *What are you sitting here*

for? You should be in your bed, and Rob said *I'm damned
if I should, I've had over much of bed. I was waiting about
for the grocer childe, but he didn't stop, though he knows
I'm home. I suppose he's still an ill-will at pro-Germans, like.*

Chris told him never to mind the grocer, and she spoke
to him roughly, in case she should weep at the sight of him;
and she told him to go out and see John Brigson. Then, soon
as he'd hirpled out with his stick she looked round the
place and started to clean it, and made a fine fire and a meal
with fresh eggs and butter, and oat-cakes and scones and
jam, she'd brought the lot from Blawearie. So when Rob
came in from his speak with Brigson, there it was waiting
him on the table, he blinked and sat down and said in a
whisper, *You shouldn't have done this, Chris quean.* But
Chris said nothing, just sat him down at the table and sat
there herself and saw that he ate; and when young Ewan
came in with old Brigson she fed them as well; and syne
Brigson set off for the farm at Auchinblae where Rob's horse
and sholtie were housed.

When he'd gone Chris set to work on the place and
opened the windows to the air and cleaned out the rooms
and dragged off the dirty linen from the bed and made it
up in a bundle to take back with her. Syne she baked oat-
cakes for Rob and told him that each day he'd get him a
pail of milk from the Netherhill, till time came when he'd
kye of his own again, she'd arranged for that. And when
John Brigson came back in the evening with horse and
sholtie Long Rob was fast asleep in his chair, they didn't
rouse him but spread him his supper, and set him his breakfast as well, and left a lamp low-burning and clear beside
him, and a hot-water bottle in his bed. Syne they left him
and rode them back to Blawearie, all three were tired, young
Ewan asleep in the arms of Chris, dear to hold him so
with his dark head sleeping against her breast and old
Brigson's shoulder seen as a dark quiet bulking against
the night.

Next morning they looked out from Blawearie and saw
Rob's horse and sholtie at graze in a park of the Mill, and
Long Rob himself, a dot in the sunlight, making slow way
to the moor land he'd wrought at so long. And as they looked

they heard, thin and remote, the sound of a song Kinraddie
had missed for many a day. It was *Ladies of Spain*.

Soon maybe the War would end, Chris had dreamt as
she listened to that singing, and they all be back in Kinraddie as once they had been, Chae and Long Rob and her
dark lad, Ewan himself. So she'd dreamt that morning, she'd
never grow out from long dreamings in autumn dawns like
those. And fruition of dream came soon enough, it was a
telegram boy that came riding his bicycle up to Blawearie.
Chris read the telegram, it was Ewan that had sent it, *Home
on leave tonight before going to France*. She stared at it and
the lad that had brought it, and he asked, *Any reply?* and
she said *Any what?* and he asked her again, and she said *No*,
and ran into the kitchen and stared at the writing in the
telegram. He was going to France.

It lingered at the back of her mind, dark, like a black cat
creeping at the back of a hedge, she saw the fluff of its fur
or the peek of its eyes, a wild and sinister thing in the
sunlight; but you would not look often or see those eyes,
how they glared at you. He was going out there, where the
sky was a troubled nightmare and the earth shook night
and day, into the lands of the coarse French folk, her Ewan,
her lad with his dark, dear face and that quick, blithe blush.
And suddenly she was filled with a weeping pity in her
heart for him, a pity that brought no tears to her eyes, he
must never see her shed tears all the time he was with her,
he'd go out to the dark, far land with memories of her and
Blawearie that were shining and brave and kind.

So all that forenoon she fled and bustled from room to
room, brightening the place, she brought out fresh sheets
and pillows for the bed she had found so lonely, she sent out
young Ewan to gather roses and honeysuckle to set in a jar
on the ledge above the bed. And she hung new curtains
there and brought out Ewan's clothes and brushed them,
he'd want to get out of his uniform, they were sick of the
khaki the men that came back. Then she made a great
baking against his coming, so much that she'd hardly time
to make dinner for young Ewan and Brigson, but they didn't
care, they were both excited as herself. She knew the train

he would come by, the half-past five, and she swept and dusted the kitchen and set his tea, and punched a great cushion ready for his chair, and dressed herself in the blue he liked and young Ewan in his brave brown cords. John Brigson cried *This is hardly the place for me with your man come home, I'll away to Bervie then for the night*.

Off he set, Chris waved to the old, kind childe as he bicycled down Blawearie brae. And then she ran back, ben to the parlour to look at herself in the mirror again, in the long glass her figure seemed blithe and slim even still, she'd be fine to sleep with yet, she supposed—oh, Ewan! Her face hadn't changed, it was flushed and fair, the eyes maybe older, but shining and bright. And she finished with that looking and went over the close to stand by the side of young Ewan, looking down the hill for his father coming up. The sun flung the long shadows of Blawearie and the beeches far in the east, and across the Den, high in the fields of Upperhill, a lost sheep baaed in the whins.

She had hardly been able to believe it him lying awake after he slept, he slept with a snoring breath and fuddled mumblings, bulging out against her so that she had but little of the bed and less of the blankets. She closed her eyes and pressed her knuckles against her teeth that the pain might waken her, that she might know Ewan hadn't come home, was still the same Ewan she'd dreamt of in the silence of the night and her own lonely bed. But he moved, flinging out an arm that struck her across the face, she lay still below it, then it wabbled away. She took her knuckles from her mouth and lay quiet then, no need for her to hurt herself now.

Drunk he had come from the station and more than two hours late. Standing at last in the kitchen in his kilts he'd looked round and sneered *Hell, Chris, what a bloody place!* as she ran to him. And he'd flung his pack one way and his hat the other and kissed her as though she were a tink, his hands on her as quickly as that, hot and questing and wise as his hands had never been. She saw the hot smoulder fire in his eyes then, but no blush on his face, it was red with other things. But she smothered her horror and laughed, and kissed him and struggled from him, and cried *Ewan, who's this?*

Young Ewan held back, shy-like, staring, and just said *It's father.* At that the strange, swaying figure in the tartan kilts laughed, coarse-like, *Well, we'll hope so, eh Chris? Any supper left—unless you're too bloody stand-offish even to have that?*

She couldn't believe her own ears. *Stand-offish? Oh, Ewan!* and ran to him again, but he shook her away, *Och, all right, I'm wearied. For Christ's sake let a man sit down.* He staggered to the chair she'd made ready for him, a picture-book of young Ewan's lay there, he picked the thing up and flung it to the other side of the room, and slumped down into the chair. *Hell, what a blasted climb to a blasted place. Here, give us some tea.*

She sat beside him to serve him, she knew her face had gone white. But she poured the tea and spread the fine supper she'd been proud to make, it might hardly have been there for the notice he paid it, drinking cup after cup of the tea like a beast at a trough. She saw him clearer then, the coarse hair that sprang like short bristles all over his head, the neck with its red and angry circle about the collar of the khaki jacket, a great half-healed scar across the back of his hand glinted putrescent blue. Suddenly his eyes came on her, *Well, damn't, is that all you have to say to me now I've come home? I'd have done better to spend the night with a tart in the town.*

She didn't say anything, she couldn't, the tears were choking in her throat and smarting and biting at her eyelids, pressing to come, the tears that she'd sworn she'd never shed all the time he was home on leave. And she didn't dare look at him lest he should see, but he saw and pushed back his chair and got up in a rage, *God Almighty, what are you snivelling about now? You always were snivelling, I mind.* And out he went, young Ewan ran to her side and flung his arms round her, *Mother, don't cry, I don't like him, he's a tink, that soldier!* She'd pressed back the tears then, *Whist, Ewan, never say that again*; and got up and cleared off the supper things and went out to the close and cried gently *Ewan!*

He cried back *All right, all right!* still angrily; and at that some anger kindled within herself, she didn't wait for him to come back but turned and took young Ewan in her arms and climbed the stairs and put him to bed, he was vexed and troubled about her, kissing her as he lay there. *Sleep with me tonight, mother.* She laughed at him, she was sleeping with his father tonight, he must be good and sleep himself, quick and quick, there'd be such fun with father the morn. He said *I'll try*, and closed his eyes and she went down the stairs, it was dark there getting on for eight. She thought Ewan was still outside but as she made for the lamp something stirred in the chair, she thought it a cat, it was Ewan. He caught her and pulled her on to his knees and said *Be stand-offish now if you can, what the devil do you think I've come home for?*

It had been like struggling with someone deep in a nightmare, when the blankets are over your head and you can barely breathe, awful she should come to think that of Ewan. But it wasn't Ewan, her Ewan, someone coarse and strange and strong had come back in his body to torment her. He laughed as he fought her there in the chair and held her tight and began to tell stories—oh, he was drunk and didn't know what he said, terrible and sickening things, he'd had women when he pleased in Lanark, he said. And he whispered of them to her, his breath was hot on her face, she saw the gleam of his teeth, he told her how he'd lain with them and the things he'd done. Sickened and shamed she had felt and then worse than that, stopping from struggling, a shameful, searing desire come on her. And he knew, he knew at once, he said *Well, now that you know you can get!*

She had picked herself up from the floor and in a dream went out to milk the kye, leaving him there. When she came back he had gone from the kitchen, she was slow to finish sieving and skimming the milk and go up to the room she'd made ready that morning, singing she had made it ready. And up there he waited her, lying in the bed, he'd carried up a lamp from the kitchen, they who'd always gone to bed in the darkness and thought it fine to lie in each other's arms in the night-glimmer from the window. But now he

grumbled *For God's sake hurry up!* and when she made to
put out the light—*I'll do that, come on!* And she lay beside
him and he took her.

She remembered that now, lying in the darkness the while
he slept, why he had left the lamp alight; and at memory
of that foulness something cold and vile turned and turned
like a wheeling mirror inside her brain. For it had been
other things than his beast-like mauling that had made her
whisper in agony, *Oh Ewan, put out the light!* The horror
of his eyes upon her she would never forget, they burned
and danced on that mirror that wheeled and wheeled in
her brain.

So that was Ewan's homecoming on leave and the days
that went by were the same as that first night foreshadowed.
He had gone away Ewan Tavendale, he came back a man
so coarse and cruel that in place of love hate came singing
in the heart of Chris—hate that never found speech, that
but slowly found lodgement secure and unshaken. For often
it seemed to her that a tortured, tormented thing looked
out from Ewan's eyes while he told them his foulest tale, ill-
used old Brigson and jeered at him, came drunken back to
Blawearie night after night—that tortured thing that was
the lost lad she had married. But the fancy wilted and
vanished as the days went by. He stayed five days, had his
breakfast in bed, and never got up till dinner-time; he
never looked at the parks or stock or took notice of young
Ewan; he dressed in his khaki and kilts alone, and to Chris's
suggestion that he wear a suit—*What, me, dress up like a
bloody conchy? I'll leave that to your friend, Rob Duncan.*

Every day he went swaggering down the road and was off
to Drumlithie or Stonehaven or Fordoun, drinking there.
Before he went he'd ask for money, Chris gave him all that
he asked, not saying a word, but he'd fancy a reluctance and
sneer at her. Wasn't he entitled to what was his own? Did
she think him still the young fool he had been, content to
slave and slave at Blawearie—*without as much as a dram to
savour the soss, or a quean or so at night to waken your
blood—nothing but a wife you hardly dared touch in case
you put her in the family way, eh Chris?*

He would say this at dinner-time, sneering and boasting, old Brigson would colour and look down at his plate and young Ewan stare and stare at his father till Ewan would say *God, what a damned glower! Eyes like your mother and a nature the same*; and he'd swear at the bairn, it was shameful to hear that. He'd made friends with Mutch, him that once he could hardly abide, and with him he went driving each night on their drunken sprees. As he went to bed John Brigson would look at Chris with trouble in his kind old eyes, but she didn't dare say a thing to him, he'd go stamping slow up above her head the while she sat down to await Ewan's return and have the hirpling note of the clock stamp each second in her heart, hating him home, wanting him home.

For after that first night he had ceased to touch her, she would lie beside him, quivering and waiting. And he'd lie quiet, she knew him awake and knew that he knew what she waited; and it was as though he were a cat that played with a mouse, he would laugh out after a while and then go to sleep, she herself to lie tortured in the hours thereafter. The last night she refused the torment, she got up near three o'clock and kindled a fire and made herself tea and watched the morning come down the hill passes—a fine summer morning, yellow and grey and lovely with its chirping of birds in the beeches. And suddenly then, as always these changes took her, she was calm and secure, putting Ewan from her heart, locking it up that he never could vex her again, she was finished with him, either loving or hating. And at that release she rose and went slow about her work, a great load had gone from her then, John Brigson coming down in the morning heard her sing and was cheery himself, cheery with relief, but she sang her release.

At nine o'clock Ewan cried down from his room. *When the hell are you bringing some breakfast?* She took no notice of that, but she sent young Ewan out to play and then went on with her work. And at last she heard a clatter on the stairs, and there he stood at the kitchen entrance, glaring at her, *Have you gone clean deaf?* She answered him then, raising her head and looking at him, *If you're in need of a breakfast—get it.*

He said *You bitch!* and he made to strike her. But she caught up a knife from the table, she had it waiting there nearby, he swore and drew back. She nodded and smiled at that, calm, and put the knife down and went on with her work.

So he made his own tea, grumbling and swearing, a fine send-off this for a man that was going to France to do his bit. And Chris listened to the catch-phrase, contempt in her heart, she looked at him with curling lip, and he saw her look and swore at her, but was frightened for all that, always now she knew she had known him the frightened one. And a queer, cold curiosity came on to her then that so she should have slaved to tend him and love him and give him the best, body and mind and soul she had given, for a gift to the body of a drunken lout from the plough-stilts.

And now that body she saw with a cold repulsion him wash and shave and dress, she could hardly bear to look at him and went out and worked in the close, cleaning pots there in the shining weather, young Ewan played douce and content with his toys, it was hay-time all down the Howe and the hens came pecking around her. She heard Ewan stamp about in the kitchen, he wanted that she should look, go running and fetch him his things. And she smiled again, cold and secure and serene, and heard him come out and bang the door; and without raising her head she saw him then. He was all in his gear, the Glengarry on his head, his pack on his shoulder, his kilts a-swing, and he went past her jauntily but she knew he expected her to stop him, to run after him and throw her arms about him: she saw in his eyes as he went by the fear that she'd pay no heed.

And none she paid, she did not speak, she did not unbend, young Ewan stopped from his playing and looked after his father incuriously, as at a strange alien that went from the place. At the gate of the close, as he banged it behind him, Ewan stooped to sort up his garters, red in the face, not looking at her still. And she paid him no heed.

He swung the pack on his shoulders then and went slow down the road to the turnpike bend, she saw that from the kitchen window, knew he believed she would cry to him at the last. And she smiled, cold and sure, that she knew him so, every action and thought, and why he stood there at last, not trying to look back. He fumbled for matches and lighted his pipe as she watched; and a cloud came over the sun and went on with Ewan, the two of them went down the turnpike then together, out of her sight in the shadow and flame of the bright sun weather, it was strange and impossibly strange. She stood long staring down at that point where he'd vanished, sharp under her breast, tearing her body, her heart was breaking, and she did not care! She was outside and away from its travail and agony, he had done all to her that he ever could now, he who had tramped down the road in that shadow that fled from the sun.

And then it was she found no salvation at all may endure for ever, or beyond the pitch that the heart may bear it, she was weeping and weeping, her arms flung over the kitchen table, weeping for that Ewan who had never come back, for the shamed, tormented boy with the swagger airs she had let go from Blawearie without a kiss or a parting word. *Ewan, Ewan!* her heart cried then, breaking and breaking, *Oh, Ewan, I didn't mean it!* Ewan—he was hers, hers still in spite of all he had done and said, he had lived more close in her body than the heart that broke now, young Ewan was his, Oh God, she had never let him go like that! And in her desolation of weeping she began to pray, she had known it useless, but she prayed and prayed for him to come back, to kiss her and hold her in kindness just once before he went down that road. She ran wild-eyed and weeping to the close and there was John Brigson, he stared dumbfounded as she cried *Oh, don't let him go, run after him, John!*

And syne he said he didn't understand, if she meant her man, it was more than an hour since Ewan had gone down the road, he'd heard long syne the whistle of his train out across the hills.

It was a month before she heard from him, and then only a scrape and a score on a thing they called a field postcard written somewhere in France; and it said no more than that he was well. No more than a whisper out of the dark cave of days into which he had gone, it yet salved her mind from the searing agony that tormented the early weeks. They would never be the same again, but some day he would come back to her, their madness forgotten, back to her and young Ewan and Blawearie when the War was done, they'd forget and forget, busy themselves in new hours and seasons, there would never be fire and gladness between them again but still undying the labour of the fields in which she now buried her days.

For she sank herself in that, the way to forget, she was hardly indoors from dawn to dusk in all the range of the harvest weather, running down the bouts behind the binder that John Brigson drove, little Ewan running and laughing beside her. He thought it a fun and a play she made, stooking and stooking so quickly then, her hands became as machines, tireless and quick and ceaseless through the long hours, she stooked so quickly that with an extra hour each evening, old Brigson helping her, she was close to the uncut rigs again. Corn and the shining hollow stalks of the straw, they wove a pattern about her life, her nights and days, she would creep to bed and dream of the endless rigs and her hands in the night would waken her, all pins and needles they would be. Once she went ben to the parlour to look in the glass and saw then why pity came often in old Brigson's eyes, she was thinner than ever she'd been, her face was thin, it seemed to her some gloss had gone from her hair, her eyes grown dull and patient and pupil-less; like the eyes of a cow.

So, hurt and dazed, she turned to the land, close to it and the smell of it, kind and kind it was, it didn't rise up and torment your heart, you could keep at peace with the land if you gave it your heart and hands, tended it and slaved for it, it was wild and a tyrant, but it was not cruel. And often, in the night-stooking with old John Brigson near, a ghost of gladness would come to her then, working under the coming of the moon before the evening dew came pringling over Kinraddie, night-birds whistling over the fields, so quiet, so quiet, stilling away the pain in her body, the pain in her heart that this reaping and harvesting had brought.

And then Long Rob of the Mill came up to Blawearie.

He came one morning as they started the yavil, he came through the close and into the kitchen, long and as rangy as ever he was, his face filled out and his eyes the same, and he cried *How's Chris? Bonny as ever!* And he caught young Ewan up on his shoulder and Ewan looked down at him, dark and grave, and smiled, and thought him fine.

Rob had come over to help, he'd no cutting to do; and when Chris said nay, he mustn't leave the Mill, he twinkled his eyes and shook his head. And Chris knew he'd have little loss, folk changed and were changing again, not a soul had driven his corn cart to the Mill since Long Rob came back. He'd had nothing to do but pleiter about from park to park and look out on the road for the custom that never came; and if any came now it could damn well wait, he'd come up to stook Blawearie.

So the two went down to the park, young Ewan went with them, and they stooked it together, the best of the crop, Rob cheery as ever it seemed to Chris. But sometimes his eyes would wander up to the hills, like a man seeking a thing he had never desired, and into the iron-blue eyes a shadow like a dark, quiet question would creep. Maybe he minded the jail and its torments then, he spoke never of that, and never a word of the War, nor Chris, all the stooking of the yavil park. Strange she had hardly known him before, Long Rob of the Mill, unco and atheist; he'd been only the miller with the twinkling eyes, his singings by morn and his whistlings by night, his stories of horses till your head fair reeled. Now it seemed she had known him always, closely and queerly, she felt queer, as though shy, when she sat by his side at the supper table and he spoke to old Brigson that night. The pallor of the jail came out in the lamp-light, under the brown that the sun had brought, and she saw his hand by the side of her hand, thin and strong, the miller's horse-taming hand.

He bedded young Ewan that night, for a play, and sung him to sleep, Chris and old Brigson heard the singing as they sat in the kitchen below, *Ladies of Spain* and *There was a Young Farmer* and *A' the Blue Bonnets are Over the Border*. Hardly anybody left in Kinraddie sang these songs, it was full of other tunes from the bothy windows now,

Tipperary and squawling English things, like the squeak of a rat that is bedded in syrup, the *Long, Long Trail* and the like. It was queer and eerie, listening to Rob, like listening to an echo from far in the years at the mouth of a long lost glen.

And she never knew when and how in the days that followed, it came on her silently, secretly, out of the earth itself, maybe, the knowledge she was Rob's to do with as he willed, she willed. She wanted more than the clap of his hand on her shoulder as they finished the bout at evening and up through the shadows took their slow way, by parkside and dyke, to the close that hung drenched with honeysuckle smell. She wanted more than his iron-blue eye turned on her, warm and clean and kind though she felt her skin colour below that gaze, she wanted those things that now all her life she came to know she had never known—a man to love her, not such a boy as the Ewan that had been or the poor demented beast he'd become.

And if old John Brigson guessed of those things that whispered so shamelessly there in her heart he gave never a sign, wise and canny and kind. And no sign that he knew did Rob give either, swinging by her side in the harvest that drew to its end. And in Chris as she bent and straightened and stooked the last day was a prayer to the earth and fields, a praying that this harvest might never end, that she and Long Rob would tramp it forever. But the binder flashed its blades at the head of the last, long bout, and Long Rob had his hand on her shoulder, *He's finished, Chris quean, and it's clyak!*

That evening she went out with him to the gate of the close, and he swung his coat on his shoulder, *Well, well, Chris lass, I've liked this fine.* And then, not looking at her, he added *I'm away to Aberdeen to enlist the morn.*

For a moment she was stupefied and stared at him silently, but she had no place in his thoughts, he was staring across Kinraddie's stooked fields. And then he began to tell her, he'd resolved on this days before, he couldn't stay out of it longer, all the world had gone daft and well he might go with the rest, there was neither trade nor trust for him here, or rest ever again till this War was over, if it ever ended at all. *So I'm giving in at last, I suppose they'll say. And this is lu-lu, Chris. mind on me kindly some times.*

She held to his hand in the gloaming light and so he looked down at last, she was biting her lips to keep down the tears, but he saw them shine brimming then in her eyes. And his own changed, changed and were kind and then something else, he cried *Why, lass!* and his hand on her shoulder drew her close, she was close and against him, held tight so that she felt the slow beat of his heart, she wanted to rest there, safe and safe in these corded arms. And then she minded that tomorrow he'd be gone, it cried through the evening in every cry of the lapwings, *So near, so near!* So this also ended as everything else, every thing she had ever loved and desired went out to the madness beyond the hills on that ill road that flung its evil white ribbon down the dusk. And it was her arms then that went round his neck, drawing down his head and kissing him, queer and awful to kiss a man so, kissing him till she heard his breath come quick, and he gripped her, pleading with her, *We're daft, Chris quean, we mustn't!* But she knew then she had won, she wound her arms about him, she whispered *The haystacks!* and he carried her there, the smell of the clover rose crushed and pungent and sweet from under her head; and lying so in the dark, held to him, kissing him, she sought with lips and limbs and blood to die with him then.

But that dark, hot cloud went by, she found herself still lying there, Rob was there, and she drew his head to her breast, lying so with him, seeing out below the rounded breasts of the haystacks the dusky red of the harvest night, this harvest gathered to herself at last, reaped and garnered and hers in her heart and body. So they were for hours, John Brigson never called out to them; and then she stood beside Rob at the head of the road again, drowsy and quiet and content. They made no promises, kissing for last, she knew already he was growing remote from her, his eyes already remote to that madness that beckoned beyond the hills. So it was that he went from her next, she heard him go step-stepping slow with that swinging stride of his down through the darkness, and she never saw him again, was never to see him again.

It had burned up as a fire in a whin-bush, that thing in her life, and it burned out again and was finished. She went about the Blawearie biggings next day singing under breath to herself, quiet and unvexed, tending to hens and kye, seeing to young Ewan's sleep in the day and the setting of old Brigson's supper ere he came at night. She felt shamed not at all, all the vexing fears had gone from her, she made no try to turn from the eyes in the glass that looked out at her, wakened and living again. She was glad she'd gone out with Long Rob, glad and content, they were one and the same now, Ewan and her.

So the telegram boy that came riding to Blawearie found her singing there in the close, mending young Ewan's clothes. She heard the click of the gate and he took the telegram out of his wallet and gave it to her and she stared at him and then at her hands. They were quivering like the leaves of the beech in the forecoming of rain, they quivered in a little mist below her eyes. Then she opened the envelope and read the words and she said there was no reply, the boy swung on his bicycle again and rode out, riding and leaning he clicked the gate behind him; and laughed back at her for the cleverness of that.

She stood up then, she put down her work on the hackstock and read again in the telegram, and began to speak to herself till that frightened her and she stopped. But she forgot to be frightened, in a minute she was speaking again, the chirawking hens in the close stopped and came near and turned up bright eyes to her loud and toneless whispering, *What do I do—oh, what do I do?*

She was vexed and startled by that—what was it she did? Did she go out to France and up to the front line, maybe, into a room where they'd show her Ewan lying dead, quiet and dead, white and bloodless, sweat on his hair, killed in action? She went out to the front door and waved to the harvesters, Brigson, young Ewan, and a tink they'd hired, they saw her and stared till she waved again and then John Brigson abandoned the half-loaded cart and came waddling up the park, so slow he was, *Did you cry me, Chris?*

Sweat on his hair as sweat on Ewan's. She stared at that and held out the telegram, he wiped slow hands and took it and read it, while she clung to the door-post and whispered and whispered *What is it I do now, John? Have I to go out to France?* And at last he looked up, his face was grizzled and hot and old, he wiped the sweat from it slow. *God, mistress, this is sore news, but he's died like a man out there, your Ewan's died fine.*

But she wouldn't listen to that, wanting to know the thing she must do; and not till he told her that she did nothing, they could never take all the widows to France and Ewan must already be buried, did she stop from that twisting of her hands and ceaseless whisper. Then anger came, *Why didn't you tell me before? Oh, damn you, you liked tormenting me!* and she turned from him into the house and ran up the stairs to the bed, the bed that was hers and Ewan's, and lay on it, and put her hands over her ears trying not to hear a cry of agony in a lost French field, not to think that the body that had lain by hers, frank and free and kind and young, was torn and dead and unmoving flesh, blood twisted upon it, not Ewan at all, riven and terrible, still and dead when the harvest stood out in Blawearie's land and the snipe were calling up on the loch and the beech trees whispered and rustled. And SHE KNEW THAT IT WAS A LIE!

He wasn't dead, he could never have died or been killed for nothing at all, far away from her over the sea, what matter to him their War and their fighting, their King and their country? Kinraddie was his land, Blawearie his, he was never dead for those things of no concern, he'd the crops to put in and the loch to drain and her to come back to. It had nothing to do with Ewan this telegram. They were only tormenting her, cowards and liars and bloody men, the English generals and their like down there in London. But she wouldn't bear it, she'd have the law on them, cowards and liars as she knew them to be!

It was only then that she knew she was moaning, dreadful to hear; and they heard it outside, John Brigson heard it and nearly went daft, he caught up young Ewan and ran with him into the kitchen and then to the foot of the stairs; and told him to go up to his mother, she wanted him. And young Ewan came, it was his hand tugging at her skirts that brought her out of that moaning coma, and he wasn't crying, fearsome the sounds though she made, his face was white and resolute, *Mother, mother!* She picked him up then and held him close, rocking in an agony of despair because of that look on his face, that lost look and the smouldering eyes he had. *Oh Ewan, your father's dead!* she told him the lie that the world believed. And she wept at last, blindly, freeingly, for a little, old Brigson was to say it was the boy that had saved her from going mad.

But throughout Kinraddie the news went underbreath that mad she'd gone, the death of her man had fair unhinged her. For still she swore it was a lie, that Ewan wasn't dead, he could never have died for nothing. Kirsty Strachan and Mistress Munro came up to see her, they shook their heads and said he'd died fine, for his country and his King he'd died, young Ewan would grow up to be proud of his father. They said that sitting at tea, with long faces on them, and then Chris laughed, they quivered away from her at that laugh.

Country and King? You're havering, havering! What have they to do with my Ewan, what was the King to him, what their damned country? Blawearie's his land, it's not his wight that others fight wars!

She went fair daft with rage then, seeing the pity in their faces. And also it was then, and then only, staring through an angry haze at them, that she knew at last she was living a dream in a world gone mad. Ewan was dead, they knew it and she knew it herself; and he'd died for nothing, for nothing, hurt and murdered and crying for her, maybe, killed for nothing; and those bitches sat and spoke of their King and country. . . .

They ran out of the house and down the brae, and, panting, she stood and screamed after them. It was fair the speak of Kinraddie next day the way she'd behaved, and nobody else came up to see her. But she'd finished with screaming,

she went quiet and cold. Mornings came up, and she saw
them come, she minded that morning she'd sent him away
and she might not cry him back. Noons with their sun and
rain came over the Howe and she saw the cruelty and pain
of life as crimson rainbows that spanned the horizons of the
wheeling hours. Nights came soft and grey and quiet across
Kinraddie's fields, they brought neither terror nor hope to
her now. Behind the walls of a sanity cold and high, locked
in from the lie of life, she would live, from the world that
had murdered her man for nothing, for a madman's gibber-
ish heard in the night behind the hills.

And then Chae Strachan came home at last on leave, he
came home and came swift to Blawearie. She met him out
by the kitchen door, a sergeant by then, grown thinner and
taller, and he stopped and looked in her frozen face. Then,
as her hand dropped down from his, he went past her with
swinging kilts, into the kitchen, and sat him down and took
off his bonnet. *Chris, I've come to tell you of Ewan.*

She stared at him, waking, a hope like a fluttering bird
in her breast. *Ewan? Chae—Chae, he's not living?* And then,
as he shook his head, the frozen wall came down on her heart
again. *Ewan's dead, don't vex yourself hoping else. They
can't hurt him more, even this can't hurt him, though I
swore I'd tell you nothing about it. But I know right well
you should know it, Chris. Ewan was shot as a coward and
deserter out there in France.*

.   .   .   .   .

Chae had lain in a camp near by and had heard of the
thing by chance, he'd read Ewan's name in some list of
papers that was posted up. And he'd gone the night before
Ewan was shot, and they'd let him see Ewan, and he'd heard
it all, the story he was telling her now—*better always to
know what truth's in a thing, for lies come creeping home
to roost on unco rees, Chris quean. You're young yet, you've
hardly begun to live, and I swore to myself that I'd tell you
it all, that you'd never be vexed with some twisted bit in
the years to come. Ewan was shot as a deserter, it was fair
enough, he'd deserted from the front line trenches.*

He had deserted in a blink of fine weather between the

rains that splashed the glutted rat-runs of the front. He had done it quickly and easily, he told to Chae, he had just turned and walked back. And other soldiers that met him had thought him a messenger, or wounded, or maybe on leave, none had questioned him, he'd set out at ten o'clock in the morning and by afternoon, taking to the fields, was ten miles or more from the front. Then the military policemen came on him and took him, he was marched back and court-martialled and found to be guilty.

And Chae said to him, they sat together in the hut where he waited the coming of the morning, *But why did you do it, Ewan? You might well have known you'd never get free.* And Ewan looked at him and shook his head, *It was that wind that came with the sun, I minded Blawearie, I seemed to waken up smelling that smell. And I couldn't believe it was me that stood in the trench, it was just daft to be there. So I turned and got out of it.*

In a flash it had come on him, he had wakened up, he was daft and a fool to be there; and, like somebody minding things done in a coarse wild dream there had flashed on him memory of Chris at Blawearie and his last days there, mad and mad he had been, he had treated her as a devil might, he had tried to hurt her and maul her, trying in the nightmare to waken, to make her waken him up; and now in the blink of sun he saw her face as last he'd seen it while she quivered away from his taunts. He knew he had lost her, she'd never be his again, he'd known it in that moment he clambered back from the trenches; but he knew that he'd be a coward if he didn't try though all hope was past.

So out he had gone for that, remembering Chris, wanting to reach her, knowing as he tramped mile on mile that he never would. But he'd made her that promise that he'd never fail her, long syne he had made it that night when he'd held her so bonny and sweet and a quean in his arms, young and desirous and kind. So mile on mile on the laired French roads: she was lost to him, but that didn't help, he'd to try to win to her side again, to see her again, to tell her nothing he'd said was his saying, it was the foulness dripping from the dream that devoured him. And young

Ewan came into his thoughts, he'd so much to tell her of
him, so much he'd to say and do if only he might win to
Blawearie. . . .

Then the military policemen had taken him and he'd
listened to them and others in the days that followed, listening and not listening at all, wearied and quiet. *Oh, wearied
and wakened at last, Chae, and I haven't cared, they can
take me out fine and shoot me tomorrow, I'll be glad for
the rest of it, Chris lost to me through my own coarse daftness. She didn't even come to give me a kiss at good-bye,
Chae, we never said good-bye; but I mind the bonny head
of her down-bent there in the close. She'll never know, my
dear quean, and that's best—they tell lies about folk they
shoot and she'll think I just died like the rest; you're not
to tell her.*

Then he'd been silent long, and Chae'd had nothing to
say, he knew it was useless to make try for reprieve, he was
only a sergeant and had no business even in the hut with
the prisoner. And then Ewan said, sudden-like, it clean took
Chae by surprise, *Mind the smell of dung in the parks on an
April morning, Chae? And the peewits over the rigs? Bonny
they're flying this night in Kinraddie, and Chris sleeping
there, and all the Howe happed in mist.* Chae said that he
mustn't mind about that, he was feared that the dawn was
close, and Ewan should be thinking of other things now,
had he seen a minister? And Ewan said that an old bit billy
had come and blethered, an officer creature, but he'd paid
no heed, it had nothing to do with him. Even as he spoke
there rose a great clamour of guns far up in the front, it
was four miles off, not more; and Chae thought of the
hurried watches climbing to their posts and the blash and
flare of the Verey lights, the machine-gun crackle from pits
in the mud, things he himself mightn't hear for long:
Ewan'd never hear it at all beyond this night.

And not feared at all he looked, Chae saw, he sat there
in his kilt and shirt-sleeves, and he looked no more than a
young lad still, his head between his hands, he didn't seem
to be thinking at all of the morning so close. For he started
to speak of Blawearie then and the parks that he would have
drained, though he thought the land would go fair to hell

without the woods to shelter it. And Chae said that he thought the same, there were sore changes waiting them when they went back; and then he minded that Ewan would never go back, and could near have bitten his tongue in half, but Ewan hadn't noticed, he'd been speaking of the horses he'd had, Clyde and old Bess, fine beasts, fine beasts—did Chae mind that night of lightning when they found Chris wandering the fields with those two horses? That was the night he had known she liked him well—*nothing more than that, so quick and fierce she was, Chae man, she guarded herself like a queen in a palace, there was nothing between her and me till the night we married. Mind that—and the singing there was, Chae? What was it that Chris sang then?*

And neither could remember that, it had vexed Ewan a while, and then he forgot it, sitting quiet in that hut on the edge of morning. Then at last he'd stood up and gone to the window and said *There's bare a quarter of an hour now, Chae, you'll need to be getting back.*

And they'd shaken hands, the sentry opened the door for Chae, and he tried to say all he could for comfort, the fore-shadowing of the morning in Ewan's young eyes was strange and terrible, he couldn't take out his hand from that grip. And all that Ewan said was *Oh man, mind me when next you hear the peewits over Blawearie—look at my lass for me when you see her again, close and close, for that kiss that I'll never give her.* So he'd turned back into the hut, he wasn't feared or crying, he went quiet and calm; and Chae went down through the hut lines grouped about that place, a farm-place it had been, he'd got to the lorry that waited him, he was cursing and weeping then and the driver thought him daft, he hadn't known himself how he'd been. So they'd driven off, the wet morning had come crawling across the laired fields, and Chae had never seen Ewan again, they killed him that morning.

.   .   .   .   .

This was the story Chae told to Chris, sitting the two of them in the kitchen of Blawearie. Then he moved and got up and she did the same, and like one coming from a far, dark country, she saw his face now, he'd been all that time but a voice in the dark. And at last she found speech herself *Never vex for me or the telling me this, it was best, it was best!*

She crept up the stairs to their room when he'd gone, she opened the press where Ewan's clothes were, and kissed them and held them close, those clothes that had once been his near as ever he'd come to her now. And she whispered then in the stillness, with only the beech for a listener, *Oh, Ewan, Ewan, sleep quiet and sound now, lad, I understand! You did it for me, and I'm proud and proud, for me and Blawearie, my dear, my dear—sleep quiet and brave, for I've understood!*

The beech listened and whispered, whispered and listened, on and on. And a strange impulse and urge came on Chris Tavendale as she too listened. She ran down the stairs and found young Ewan and kissed him, *Let's go a jaunt up to the hill.*

Below them, Kinraddie; above, the hill; the loch shimmering and sleeping in the autumn sun; young Ewan at her feet; the peewits crying down the Howe.

She gave a long sigh and withdrew her hand from the face of the Standing Stone. The mist of memories fell away and the aching urge came back—for what, for what? Sun and sky and the loneliness of the hills, they had cried her up here —for what?

And then something made her raise her eyes, she stood awful and rigid, fronting him, coming up the path through the broom. Laired with glaur was his uniform, his face was white and the great hole sagged and opened, sagged and opened, red-glazed and black, at every upwards step he took. Up through the broom: she saw the grass wave with no press below his feet, her lad, the light in his eyes that aye she could bring.

The snipe stilled their calling, a cloud came over the sun. He was close to her now and she held out her hands to him, blind with tears and bright her eyes, the bright weather in their faces, her voice shaping a question that she heard him answer in the rustle of the loch-side rushes as closer his soundless feet carried him to her lips and hands.

Oh lassie, I've come home! he said, and went into the heart that was his forever.

EPILUDE

THE UNFURROWED FIELD

Folk said that winter that the War had done feint the much good to Mutch of Bridge End. In spite of his blowing and boasting, his silver he might as well have flung into a midden as poured in his belly, though faith! there wasn't much difference in destination. He'd gone in for the Irish cattle, had Mutch, quick you bought them and quick you sold and reaped a fine profit with prices so brave. More especially you did that if you crammed the beasts up with hay and water the morning before they were driven to the mart, they'd fairly seem to bulge with beef. But sometimes old Aitken of Bervie, a sly old brute, would give a bit stirk a wallop in the wame and it would belch like a bellows, and Aitken would say, *Ay, Mutch, the wind still bloweth as it listeth*, I see, he was aye quoting his bits of poetry, Aitken.

But he'd made silver for all that, Mutch, and many an awful feed had his great red lugs overhung, there in the Bridge End while the War went on. For that was how it struck him and his family, they'd gorge from morn till night, the grocer would stop three times a week and out to him Alec and his mistress would come, the bairns racing at the heels of them, and they'd buy up ham and biscuits and cheese and sausage, and tins of this and tins of that, enough to feed the German army, folk told—it that was said to be so hungry it was eating up its own bit corpses, feuch!

Though faith! it was little more than eating their own corpses they did at Bridge End. And what little they left uneaten they turned to drink, by the end of the War he'd got him a car, had Alec, it was only a Ford but it clattered up and down the road to Drumlithie every day of the week, and back it would bump to the Bridge End place with beer in crates and whisky in bottles wagging drunken-like over the hinder end. But Alec would blow and boast as much as ever, he'd say the Bridge End was a fine bit place and could

241

easily stand him a dram—*it's the knack of farming you want, that's all.*

Mutch had just got up and come out blear-eyed that day when the postman handed him the letter from Kinraddie House. So he had one read of it and then another, syne he cried to his wife *Nine hundred pounds—have YOU got nine hundred pounds, you?* And she answered him back, canty and cool, *No, I've seen neither silver nor sense since I married you. Why do you need nine hundred pounds?* So Alec showed her the letter, 'twas long and dreich and went on and on; but the gist of it was the Trustees were to sell up Kinraddie at last; and the farmers that wanted them could buy their own places; and if Mutch of Bridge End still wanted his the price was nine hundred pounds.

So that was how the Mutches left Kinraddie, they said never a word about buying the place, Alec sold off his stock fell quietly and they did a moonlight flit; some said they heard the Ford that night go rattling up by Laurencekirk, others swore that Mutch had gone north to Aberdeen and had got him a fine bit job in a public-house there. North or south, feint the thing more folk saw of him; and before the New Year was out old Gordon of Upperhill had bought up the Bridge End forbye his own place, he said he would farm the fields with a tractor. But damn the tractor ever appeared, he put sheep on the place instead, and sometimes the shepherd would wander into the kitchen where that gley-eyed wife of Mutch had sat to smoke her bit cigarettes; and he said that the smell of the damned things lingered there still, they'd been as unco at changing their shirts, the Mutches, as ever old Pooty had been.

What with his Germans and ghosts and dirt, he'd fair been in a way, had old Pooty. Long ere the War had finished he'd have nothing to do with the mending of boots, he wouldn't let the grocer up to the door, but would scraich at him to leave the messages out by the road. And at last he clean went over the gate, as a man might say, he took in his cuddy to live with him there in the kitchen, and the farmer lads going by on their bicycles of a Saturday night would hear the two of them speaking together, old Pooty they'd hear, thinking himself back at some concert or other in the olden days, reciting his TIMROUS BEASTIE, stuttering and stammering at the head of his voice. And then he'd be heard to give the donkey a bit clout, and *Damn you! Clap, you creature!* he'd cry; and it was a fair entertainment.

But at last it grew overmuch to bear, that was just about the month when the letters went out from the Trustee childes, and folk said that fell awful sounds were heard coming from the Pooty place, the creature was clean demented. Not a body would do a thing till at last old Gordon did, he roaded off with his foreman, they went in old Gordon's car, it was night, and the nearer they came to Pooty's the more awful came the sounds. The cuddy was braying and braying in an awful stamash, they tried to look through the window, but there was a thick leather blind there and feint the thing could they see. So the foreman tried the door and it wouldn't budge, but the braying of the cuddy grew worse and worse; and the foreman was a big bit childe and he took a great run at the door and open it flew and the sight he saw would have scunnered a sow from its supper, the coarse old creature was tormenting the donkey this way and that with a red-hot poker, he scraiched the beast was a German, and they had to tie him up.

So the foreman went back for his gun and to send a message to bring the police; and when the police came down the next day the donkey was shot, and some said old Pooty should have been instead. But they took the old creature away to the madhouse, fair a good riddance to Kinraddie it was. For a while after that there was speak of the Upperhill's foreman biding at Pooty's, he wanted to marry and it would be fine and close for his work. And the foreman said the place was fine if you thought of breeding a family of swine; but he was neither a boar himself nor was his quean a bit sow.

So the place began to moulder away, soon the roof went all agley and half fell in, it was fit for neither man nor beast, the thistles and weeds were all over the close, right they'd have pleased old Pooty's cuddy if he'd lived to see them. It looked a dreich, cold place as you rode by at night, near as lonesome as the old Mill was, and not near so handy. For the Mill was a place you could take your quean to, you'd

lean your bicycles up by the wall and take a peek through
the kitchen window; syne off you'd go, your two selves, and
sit inside the old Mill itself; and your quean would say
Don't! and smooth her short skirts; and she'd tell you you
would be lucky if you got two dances at the Fordoun ball,
John Edwards was to take her there in his side-car, mind.

For Long Rob had never come back to the Mill. It had
fair been a wonder him joining the soldiers and going off
to the War the way he did—after swearing black was blue
that he'd never fight, that the one was as bad as the other,
Scotch or German. Some said it was just plain daft he had
gone, with no need for him to enlist; but when Munro of
the Cuddiestoun told that to Chris Tavendale up at Blawearie she said there had been more sweetness and sense
in Rob's little finger than in all the Munro carcases clecked
since the Flood. Ill to say that to a man of an age with your
father, it showed you the kind of creature Chris Tavendale
was, folk shook their heads, minding how she'd gone near
mad when her man was killed; as if he'd been the only one!
And there was her brother, Will was his name, that had
come from the War in a queer bit uniform, French he had
said that it was; but them that were fine acquainted with
uniforms weren't so sure, the Uhlans had worn uniforms
just like that.

They had been the German horse-billies away back at the
War's beginning, you minded, and syne shook your head
over that, and turned to thinking of Long Rob again, him
that was killed in the April of the last year's fighting. He'd
been one of the soldiers they'd rushed to France in such
hurry when it seemed that the German childes were fair over
us, and he'd never come back to Kinraddie again, just notice
of his death came through and syne a bit in the paper about
him. You could hardly believe your eyes when you read it,
him such a fell pacifist, too, he'd been killed in a bit retreat,
that they made, him and two-three more billies had stood
up to the Germans right well and held them back while the
Scots retreated; they'd held on long after the others had
gone, and Rob had been given a medal for that. Not that
he got it, faith! he was dead, they came on his corpse long
after, the British, but just as a mark of respect.

And you minded Long Rob right well, the long rangy childe, with his twinkling eyes and his great bit mouser and those stories of his that he'd deave you with, horses and horses, damn't! he had horses on the brain. There'd been his coarse speak about religion, too, fair a scandal once in the Howe, but for all that he'd been a fine stock, had Rob, you minded him singing out there in the morning, he'd sung—— And you couldn't mind what the song had been till maybe a bairn would up and tell you, they'd heard it often on the way to school, and Ay, it was *Ladies of Spain*. You heard feint the meikle of those old songs now, they were daft and old-fashioned, there were fine new ones in their places, right from America, folk said, and all about the queer blue babies that were born there, they were clever brutes, the Americans.

Well, that was the Mill, all its trade was gone, old Gordon bought up its land for a two-three pounds, and joined the lot on to Upperhill. Jock Gordon came blinded back from the War, they said he'd been near demented at first when he lost the use of his eyes. But old Gordon was making silver like dirt, he coddled up Jock like a pig with a tit, and he'd settled down fell content, as well the creature might be, with all he could smoke or drink at his elbow, and his mother near ready to lick his boots. Fell gentry and all they were now, the Gordons, you couldn't get within a mile of the Upperhill without you'd hear a blast of the English, so fine and genteel; and the ploughmen grew fair mad when they dropped in for a dram at Drumlithie Hotel and some billy would up and ask, *Is't true they dish you out white dickies at Upperhill now and you've all to go to the Academy?*

He was one of the folk that broke up the ploughmen's Union, old Gordon, right proud he was of it, too; and faith, the man was but right, whoever heard tell of such nonsense, a Union for ploughmen? But he didn't get off scot-free, faith, no! For what should happen in the General Election but that the secretary of the Farm Servants' Union put up as a candidate for the Mearns; and from far and near over Scotland a drove of those socialist creatures came riding to help him, dressed up in specs and baggy breeks and stockings with meikle checks. Now, one of them was a doctor childe and up to the Upperhill he came on a canvass, like, when old Gordon and the wife had driven off to lend help to the Coalition. The door was opened by Maggie Jean, she'd grown up bonny as a flower in spring, a fine quean, sweet and kind, with no English airs. And damn't if they didn't take up, the doctor and her, all in a minute, the doctor forgot about the bothy he'd come to canvass and Maggie Jean had him in to tea, and they spoke on politics for hours and hours, the servant quean told, she said it was nothing but politics; and there have been greater miracles.

Well, the next thing was that old Gordon found his men being harried to vote for the Labour man, harried by his own lass Maggie Jean, it sent him fair wild and the blind son too. But Maggie Jean didn't care a fig, the doctor childe had turned her head; and when the election was over and the Labour man beaten she told her father she wasn't going on to the college any longer, she was set on marrying her Labour doctor. Gordon said he'd soon put his foot on that, she wasn't of age and he'd stop the marriage. But Maggie Jean put her arms round his neck, *I know, but you wouldn't like people to point at you and say 'Have you heard of old Gordon's illegitimate grandchild?'* And at that they say old Gordon fair caved in, *Oh, my lass, my Maggie Jean, you haven't done that!* For answer Maggie Jean just stood and laughed, shaky-like, though, till ben came Mistress Gordon herself and heard the news, and started in on the lass. Syne Maggie Jean grew cool as ice, *Very well, then, mother, I hear there's a good bed in Stonehaven Workhouse where women can have their babies.*

So she won in the end, you may well be sure, the Gordons fair rushed the marriage, and every now and then the doctor and Maggie Jean would take a bit look at each other and laugh out loud, they weren't a bit ashamed or decent. And when the wedding was over Mistress Gordon said *It's glad I am that you're off from Kinraddie to Edinburgh, where the shame of your half-named bairn won't aye be cast in my face.* And Maggie Jean said *What bairn, mother? I'm not to have a baby yet, you know, unless George and I get over-enthusiastic tonight.* Fair dumbfoundered was Mistress Gordon, she gasped, *But you said that you were with a bairn!* and Maggie Jean just shook her head and laughed, *Oh, no, I just asked father if he'd like to grandfather one. And I don't suppose that he would. I won't have time for babies for years yet, mother, I'm to help ORGANIZING THE FARM SERVANTS!*

Ah well, folk said there was damned little chance of Nellie, the other bit daughter, ever having anything legitimate or illegitimate, she was growing up as sour and wizened as an old potato, for all her English she'd sleep cold and unhandled, an old maid all her days. But faith! you're sure of nothing in this world, or whoever would have guessed that Sarah Sinclair, the daft old skate, would go marrying? It all came through the War and the stir at the Netherhill when old Sinclair bought up the Knapp and his own bit place all at one whip. Soon's she heard of that Sarah went to him and said *You did plenty for Kirsty and she'll not be needing the Knapp any more, you can bravely settle me there!*

Old Sinclair, he was nearly ninety and blind, he stared at her like a stirk at a water-jump, and then cried for his wife. And Sarah told them she meant what she said, Dave Brown, the Gourdon childe, would marry her the morn if they'd Peesie's Knapp to sit down in.

And she got her way, but she didn't get the land, old Sinclair pastured his sheep on it, and Dave stayed on as a Netherhill ploughman. So Sarah was married off at last and taken to bed in the house that had been her sister's. She soon had her man well in hand, had Sarah, folk said she'd to take him to bed by the lug the first night, but there are aye coarse brutes to say things like that. And damn it, if before a twelvemonth was up she didn't have a bairn, a peely-wally girl, but a bairn for all that. It wasn't much, but still it was something, and when old Sinclair heard the news he got it all mixed, he was in bed by then and sinking fast, he thought it was Kirsty's first bairn that they told of, and all the time he kept whispering *Chae!* he wanted his good-son, Chae, that had married Kirsty long syne.

But Chae had been gone long ere that, he was killed in the first fighting of Armistice Day, an hour before the guns grew quiet. You minded him well and the arguings he'd

have with Long Rob of the Mill; he'd have been keen for
the Labour candidate, for Rich and Poor were as far off
being Equal as ever they'd been, poor Chae. Ay, it struck
you strange that he'd gone, fine childe he had been though
a bit of a fool that you laughed at behind his back. In his
last bit leave folk said he'd been awful quiet, maybe he
knew right well he would never come back, he tramped the
parks most of the time, muttering of the woods they'd cut
and the land that would never get over it. And when he said
good-bye to Kirsty it wasn't just the usual slap on the
shoulder and *Well, I'm away!* He held her and kissed her,
folk saw it at the station, and he said *Be good to the bairns,
lass.* And Kirsty, the meikle sumph, had stood there crying
as the train went out, you'd have thought she'd have had
more sense with all the folk glowering at her. And that was
the last of Chae, you'd say, except that in the November
of nineteen-eighteen they sent home his pocket-book and
hankies and things; and they'd been well washed, but blood
lay still in a pouch of the pocket-book, cold and black, and
when Kirsty saw it she screamed and fainted away.

Women had little guts, except one or two, said Munro
of the Cuddiestoun, as though he himself had been killing
a German for breakfast every day of the War. And maybe
that's what he'd liked to think as he chased the hens and
thrawed their necks for the hospital trade, or swore at the
daftie, Tony, over this or that. Feint the much heed paid
Tony, though, he'd just stand about the same as ever, staring
at the ground and driving Mistress Munro fair out of
her senses when she'd sent him to lower the heat in one
incubator or raise it up in another. For it was more than
likely the creature would do clean the opposite of what he'd
been told, and syne stand and glower at the ground a whole
afternoon till somebody came out to look for him and would
find every damned egg hard-boiled or stone cold, as the
case might be. Some said he wasn't so daft, he did it for spite,
but you'd hardly believe that a daftie would have the sense
for that.

But nobody could deny the Munros had got on, they'd
clean stopped from farming every park except one to grow
their potatoes in, all the rest were covered with runs and rees

for the hens, they'd made a fair fortune with their poultry and all. You'd never hear such a scraich in your life as when night-time came and they closed up the Cuddiestoun rees, it was then that Mistress Munro would nip out a cockerel here and an old hen there and thraw the creature's neck as quick as you'd blink and syne sit up half the night in the plucking of the birds. They'd hardly ever a well-cooked meal in the house themselves, but if their stomachs had little in them their bank books knew no lack, maybe one more than consoled for the other. But Ellison said that they made him sick, the only mean Scotch he'd ever met, and be damned if they didn't make up for all the free ones.

Though that was only the kind of speak you'd expect from an Irish creature, he still spoke like one, fell fat he'd grown, his belly wabbled down right near to his knees and his breeks were meikle in girth. When the Trustees sent out their notice to buy, folk wondered what he'd do, there'd be an end to Ellison now, they said. But sore mistaken they found themselves, he bought up the Mains, stock and all, he bought up the ruins of Kinraddie House, and he bought Blawearie when there were no bids, he got it for less than two hundred pounds. And where had be got all that money except that he stole it?

Fair Kinraddie's big man he thought himself, faith! folk laughed at him and called him the waiter-laird, Cospatric that killed the gryphon would have looked at him sore surprised. He spoke fell big about tractors for ploughing, but then the slump came down and his blowing with it, he bought up sheep for Blawearie instead. And that was the way things went in the end on the old bit place up there on the brae, sheep baaed and scrunched where once the parks flowed thick with corn, no corn would come at all, they said, since the woods went down. And the new minister when he preached his incoming sermon cried *They have made a desert and they call it peace;* and some had no liking of the creature for that, but God! there was truth in his speak.

For the Gibbons had gone clean out of Kinraddie, there'd be far more room and far less smell, folk said, Stuart Gibbon had never come back from the War to stand in the pulpit his father had held. Not that he'd been killed, no, no, you might well depend that the great, curled steer had more sense in him than that. But the gentry liked him in Edinburgh right well in his Chaplain's uniform, and syne he fell in with some American creatures that controlled a kirk in New York. And they asked him if he'd like to have that kirk, all the well-off Scots went to it; and he took the offer like a shot and was off to America before you could wink, him and that thin bit English wife of his and their young bit daughter. Well, well, he'd done well for himself, it was plain to see; no doubt the Americans would like him fine, they could stand near anything out in America, their stomachs were awful tough with all the coarse things that they ate out of tins.

As for the father, the old man that had had such an ill-will for the Germans, he'd grown over-frail to preach and had to retire; and faith! if the British armies had killed half the Germans with their guns that he did with his mouth it would have been a clean deserted Germany long ere the end of the War. But off he went at last and only two ministers made try for the pulpit, both of them young, the one just a bit student from Aberdeen, the other new out of the Army. There seemed little to choose between the pair, they'd no pulpit voices, either of them, but folk thought it only fair to give the soldier billy the chance.

And it was only after he headed the leat, Colquohoun was his name, that the story went round he was son to that old minister from Banff that made try for Kinraddie before the War and was fair out-preached by the Reverend Gibbon. You minded him, surely?—he'd preached about beasts and the Golden Age, that the dragons still lived but sometime they'd die and the Golden Age come back. Feuch ay! no sermon at all, you might say. Well, that was him and this was the son, thin and tall, with a clean-shaven face, and he lectured on this and he wrote on that and he made himself fair objectionable before he'd been there a month. For he chummed up with ploughmen, he drove his own coal, he never wore a collar that fastened at the back, and when folk called him the Reverend he pulled them up sharp— *reverent, I am, no more, my friend.* And he whistled when he went on a Sunday walk and he stormed at farmers for the pay they paid and he helped the ploughmen's Union; and he'd preach just rank sedition about it, and speak as though Christ had meant Kinraddie, and folk would grow fair uncomfortable

You couldn't well call him pro-German like, for he'd been a plain soldier all through the War. Folk felt clean lost without a bit name to hit at him with, till Ellison said he was a Bolshevik, one of those awful creatures, coarse tinks, that had made such a spleiter in Russia. They'd shot their king-creature, the Tsar they called him, and they bedded all over the place, folk said, a man would go home and find his wife commandeered any bit night and Lenin and Trotsky lying with her. And Ellison said that the same would come in Kinraddie if Mr Colquohoun had his way; maybe he was feared for his mistress, was Ellison, though God knows there'd be little danger of *her* being commandeered, even Lenin and Trotsky would fair be desperate before they would go to that length.

Well, that was your new minister, then; and next there came scandalous stories that he'd taken up with young Chris Tavendale. Nearly every evening of the week he'd ride up to Blawearie, and bide there all the hours of the night, or so folk said. And what could he want with a common bit quean like the Tavendale widow? Ministers took up with ladies if they meant no jookery-packery. But when Munro said that to old Brigson the creature fair flew into a rage; and he said that many a decent thing had gone out of Kinraddie with the War but that only one had come in, and that was the new minister. Well, well, it might be so and it mightn't; but one night Dave Brown climbed up the hill from the Knapp, to see old Brigson about buying a horse, and he heard folk speaking inside the kitchen and he took a bit keek round the door. And there near the fire stood Chris herself, and the Reverend Colquohoun was before her, she was looking up into the minister's face and he'd both her hands in his. And *Oh, my dear, maybe the second Chris, maybe the third, but Ewan has the first forever!* she was saying, whatever she meant by that; and syne as Dave Brown still looked the minister bent down and kissed her, the fool.

Folk said that fair proved the stories were true, but the very next Sunday the minister stood up in the pulpit, and, calm as ever, read out the banns of Upperhill's foreman and his quean from Fordoun, and syne the banns of *Robert Colquohoun, bachelor of this parish, and Christine Tavendale, widow, also of this same parish.*

You could near have heard a pin drop then, so quiet it was in the kirk, folk sat fair stunned. And there'd never been such a claik in Kinraddie as when the service was over and the congregation got out—ay, Chris Tavendale had feathered her nest right well, the sleeked creature, who'd have thought it of her?

And that made the minister no more well-liked with Kinraddie's new gentry, you may well be sure. But worse than that came; he'd been handed the money, the minister, to raise a memorial for Kinraddie's bit men that the War had killed. Folk thought he'd have a fine stone angel, with a night-gown on, raised up at Kinraddie cross-roads. But he sent for a mason instead and had the old stone circle by Blawearie loch raised up and cleaned and set all in place, real heathen-like, and a paling put round it. And after reading out his banns on that Sunday the minister read out that next Saturday the Kinraddie Memorial would be unveiled on Blawearie brae, and that he expected a fine attendance, whatever the weather—*they'd to attend in ill weather, the folk that fell.*

Fine weather for January that Saturday brought, sunny, yet caller, you could see the clouds come sailing down from the north and over the sun and off again. But there was rain not far, the seagulls had come sooning inland; for once the snipe were still. Nearly every soul in Kinraddie seemed climbing Blawearie brae as the afternoon wore on, a fair bit stir there was in the close, the place was empty of horses and stock, Chris would be leaving there at the term. Soon she'd be down at the Manse instead, and a proud-like creature no doubt she'd be.

Well, up on the brae through the road in the broom there drew a fell concourse of folk, Ellison was there, and his mistress, and the Gordons and gentry generally, forbye a reischle of ploughmen and queans, lying round on the grass and sniggering. There was the old circle of the Standing Stones, the middle one draped with a clout, you wondered what could be under it and how much the mason had charged. It was high, there, you saw as you sat in the grass and looked round, you could see all Kinraddie and near half the Howe shine under your feet in the sun, *Out of the World and into Blawearie* as the old speak went. And faith! the land looked unco and woe with its woods all gone, even in the thin-sun-glimmer there came a cold shiver up over the parks of the Knapp and Blawearie, folk said that the land had gone cold and wet right up to the very Mains.

Snow was shining in the Grampians, far in the coarse hills there, and it wouldn't be long ere the dark came. Syne at last the minister was seen coming up, he'd on the bit robes that he hardly ever wore, Chris Tavendale walked by the side of him and behind was a third childe that nobody knew, a Highlander in kilts and with pipes on his shoulder, great and red-headed, who could he be? And then Ellison minded, he said the man had been friend to young Ewan Tavendale, he'd been the best man at Ewan's marriage, McIvor his name was.

The minister held open the gate for Chris and through it she came, all clad in her black, young Ewan's hand held fast in hers, he'd grown fair like his father, the bairn, dark-like and solemn he was. Chris's face was white and solemn as well except when she looked at the minister as he held the gate open, it was hardly decent the look that she gave him, they might keep their courting till the two were alone. Folk cried *Ay, minister!* and he cried back cheerily and went striding to the midst of the old stone circle, John Brigson was standing there with his hands on the strings that held the bit clout.

The minister said, *Let us pray,* and folk took off their hats, it smote cold on your pow. The sun was fleering up in the clouds, it was quiet on the hill, you saw young Chris stand looking down on Kinraddie with her bairn's hand in hers. And then the Lord's Prayer was finished, the minister was speaking just ordinary, he said they had come to honour the folk whom the War had taken, and that the clearing of this ancient site was maybe the memory that best they'd have liked. And he gave a nod to old Brigson and the strings were pulled and off came the clout and there on the Standing Stone the words shone out in their dark grey lettering, plain and short:

FOR : THE : MEMORY : OF :

CHARLES : STRACHAN : JAMES :

LESLIE : ROBERT : DUNCAN : EWAN :

TAVENDALE :

WHO : WERE : OF : THIS : LAND :

AND : FELL : IN : THE : GREAT : WAR :

IN : FRANCE :

REVELATION : II CH : 28 VERSE

And then, with the night waiting out by on Blawearie brae, and the sun just verging the coarse hills, the minister began to speak again, his short hair blowing in the wind that had come, his voice not decent and a kirk-like bumble, but ringing out over the loch:

FOR I WILL GIVE YOU THE MORNING STAR

In the sunset of an age and an epoch we may write that for epitaph of the men who were of it. They went quiet and brave from the lands they loved, though seldom of that love might they speak, it was not in them to tell in words of the earth that moved and lived and abided, their life and enduring love. And who knows at the last what memories of it were with them, the springs and the winters of this land and all the sounds and scents of it that had once been theirs, deep, and a passion of their blood and spirit, those four who died in France? With them we may say there died a thing older than themselves, these were the Last of the Peasants, the last of the Old Scots folk. A new genera-

tion comes up that will know them not, except as a memory in a song, they passed with the things that seemed good to them with loves and desires that grow dim and alien in the days to be. It was old Scotland that perished then, and we may believe that never again will the old speech and the old songs, the old curses and the old benedictions, rise but with alien effort to our lips. The last of the peasants, those four that you knew, took that with them to the darkness and the quietness of the places where they sleep. And the land changes, their parks and their steadings are a desolation where the sheep are pastured, we are told that great machines come soon to till the land, and the great herds come to feed on it, the crofter has gone, the man with the house and the steading of his own and the land closer to his heart than the flesh of his body. Nothing, it has been said, is true but change, nothing abides, and here in Kinraddie where we watch the building of those little prides and those little fortunes on the ruins of the little farms we must give heed that these also do not abide, that a new spirit shall come to the land with the greater herd and the great machines. For greed of place and possession and great estate those four had little heed, the kindness of friends and the warmth of toil and the peace of rest—they asked no more from God or man, and no less would they endure. So, lest we shame them, let us believe that the new oppressions and foolish greeds are no more than mists that pass. They died for a world that is past, these men, but they did not die for this that we seem to inherit. Beyond it and us there shines a greater hope and a newer world, undreamt when these four died. But need we doubt which side the battle they would range themselves did they live today, need we doubt the answer they cry to us even now, the four of them, from the places of the sunset?

And then, as folk stood dumbfounded, this was just sheer politics, plain what he meant, the Highland man McIvor tuned up his pipes and began to step slow round the stone circle by Blawearie Loch, slow and quiet, and folk watched him, the dark was near, it lifted your hair and was eerie and uncanny, the *Flowers of the Forest* as he played it:

It rose and rose and wept and cried, that crying for the
men that fell in battle, and there was Kirsty Strachan weeping quietly and others with her, and the young ploughmen
they stood with glum, white faces, they'd no understanding
or caring, it was something that vexed and tore at them, it
belonged to times they had no knowing of.

He fair could play, the piper, he tore at your heart marching there with the tune leaping up the moor and echoing
across the loch, folk said that Chris Tavendale alone shed
never a tear, she stood quiet, holding her boy by the hand,
looking down on Blawearie's fields till the playing was over.
And syne folk saw that the dark had come and began to
stream down the hill, leaving her there, some were uncertain
and looked them back. But they saw the minister was standing behind her, waiting for her, they'd the last of the light
with them up there, and maybe they didn't need it or heed
it, you can do without the day if you've a lamp quiet-lighted
and kind in your heart.

COMMENTARY

by

J. T. LOW

THE AUTHOR

James Leslie Mitchell was born, the youngest of three sons, in the croft of Hillhead of Segget, Auchterless, Aberdeenshire, on 13 February, 1901. When he was eight years of age, the family moved to the farm-croft of Bloomfield on the Reisk road, two miles above the village of Arbuthnott, in an area of farmland dotted with crofts and situated between Inverbervie and Drumlithie in Kincardineshire. Even as a pupil in the middle primary school Leslie Mitchell was interested in history and prehistory which he could study at first hand, for the district around Bloomfield abounds in relics of the recent and distant past. The church at Arbuthnott ('the Kirk of Sanct Ternan Arbuthnott'), whose oldest existing buildings date from 1242, is a reminder of still earlier times: it was dedicated in the name of a Pictish saint in the fifth century; and throughout the district there are stone circles, standing stones, and cairns indicating the sites of battles and camps. It was not until Mitchell was twelve that he showed signs of skill in writing, however; and there seems little doubt that he was greatly encouraged and stimulated by Alexander Gray who became headmaster of Arbuthnott School in 1913.

Despite his promising start at Arbuthnott, Leslie Mitchell did not flourish when he moved to Mackie Academy, Stonehaven; and after some awkward scenes at home and in school he left the Academy and found for himself a job as junior reporter with the *Aberdeen Journal*. It was at this period in his career that he became interested in economic and social problems and in left-wing politics. From Aberdeen Mitchell went to Glasgow to be a reporter with the *Scottish Farmer*. Here he seems to have done well to begin with but his distaste for Glasgow and trouble with his editor eventually led to dismissal from the post, and he found himself for a time back home at Bloomfield with his family, facing an uncertain future.

On 26 August 1919, Leslie Mitchell enlisted with the
Royal Army Service Corps. He was sent to Mesopotamia
(Iraq) and was soon involved in an Arab rebellion. In the
years of service that followed he travelled in Persia, India,
and Egypt, and visited Jerusalem and Constantinople. He
was later to turn these experiences to good account both
in his novels and in his archaeological studies. As a boy
he had become friendly with a neighbouring crofter Robert
Middleton of Hareden on whom the character Long Rob
of the Mill is based; and his friendship with Rebecca,
Middleton's daughter, continued despite interruptions and
blossomed eventually into a love affair. After leaving the
army in 1923, Mitchell tried to earn a living by free-lance
journalism but was obliged after five months to join the
Royal Air Force as a clerk. Things began to improve for
him after this. He won first prize in a short story competition
in 1924; on 15 August 1925 he married Rebecca Middleton;
and in 1927 he was promoted Corporal. In the last two years
of his service with the R.A.F., particularly from 1928 onwards, it was clear Leslie Mitchell was finding his métier
as a writer. The first of twelve stories was accepted for
publication by the *Cornhill Magazine* ('For Ten's Sake')
in April 1928 (and eventually published in 1929), and his
first book *Hanno or The Future of Exploration* was published by Kegan Paul in June 1928.

After a struggle Leslie Mitchell's first novel *Stained
Radiance* was published by Jarrolds in September 1930.
By this time he had left the R.A.F. and had settled down
with his wife in London, reading and studying archaeology
at the British Museum, and determined to carve for himself a career as a writer. In the crowded years that followed
Mitchell wrote articles on archaeology and exploration as
well as stories and novels, becoming particularly interested
in the origins of civilisation and the ancient Mayan people
of Central America. He was greatly attracted to the theory
of *diffusionism*[1]—roughly, the notion that primitive man,
far from being savage, was essentially peaceful and sane
and happy, only becoming savage and corrupted by the
spread of 'civilisation'. Mitchell's 'diffusionist' ideas are not

[1] See Appendix A, p. 293.

only reflected in his archaeological study *The Conquest of the Maya* (1934), but are also interwoven with the narrative in his 'English' novels *The Thirteenth Disciple* (1931), *Three Go Back* (1932), *The Lost Trumpet* (1932), and *Image and Superscription* (1933). They are less in evidence in *Gay Hunter* (1934).

Leslie Mitchell was prolific in output. Under his own name he continued to write novels and articles, but in 1932 he turned to Scottish themes and scenes. He used his home background, his childhood memories, and his detailed knowledge of the north-east crofter's life in writing *Sunset Song* and in planning the other two parts of the trilogy *Cloud Howe* (1933) and *Grey Granite* (1934). His 'Scottish' works—these three novels that make up *A Scots Quair* and his short stories 'Greenden', 'Smeddum', 'Clay', 'Forsaken' and 'Sim'—were published under the pseudonym Lewis Grassic Gibbon which is based on his mother's name Lilias Grassic Gibbon.

Most critics agree that the Scottish novels represent Mitchell's greatest achievement. They capture the flavour of the life and speech of a community whose ways were being threatened (and were partially destroyed) by the forces of modern war and 'civilisation'. There are indeed traces of the 'diffusionist' theory in the Scottish novels (the sermon preached by old Colquohoun for instance[1]); but their great achievement is the portrayal of the setting and people of the Mearns by means of a sharply and poetically recreated impression of folk speech rhythms partly Scots, partly English.

Mitchell continued to write and lay plans for other works after the success of the three novels that make up his Scottish trilogy; but he was being more and more incapacitated by gastric trouble. Confined to bed for a time in the winter of 1934, he yet managed to correspond with his friends and publishers, and looked forward to resuming his work. Just after the new year of 1935 however, when he seemed to have recovered a little, he was taken violently ill; and in Welwyn Garden City Hospital he died of peritonitis on 7 February, not quite 34 years old. It was fitting that the casket

[1] See p. 57 of the text.

containing his ashes should have been taken back to the churchyard at Arbuthnott.

Leslie Mitchell's death at such a young age was a tragedy not only to his family but also to literature. There is no saying what works he would have produced had he lived. (Selections from the opening of a new novel of the Mearns are printed in *A Scots Hairst*.) As it is, his contribution is to be ranked with that of the great novelists of the twentieth century and with those writers who helped to stimulate a renaissance in Scottish letters that began just after the first war and has continued to our own day.

THE SCOTTISH LITERARY REVIVAL

Grassic Gibbon's name will always be linked with Hugh MacDiarmid's; for those two writers, the one a great novelist the other a great poet, collaborated to produce one of the most controversial books ever written on Scotland—*Scottish Scene or The Intelligent Man's Guide to Albyn* (1934). This work contained a series of impressions and writings on Scotland and Scottish life, contradictory, derogatory, irreverent. MacDiarmid's contributions tended to reflect a belief in Scotland, Gibbon's reflected the opposite. The book is remarkable too for containing Gibbon's essay 'The Land' and his five Scottish short stories. (This essay, these stories, and other essays published in *Scottish Scene*, also appear in *A Scot Hairst*.) Hugh MacDiarmid himself (C. M. Grieve, born 1892) had already become well known as the writer of Scots lyrics of cosmic range and as the author of *The Drunk Man Looks at the Thistle* (1926), a satirical vision of Scotland within a world setting, an attempt to use Scottish verse for serious critical purposes. MacDiarmid has continued to write his political poems, satires and commentaries, experimenting at first with Scots, but later using also standard English. Today he is regarded as the greatest living Scottish poet, by some as the greatest living poet writing in English.

Edwin Muir was another Scot who was making a name for himself as poet and critic at the time Grassic Gibbon was writing; and like Gibbon he seemed not to believe in a distinctly Scottish literature. His poems, many of them deriving their strength from his Orkney background, are all written in English, in contrast to the works of Sydney Goodsir Smith, who fashioned for himself a particularly rich and virile form of Scots. Goodsir Smith's long work *Under the Eildon Tree* (1948) is a kind of satirical love poem, a cycle of twenty-four 'elegies', the ground theme taken from the Thomas the Rhymer story. Amongst the other poets who have written in Scots are William Soutar, in whom the influence of the ballad is strong, and Douglas Young, whose poems have a typically Scottish directness and humour. George Bruce and George Mackay Brown write some of their best works as a reflection of their home background— Bruce in terms of the Buchan area and Mackay Brown in terms of Orkney. Norman MacCaig produces poems on the Edinburgh scene and on the highlands in a witty meta-physical style.

In drama between 1928 and 1950 James Bridie (Dr O. H. Mavor) wrote his plays about Scottish doctors, Biblical characters, and Scottish professional men. In the revival of interest in Scottish drama in the fifties three other names stand out—Robert Kemp, Alexander Reid, Robert Mac-Lellan; and with Bridie these writers played a big part in vitalising theatre in Edinburgh and Glasgow, and in encouraging the drama side of the Edinburgh International Festival. It is interesting that there should have been a correspondence between Bridie and Grassic Gibbon in 1934 in the course of which Bridie urged Gibbon to write plays since he had 'a hell of a grip on the spoken word'.[1]

At the time the Grassic Gibbon novels of the Mearns countryside were appearing, other Scottish writers were turning to Glasgow as a setting for their novels. Dot Allan wrote *Hunger March* in 1931, Edwin Muir *Poor Tom* in 1932, and Alexander McArthur *No Mean City* in 1936. Perhaps the best of the novels of Glasgow life of this period is *The Shipbuilders* by George Blake. Like Gibbon, Blake is interested in the contrast between the Anglified Scot and

[1] Quoted in Ian S. Munro's biography *Leslie Mitchell: Lewis Grassic Gibbon*, p. 195.

the Scot who remains true to his origins; but the contrast becomes one between classes rather than a conflict within the personality as in Gibbon. Apart from historical novels and novels of the highland clearances by writers like Naomi Mitchison and Tom MacDonald ('Fionn MacColla'), the works of two Scottish novelists of the 'thirties and 'forties stand out—those of Eric Linklater and Neil Gunn. Linklater's novels such as *White Maa's Saga* (1929) and *Magnus Merriman* (1934) are coloured by his impressions of Orkney; and Neil Gunn's works like *Highland River* (1937) and *The Silver Darlings* (1941) are concerned with the folk-history and the social patterns of life in the highlands. Leslie Mitchell could turn from *Spartacus*, his novel on the Roman slave leader, and his diffusionist novels to become Lewis Grassic Gibbon and take part in this developing interest in the Scottish scene, Scottish society and Scottish character. *Sunset Song*, when viewed in this context of literary activity in Scotland, can be seen to fulfil a vital role in the development of the Scottish novel.

THE SETTING

The novel is set in the author's own home territory—that part of east Kincardineshire or the Mearns that lies south of Stonehaven towards Bervie and Gourdon and westward as far as Drumlithie and Laurencekirk—perhaps coloured by impressions of an area near Echt in Aberdeenshire with its higher hills, stone circles and loch. It has a varied enough landscape—field, farmcroft, howe, hill, kirk, river, occasional loch, sea. It is a countryside where you can feel remote in the 'parks' and hillsides that echo to the cry of the 'peesie' (lapwing), yet you are never far from the sea. In *Sunset Song* Chris returns again and again to the hills for sanctuary, but behind her there is 'the shimmer of the North Sea' or the sound of the foghorn down by Kinneff, as she reaches her Standing Stones.

Chris and Ewan have holiday jaunts to Stonehaven and Dunnottar; and there are references to Laurencekirk, Drumlithie, Fordoun, Edzell, Brechin. But the true setting of the novel is given the fictitious name 'Kinraddie',[1] which is described as an estate dating back to the days of William the Lion of Scotland when it had come into the hands of the 'Norman childe' Cospatric, and now at the opening of the novel in 1911 a community of nine farms leased from the trustees of his half-witted descendant. We notice how systematically and yet humorously Gibbon at the beginning describes each of the nine farm-crofts of 'Kinraddie'—Mains the largest held by the Irishman Ellison, Peesie's Knapp farmed by Chae Strachan, Blawearie that the Guthries come from Aberdeenshire to farm, Munro's place Cuddiestoun, Netherhill occupied by the Sinclairs, the Mill run by Long Rob, the Gordons' place Upperhill, Pooty's little croft, and Bridge End farmed by Alec Mutch. The tradition of referring to a man by the name of his farm is illustrated throughout *Sunset Song*.

Although there are references (and some of them not very complimentary!) to people outside the crofting circle—the minister, the schoolmaster, the doctor, it is the world of Kinraddie and in particular the world of Blawearie, Chris's world, that we are concerned with. This might give us the impression we are cut off in a restricted setting, but in fact the feeling for field and moorland, for air and sea, for the power of life throbbing in humans and animals and crops, gives us the opposite impression: we feel with Chris at the very centre of life. The setting has a universal quality as well as a particular reference. Life in this part of Scotland may seem remote to some people but one is nearer the heart of things here than in big cities. Yet even this life is subject to change, violent change when the first war strikes. A large part of the skill and power of this book lies in the way the author shows how the corruption of outside forces, particularly a world war, destroys the ancient patterns of living on the land in such a setting as Kinraddie of the Mearns.

For by the end of the book the setting is destroyed or at least changed, utterly changed. The woods that protected and nourished the land have been cut down to provide timber for the war. Chae Strachan during his leave goes about lamenting their destruction. At the end of the war

[1] See the sketch map on p. ix.

the trustees at Kinraddie House decide to sell up the crofters' land. The Mutches at Bridge End for all their boasting and high living are unable or unwilling to buy their place for £900 and off they go on a moonlight flit to Aberdeen. Pooty has become insane living with his cuddy and has to be taken to the madhouse. Both Pooty's and the Mill fall into ruin; but the land round the mill is bought by old Gordon of Upperhill and joined on to his place. Another to prosper is old Sinclair who buys up both his own place Netherhill and Chae Strachan's Peesie's Knapp. Munro of Cuddiestoun also prospers but only by stopping farming and turning over to poultry. Ellison of the Mains, as is to be expected, is able to buy his Mains and more besides—the ruins of Kinraddie House and Blawearie itself. How serious his avowed intention was to plough the land with tractors we hardly know; but the slump comes and he peoples Blawearie with sheep instead. The change in Blawearie— at the very heart of the setting of *Sunset Song*—is summed up in Lewis Grassic Gibbon's own words:

> And that was the way things went in the end on the old bit place up there on the brae, sheep baaed and scrunched where once the parks flowed thick with corn, no corn would come at all, they said, since the woods went down.

This theme of a changed setting and a changed way of life is developed strikingly in the sermon that Colquohoun preaches during the memorial service at the Standing Stones towards the end of the book. Here the author makes us aware of how closely the character of a people is affected by their attitude to the land:

> . . . here in Kinraddie where we watched the building of those little prides and those little fortunes on the ruins of the little farms we must give heed that these also do not abide, that a new spirit shall come to the land with the greater herd and the great machines. For greed of place and possession and great estate those four had little heed, the kindness of friends and the warmth of toil and the peace of rest–they asked no more from God or man,·and no less would they endure.

The setting therefore is central to the main theme of *Sunset Song*: the tragic element is closely bound up with the destruction of the way of life that comes as a result of the almost savage changes to the land. The woods have been cut down; sheep graze where the land was once cultivated; and the farm-crofts of the men who gave their lives for their country (and their way of living) are by the irony of history swallowed up in the new large-scale mechanised farming. Only the Standing Stones remain untouched, except for one that becomes a war memorial to Chae Strachan, James Leslie, Long Rob, and Ewan Tavendale.

STRUCTURE: MAIN LINES OF DEVELOPMENT

Lewis Grassic Gibbon was greatly interested in history and pre-history, in the links between past and present; but in tracing history he was as interested in the marks left on the land and in people as in history books. As we have seen, he begins by outlining the history of Kinraddie from Norman times to 1911, and then giving an account of life on the nine crofts left on the estate. This forms the Prelude to The Song—sub-headed 'The Unfurrowed Field'. The same sub-heading is given to the Epilude where we are told of the disintegration of the nine crofts. In between the Prelude and the Epilude comes the book—'The Song'—consisting of four chapters, each with a heading appropriate to the setting and the personal story—Ploughing, Drilling, Seed-Time, Harvest. Each chapter begins with a scene at the Standing Stones where Chris has come for rest and relaxation, relief or respite. From here she can review the events of each stage of her life.

The first chapter 'Ploughing' presents Chris as a young lassie seeking refuge from the drought at the Standing Stones, musing on the life in Kinraddie and going back in memory to the early days in Aberdeenshire. The chapter ends a few minutes later with the breaking of the drought and Chris flying down the hill; but in between we have had the first part of her story—the study of her mother and father in their young days, the account of their early family life at Cairndhu, Echt, an impression of John Guthrie as an outspoken independent Scot, the description of the winter journey over the Slug road from Aberdeenshire into the Mearns, and above all the impressions of Chris growing up torn between the Anglicising life of schooling and the hard Scottish life on the croft close to the land.

At the beginning of the second chapter 'Drilling' Chris is again at the Standing Stones, but this time there is a real need for sanctuary. She has come to escape from the tyranny of her sick father. A few moments later she has to answer his call; but in between the second part of the story is unfolded, even more intensely from the mind of Chris. The highlights of this second chapter are the pathos of the mother's suicide, the excitement of the fire at Peesie's Knapp, the high spirits of the New Year scene, and the story of Chris's brother Will—his love affair with Mollie Douglas and the conflict with his father. But the real climax is not so much Will's departure as John Guthrie's breakdown and the effect this has on Chris's life: now she has the full burden of running the croft and looking after her father.

The third chapter 'Seed-time' begins with a description of Chris stumbling towards the Standing Stones in great mental turmoil, almost ready to kill herself. This chapter —the longest in the book—ends 'a quarter of an hour, half an hour' later when Ewan comes seeking her, fearing she might have drowned herself in the loch: 'she called to him and he came'. In between we have the first great personal climaxes in the life of Chris—her double liberation and her fulfilment. She is liberated from family bondage by the death of her father, and she breaks free from her relations by deciding to stay on and work the croft by herself. (There is a similarity here with the story of Bathsheba Everdene in Thomas Hardy's novel *Far from the Madding Crowd*.) The fulfilment comes rapidly after the funeral when Chris and Ewan Tavendale, the foreman from Upperhill, a high-lander, meet again, fall in love, and get married. The central scene in 'Seed-time' is the wedding at Blawearie—the cere-mony in the parlour and the celebration in the barn. This is the longest and most detailed scene in the book, rooted in old Scottish ways and traditions. The pace of the chapter slackens in the account of the holiday that Chris and Ewan give themselves in the following March; and this account is interesting for the descriptions of the Mearns countryside and the little Mearns towns—Drumlithie Fordoun, Laurencekirk. As they look over the countryside by Edzell and Drumtochty, thoughts of the history and legends of the scene pass through Chris's mind: it is one of the characteristic moments of suspension that give the novel its quality of timelessness and universality. But the pace quickens as the story is resumed. There is a build up by way of Chris's discovery she is pregnant and her first quarrel with Ewan to the final scene at the Standing Stones.

There is deep pathos at the beginning and end of the final chapter 'Harvest': the standing stone she touches is 'cold to her hand', and this coldness is within her heart as she prays for 'that Ewan whose hand lay far from hers'. The chapter traces the events of the years between the birth of young Ewan and the news of the death of Ewan himself in France. Two themes are interwoven in this chapter—the main Chris-as-mother-and-wife theme and the off-stage theme of the war. This war theme is heard from afar: we are more concerned with the pain and anguish that Chris undergoes before the birth of her son. Thereafter the tension relaxes and we have the humorous treatment of Kinraddie gossip from the point of view of a member of the community— the 'folk voice'; but the power of the writing resides in the way the author gradually makes the war theme dominate everything else until all the young crofters are engulfed— James Leslie, Chae Strachan, Ewan, then finally Long Rob himself. This chapter is richly textured in other ways too. Following scenes of tenderness come scenes of harshness— the return of Ewan on leave, a debased drunken creature, and the turning of the community against Rob for not enlisting; but there are also scenes of great human power —the brief love affair between Rob and Chris, and the scene as reported by Chae Strachan of Ewan's vision and desertion and return to sanity before he is shot as a deserter. The poetic quality of the writing here is reflected also in the sequel that ends the chapter and returns us to its beginning—the fusion of reality and fantasy, of past and present, as Chris sees at the Standing Stones the ghost that was her husband.

So we see something of the skill of the writer in observing his structural method, particularly his use of the flash-back from present to past. Each chapter begins and ends with Chris at the Standing Stones; but the method, used with poetic subtlety, enables the author to mark the stages in the development of the story and to underline the timeless quality of the setting. The Standing Stones representing something that endures become for Chris a haven where she can escape from the pressures of life and from time itself.

We have seen how the novel is flanked at the beginning and at the end by the half-serious, half-mocking account of life in the nine croft-farms of Kinraddie; but we have to consider also the effect of that concluding elegy, the sermon preached by Robert Colquohoun. Perhaps we can best realise its importance and place in the structure of the novel if we think of it in terms of great music—as a coda or a sequence of chords that bring a symphony to a fitting conclusion. It might also be compared to a concluding speech in a Shakespeare play or a great ode spoken by the Chorus in Greek drama. In this sermon or elegy or requiem by Colquohoun Grassic Gibbon is placing the theme of this Scottish story in a universal context. What we have read and felt in the novel is revealed as an expression of compassion and understanding for ordinary people whose way of living and social patterns are first interrupted and then destroyed by alien forces.

THE CHARACTERS

Dominating the whole book is the figure of Chris Guthrie, crofter's daughter and crofter's wife. In the early part of the book she is depicted as an intelligent lassie in her teens attending Duncairn College; and she is attracted to some aspects of learning—history, Latin, French and Greek, but she has no high regard for her schoolmasters. Through her Lewis Grassic Gibbon satirises public education and the snobbery of schoolmasters: Duncairn College is 'a little ugly place . . . ugly as sin and nearly as proud'; and the teachers, although mostly 'sons and daughters of poor bit crofters and fishers themselves', 'loved the gentry', and were 'right condescending . . . with Chris, daughter of a farmer of no account, not that she cared, she was douce and sensible she told herself'.

In some ways Chris is Everywoman, learning from her mother, sensitive to the needs of those about her, aware of her development as a woman and her need for fulfilment as wife and mother. In other ways she is the Scot—the Scottish peasant—torn by an internal conflict. At one time she will be despising the land and the *clartiness* of crofting life, keen on her books and learning—the 'English' Chris; but at other times she returns to her Scottish self and its concern with real living and with the rhythms of the seasons. When her father dies, she thinks briefly of the possibilities of giving up Blawearie and going to college to train as a teacher; but she realises deep down within herself ·that reality and fulfilment for her lie in the life of the soil. She feels then and throughout the book too much a part of the setting, is too much aware of the attraction of the land and its links with past and eternity. More and more we realise that Chris derives her strength of character from the roots deep in the Scottish earth that nourish her.

She is partly but not entirely type or symbol: she exists in her own right as a human being too. She is compassionate towards her mother and understanding towards her brother Will in his love affair and in his conflict with his father. She comes to hate her father for the bondage he places upon her, but at his death her clear-sighted compassion returns. She has a fine sturdy independence of mind that is clearly illustrated by the way she handles her relations and the Stonehaven lawyer in Chapter III: she announces she is going to transact her own business, and quietly holds to her decision to live on at Blawearie. She shows similar cool independence of mind under more difficult circumstances when she has to deal with Ewan as a drunken bullying lout arrogant in his soldier's uniform. But as a contrast to this she can be highly strung, emotional, sensitive to pain and

anguish, as in her brush with Kirsty Strachan after her
father's collapse, as in the quarrel she has with Ewan before
she reveals her pregnancy, as in her break-down at the
Standing Stones after hearing about Ewan's death.

But her outstanding human qualities—compassion, coolness, deep feeling—cannot be separated from the great
developing maturity that enables her to see beyond the
pretences of position and education to the eternal aspects of
life made tangible in the land. In the crisis of her life when
she has to decide whether or not to give up Blawearie,
whether or not to be herself independent, she goes out into
the wet fields and has that 'queer thought':

> . . . that nothing endured at all, nothing but the land she
> passed across, tossed and turned and perpetually changed
> below the hands of the crofter folk . . .

The greatness of Gibbon's conception of Chris lies in the
way her personal character fuses with forces greater than
herself. We have seen how she deliberately chooses to remain
the Scottish Chris; and we have seen how closely she identi-
fies herself with the life of crofting. When she is asked to
sing at her own wedding she chooses 'The Flowers of the
Forest', Scotland's national lament; and we have noticed
the persistence of one theme that runs through her mind—
that nothing endures at all except the land. Chris Guthrie
is thus more than a character: in *Sunset Song* and in the
two works that follow and complete the trilogy she is seen
to be an allegorical figure who personifies the history of
Scotland and the Scot, and perhaps also more generally the
relationship between Woman and the Land.[1]

The other characters are vividly presented, some lightly
sketched, others developed at greater length to take their
place in the universal and allegorical pattern of the novel.
Chris's mother Jean Guthrie is a wise gentle soul who is
yet capable of a stinging reply to her God-fearing, incon-
siderate husband: 'No doubt your friend Jehovah will see
to it all'. Life with John Guthrie is too much for Jean
Murdoch: she kills her twins and commits suicide. She lacks

[1] See Appendix B, p. 295.

Chris's strength, her balance and ability to withdraw and survive; yet she bequeaths to Chris that love of the country-side—and that feeling of identification with it—that become such a powerful motif in the book:

> Oh, Chris, my lass, there are better things than your books or studies or loving or bedding, there's the countryside your own, you its, in the days when you're neither bairn nor woman.

John Guthrie has the strength and weakness of the Scot at his best and worst. His fierce independence of mind and his pride are illustrated in his dealings with the agent at Banchory, the 'dowp-licking clerk' who insulted him during negotiations for the croft at Banchory, and in his handling of Maitland, the foreman of Mains, whom he found shooting on his land at Blawearie. He reveals a narrowness of mind and an insensitivity towards his wife when she objects to more child-bearing and towards Will his son when he shows signs of independence and rebellion. Yet there is evidence that he was capable of friendship and bonhomie in company, as we see, for example, in the welcome he gives Rob and Chae in the New Year scene. As he declines in strength, he becomes more of a tyrant; and the passion within him twists and debases him to the point of making him demand an incestuous relationship with Chris. Yet it is the vigour and the honesty and the pride—the positive qualities—that Chris remembers as she mourns him. Will his son has the same independence of spirit and a courage to stand up against his father. Between Will and Chris there is a friendship that reflects the quality of sympathy and understanding common to both.

Long Rob and Chae Strachan are attractive, complementary characters. Chae believes that socialism and practical politics will bring about a more equitable economic system, but Long Rob is sceptical about it all. Chae has beliefs where Rob has doubts; but both have a friendliness and warmth of personality that are frequently directed towards Chris. Chae and Rob are characteristic of the Scot who loves argument and yet has an artistic, sensitive side to his nature. At the wedding they argue about machines and the socialist state; and the next minute they are providing music for the dancing in the barn—Chae at his melodeon, Rob at his fiddle. Chae enlists willingly, believing that tyranny must be broken; Rob's independent mind rebels against conscription but in the end his spirit is broken and he too is obliged to yield to the pressures of society.

Ewan Tavendale has the hard-working quality of John Guthrie and something of his stubbornness too. His is a simple, straightforward mind, not lively or imaginative like Chris's. He is at his best as a happily married man working his croft; but when the accustomed pattern of his life is destroyed he disintegrates. He falls easy prey to the temptations of war-time life away from home, and attempts to cover up by showing off, by bullying Chris, by acting the big man. Deep down he is the eternal countryman and the Celt—affected by the seasons and their rhythms. His desertion may be in one way an attempt to escape from a nightmare; in another way it represents a desire to resume the natural patterns of living. It is also, as I suggest in the notes, a form of expiation for his cruelty to Chris.

Four women stand out as contrasting Kinraddie types— Kirsty Strachan the feckless simpering wife of Chae who is chastened into sense by the war and her husband's death, Mistress Gordon who is cured of her pride by the blinding of her son in the war, Mistress Mutch the 'slummock' who becomes harder with the passing of time, smoking her cigarettes and mocking her man for playing at war, and Mistress Munro who goes on making money, becoming more like a weasel than ever, and yet always ready to use her skill as a midwife. Ellison of the Mains is the shrewd business man, resourceful and friendly on occasion, but always acting the big man and getting fatter and more prosperous with the years. Mutch of the big ears and little intellect proves a boaster and a glutton; Sinclair and Gordon give the impression of meanness and prejudice hardening in old age. Munro of the unwashed neck and the 'meikle' feet makes money but remains unfed; and Stuart Gibbon is the hypocritical, oversexed glib minister, quick to change his tune and take advantage of the times. More honest, refreshing touches come from Maggie Jean the cheerful daughter of old Gordon who marries her Labour doctor and goes off to organise the farm servants' union, and from Tony the daftie who can suddenly become quite sane and make the wisest remarks. John Brigson and Mistress Melon represent the honest hard-working servant class; and Auntie Janet and Uncle Tom represent the narrow-minded opportunist relations. Hovering above all the named characters, however, there is that community figure who purveys gossip, retails scandal, and at times, especially towards the end, reveals a shrewdness and a humanity.

What we have throughout *Sunset Song* is a kind of portrait gallery of common Scottish rural types, reminiscent in some ways of the characters to be found in William Alexander's novel of North-East Scotland *Johnny Gibb of Gushetneuk* (1871). But the universality and symbolism of *Sunset Song* extend the range and add a dimension to characterisation in the Scottish novel.

LANGUAGE, STYLE AND TECHNIQUE

The remarkable thing about the language of *Sunset Song* is that Lewis Grassic Gibbon can use so many Scottish words and turns of speech without either interrupting the rhythms and flow of the work or giving us the impression he is writing in a difficult, strange-sounding idiom. English and American readers have been as much impressed and moved by the work as Scots, and the reason lies in the way the author, using a powerfully rhythmic and poetic prose, has taken us into the thoughts and hearts of the people and into the atmosphere of the setting itself.

The style is an intimate earthy one: it has a human knowingness about it but nothing of the superiority and cold remoteness of the omniscient author. There is at times an echo of the ballads in the direct and vivid quality of the writing. Near the beginning of the novel occurs this rhythmic quick-moving narrative passage:

> So Cospatric got him the Pict folk to build a strong castle there in the lithe of the hills, with the Grampians bleak and dark behind it . . . And his son took the name Kinraddie, and

looked out one day from the castle wall and saw the Earl
Marischal come marching up from the south . . .

The scene is dramatically sketched: 'lithe of the hills',
'Grampians bleak and dark behind it'; and there are sugges-
tions of ballad rhythms and images: 'looked out . . . from
the castle wall', '. . . saw the Earl Marischal come marching
up'. And always the person behind the narrative is of the
community. Often he represents the communal mind aware
both of the history and the 'speak' of the place, so that the
comments are sometimes factual, sometimes gossipy. (It is
a kind of Greek chorus, reminding us of the gossiping of
the 'bodies' in George Douglas Brown's *The House with
the Green Shutters*.) Here is the folk voice telling us a little
of the history of Kinraddie:

> Next door the kirk was an olden tower, built in the time of
> the Roman Catholics, the coarse creatures, and it was fell old
> and wasn't used any more except by the cushat-doves and they
> flew in and out the narrow slits in the upper storey and nested
> there all the year round and the place was fair white with their
> dung. In the lower half of the tower was an effigy-thing of
> Cospatric de Gondeshil, him that killed the gryphon, lying
> on his back with his arms crossed and a daft-like simper on his
> face . . .

We note here how the factual is set alongside touches that
satirise religious prejudice—'the coarse creatures', or that
humorously introduce realism—'fair white with their
dung', 'daft-like simper on his face'. When the author comes
to deal with the present and with living characters the note
of the 'gossipy' is perhaps stronger but the intimate style is
flexible enough to allow sharp glimpses of character to
appear:

> And Rob said he'd rather be a thorn than a sucker any day,
> for he didn't believe in ministers or kirks, he'd learned that
> from the books of Ingersoll though God knows if the creature's
> logic was as poor as his watches he was but a sorry prop to lean
> on. But Rob said he was fine, and if Christ came down to
> Kinraddie he'd be welcome enough to a bit meal or milk at the
> mill, but damn the thing he'd get at the Manse. So that was
> Long Rob and the stir at the Mill, some said he wasn't all there
> but others said Ay, that he was, and a bit over.

Sometimes we shift to the point of view of one of the characters—John Guthrie, Will, Chae Strachan, Mistress Mutch. When Chae comes home on leave from the war he goes to visit the people of the district and calls in at Bridge End. Here we have life (and war) from Mistress Mutch's viewpoint, but we have also something of Chae's idealism:

> But Mistress Mutch was there and she sat and smoked at a cigarette and told him that Alec was still a fell patriot, he'd enrolled in the volunteers of Glenbervie and every other night went down to Drumlithie for drill, a sight for sore eyes, the gowks, prancing about like dogs with diarrhoea, that's what they minded her of. And she asked Chae when the War was to end, and Chae said *God only knows* and she asked *And you still believe in Him?* And Chae was real shocked, a man might have doubts and his disbelief, you expected a woman to be different, they needed more support in the world . . .

Grassic Gibbon thus uses his folk or character voices to evoke atmosphere, to give flesh and blood to his historical sequences, and to enliven and satirise the contemporary scene. But always the movement of the novel is back towards Chris: the narration is continually focusing on her mind and thoughts. It is from her consciousness that we view the Kinraddie scene and the different phases of her own personal life. The style remains conversational and flexible, but it has at these points a greater firmness and discipline that prevent the latent pathos from becoming sentimental:

> It was not mother only that died with the twins, something died in your heart and went down with her to lie in Kinraddie kirkyard—the child in your heart died then, the bairn that believed the hills were made for its play, every road set fair with its warning posts, hands ready to snatch you back from the brink of danger when the play grew over-rough. That died, and the Chris of the books and the dreams died with it, or you folded them up in their paper of tissue and laid them away by the dark, quiet corpse that was your childhood.

It would seem then that the characteristic narrative patterning of *Sunset Song*, at times relaxed and satirical, at times intense and emotional, at times vibrant with compassion, comes from the interaction of the minds of the folk as a whole and of the particular characters with the deeper thoughts of Chris's consciousness. It is in this way that Lewis Grassic Gibbon fashions and exploits his own form of 'stream of consciousness' technique.

One feature that keeps *Sunset Song* flowing and easy to read is the non-dialectal spelling of Scots words—*cushat-doves* for *cooshie-doos*, *creature* for *cratur*, *clout* for *cloot*. Another is the author's unusual way with punctuation. He uses commas freely (too freely some might say) and he substitutes italics for quotation marks. It is easy to understand why he does this: the flow is maintained and the thought and commentary of the narrative move and merge easily into the spoken words:

> Most said it was a coarse thing, learning, just teaching your children a lot of damned nonsense that put them above themselves, they'd turn round and give you their lip as soon as look at you. But Chae was sitting down himself by then and he wouldn't have that. *Damn't man, you're clean wrong to think that. Education's the thing the working man wants to put him up level with the Rich.* And Long Rob of the Mill said *I'd have thought a bit balance in the bank would do that.* But for once he seemed right in agreement with Chae—*the more education the more of sense and the less of kirks and ministers.*

We notice here that the narrative style, while retaining its gossipy conversational flavour—'coarse thing, learning', 'a lot of damned nonsense', has also a more formal quality— 'But for once he seemed in agreement . . .'

It is relatively easy to use dialectal words and phrases with a hard conversational style and rhythm to depict the life and characters on the periphery. It requires more subtlety to use these resources to animate the setting and reveal its inner life. We have seen how the style becomes firmer at moments of crisis for Chris. Now let us see what happens to the style at those points in the novel when the notion central to the book is being illuminated—Chris's realisation that only the land endures and her feeling of identity with the land. After her father's death, it looks as if she might be dominated by aunt and uncle, and leave Kinraddie to train as a teacher. But she goes out into the fields and surveys the scene:

> And then a queer thought came to her there in the drooked fields, that nothing endured at all, nothing but the land she passed across, tossed and turned and perpetually changed below the hands of the crofter folk since the oldest of them had set the Standing Stones by the loch of Blawearie and climbed there on their holy days and saw their terraced crops ride brave in the wind and sun . . .
>
> She walked weeping then, stricken and frightened because of that knowledge that had come on her, she could never leave it, this life of toiling days and the needs of beasts and the smoke of wood fires and the air that stung your throat so acrid, Autumn and Spring, she was bound and held as though they had prisoned her here.

There is a fine poetry about the rhythms here, about the quick series of images actual and historical and about the reverberations of feeling that these touch off. Indeed it seems to me that the cadences frequently reflect an *animism* that gives the setting and the land their central place in the novel:

> But for days now the wind had been in the south, it shook and played in the moors and went dandering up the sleeping Grampians, the rushes pecked and quivered about the loch when its hand was upon them, but it brought more heat than cold, and all the parks were fair parched, sucked dry, the red clay of Blawearie gaping open for the rain that seemed never-coming. Up here the hills were brave with the beauty and the heat of it . . .

The wind here is a living thing, as are the rushes and the 'parks' that are gasping for rain; and there is almost a feeling of pride and enjoyment in 'brave with the beauty and the heat of it'. Perhaps however it is at the very end of the novel where the motifs and themes are universalised in the requiem to the four men who perished in the war that we become most aware of the powerful rhythms; and here these rhythms, allied with the characteristic imagery of the land, are used most effectively to convey the tragic message:

> And the land changes, their parks and their steadings are a desolation where the sheep are pastured, we are told that great

K

machines come soon to till the land, and the great herds come to feed on it, the crofter has gone, the man with the house and the steading of his own and the land closer to his heart than the flesh of his body . . .

They died for a world that is past, these men, but they did not die for this that we seem to inherit. Beyond it and us there shines a greater hope and a newer world, undreamt when these four died. But need we doubt which side the battle they would range themselves did they live today, need we doubt the answer they cry to us even now, the four of them, from the places of the sunset?

THE ACHIEVEMENT

A serious novel is not restricted to the preoccupations or outcome of its story; nor is it limited to the commentary it may make on its characters or social scene. Some kind of interpretation of life may emerge from the work, implicitly or explicitly. *Sunset Song* measures up to this test. It tells the personal story of Chris Guthrie and her family, her love for Ewan Tavendale, and her relationship with the people of Kinraddie. It also sketches for us the social and agricultural life of that community, and traces the stages by which the way of living is destroyed by war and outside forces. But above and beyond the temporal aspects there is the eternal aspect of the story—its mythological and symbolic plane. The Land endures and there is a longing within Chris to be at one with it. The novel therefore celebrates the myth of woman's identification with the earth in the cycle of the seasons, in the rhythms of ploughing, sowing and harvest, in the rhythms of birth, marriage, death and rebirth. The symbolism interprets Scotland's history and tragedy too: Chris's first marriage symbolises the union of lowlander and highlander; Ewan's desertion from the trenches and his death may represent the retreat from Derby —the desire of the highlander to resume the pattern of his social life broken by the '45—and the destruction of the highland way of living. Chris's second (coming) marriage with Colquohoun symbolises Scotland's strong ties with religion and the Kirk; and her return time and again to the

Standing Stones symbolises the long history of Scotland and the links between past and present. At the end of *Grey Granite*, the third book of the trilogy, Chris goes back to her original home in Aberdeenshire, climbs the Barmekin Hill, and there dies or merges with—becomes the Land itself. The dominating part she plays in *Sunset Song* is clearly a preparation for this; and it is she who unifies the work and best illustrates its three planes—the personal, the social and the symbolic, because she *is* Scotland personified.

NOTES

*The notes in this edition are intended
to serve the needs of overseas students
as well as those of British-born users*

Page

3 *Cospatric de Gondeshil . . . William the Lyon:* William
the Lion, so called from the lion painted on his shield,
reigned in Scotland from 1165 to 1214. The Cospatrics
or Gospatrics, related to the Scottish kings Duncan and
Malcolm Canmore, first appear in Scottish history about
1069. Gospatric I was appointed Earl of Northumbria by
William the Conqueror; Gospatric II became the first Earl
of Dunbar, and is mentioned, along with a Cospatric *vice-
comes*, in a charter issued by Earl David (afterwards King
David) in the reign of Alexander I.

gryphons: the gryphon or griffin was a legendary creature
with a lion's body and an eagle's beak and wings.

Aberlemno's Meikle Stane: this refers to a cross slab of sand-
stone that stands in Aberlemno churchyard, Angus, remarkable as having an 'elaborate interlaced pattern in
sculptured stonework' on the front, and, on the reverse, a
battlefield scene 'unique in Pictish art' (See *The Picts:*
Isabel Henderson). Aberlemno was the scene of a battle at
which the Danes were defeated by Malcolm II (1005–34).

4 *battle that was fought at Mondynes:* Duncan II (a son of
Malcolm Canmore) was defeated and slain at Mondynes in
the Mearns in 1094 by Donald Bane (Malcolm's brother)
and Edmund (another son of Malcolm's) who reigned
jointly until 1097.

Dunnottar Castle: this stands, a magnificent ruin set on a
rock, on the coast a few miles south of Stonehaven. Built
just before 1394, it has featured frequently in Scottish
history. The Honours of Scotland (crown, sceptre and
sword of state) were placed there for safety in the time of
Cromwell; and in the 'Killing Time' (1685–87) all the im-
prisoned Covenanters (about two hundred of them) were

placed in a vault in Dunnottar ankle-deep in mud with only one window for air. Many died. See also pp. 125–6—the visit by Chris and Ewan to Dunnottar.

5 *Abbey of Aberbrothock:* Arbroath Abbey was founded by William the Lion in 1178 in honour of St Thomas Beckett.

The First Reformation: the Reformation, which reached Scotland in the mid-sixteenth century, was led by George Wishart and John Knox, and resulted in much civil strife between Mary Queen of Scots and her Protestant lords. The conflict between Mary and John Knox is recalled on p. 7: 'he would glower across at Kinraddie House like John Knox at Holyrood'.

Dutch William . . . the Covenant: William of Orange was called upon to take over the English and Scottish crowns in 1688 to displace James II who was believed to be aiming at establishing Catholic supremacy. The National Covenant, defending the (Scottish) Protestant Reformation, was signed by large numbers of the Scottish people in 1638; and in subsequent decades the Covenanters had to defend their religion against the Stuarts and such military figures as Montrose and John Graham of Claverhouse. Two Scottish historical novels deal with the Covenanters from different viewpoints—Scott's *Old Mortality* and Galt's *Ringan Gilhaize*.

5 *the creatures Johnson and James Boswell:* James Boswell (1740–95), who accompanied Dr Samuel Johnson on his tour of the Hebrides in 1773 and published his *Life of Johnson* in 1791, far from being merely the sycophant and sot of the Macaulay tradition, was a very colourful personality as well as a skilful biographer, as recent studies have shown. He was however inclined to have bouts of womanising, as Grassic Gibbon's Anglo-Greek fragment about Betty Dundas indicates.

the Auld Kirk: the Established Church of Scotland.

called himself Jacobin: a supporter of the French Revolution. The Jacobins, a political society formed during the French Revolution, were so called because they met in a building in the Rue St Honoré in Paris belonging to the Dominican or Jacobin Order. They included such revolutionaries as Danton, Robespierre, Carnot and St Just, and became more and more extremist as the Revolution gained momentum; but their influence declined with the death of Robespierre.

Page

8–9 *the Turra Coo:* a reference to the story of Paterson of
Lendrum, a farmer of Turriff, Aberdeenshire, who refused
to pay the new insurance stamps for his men. One of his
cows was impounded by the authorities, but was bought
back for him by his friends and returned to Paterson in
triumph garlanded and bedecked with ribbons. The incident has been celebrated in songs. For the Insurance Acts
of 1908 and 1912, see note to p. 98.

14 *circle of stones . . . Druid stones:* as can be seen from the
map on p. ix, there are many stone circles in Aberdeenshire and Kincardineshire, which are popularly believed
to have been the haunts of the Druids, the priests of the
ancient Celts. Mrs Mitchell tells me the author was particularly interested in the Stone Circle west of Echt above
Sunhoney farm—a circle consisting of eleven upright
stones, the two largest flanking a recumbent stone.

15 *if you turned east . . . along the Auchinblae road first on your
right was Cuddiestoun:* Auchinblae is west of the Drumlithie area. If we substitute *Kinraddie* for *Auchinblae* and
accept the revised compass indications, we can follow this
description (and the others that follow) quite clearly on
the sketch map. (Mr Geoffrey Wagner discusses these geo-
graphical problems in *The Bibliotheck*, Vol. I, No. 1.
Autumn 1956, p. 5.)

18 *Calgacus . . . that chased the Romans . . . at the battle of
Mons Graupius:* Calgacus was the leader of the Caledonians
in their struggle against the Romans under Agricola in
A.D. 84 amongst the Grampian Mountains. See note to
pp. 248–9.

19 *Ingersoll:* the author is (perhaps deliberately for comic
effect) confusing two different Ingersolls. Robert Hawley
Ingersoll (1859—1928) was the U.S. business man who mar-
keted the (Waterbury) dollar watch in 1892. Robert Green
Ingersoll (1833–99) was the U.S. lawyer, soldier and lecturer
who questioned the whole basis of Christianity and became
known as the great agnostic.

25 *the Scots countryside itself, fathered between a kailyard and
a bonny brier bush in the lee of a house with green shutters:*
the kailyard school of nineteenth-century Scottish novel-
writing was notorious for its sentimentalised misrepre-
sentation of Scottish life and character. Apart from
J. M. Barrie whose works are redeemed by superior crafts-
manship, the best examples of the kailyard school are

perhaps *Beside the Bonnie Brier Bush* (by 'Ian Maclaren'—
the Rev. John Watson) which has as inscription a couplet
that explains Grassic Gibbon's allusion:

> There grows a bonnie brier bush in our kail-yard,
> And white are the blossoms on't in our kail-yard,

and S. R. Crockett's novel *The Lilac Sunbonnet.* Crockett
could write a good tale of adventure in the Stevensonian
manner, as can be seen by *The Raiders,* but *The Lilac
Sunbonnet,* like *The Bonnie Brier Bush,* presents the
Scottish countryside and the ways of the Scottish people in
too sweetie-pink a style. George Douglas Brown's *The
House with the Green Shutters* (1901) sounded a counter-
blast to the kailyard: it gave a harshly realistic, starkly
tragic view of Scottish small-town life and character. These
are the two extremes; and it may be said that Grassic
Gibbon's Scottish novels, particularly *Sunset Song,* at-
tempted to give a more balanced, more truthful view.

29 *Gladstone:* William Ewart Gladstone (1809–98) four times
Liberal Prime Minister of Great Britain. His foreign policy
made him at times unpopular; but in domestic affairs his
humane measures gained wide support. He fell foul of the
House of Lords in trying to bring about Home Rule for
Ireland.

30 *the Army and the Prince of Wales' rheumatics:* the author
is here making Long Rob satirise the habit some preachers
have of mixing politics with religion in their prayers.

31 *the Barmekin:* a striking hill of conical shape 900 feet high
near the village of Echt in Aberdeenshire. The rings of
stones—'concentric intrenchments'—near its summit indi-
cate it was one of those Iron Age hill forts to be found in
various parts of N.E. Scotland. In the closing scene of *Grey
Granite* Chris goes back to Aberdeenshire and surveys the
land for the last time from the top of the Barmekin.

Kildrummie: a parish on Donside, Aberdeenshire, famous
for its castle that goes back to the thirteenth century.

37 *Wallace . . . Bannockburn . . . Flodden:* these references
to Scotland's hero in the War of Independence and to the
battles of 1314 and 1513 remind us how patriotic and
nationalistic young Scottish children can be in school. The
reference to 'The Flowers of the Forest'—the lament for
Flodden—has a double significance: it enshrines the tragedy
of Scotland and Chris's (or Kinraddie's) coming tragedy.

Page

40 *the Slug road:* this runs from near Banchory on Deeside to
Stonehaven. It reaches its highest point 757 feet up on the
shoulder of Cairnmonearn. In winter it can be a lonely
bleak road.

42 *The ships of Pytheas:* this dream of Chris's illustrates the
author's interest in history and exploration, and also his
feeling for the continuity of life. Pytheas was a Greek
navigator of the fourth century B.C. who sailed round the
east coast of Britain. The notion that he visited Thule
(the Orkneys and Shetlands) is attractive, but probably
inaccurate.

53–54 *Bonny wee thing:* this is one of the loveliest of Burns's
songs. A delicate touch this: the daftie is subdued (and
Maggie Jean saved) by the 'blithe lilt' of the man's song
from across the fields.

57 *and he pictures the dark, slow tribes . . . howes and hills
of Scotland:* this is an echo of Leslie Mitchell's 'diffusionism'—his belief in a Golden Age destroyed by the lust
and cruelty of 'civilisation'. This sermon is preached
by the father of the man who becomes Chris's second
husband.

58 *it was out of the Song of Solomon . . . salvation in the
next:* Song of Solomon IV describes the Church in terms of
a beautiful woman. This sermon and text turn out to be an
appropriate anticipation of the Rev. Stuart Gibbon's less
clerical interests.

62 *Religio Medici:* a work of great erudition by Sir Thomas
Browne (1605–82) on mainly religious subjects. It is not
surprising that the young Chris 'nearly yawned her head off
with the reading of it'.

64 *Aberdeen University, getting her B.A.:* this may be another
deliberate error. It is well known that Aberdeen University
awards the M.A. as a first degree.

85 *since Nebuchadnezzar went out to grass:* with Rob's free
thinking goes a sound knowledge of the Bible. Nebuchadnezzar, king of Babylon, captured Jerusalem, set up the
golden image, but was humiliated by being driven out to
the fields to eat grass like the oxen (Daniel IV, 33).

90–92 *Peesie's Knapp would be all in a blaze in a minute . . .
smell roasting beef again:* this recalls the description of the
burning of the Breadland in Galt's *Annals of the Parish*
(Chapter VII) but Grassic Gibbon's description is much
more detailed and contains the episode describing the

attempt to save the cattle—a moving episode that illustrates Long Rob's love of animals.

95 *And there he was . . . can't sleep there:* the New year scene reflects a Scottish vigour and heartiness, and brings out the more human side of John Guthrie's nature.

98 *he'd support the Insurance and to Hell with the House of Lords:* behind these references in this description of the bye-election meeting lie the burning political questions of the pre-war era—1909–14. The Lloyd George budget introducing a steeply graduated income tax and other taxes on the rich and on landlords to pay for social reform was finally enacted in 1910, despite opposition by the House of Lords and the Conservatives. The battle over the Parliament Bill that aimed at curbing the power of the Lords ended in 1911 when it became law. This was the era of social legislation—particularly the acts of 1908 which established funds to provide medical care for children and old-age pensions, and the National Insurance Act of 1912 which provided health and unemployment benefits for workers.

104 *Up in the Morning:* another of Burns's songs. It is sung by Chae at Chris's wedding. (See p. 163.)

109 *whispering her to come to him, they'd done it in Old Testament times:* see Genesis XIX, 30–8. This brings out an ugly side to the religious bigot that was John Guthrie.

116–117 *words that promised Resurrection . . . how he'd smiled at her:* in this description of Chris's reactions at her father's funeral, New Testament images are thrown alongside touches that are half-realist, half-imaginative, and that lead to a moving vision of her father at his best. Compare, on a much grander scale, Cleopatra's vision of Antony as he was or might have been in Shakespeare's *Antony and Cleopatra*, v. ii, 76–99.

120 *Brechin . . . with its ancient tower:* Brechin was mentioned in records first in 990 in the reign of Kenneth III and again about 1012 just after the defeat of the Danes by Malcolm II at Aberlemno. It is the seat of a cathedral founded about 1150 by David I. The 'ancient tower', one of two Scottish examples of round tower, may have been built by Kenneth III between 971 and 994.

120 *Πάντα ρεῖ:* literally—'everything flows on'. From *On Nature*, a work by Heraclitus, a Greek philosopher (535–475 B.C.). The main theme of the work is that everything in the

Page

universe is in a state of continuous flux, so that nothing can escape change or destruction.

And then a queer thought . . . learning: this could be regarded as the spiritual crisis of the novel. Chris becomes aware of the power of the land, becomes more and more identified with it, and realises here that to break from it is to break from herself.

124–125 *it was a sore shame there wasn't somebody about to heed to the Guthrie girl from the hands of that coase tink brute, Ewan Tavendale:* this seems to be an example of faulty or incomplete syntax natural to an author who is more concerned with ideas and rhythms than with exact structure. There seems to be something missing between 'girl' and 'from'—perhaps words like 'and keep her safe'. The problem would be solved if we substituted 'to keep' for 'to heed to'.

136 *the Blue Wyandotte:* a breed of domestic fowl originally from America.

146 *She sat by the window . . . far in the times to be:* this is yet another point at which the story goes beyond its realistic or social frame into timelessness. A good example too of Grassic Gibbon's poetic prose bright and crackling with cosmic imagery.

151–153 *and when she came down again . . . shaking their hands:* this description of Chris's wedding has a direct, intimate and vivid quality. Its effect comes from the suppleness of the conversational style, yet its beauty has something more formal, a kind of natural rhetoric that sometimes deepens to the personal and sometimes opens out to wider vistas.

155–156 *Up at Rob's table an argument rose . . . socialist tomorrow:* just as Chris struggles between the two sides of her nature Scots and English, so the company here struggles with the two aspects of Scottish life—the attempt to hold on to Scottish words and ways and the feeling that it is the English words that must be used and the new ways that must be introduced. It is a paradox that Chae's idealism should be thrown against Rob's realism here, for Chae is for change whereas Rob is for the old ways.

156–157 *And the red Highlander, McIvor, got up to his feet . . . music of the stars:* McIvor's speech, full of the imagery of the seasons and life after death, has a Celtic mysticism that contrasts with the earthiness of the Lowlanders' argument.

Page

It contrasts also with the worldly-wise style of Long Rob's speech that follows (p. 157).

162–165 *No sooner was the dancing done . . . that made the songs:* in this impromptu concert that takes place during a lull in the wedding celebrations, we note how in the Scottish songs that are sung—'The Lass that Made the Bed to Me', 'Up in the Morning', 'Auld Robin Gray'—realism jostles with pathos until at the climax—Chris's own singing of 'The Flowers of the Forest'—the two aspects combine and deepen to express the sadness of Scotland's story—'Scotland of the mist and rain and crying sea'.

172 *Thomas the Rhymour:* Thomas of Erceldoune (Earlston-a village in Berwickshire, four miles from Melrose), half-legendary seer and poet of the thirteenth century about whom many stories are told. The ballad 'Thomas the Rhymer' tells how at the Eildon Tree, beneath the Eildon Hills near Melrose, he met the 'Queen o' Fair Elfland' who took him to fairyland to serve her seven years.

Edzell Castle: the oldest part of Edzell Castle, the tower-house, dates from the early sixteenth century. The castle was at one time the home of the Lindsays of Glenesk.

185 *One night, the mid-days of August . . . Germany:* the outside world, 'civilisation', impinges for a moment on the natural rhythms of harvest and child-birth. This is the first hint of the outside forces that are to destroy the age-old ways of living in Kinraddie.

190 *For it was on . . . progress for ever:* with a grim kind of antithesis, the black theme of war is thrown against the bright background of the birth of Chris's son.

194–195 *a jade called Jael . . . scudding in chase:* for the biblical reference see Judges IV. Now the community of Kinraddie, stirred up by the preaching of the Rev. Stuart Gibbon to take action against 'traitors', reflect the correct attitude to the war; but Long Rob reveals here both his independence of mind and his courage in the face of mob hysteria.

198 *Ay, man, Rob . . . Ay, man, Ewan . . . herself daft:* a view of friendship as it is for a moment and ideally should remain; but alongside this is set a prophetic vision: Chris sees these men become 'mirages . . . dreamt by a land grown desolate against the changing sky'. Chris is again suddenly given a wisdom and an identity beyond her physical self.

205–206 *And it was there . . . a Calgacus' man from the Graupius battle . . . Glenlivet:* Chae's vision or hallucination, another

Page

illustration of the author's preoccupation with the links between past and present and the ancestral memory, suggests
a feeling of fellowship between the Roman and the Scot
caught in different eras in the toils of wars waged in the
name of 'civilisation'. (Cf. the vision that Chris has on the
Slug road. See p. 42 and note.)

206 *the Conscription Act:* the Military Service Act of January
1916 that imposed universal conscription in Great Britain.
In the story of Long Rob's resistance to it (p. 217) we
have an impression of how harshly it could operate. A
happy contrast is the help Chris gives Rob in defiance of
public opinion (p. 218).

208–211 *And to Chris . . . Ewan would be fine:* Grassic Gibbon
so constructs his novel as to give at this point a striking
example of the triumph of the destructive element in life
over the creative; and we have here too a glimpse of the uncertain, worried, morose person Ewan is becoming under
the stress of war and public opinion.

220–223 *She had hardly . . . wheeled in her brain:* this shattering
change in Ewan's character has been criticised as coming
too suddenly and being too harsh and cruel; and it is true
that Ewan's character is made to degenerate rapidly before
he has experienced the horrors of war. On the other hand,
he is suddenly torn from his simple natural life and exposed
to the evils of war-time as a soldier about to be ordered to
the front; and it is conceivable that this savage uprooting
would have had a savage effect on his character. The change
is to be viewed too in the wider context of the destruction
of natural man in the cataclysm released by 'civilisation'.

228–229 *There was a Young Farmer . . . Tipperary:* the folk-
songs, arising out of the setting and its history, have given
way to imported artificial 'squawling English things'. Here
we have a glimpse of the old ways that are passing: Long
Rob briefly revives the old songs–'from far in the years at
the mouth of a long lost glen'.

229 *He's finished, Chris quean, and it's clyack . . . to enlist the
morn:* an interesting structural parallelism here. Long
Rob's decision to give in, to go 'daft with the rest', comes
at the end of harvest just when Chris realises her love and
need for him. The love comes to its climax and dissolves
quickly into the war. Compare the earlier episode of Ewan's
sudden going that frustrates Chris's plan to have a second
child (see pp. 208–11).

Page

236 *Chris lost to me . . . the Howe happed in mist:* the clarity
and moral cleanliness that come upon Ewan in this
reported incident represent a return to the sanity of his
natural life with Chris. His desertion is seen now as an act
of expiation. This is fully understood by Chris—see pp.
237–8.

236 *Verey lights:* the Verey or Very light was a kind of flare
projected from a pistol to illuminate part of a battlefield.
It was invented by Samuel W. Very in 1877.

242–252 *What with his Germans . . . the folk that fell:* the folk
mind moves over the Kinraddie post-war scene, purveying
gossip and scandal yet revealing also something of the truth
of the harsh changes that have come over land and people.

244 *Uhlans . . . German horse billies:* the Uhlans were originally
Polish and later Prussian cavalry regiments armed with the
lance and wearing distinctive uniforms.

248–249 *Woman had little guts . . . call it peace:* the wild pace
of the farcical satire on the post-war opportunism of the
Munros and Ellison is suddenly halted by the text that
sums up the lesson: 'They have made a desert and they call
it peace.' Significantly enough, the Roman historian Tacitus
(55–117) in his *Agricola* puts these words—'*Ubi solitudinem
faciunt, pacem appellant*'—into the mouth of Calgacus.

250–251 *Colquohoun was his name . . . Golden Age . . . ploughman's Union:* so the wheel comes round full circle. The
old Colquohoun preached and lost but the son succeeds;
and we note the reference to the Golden Age alongside
references to the radicalism of the new minister.

252 *the banns of Robert Colquohoun . . . and Christine
Tavendale:* the coda to *Sunset Song* contains the seed for
the next novel *Cloud Howe.* Chris's new role as minister's
wife is foreshadowed.

252–256 *Fine weather . . . in your heart:* the last scene in the
coda or epilude—the unveiling of the war memorial—takes
place appropriately at the Standing Stones. The inscription
that is unveiled on one of the stones recalls the inscription
to the Covenanters at Dunnottar Castle: both texts are
taken from Revelation II, the one referring to 'the sharp
sword with two edges', and the second to 'the morning
star'. Colquohoun's memorial sermon reviews the destruction of the crofters' way of life and the desolation of the
scene but goes on to hint the possibility of 'a greater hope
and a newer world'. There is the aura of sunset, requiem

Page

and lament; and 'The Flowers of the Forest' played by McIvor harks back to Chris's wedding song and epitomises Scotland's tragedy. But the last words suggest a new light and life to come, even if there is a touch of the sentimental: 'you can do without the day if you've a lamp quiet-lighted and kind in your heart'.

APPENDIX A

According to the theory of diffusionism or the diffusion of culture, as developed by writers such as Sir Grafton Elliot Smith and H. G. Massington, civilisation originated in Egypt, perhaps as early as 4000 B.C., when the process of the artificial irrigation of the Nile valley began to be practised regularly. This meant that agriculture as a settled method of providing food was established and that a settled form of life in villages took the place of a nomadic existence. From this there developed an interest in house building, land measurement, carpentry and shipbuilding, and so on; and people became more aware of the importance and value of materials like timber and gold and copper in the context of this new form of society. Control of irrigation came to be concentrated in the hands of one man who was looked upon as the giver of life, the Sun-God, and thus arose autocratic forms of government and religion. The methods, activities, and ideas that characterised the agricultural economy spread outwards east and west. In other words 'civilisation', with all its attendant evils, was diffused throughout the rest of the world.

Before this time mankind had, according to the theory, been living as an essentially happy and peaceful society of nomadic hunters; but when they became affected by the spread of this 'civilisation', they lost their innocence and freedom and found themselves caught in the corruptions of a new way of life. Many were enslaved in building projects: Professor Elliot Smith tells in his book *The Diffusion of Culture* how the idea of building pyramids spread from Babylonia to India, Java and America, and led to a great abuse of human labour everywhere.

As Geoffrey Wagner states in a footnote in his article 'The Greatest since Galt' (see *Essays in Criticism*, Vol. 2, 1952), Gibbon did not publicly accept the theory of the diffusion of culture from Egypt, but there is no doubt about the effect it had on his novels. In *Sunset Song* we are aware of the sharp criticism levelled at 'civilised' society, especially as organised in war-time, and at the church, especially as represented by the Rev. Stuart Gibbon; and we have noticed references to a Golden Age, especially in the sermon preached by old Mr Colquohoun which Chris 'thought fine'. Old Colquohoun spoke of 'dark, slow tribes' who 'hunted and fished and loved and died, God's children in the morn of time'. He then pictured the bringers of 'civilisation'—'the first voyagers sailing the sounding coasts . . . the Golden Age was over and past and lust and cruelty trod the world'.

On the other hand Gibbon seems at times to be seeking for a new Golden Age, or at least a new kind of world, if we assume that the Rev. Robert Colquohoun (the son) is speaking for the author in the requiem at the end of *Sunset Song*. This seems to be an echo from the end of the father's sermon: after the vision of the past Golden Age, the old man, it will be remembered, spoke of 'the cosmic light far off in Palestine, the light that would yet shine as the sun on all the world'.

It is characteristic of Gibbon that he should use his ideas of diffusionism to enrich and extend, rather than restrict, the background of his novel.

APPENDIX B

THE SYMBOLISM OR ALLEGORICAL PATTERN
OF 'SUNSET SONG'

Within the allegorical treatment of the character of Chris
Guthrie in *Sunset Song* there lie landmarks in the long history
of Scotland. Her first marriage with the highlander Ewan Tavendale symbolises the original Celtic settlement of Scotland. Young
Ewan, the son, represents the racial stock of Scotland persisting.
Chris's second marriage with the minister Robert Colquhoun
symbolises the identification of the Protestant Kirk with Scotland. From another allegorical angle, the Rev. Robert Colquohoun may be taken to embody the stricter Protestant influence
and its concern with the social well-being of the nation, while
the Rev. Stuart Gibbon may stand for the more worldly Scottish
cleric, especially of the pre-Reformation era.

Chris's parents John Guthrie and Jean Murdoch take us
farther back in time. Guthrie is the aboriginal peasant—the Pict
—concerned with breaking in the land, scarcely aware of life
beyond the fields, his religion narrow—almost a superstition.
Jean Murdoch is, even more than Chris, Woman personified,
restricted to the function of child-bearing, Mother Eve closely
linked to the earth. Ewan Tavendale, representing the Gael, is
seen to be at first distorted and then destroyed by the forces of
history. As already suggested, his desertion from the trenches
may symbolise the retreat from Derby and his death the end of
the highland way of life after the '45. Chae Strachan stands for
the radical Scot reacting against the feudal past and seeking a
juster economic system. Long Rob is the Scot of independent
mind, the poet and the singer of songs, the thinker and the artist.
Mr David Murison thinks that he may personify Robert Burns
himself.

In the later books of the trilogy, the historical symbolism is
continued. Ewan Tavendale the younger comes to stand for the
Scottish people as against the land that is Chris. He is the Scot
on the move—like Will, Chris's brother, who personifies the
old Scottish soldier of fortune. Ake Ogilvie, Chris's third husband, represents the industrial or proletarian phase that Scotland

has to pass through. It is significant that this third marriage is sterile. Ogilvie later becomes an emigré Scot whose love of Scotland is not strong enough to keep him at home. On the other hand, it is appropriate for the historical allegory that Chris as Scotland remains essentially unaffected by any political or religious dogma or experience. As a person she stands for the natural unspoiled woman of the Golden Age before the coming of 'civilisation'.

BIBLIOGRAPHY

Books marked with an asterisk are specially recommended for further reading.

GIBBON, LEWIS GRASSIC. *Sunset Song.* Jarrolds, First edition, 1932 and Jackdaw Library edition 1937

* GIBBON, LEWIS GRASSIC. *Cloud Howe.* Jarrolds, Jackdaw Library, 1937

* GIBBON, LEWIS GRASSIC. *Grey Granite.* Jarrolds, Jackdaw Library, 1937

* GIBBON, LEWIS GRASSIC. *A Scots Quair.* 8th imp., Hutchinson, 1969

* MUNRO, IAN S. *Leslie Mitchell: Lewis Grassic Gibbon.* Oliver & Boyd, 1966

* GIBBON, LEWIS GRASSIC. *A Scots Hairst,* ed. Ian S. Munro, Hutchinson, 1967

* WITTIG, KURT. *The Scottish Tradition in Literature.* Oliver & Boyd, 1958

BLAKE, GEORGE. *Barrie and the Kailyard School.* Barker, 1951

CAIRD, JAMES B. 'Lewis Grassic Gibbon and his Contribution to the Scottish Novel', *Essays in Literature.* Oliver & Boyd, 1936

WAGNER, GEOFFREY. 'The Greatest since Galt', *Essays in Criticism.* Vol. 2. Blackwell, Oxford, 1952

* MITCHELL, J. LESLIE. *Spartacus.* Jarrolds, Jackdaw Library, 1937

MACLAREN, IAN. *Beside the Bonnie Brier Bush.* Hodder & Stoughton, 1895

CROCKETT, S. R. *The Raiders* and *The Lilac Sunbonnet,* ed. G. Blake, Collins, 1954

* (BROWN), GEORGE DOUGLAS. *The House with the Green Shutters.* Nelson (undated edition). First published 1901

* GUNN, NEIL. *The Silver Darlings.* Faber, Paperback Edition, 1969

LINKLATER, ERIC. *Magnus Merriman.* Penguin, 1959

The Oxford Book of Scottish Verse, ed. John MacQueen and Tom Scott, Oxford, 1966

A Book of Scottish Verse. Selected R. L. Mackie, revised M. Lindsay, O.U.P., 1967

The Scottish Literary Revival, ed. George Bruce, Collier-Macmillan, 1968

* BROWN, P. HUME. *Scotland: a Short History.* (new edition H. W. Meikle), Oliver & Boyd, 1955

MAXWELL, D. *Bygone Scotland:* (originally published in 1894) Reprint by S.R. Publishers, 1970

HAYES, CARLTON J. H. *A Political and Cultural History of Modern Europe,* Vol. II. New York, Macmillan, 1939

JERVISE, A. *Memorials of Angus and the Mearns.* (revised J. Gammack) David Douglas, 1885

SIMPSON, W. DOUGLAS. *The Ancient Stones of Scotland.* Hale, 1965

* RITCHIE, R. L. GRAEME. *The Normans in Scotland.* E.U.P., 1954

The Problem of the Picts, ed. F. T. Wainwright. Nelson, 1955

* HENDERSON, ISABEL. *The Picts.* Thames & Hudson, 1967

HENDERSON, G. A. *The Kirk of St. Ternan Arbuthnott.* Oliver & Boyd, 1962

SKENE, JAMES (of Rubieslaw). 'An Account of the Hill Fort of the Barmekyne in Aberdeenshire', *Transactions of the Society of the Antiquaries of Scotland.* Vol. II, Part I. William Blackwood, 1818

SMITH, SIR GRAFTON ELLIOT. *The Diffusion of Culture.* Watts & Co., 1933

WAGNER, GEOFFREY. 'James Leslie Mitchell/Lewis Grassic Gibbon: a chronological check-list', *The Bibliotheck,* Vol. I, No. 1, Autumn 1956. The Scottish Group, The University and Research Section of the Library Association

The Scottish National Dictionary, ed. William Grant and David Murison, Scottish National Dictionary Association, Edinburgh 1929–   )

GLOSSARY

Note: The dialect form—Sc.—has been added in brackets where the author anglicises

Affronted	put to shame, humiliated
Agley	off the straight, awry
Ayont	beyond
Bairns	children
Bap	a floury roll
Beasts	animals in general, apart from humans, especially farm animals
Ben	(right) inside, within, through, towards (the speaker)
Bent	a hill-slope or sandy hillock in coarse grass
Bided	stayed, remained
Biggings	buildings
Billies	fellows (friends)
Blatter	a loud rattling sound
Blithered (Sc. *Blethered*)	talked foolishly
Blow (Sc. *Blaw*)	to boast, brag
Bout	a stretch of land ploughed or a stretch of corn or hay cut
Brave (Sc. *Braw*)	handsome, fine
Breeked	put into *breeks* or trousers
Bree	the liquid in which meat or vegetables are boiled
Bristling	scorching, burning
Brose	oatmeal or peasemeal mixed with boiling water
Bruised	squeezed, crushed
Bubbly-Jock	turkey-cock
Buchts	pens, sheepfolds
But and ben	a two-roomed cottage
Byre	cow-house
Caller	fresh, cool, refreshing

Canny	agreeable, cautious, natural (*not canny*: somewhat sinister)
Canty	lively, neat, pleasant
Cap	a wooden bowl
Cateran	(originally) a highland marauder or reiver; (humorously) rascal, rogue
Champ	stretch of ground trodden into a miry state; to trample down
Chancy	lucky (generally used with the negative)
Chap of eight	as eight o'clock was ringing, at eight o'clock exactly
Chapping	knocking
Chave	a task, struggle; to struggle, toil
Chief (-like)	friendly, intimate
Childe (Sc. *Chiel*)	(generally) a (young) man, a 'fellow', with sense of affection, contempt, or familiarity
Claik	a gossip, a gossiping woman
Clairted	besmeared, dirty
Clart	a muck-rake
Clamjamfried	crowded, cluttered (up), plastered (by extension)
Clecking	hatching, bringing forth, inventing
Clip Clouts	(lit.) cut cloths; *a tongue that would* . . . i.e. a very sharp tongue
Clipped	clasped, embraced
Close	courtyard, farmyard
Clout (Sc. *Cloot*)	a cloth, piece of cloth; to slap, strike
Clyack	the end of harvest (the last handful of corn cut in the harvest field)
Coarse	rough, foul, hard, disagreeable, wicked, bad (a favourite word of the author's)
Coldrife (Sc. *Cauldrife*)	very cold, chilly
Coles (Sc. *Coiles*)	haycocks
Cotters	peasants occupying cottage and renting small plot of land from a landlord. Married dependants on a farm occupying cottage as part of their contract
Coulter	a humorous name for the nose; an iron cutter in front of a ploughshare
Coup	capsize, knock over, overbalance
Couthie	kind, pleasant, sympathetic

Cravat (or *Gravat*)	scarf, comforter for the neck
Creash	grease, fat
Creature (Sc. *Cratur*)	a (living) 'thing' (used contemptuously or sympathetically)
Cushat-Doves (Sc. *Cooshie-doos*)	ring-doves, wood-pigeons
Daftie	a half witted person, fool, imbecile
Dander	temper, anger, spirit
Dander	saunter, stroll
Dawtie	darling, pet
Deaved	deafened
Dirl	to vibrate noisily, reverberate
Doiter	to totter, move unsteadily
Dominie	schoolmaster
Douce	quiet, respectable, gentle, neat
Dour	hard, sullen, stubborn
Dove's flitting	a mistake for *dove's clecking* or *sitting*: a family of two
Dowp	the buttocks
Dreich	dull, dreary
Drooked	soaked, drenched
Dyke	a low wall of stones
Eightsome (Sc. *Echtsome*)	a Scottish dance, a reel for eight dancers
Fairlies	strange sights, wonders, creatures seen in hallucinations
Feared (Sc. *Feart*)	afraid
Feckless	ineffective, spiritless, incompetent
Fee	a servant's wages, engagement as servant; to engage or hire
Feint the	(as a strong negative) 'devil the' (i.e. none at all)
Fell	very (much), exceedingly
Feuch	an exclamation of disgust
Fiddley-faddles	trifles
Fleering	mocking, making a wry face, ogling
Fliting	scolding, railing at
Forbye	besides
Fore-winter	early winter
Fusionless	feeble, dull, flat, weak, spiritless
Futret	weasel
Futret with kittle	weasel with (unborn) young

Gait (or *Gate*)	way, road
Gang	go
Gey	wild, 'great', 'fast' (loose-living); rather
Girned	complained, snarled, raged
Glaur	soft sticky mud
Glegs	gadflies, horseflies
Gley	to glance sideways, squint
Glinting	glancing (slyly), looking furtively
Gloaming	evening twilight, dusk
Glooming	frowning, scowling, sulking
Glower	to look threateningly, scowl, stare, gaze intently
Glunching (or *Glumching*)	frowning, grumbling
Golochs	earwigs, beetles (or similar insects)
Gomerils	blockheads, stupid persons
Gowking	staring idly or foolishly
Gowks	cuckoos, (by extension) fools
Graip	three- or four-pronged iron fork used in farming
Greeve	(of weather) stormy
Greip (or *Gruip*)	an open trench or drain for carrying off water
Growked	growled, grumbled, looked suspiciously (of a niggardly person)
Guff	(bad) smell
Gutsy	greedy for food, gluttonous
Hack-stock	a butcher's block or a block on which to hack wood with an axe
Handless	awkward, clumsy
Hantle	a good deal, much, very
Hantled (or *Handled*)	impressive
Happed	covered, enfolded
Haughs	level ground, meadows, river meadow land
Haver (or *Haiver*)	to talk nonsense, talk in a foolish manner
Heuch	a pit, crag, deep glen, cliff
Heuch (p. 9)	a variant of *heuk*, a sickle
Hiddling	nestling closely, taking shelter
Hinder end	back or rear portion
Hippens	baby's napkins
Hirpled	limped, hobbled, walked painfully
Hoasts	coughs
House nor hall	no refuge or place of shelter

Hotter	to boil away, bubble, seethe
Howe	a vale, a flat tract between hill ranges
Hurled	drove, trundled
Ill	unkind, difficult
Ill-fashionce	bad manners, (vulgar) curiosity
Ill-like	not very well
Ill-marled	badly mottled, marked or streaked
Jookery-packery	double dealing, trickery
Keek	a spectacle, an odd sight; to peep
Kirk	church
Kist	chest, box, trunk
Kittle	unsteady, fickle, not easily managed
Kittled up	livened up, stimulated
Kye	cows, cattle
Laired	bogged, stuck fast (in mud, snowdrift, etc.), deep in mud; covered or stained (with mud)
Leat (or *Leet*)	a list of candidates or nominees eligible for a post
Lemans	mistresses (originally sweethearts, lovers)
Ley	grasslands, pasture
Libbed	castrated, gelded, emasculated
Lilt	a song, tune, air, cadence
Limmer	(originally) a rogue or loose woman; (now applied more generally) hussy, jade; a half-contemptuous, half-playful term for any female
Lithe	shelter(ed)
Longer (or *Langour*)	boredom, ennui
Loosed (Sc. *Loused*)	unyoked, untied
Losh	Lord
Louping	leaping, springing
Louring	skulking, lurking, threatening (rain)
Lowe (or *Low*)	glow, flame, blaze
Lugs	ears
Lum hat	a top hat
Marled	mottled, streaked, chequered
Mart	market, building used for auctioning livestock
Meat	food; to feed
Meikle (or *Muckle*)	large, big, much
Midden	dung-hill, refuse-heap

Minded	remembered, recollected
Mirk	darkness
Mischieve	to injure, hurt, damage
Mislike (Sc. *Mislek*)	dislike
Moonlight flit	removal at night-time with household goods to escape payment of debts
Mouser	moustache
Muck	to clean out, remove dung
Neb	snout, nose
Neuk	corner, corner-seat, nook
Nicked	stole
Nicker	whinny, neighing
Ongoing (Sc. *Ongaun*)	goings-on, events, behaviour
Orra	spare, extra, odd, disreputable
Orra men	men doing odd jobs on a farm
Over (Sc. *Ower*)	too, over-much, excessively
Oxter	armpit; to embrace, cuddle
Paichs	gasps, pants of breath
Park	a field
Pecked up (perhaps *Peeked*)	thrust forward
Peeked	decked out, made (herself) neat
Peesie (or *Peesweep*)	peewit, lapwing
Pelted	thrashed, belaboured
Pernickety	very fastidious, fussy
Plaid	piece of (tartan) woollen cloth worn over the shoulders; tartan cloth used as a blanket
Pleitering	wading through mud or wet ground
Ploy	occupation, employment
Pouch	pocket
Pow	head of human being or animal
Prigged out =*Prinked out*	pushed out, decked out (of hair)
Prigging	pleading, entreating
Pringle	a tingling sensation; to tingle
Queered	puzzled
Queans	girls
Rampage	an outburst of rage, violent **wild behaviour**
Rax	stretch

Redd up	tidied up
Ree	enclosure, pen, (perch)
Reek	smoke
Reischle	rustling noise; a large (noisy) gathering
Rickle, Ruckle	a loose collection, a carelessly thrown together pile
Rigs	ridges, strips of ploughed land
Rip	unbound sheaf of corn, a handful of stalks of unthreshed grain
Rived	tore, broke, burst
Roaded up	put on the way to, directed on to a road
Roup	to sell by public auction
Sark	a shirt
Schlorich	a mess, untidy mass
Scraich	screech, yell, shriek
Scunner	a feeling of aversion or disgust
Sharn	cow-dung
Shaws	leaves or stalks of potatoes, turnips, etc
Shelvin(g)	an additional board fixed to a cart to increase its capacity
Sholtie	(Shetland) pony
Silver (Sc. *Siller*)	money in general
Skelp	strike, beat, whip
Skilly	handy, skilful
Skirled	shrieked, screamed
Skite	mad, queer, insane
Sleeked	smooth, hypocritical, sly, flattering
Sleeking	walking or moving in a sly manner
Slummock	a dirty untidy person, a slut, a slattern; sly
Smore	(of sleet) a dense fall; to choke
Sneck	door-latch
Snickered	sniggered
Sniftering	snuffling, sneering, sobbing
Sock	ploughshare
Sonsy	plump, fat, buxom; happy, placid
Sooning	floating, crying(?)
Sore-made	overworked, harassed, overwrought
Soss	a state of dirt or mess; to pet
Sotter	a filthy mess
Soughing	sighing
Sourocks	sorrel; a surly person
Sow (Sc. *Soo*)	an oblong stack (of straw or hay)
Speak	a subject of conversation, gossip

Spleiter	splash, mess
Spunk	spark of life, spirit, courage; a match
Stamash (or *Stramash*)	tumult, uproar
Stammy-gaster	(to affect with) disagreeable surprise
Steadings	farm buildings
Stew	commotion, excitement
Stirk	steer, young ox or cow
Stite	nonsense
Stiter	stagger, totter
Stock	(generally) a person (sometimes as a term of pity or contempt or affection)
Stook	pile of sheaves of corn set up in a field
Store the kiln	last out, survive
Stour	dirt, dust, commotion
Sumph	blockhead, simpleton
Sutor	shoemaker, cobbler
Swackest	most agile, nimblest
Sweirty	laziness
Swick	a fraud, cheat
Swipe	heavy driving stroke
Swither	a flurry; a luxuriant mass; to hesitate, be undecided; to stagger, totter
Syne	since, then
Taik	stroll
Thole	stand, suffer, endure
Thrapple	windpipe
Thrawn	stubborn, perverse
Ticed	invited kindly, coaxed
Tink	a tinker; a vagabond
Tocher	dowry
Toun	farm
Trig	neat, smart
Tune	state, temper
Tweeted	piped, cheeped
Tyne	to lose
Uncanny	ominous
Unchancy	unlucky, ill-omened
Unco	uncouth, weird, strange; very
Uncouthy	unfriendly
Unsnecked	lifted the latch
Wabbled	wobbled
Wame	stomach, belly

Waster (or *Wasterie*)	heedless spending, extravagance
Wean	child
Weeked	squeaked
Well-kenspeckled (or *Kenspeckle*)	well-known, easily recognisable
Wheep	a whistling sound
Wheeber	whistle
Wheest	hush
Whimsy	fanciful idea
Wight	fault, blame
Yavil (*park*)	a field with a second crop of grain
Yammer	talk loudly and continuously, drive out with the tongue; whimpering, whining